# DETERMINED SOULS

THE JOSEPH CHRONICLES
BOOK 2

WILL MARLER

*To my grandson Mason, whose intense passion inspires me.*

# PROLOGUE

Northwest Pakistan—Two Years Before

Through military-grade optics, Faraz Qureshi watched a ghost return to the place he'd burned down thirteen years ago.

From a thousand meters, the rangefinder held steady on the blackened timbers jutting from the Christian compound's ruins. A solitary figure moved through the destruction, his white shalwar kameez bright against charred stone—Hassan Awan, the missionary's former assistant. The traitor who'd chosen infidels over his national faith.

Sweat soaked through Faraz's uniform, but he didn't blink. Didn't shift position despite rocks digging into his elbows. A hawk circled overhead, riding thermals thick with dust and wild sage.

*Thirteen years since I cleansed this place. And now he's returned?*

Awan had worked at the mission for years before the attack. According to rumors, he had risked everything to guide William Freeman's son through an escape tunnel while the parents stayed behind to face death. To Faraz, this was an unforgivable betrayal—a Pakistani Muslim loyal to Christian missionaries.

"So you've returned." Faraz's whisper carried no farther than the hot wind. "Like a dog to its vomit."

The question that had haunted him for thirteen years surfaced again. Where was the boy? The boy would be a young man now, twenty-two or twenty-three. Old enough to have inherited his father's charisma, his ability to win hearts and build influence among the vulnerable people near the Shingli Payeen Village of Northwest Pakistan.

Faraz surveyed what remained of his most significant accomplishment. Few at the Federal Investigation Agency (FIA) knew of his militant past with Tehreek-e-Labbaik Pakistan—his personnel file mentioned only "security experience." A scrubbed history, maintained through careful networking and Rahman's protection. If the truth emerged, everything would collapse.

Hassan's careful preparation below suggested this wasn't a casual visit. This was reconnaissance for a greater threat. Perhaps the son's return.

Faraz's left cheek flared—the familiar burn whenever his past threatened his present. He touched the scar tissue, feeling the ridged line where flames had marked him that night. Rahman had cauterized the wound himself, turning disfigurement into a badge of service.

From TLP raider to FIA Director. He'd spent thirteen years building this new identity, all while maintaining his devotion to Rahman's vision—a Pakistan purified of Christian influence. A scorpion scuttled across the rock beside him, its tail curved defensively. Faraz watched it disappear into a crevice. Silent. Deadly. Patient.

Like him.

He shifted his position, careful not to dislodge any loose stones that might betray his presence. His government vehicle waited a kilometer away, where the dirt road ended. No official reason explained why he was here today. This was personal reconnaissance, conducted with resources only his rank afforded.

Through the binoculars, he watched Hassan pause at what had once been the chapel's entrance. The infidel knelt, running his fingers over the scorched foundation, his head bowed in what Faraz recognized as prayer. Rage ignited in his chest.

*Still clinging to his false Son of God. Yet where was this Christ when we burned their sanctuary to the ground?*

A text message vibrated silently against his hip. He ignored it, knowing only Rahman would contact him on this secure line. Their communication had grown more cautious lately—the sheikh had expressed concern about Faraz's "divided loyalties," questioning whether government service had softened his commitment to their cause. This surveillance would prove otherwise.

Hassan stood and moved to what had once been the mission's garden, his steps sure despite the tangled undergrowth. He seemed to know where he was going, as if he'd memorized every corner of this place before its destruction. He knelt again, clearing away weeds and stones from a particular spot with gentle, reverent movements.

Faraz adjusted the binoculars, tightening his focus on Hassan's hands as they worked the soil. The Christian reached into his bag and withdrew a small canteen. A dust devil swirled across the compound, stirring ash and debris. Hassan waited for it to pass, then poured water onto whatever he had uncovered.

Adjusting the binocular's focus ring, Faraz magnified the

image. A small green shoot pushed through the blackened soil, its leaves bright against the damp earth. Some kind of plant that had returned despite the devastation.

"What are you nurturing, traitor?" he whispered, though he already understood.

The memory of that day thirteen years ago surged unbidden. The shouting, the gunfire, the crackling flames that had devoured the structures. He remembered the missionaries' terrified faces illuminated by the inferno, the woman's screams as she called for her God. The boy he'd never laid eyes on—nine or ten years old—who had somehow escaped with Hassan's help while his parents died defending their schoolhouse.

Joseph Freeman. The one who got away.

Hassan shifted position, giving Faraz a clear view of what the man had been protecting. The plant was small but healthy, its leaves bright against the damp soil. Around its base, a perfect circle—a tiny sanctuary in the midst of destruction.

"You think something can grow here again," Faraz muttered. "You think you can resurrect what we destroyed."

The thought chilled him more than he cared to admit. He had built his reputation on thoroughness, on leaving no loose ends. The mission raid should have been complete— the buildings burned to rubble, the missionaries killed, their influence eradicated. Yet here was Hassan, suggesting that perhaps Faraz's greatest victory had not been as final as he'd believed.

Hassan finished his work and stood, scanning the ruins before gathering his things. The Christian paused at what had once been the entrance to the compound. He bowed his head in prayer, then turned and walked away along the dirt path that led back to the nearest village.

Faraz remained motionless until Hassan was well out of sight. Only then did he slip the binoculars into their case and secure it in his pack.

He stretched his stiff joints before departing his observation post, then took a last look at the ruins below. From this distance, without magnification, the compound appeared completely desolate—just another abandoned place reclaimed by nature and time. No one passing by would notice the new growth pushing through the hard earth.

But Faraz knew. And Faraz would not allow such things to grow.

He reached his government SUV, parked discreetly behind an outcropping of rocks. His driver was absent— some matters about his past must remain secret.

"This is not over," he promised the empty air, his voice carrying absolute conviction. "This will never be over until every trace is gone."

He checked his watch—he had a meeting with local officials in twenty minutes. Director Qureshi would be punctual, professional, respected. No one would guess that beneath his administrator exterior lay the same zealot who had led the charge against this mission thirteen years ago.

His scar pulsed one final time as he started the engine— a warning, perhaps, that the past was never truly buried, only waiting for the right moment to resurrect itself.

# PART I

# ONE

## The Fundraiser

Joseph Freeman pressed his back against the paneled wall, scanning the crowd of potential donors. Familiar faces mixed with strangers, all here to learn of his plans to return to Pakistan.

The printed program trembled in his hand. There they were, smiling up from the glossy paper—his parents, forever frozen in a photograph taken weeks before the attack. William and Lyla Freeman, standing before the mission compound they'd built with their own hands, the compound that extremists had burned to the ground fifteen years ago.

The mission was more than buildings—it was their legacy. Their sacrifice. And now, with so much uncertainty about permits and funding, everything he'd worked toward for the past two years hung in the balance. Three churches had already withdrawn pledges, citing "security concerns."

The $130,000 he'd raised would evaporate if he couldn't break ground by December.

This wasn't just about honoring the dead. It was about believers meeting in cellars, families beaten for their faith, children denied education because the village's only school lay in ashes. Without the mission, many had abandoned the Gospel, Hassan had written.

"They'd be proud of you, you know."

Joseph looked up to find Uncle David beside him, his face softened with a smile. His uncle had accompanied him from Gulfport, leaving his pastoral responsibilities at Victory Chapel to support the mission.

"I hope so," Joseph said. "The opposition is stronger than I expected."

His phone buzzed in his pocket. He ignored it.

"Second thoughts are normal," Uncle David said, squeezing his shoulder. "What your parents started wasn't easy. Rebuilding won't be either." His hand swept toward the crowded room. "But look around you. All these people came tonight because they believe in your mission."

Joseph's eyes caught on Jerome Phillips, Lamar County Chamber of Commerce president, whose furrowed brow and tight lips suggested otherwise. Not everyone was convinced.

"It's almost time," Uncle David said, checking his watch. "Are you ready?"

"As I'll ever be." Joseph straightened his shoulders.

The microphone feedback pierced the room as David stepped to the podium, calling the crowd to attention. Conversations tapered off, chairs scraped against the floor. All eyes turned forward.

Joseph moved to the microphone, heart pounding. He'd

given this presentation a dozen times already in churches across three states, but tonight felt different. This gathering represented assemblies and businesses throughout the Pine Belt—people who had known his family, who had financed his parents from the beginning.

"Thank you all for coming," he began, touching the small silver cross his mother had given him the night she died. His voice steadied. "Many of you knew my parents, William and Lyla Freeman. You saw their passion for the work they were doing and supported them." He clicked to the first slide—a photograph of the mission compound as it once stood, nestled against the foothills, its white walls gleaming in the sun.

"This was their life's work. A place where Christians and Muslims worked side by side. Where children learned to read, where the sick found healing, where hope took root." He clicked to the next slide, showing the charred ruins after the militant assault. "And this—is what remains."

A murmur rippled through the audience. Joseph scanned their faces—some pained, some sympathetic, others visibly skeptical. Mr. Davidson from First Baptist shifted uncomfortably, whispering to his wife. In the back row, the representative from Hattiesburg Christian Coalition checked his watch.

"What you're seeing is the aftermath of an attack by Tehreek-e-Labbaik Pakistan, or TLP," Joseph explained. "The group targets religious minorities, particularly Christians. Fifteen years ago, they surrounded my parents' mission, set fire to the buildings, and..." He paused, swallowing hard. "My parents gave their lives that night, along with several Pakistani believers who refused to deny Christ."

Mrs. Landry from Petal Methodist dabbed at her eyes.

"I could walk away," Joseph continued. "Say it was a noble effort that ended in tragedy. But I can't do that. Not when there are still people there who need a place to worship, who need education, medical care, and spiritual guidance."

He clicked to his final slide—a rendering of the rebuilt mission.

"This isn't just about restoring buildings. It's about restoring hope. About showing that love is stronger than hate, that faith is stronger than fear." He met the eyes of those watching. "My parents believed that with everything they were. And so do I."

The applause that followed was polite but measured. As Joseph stepped away from the podium, David thanked the audience and invited everyone to the refreshments at the back of the room. The donors hovered near the table, their voices mixing with the clink of coffee cups.

Mrs. Landry appeared, pressing a check into his hand, her eyes still wet. "Your mother was the loveliest person," she whispered. "I met her when she came to my church on one of their visits."

A young couple from Laurel peppered him with questions about volunteer opportunities. "We've been looking for a way to make a real difference," the woman said.

But as the initial crowd thinned, Jerome Phillips approached, his expression grave. "Quite a presentation."

"Thank you, sir." Joseph noted the coolness in the older man's grip.

"Walk with me a moment, would you?" Phillips gestured toward the quieter corner of the room. Away from the others, he didn't waste time. "I admired your parents greatly. Their courage was remarkable. But I have to ask—have you truly counted the cost of what you're proposing?"

Joseph stiffened. "I've spent the last two years planning this."

"Planning is one thing. Reality is another." Phillips's eyes narrowed. "That area is more volatile now than when you left. The TLP is more powerful, more organized. And you're asking not just for financial support, but potentially putting other lives at risk."

"We've consulted with security experts—"

"Protocols didn't save William and Lyla." The words landed like a punch. "I'm sorry to be blunt, but it's the truth. Have you considered the bureaucratic obstacles alone? Pakistan's religious laws make it nearly impossible to get permits for Christian buildings. Your father spent three years just getting permission, and that was before the political climate deteriorated." He lowered his voice. "And let's be frank about your unique situation. Your mother's family still has connections in that region, don't they? Powerful Muslims won't appreciate their nephew returning to rebuild a Christian ministry."

Joseph's pulse quickened. "How do you know about my mother's family?"

"The business community talks, son. Your uncle's congregation may see this as a spiritual endeavor, but there are economic interests at stake. American investments in that area are closely watched." Phillips straightened his tie. "Continental Petroleum has spent years cultivating relationships with local officials. The TLP has left our operations alone because we maintain a delicate balance. Your mission could disrupt that balance, becoming a lightning rod for extremist sentiment that would spread beyond your compound walls."

"So this isn't about concern for my safety at all." Heat rose in Joseph's chest.

Phillips's expression hardened. "It's about everyone's safety. And practicality. Your dual heritage makes you a particular target—not fully accepted by either world. The TLP will see you as a traitor to your Pakistani roots."

"My father knew the risks. He went anyway because he believed the work mattered more than his safety."

"And he paid the ultimate price for that belief." Phillips sighed. "No one questions your sincerity or your faith. But good intentions aren't enough. Think carefully before you ask others to follow you into that fire."

Before Joseph could respond, Mrs. Baxter approached, her husband hovering behind her.

"Such a lovely presentation, Joseph," she said, though her smile didn't quite reach her eyes. "But I do worry about the timing. With all the reports of increased persecution in that region...wouldn't it be wiser to wait until things stabilize?"

"Or perhaps consider a different location?" Mr. Baxter added. "Somewhere safer?"

Joseph forced a smile. "I appreciate your concerns. But the need is greatest where the challenge is greatest."

"But you're an American now," Mrs. Baxter persisted. "You've been here since you were ten."

"I'm both American and Pakistani," Joseph said. "That's precisely why I'm equipped for this work. I understand both worlds."

By the time the evening wound down, Joseph felt the weight of every conversation, every objection, every doubtful glance. The energy of his presentation had given way to the grinding reality of opposition.

As people began filtering out, Joseph stepped onto the hotel's covered veranda, breathing in the humid Mississippi night. He finally pulled out his phone to check the messages that had been buzzing throughout his presentation.

Three missed calls and two texts from his Aunt Sarah, who worked as a cultural attaché at the U.S. Embassy in Islamabad. His pulse quickened as he opened the first—

*Joseph, contact me immediately. There are rumblings about your permit applications.*

Uncle David joined him, loosening his tie. "You handled yourself well in there. Phillips was testing you."

"Was I too defensive?" Joseph asked, still staring at his phone.

"You stood your ground without being combative. That's what matters." David leaned against the railing. "What's wrong?"

Joseph held up his phone. "Aunt Sarah says there are issues with my permit application."

"That shouldn't surprise you," David said. "You knew the Pakistani government would scrutinize this carefully."

Joseph nodded, then noticed a new email notification. The sender—Tehsil Municipal Administration.

"Look at this." He turned his phone toward his uncle. "It's about my permit. I applied months ago."

David leaned closer. "That's the response you've been waiting for."

Joseph's thumb hovered over the notification. After all the presentations, all the planning, all the prayers—this email could change everything. He tapped the screen.

The message loaded slowly on the hotel's weak WiFi. The first line appeared—"Regarding Application #P-2275-C for Christian Mission Reconstruction..."

Then the second—"*After careful review of your proposal submitted on behalf of the Freeman Foundation...*"

Joseph held his breath.

"Your application has been APPROVED, subject to the following terms and limitations…"

His breath caught. *Approval. They'd granted approval.*

But as he scrolled through the document, his momentary elation began to crack.

"—Total building footprint not to exceed 1,200 square feet (approximately 111 square meters), a reduction of 60% from submitted plans."

He looked up from the screen. The chapel alone had been designed for 1,800 square feet.

"—No exterior religious symbols visible from roads or neighboring properties."

The mission compound he remembered from childhood had featured a modest wooden cross visible from the main road—a quiet beacon of hope. Now even that would be forbidden.

"—No public worship services permitted; religious activities restricted to registered residents and approved visitors only.

"—Regular inspections to be conducted bi-weekly with minimal advance notice."

The document continued with a dozen more restrictions —limitations on staff size, operating hours, sound levels, distribution of materials—each one crafted to cripple any meaningful ministry while maintaining the illusion of permission.

"Joseph?" Uncle David's voice pulled him back. "What does it say?"

"They approved it," Joseph said, his voice flat. "With conditions." He handed the phone to his uncle.

David's eyes moved across the screen, his expression darkening with each line. When he reached the end, he looked up. "These restrictions are designed to make your mission fail."

"I know." Joseph took the phone back, reading the final page—an official letterhead with a personal message beneath the bureaucratic seal.

*This approval comes with the understanding that any deviation from the stated terms will result in immediate revocation of permissions. We trust you understand the sensitive nature of religious facilities in our region and will conduct yourself accordingly.*

*—A. Qadir, Deputy Commissioner*

The name meant nothing to Joseph, but the tone meant everything. This bureaucrat wanted him to understand that permission was provisional, fragile, and could be withdrawn at any moment.

"Sixty percent smaller," Joseph said, looking out at the parking lot. "No cross. No public worship. What's the point of rebuilding if we can't actually minister to people?"

Uncle David was quiet for a moment, studying the restrictions. "What if these aren't obstacles but parameters?" he finally said. "God doesn't need a large compound to change hearts. Think about it. The early church met in homes, in caves. They whispered their prayers when praying aloud meant death."

Joseph turned to face him. "You think we should accept these terms?"

"I think a foothold is still a foothold, no matter how small. Jesus started with eleven disciples." David handed the phone back. "Your father built the mission from nothing, starting with just a tent and medical supplies. People came for healing and stayed for the message."

"If we accept these terms, we'd have to be incredibly creative. We couldn't do anything openly."

"The most powerful ministries often begin in whispers, not shouts," Uncle David said. "Remember Paul's letter to the Colossians? 'Whatever you do, work at it with all your heart, as working for the Lord.' These restrictions limit what you can do in the open, but they can't limit what God does through you."

Joseph looked down at the email again. Qadir's note stared back at him, its careful bureaucratic language barely concealing the threat beneath.

"We could build relationships first," Joseph said, thinking aloud. "Focus on meeting needs, being present in the community. Healthcare. Clean water. Education. Things no one can object to."

"Exactly." Uncle David's approval was evident. "And remember, Jesus himself often said, 'Tell no one about this'—yet the news of his works spread anyway. Build what they allow. Serve faithfully. Trust God with the rest."

Joseph stared at Qadir's signature, at the official seal that made these restrictions law. The deputy commissioner expected him to refuse the terms or fail under their weight. Either way, Qadir would win.

Unless Joseph chose a different path.

"I need to think about this," Joseph said. "Pray about it."

"Of course." David squeezed his shoulder. "But remember—opposition isn't always a sign you're on the wrong path. Sometimes it's confirmation you're headed in the right direction."

———

Two hours later, Joseph's apartment in Gulfport hummed with the quiet of late night. He stood before the large map of Pakistan above his couch, tracing the borders he'd studied a thousand times. Peshawar pulled at him like a gravitational center—the place where his old life had ended and where something new might begin.

On the table beside him lay the architectural rendering of the mission, now impossible in its original form. Beside it, the email from Qadir with its suffocating restrictions. And tucked into his Bible, a card he'd kept for three years.

Joseph pulled out the card, its edges worn from handling. Watercolor flowers framed "Thank You" in careful calligraphy. He opened it, finding comfort in the familiar handwriting inside—

*Dear Joseph,*

*The doctors say I'm a medical miracle, but Dad, Grace, and I know better. God worked through your hands that day. They said I was gone, but you brought me back.*

*I danced in my recital last week! I'm including a picture. Grace says I have "exceptional potential" (her words, not mine!). No more insulin shots, no more scary numbers. Just dancing.*

*Thank you for giving me my life back.*

*Love, Lily*

A smaller note was paper clipped to the card, in Lily's neat handwriting—

*P.S. Dad says you were put on this earth to help people like me. I pray for you every night—that God keeps you safe wherever you go.*

Joseph traced the edge of the small ballet photo. The contrast between Qadir's threat and Lily's gratitude couldn't be sharper—darkness and light, destruction and healing. This was why he had to go back. For every Qadir determined to destroy, there were children waiting for hope.

He thought of the Christian families in Shingli Payeen who'd survived the massacre. Without the mission's clinic, they'd continue traveling thirty miles for basic healthcare, risking harassment at checkpoints. Without the school, another generation would grow up uneducated, trapped in poverty that made them vulnerable to extremists. And without the chapel—without that visible symbol of faith—the message was clear: *You are forgotten.*

Joseph crossed to the table and found a marker—thick, black, permanent. He uncapped it and drew a circle around Peshawar on the map. Not neat. Not measured. A mark of decision.

Then he wrote beside it, in firm block letters—"I'm coming."

He capped the marker and set it down, his hand steady. The restrictions were real. The opposition was real. But so was the calling.

Outside, Gulfport slept beneath a faded sky. And on the other side of the world, someone was waiting.

Joseph knelt beside his bed. "Not my strength, but Yours," he whispered. "Show me how to build within their constraints. How to serve in their shadows. How to be the light they can't extinguish."

He opened his laptop and began typing his response to the Bureau of Religious Affairs. The words came with surprising clarity.

*Deputy Commissioner Qadir,*

*I acknowledge receipt of the approved permit with outlined restrictions. The William Freeman Foundation accepts these terms and will comply fully with all regulations. We look forward to working cooperatively with your office.*

*We understand the sensitive nature of our work and commit to conducting ourselves with the utmost respect for local customs and laws.*

*Respectfully, Joseph Freeman, Director, William Freeman Foundation*

He hit send before he could second-guess himself.

The die was cast. Qadir had given him an impossible set of restrictions, expecting surrender or failure. Instead, Joseph had accepted them.

Now he had to figure out how to succeed.

# TWO

## The Attic

*Gulfport, Mississippi—Two Days Later*

The knock on Joseph's door came early—too early for anyone but family.

Uncle David stood on the doorstep holding two to-go cups from PJ's Coffee, his shirt already rumpled though it wasn't even seven.

"Brought breakfast," David said, lifting the cups slightly.

Joseph stepped aside to let him in. His uncle looked like he'd slept about as well as Joseph had—which was to say, not at all.

David set both cups on the kitchen counter, then reached into his jacket pocket. When his hand emerged, a small brass key rested in his palm.

"This arrived about a year after you came to live with me," David said quietly. "Hassan sent it from Pakistan with your father's things. I've been waiting for the right time to give it to you."

Joseph's coffee sat forgotten. "What is it?"

"A key to the past." David's fingers closed around it briefly before extending his hand. "And maybe to your future. There's something at my house you need to see."

———

The drive to Uncle David's house in Biloxi took twenty minutes but felt longer. Joseph's coffee sat untouched in the cup holder as questions tumbled through his mind. What had his father left behind? Why had Uncle David waited fifteen years to mention it?

Inside the familiar two-story home where Joseph had lived from age ten to adulthood, David led him up the narrow stairs to the attic. The mustiness hit Joseph first, carrying with it the scent of old wood and forgotten memories. Morning light filtered through a single window, illuminating towers of cardboard boxes that had become monuments to grief.

Each box bore Uncle David's precise handwriting—" William—Sermon Notes," "Lyla—Ministry Records," "Pakistan—Photos," "Personal Effects—Handle with Care."

Joseph had been through most of them over the years, cataloging his sorrow alongside his parents' possessions. But Uncle David moved past the familiar boxes toward the far corner, where a faded red and yellow quilt covered something Joseph had somehow missed in all his previous explorations.

"I moved it here soon after it arrived," David said, lifting the quilt. "You were still too young to understand its significance."

Beneath the fabric sat a cedar chest with brass hinges gleaming despite the dust. Dovetail joints spoke of careful craftsmanship. His father's initials were carved into the lid—WJF. William James Freeman.

Joseph's breath caught.

"Your father chose this wood himself," David said. "Told me once it would outlast us all."

Joseph knelt beside the chest, his fingers brushing the familiar letters. How had he missed this all these years? The brass key was cool in his palm as he fitted it into the lock. The mechanism turned with a soft click.

The hinges protested as he raised the lid, releasing the rich scent of cedar mingled with something else—something acrid and faintly chemical. Smoke. The preservation of tragedy.

On top lay a Bible, its leather cover darkened with soot around the edges, water stains rippling across its surface like tears frozen in time. Joseph lifted it carefully, feeling its weight—more than just pages and binding.

This was his father's Bible. The one he'd preached from every Sunday morning at the mission, the one that had rested beside his parents' bed when the attack came.

The Bible had survived—protected somehow in the chaos. Hassan had gathered what he could from the ruins days later, once it was safe to return. He'd risked everything going back to the compound, collecting these fragments of lives lived in service.

Inside the front cover, his father's deliberate script filled the margins—*Property of William Freeman, Peshawar Mission, Pakistan. If found, please return to the hands of my son, Joseph. May he continue what we began.*

Joseph's throat tightened. "How did you know?" he whispered. "How did you know I'd need this?"

The inscription was dated three months before the attack. His father had somehow sensed the coming storm, had prepared for the possibility that Joseph would need guidance after his parents' voices were silenced.

"He knew the risks," Uncle David said softly. "He always knew."

Joseph set the Bible aside with careful hands and reached back into the chest. Next came a slim volume bound in faded blue fabric—his mother's diary. He'd seen her writing in it countless times, perched on the mission veranda as evening cooled the Pakistani air, her pen moving steadily across the pages while she watched the sun disappear behind the mountains.

Opening to a random page, he found not the personal reflections he'd expected, but testimonies—dozens of them, each beginning with a name, age, and village.

*Aisha, 8, from Darra Adam Khel. Came to know Jesus after her brother was healed at our clinic. Says she dreams of teaching other children about "the God who sees her." Her father initially opposed her baptism but was moved by her joy. Now, the whole family asks questions about Christ.*

*Tariq, 12, son of a tanner and Joseph's best friend. Baptized last spring in the irrigation canal behind the compound. Has memorized the entire Book of John and reads Scripture to his grandmother who is blind. Plans to study at seminary when he's older.*

*Samina, 23, Hassan's wife. Secretly attended worship for two years before openly professing her faith. Her parents disowned her, but she says "Jesus has given me a greater family." She now leads a women's group in her home.*

Page after page documented lives transformed, families changed, communities awakening to the Gospel message. This wasn't just a record of religious conversion—it was evidence of a movement that had taken root in the most unlikely soil.

Joseph flipped to the final entries, dated just weeks before the attack. His mother's handwriting grew more urgent here, as if she sensed time running short:

*The opposition grows stronger. TLP's influence spreads across the region. Some of our converts have been threatened, their children barred from local schools. William believes we must prepare for the worst. We've discussed evacuation, but so many refuse to leave. "This is our home now," Samina told me today. "If Jesus can stay with us in His suffering, we can stay with Him in ours."*

*William has been working on contingency plans—ways to continue worship even if the main chapel is compromised. He says the church isn't a building but a people, and people can gather anywhere. I pray we never need to test that truth.*

Joseph's hands trembled as he turned the page, but there were no more entries. The diary ended there, three weeks before the attack that would claim his parents' lives.

Beneath the diary lay a few photographs showing village celebrations and baptisms, and letters from supporters back in America. At the very bottom, wrapped in fabric that had once been white but now bore the stains of smoke and ash, he found his mother's jewelry.

Not valuable pieces, but meaningful ones. Her wedding ring, a simple gold band that had never left her finger in fourteen years of marriage. A locket containing a photo of three-year-old Joseph, grinning gap-toothed at the camera during a visit to Biloxi.

"Hassan gathered what he could," Uncle David said quietly. "Piece by piece from the ruins. He risked his life going back."

Joseph closed his eyes, overwhelmed. These weren't just objects—they were pieces of lives lived in service, in sacrifice, in unwavering faith.

"Why now?" he finally asked. "Why wait fifteen years to show me this?"

Uncle David settled onto an old trunk. "Because you weren't ready. For years, you were running from Pakistan, from the memories, from the calling. I couldn't give you these until you'd made the decision to return on your own. Otherwise, they would have been just painful reminders of what you'd lost, not tools for what you're meant to build."

Joseph looked down at his father's Bible, its pages marked with years of study—creased corners, faded ink, margins filled with notes. He opened it to a random page in Ezra, finding a passage his father had underlined multiple times in different colors of ink:

*"The people could not distinguish the sound of the joyful shouting from the sound of the people's weeping, because the people shouted with a loud shout, and the sound was heard far away."*

Beside it, in his father's handwriting: *When we rebuild, both joy and grief will be present. Both are holy.*

"He knew," Joseph whispered. "He knew what it would cost, and he knew someone would have to come back and finish it."

"He hoped it would be you," David said. "But he also knew he couldn't force that choice. It had to come from your own conviction."

Joseph carefully gathered the Bible and diary, holding them against his chest. "I'm taking these with me. To Texas, and then to Pakistan."

"I thought you might." Uncle David smiled. "That's why I knew it was time to show you. You're not just going back to rebuild buildings, Joseph. You're continuing their work. And these—" he gestured to the chest, "—these are your inheritance. Not just objects, but the testimony of what God can do when people are willing to pay the cost."

Joseph stood, the Bible and diary secure in his arms. Tomorrow he would fly to Texas to meet with Alexander Mercer. In his luggage would be architectural plans, financial projections, security assessments—all the practical tools needed to convince a billionaire to fund his mission.

But in his hands he held something more valuable than any of those documents. He held the spiritual foundation upon which everything else would be built.

"Thank you," he said. "For keeping these safe. For knowing when I was ready."

"Your father would be proud of the man you've become," David replied. "And your mother would be thrilled to know you're finally going home."

As they descended the attic stairs, Joseph glanced back at the cedar chest, now empty of its most precious contents but somehow still full of meaning. His parents' legacy wasn't locked in that box—it was alive in the testimonies his mother had recorded, in the Scripture his father had marked, in the lives they had touched across an ocean.

And now, if Joseph could find the courage and the resources, that legacy would live again.

————

That evening, Joseph sat at his kitchen table, his father's Bible lay open. The pages fell naturally to well-worn sections—passages his father had returned to again and again.

In the margins of Nehemiah, he found notes in his father's precise handwriting:

*Opposition is not evidence of failure, but of importance. The enemy only bothers to resist what threatens him.*

*Chapter 4:14 - "Don't be afraid of them. Remember the Lord, who is great and awesome, and fight for your families, your sons and your daughters, your wives and your homes."*

And beneath that, in different ink, added later: *If they come for us, we stand firm. If they scatter us, we regroup. The mission is bigger than any building.*

Joseph ran his finger over the words, feeling connected across time and distance to the father he'd lost. William Freeman had known the risks. He'd prepared for opposition. He'd planned for the possibility that his work would need to continue even after he was gone.

And he'd believed—trusted with everything in him—that Joseph would be the one to carry it forward.

Joseph closed the Bible and reached for his mother's diary, reading again the testimonies she'd so carefully recorded. Each name represented a life changed, a family transformed, a light kindled in darkness.

Tariq, his childhood friend, who'd memorized the Book of John at age twelve. What had become of him? Did he still believe, or had the persecution that followed stolen his faith along with his father's life?

Samina, Hassan's wife, who'd risked everything to follow Christ. Was she still leading that women's group, or had fear driven it underground?

These weren't just stories from the past. They were lives that continued, faith that endured, hope that refused to die despite fifteen years of opposition.

Joseph pulled out his phone and opened his notes app, typing a new entry:

*Meeting with Mercer tomorrow. Taking Dad's Bible and Mom's diary. Not to show him—these aren't for display. But to* remind myself what this is really about. Not buildings or budgets, but people. Lives. Legacy.

Dad wrote: "The mission is bigger than any building." Need to remember that when Mercer starts talking about ROI and market access.

He set the phone down and picked up the Bible again, this time turning to the inscription his father had written three months before his death:

If found, please return to the hands of my son, Joseph. May he continue what we began.

"I will, Dad," Joseph whispered to the empty room. "I promise."

Outside, the Mississippi night pressed against his windows, warm and still. But inside, something had shifted. Joseph no longer felt like he was chasing a ghost or trying to fill shoes too large for his feet.

He was continuing a work that had never truly ended. A mission that had survived fire and persecution and fifteen years of silence.

And tomorrow, when he sat across from Alexander Mercer and made his case for funding, he wouldn't be asking for charity. He would be inviting the billionaire to invest in something that had already proven its worth in the lives his parents had touched.

The legacy was real. The testimony was written. The foundation was laid.

Now it was time to build.

# THREE

**Alexander Mercer**

*BROWNSVILLE, TEXAS*

The glass doors of Stellarion's administration building opened with a soft whoosh onto marble floors that gleamed under recessed lighting. Joseph breathed in air that smelled clean and cold, mixed with hints of ozone and coffee. Uncle David walked beside him, a steady presence against Joseph's racing pulse.

In his messenger bag, tucked between architectural plans and financial projections, rested his father's Bible. Joseph had packed it that morning, not to show Mercer—the tech billionaire wouldn't care about Scripture—but as a reminder. *The mission is bigger than any building,* his father had written in the margins. Joseph would need to remember that today.

A man approached from the far end of the corridor. Late thirties, dark eyes, olive skin, thick black hair graying at the temples. He wore a tailored suit with an ID badge clipped to his jacket pocket.

.

"Mr. Freeman, Pastor David." He extended his hand to Joseph first. "I'm Christopher Rashid, Director of Security. I'm responsible for Mr. Mercer's personal protection." His tone was professional but warm, eyes bright with curiosity. "Welcome to Stellarion. I've been looking forward to meeting you since Dr. Marshall mentioned your work."

Heat flushed through Joseph's cheeks. "Dr. Marshall? From River of Life?"

Christopher nodded. "Family friend. He taught my younger brother at seminary in New Orleans. When he told me about your mission..." He paused briefly. "I knew I had to make this meeting happen."

Something flickered across Christopher's face—personal and raw—before his professional composure returned. "My family left Peshawar when I was eight. My father was a lawyer who represented Christians in blasphemy cases. The threats eventually became too dangerous to ignore."

The casual revelation carried weight. Christopher wasn't just facilitating this meeting—he had skin in the game.

"I'm sorry," Joseph said.

"Don't be." Christopher's smile was tight. "My father got us out safely. Others weren't so fortunate. That's why your work matters." He gestured down the corridor. "Please, this way."

As they walked, glass walls displayed arrays of advanced technology—rovers, AI models, screens showcasing innovations Joseph couldn't decipher. His collar suddenly felt too tight. This sleek environment was worlds away from the dusty streets of Peshawar that haunted his dreams.

"Stellarion was founded on pushing boundaries," Christopher explained, guiding them past a lab where scientists in white coats worked. "Innovative energy solutions, satellite internet, aerospace exploration." He gestured toward a large display showing a network of satellites orbiting Earth. "That's our constellation—bringing connectivity to remote regions. In Rwanda, our pilot program connected rural clinics to specialists in Kigali."

The corridor ended at an imposing conference room. Christopher opened the door.

The sun-drenched space stretched before them, its mahogany table dwarfed by walls of glass. Through floor-to-ceiling windows, the corporate campus unfolded in geometric patterns below—parking lots, office buildings, walkways threading between them like veins.

At the table sat Alexander Mercer. The tech billionaire Joseph had only seen in articles and videos. Mercer radiated controlled energy, his posture suggesting he was always one calculation away from his next move.

"You must be Joseph." Mercer's eyes assessed him. "Christopher tells me you have an interesting proposition." He gestured to the chairs. "Please, sit."

Joseph approached, sliding his messenger bag off his shoulder. Christopher took position by the wall, arms crossed, expression unreadable.

"Mr. Mercer, thank you for seeing us. I know your time is valuable."

"It is." Mercer's fingers drummed once on the table. "Christopher speaks highly of your work. Though I make exceptions for causes with merit, I'm curious what specific community needs your ministry addresses beyond the spiritual."

Joseph had rehearsed this pitch dozens of times, but sitting across from a man worth billions made his prepared words feel inadequate. He thought of his father's Bible in his bag. *Not my strength, but Yours.*

"My parents built a mission in Northwest Pakistan that served over a thousand people," Joseph began. "Medical care, education, clean water, agricultural training. When militants destroyed it fifteen years ago, they didn't just burn buildings—they eliminated the only support system for Christian families in the region."

Mercer listened with polite detachment, occasionally glancing at his watch.

"Those families are still there," Joseph continued, finding his rhythm. "Meeting secretly in cellars, unable to worship openly. Without education, without healthcare. I've raised funds to rebuild, but I need a partner who understands the strategic value of establishing presence in that region."

"Strategic value." Mercer leaned forward. "Elaborate."

"The area is underserved—perfect for testing infrastructure in challenging environments. Difficult terrain, limited existing networks, security concerns. If technology works there, it works anywhere."

Interest replaced detachment in Mercer's eyes.

"Christopher mentioned you've secured some funding already," Mercer said.

"A hundred and thirty thousand from churches and individual donors. Enough to begin, not enough to complete."

"And permits?"

Joseph's jaw tightened. "Approved, with significant restrictions. Sixty percent size reduction, no exterior religious symbols, no public worship services."

"But approved." Mercer nodded. "That's more than most achieve." He stood and walked to a large screen mounted on the wall, adjusting it with a touch. The display showed Northwest Pakistan's mountainous terrain. "Let me be frank with you. Stellarion wants to establish satellite internet service throughout Pakistan. The area needs connectivity, but politics are delicate. Infrastructure development there presents particular challenges."

He turned back to Joseph. "If I were to support a humanitarian effort in that region—your mission, for instance—it could provide the foothold we need."

The cold truth settled in Joseph's stomach. "So you'd help us to access Pakistani markets?"

"I prefer to think of it as mutually beneficial." Mercer returned to his seat. "You get your mission rebuilt. The local community gets improved infrastructure and connectivity. Stellarion gains market access." He spread his hands. "Everyone benefits."

Joseph's fingers curled against his thigh. His parents hadn't died so a tech company could sell internet packages. But without Mercer's millions, the mission would remain ruins.

"Your support would come with conditions," Joseph said carefully.

"Naturally. Any investment of this magnitude requires accountability." Mercer pulled out a tablet, swiping through documents. "Full financial transparency—monthly expenditure reports to our auditors. Every dollar accounted for."

Joseph nodded. "That's reasonable."

"Milestone-based disbursements. You'll receive twenty percent initially to secure property and begin planning. The remainder releases as you achieve specific benchmarks—breaking ground, completing the first building, establishing community programs."

"What happens if we fall behind schedule?"

"Subsequent funding could be delayed," Mercer said.

"But the timeline will be realistic. We understand construction challenges in that region."

Uncle David, who had been silent until now, leaned forward. "What kind of benchmarks?"

"Nothing unreasonable." Mercer swiped his tablet again. "Securing property within sixty days. Breaking ground within ninety. First structure completed within six months. These are aggressive but achievable targets for a motivated team."

Joseph pulled out his own notebook and started scribbling. The terms were tighter than he'd hoped, but not impossible.

"Third condition," Mercer continued. "Media access. We'll document the mission's progress—for public relations and stakeholder transparency."

Joseph's pen stopped mid-stroke. His mind flashed to his junior year—the football field, the opposing player lying motionless, Joseph's hands on the boy's chest, that strange warmth flowing through his palms. The player gasping back to life. The video spreading across the internet like wildfire. The accusations that followed. *Fake. Staged. Cult activity.*

"What kind of media access?" Joseph asked, keeping his voice neutral.

"A small team—one or two people—visiting periodically to photograph and document rebuilding efforts. Nothing intrusive."

"The Christians there are already vulnerable," Joseph said. "Media attention could identify them, make them targets."

"We'll be sensitive to that," Mercer assured him. "No identifying information published without consent. This is about creating a narrative of progress, not endangering people."

Joseph glanced at Uncle David, who gave a slight nod. The concern was real, but so was the need for funding.

"I can accept that, with the understanding that we maintain final approval over what's published."

Mercer's eyes narrowed slightly. "That's not how media partnerships typically work."

"Then perhaps this isn't a typical partnership." Joseph held his ground. "These people have survived fifteen years of persecution. I won't compromise their safety for positive press."

A beat of silence stretched between them. Christopher's hand moved to his pocket, the small gesture drawing Mercer's glance.

"Final approval over anything that could identify specific individuals," Mercer conceded. "But Stellarion maintains editorial control over general progress documentation. Fair?"

Joseph considered. It wasn't everything he wanted, but it protected the people most at risk. "Fair."

"Good." Mercer swiped his tablet again. "Final condition, and this one is non-negotiable. A withdrawal clause."

"Meaning?"

"If conditions become too dangerous—credible threats against you or your team—you must agree to halt operations and withdraw to safety. No exceptions."

Joseph's spine stiffened. "My parents didn't leave when things got dangerous."

"And they paid with their lives." Mercer's tone hardened. "I won't fund a suicide mission. If our security assessment determines the risk is unacceptable, you pull out. Otherwise, no deal."

Joseph thought of his father's final entry in the Bible: *If they come for us, we stand firm. If they scatter us, we regroup.*

But his father had also sent Joseph away, ensuring someone would survive to continue the work.

"Who makes that assessment?" Joseph asked. "Your security team?"

"In consultation with you," Mercer said. "But ultimately, if Christopher's team says it's too dangerous, you withdraw. That's the deal."

Joseph looked at Christopher, whose expression remained neutral but whose eyes conveyed something else —understanding, perhaps. Or warning.

"What if withdrawing means abandoning people who can't leave?" Joseph pressed. "Local believers who don't have American passports?"

"Then we work with organizations experienced in extraction and asylum," Christopher said, speaking for the first time since the meeting began. "But we don't sacrifice additional lives trying to save people who won't leave."

The calculation was cold but honest. Joseph's parents had died because they'd stayed when they should have fled. Would Joseph repeat their mistake, or would he choose survival over martyrdom? "I need to think about this."

Mercer stood. "Of course. But I'll need an answer by Friday. The funds could transfer as early as next week if you agree."

He moved toward the door, then paused. "One more thing. I'd recommend you stop in England on your way to Pakistan. There's someone there who might prove valuable —Reverend Imran Ashraf at Oxford University."

Joseph straightened. "I've heard that name."

"He worked with your parents before the attack," Mercer said. "He's become a leading authority on Christianity in South Asia. More importantly, he maintains connections with underground churches throughout Pakistan." Mercer glanced at Christopher. "My security director thought you might benefit from his expertise."

"I'd very much like to meet him," Joseph said.

"Christopher will arrange it." Mercer extended his hand. "Think carefully about my offer, Joseph. What you're proposing is ambitious. Success requires both conviction and pragmatism."

After Mercer left, Christopher approached with a business card. "My direct line. If you have questions about the security provisions, call me."

"Thank you for advocating for this," Joseph said.

Christopher's expression softened slightly. "I have family in Lahore—my mother's side. I've seen how conditions for minorities have deteriorated. When your proposal crossed my desk, I recognized its value beyond the business angle." He paused. "Mr. Mercer sees potential in emerging markets. The mission serves multiple purposes. That doesn't make it less valuable."

"Just more complicated," Joseph said.

"Everything worth doing is complicated." Christopher handed him another card. "Reverend Ashraf's contact information. He's expecting to hear from you."

———

Outside in the parking lot, Uncle David loosened his tie as they walked to the rental car. "That was..."

"A business negotiation disguised as charity," Joseph finished.

"Is that necessarily wrong?" David unlocked the car. "Your father accepted support from donors who had expectations about how funds would be used."

Joseph slid into the passenger seat, pulling out his

father's Bible from his bag. He opened to the Nehemiah passage his father had marked: *Opposition is not evidence of failure, but of importance.*

"Dad believed in accountability," Joseph said. "But he never let donors dictate the mission's purpose."

"Has Mercer done that?" David started the engine. "Or has he simply required practical safeguards for a significant investment?"

Joseph stared at the Stellarion building receding in the side mirror. "I don't know. Maybe both."

His phone buzzed. A text from Christopher: *Spoke with Imran. He's eager to meet. Can arrange video call this week if you'd like to discuss before deciding on Mercer's offer.*

Joseph typed a quick reply: *Yes. Tomorrow if possible.*

"What are you going to do?" Uncle David asked.

Joseph closed the Bible, his father's words echoing in his mind. "I'm going to talk to someone who knew Mom and Dad. Someone who understands what we're walking into. Then I'll decide."

# FOUR

**Imran Ashraf**

"Joseph Freeman. At last we meet."

Reverend Imran Ashraf's voice carried through the laptop speakers—melodic, warm, tinged with the accent of the subcontinent softened by years in Britain. Behind him, floor-to-ceiling bookshelves framed his study at Oxford. In his sixties, with silver-streaked dark hair and kind eyes behind wire-rimmed glasses. Afternoon light streamed through tall windows.

Joseph sat at the hotel room desk in Brownsville, Uncle David in the chair beside him. Three months had passed since Oxford. Three months of planning, preparing, assembling the team. Now, days before his flight to Pakistan, he needed wisdom from someone who'd walked this path before.

"Thank you for taking the time," Joseph said. "Christopher Rashid said you might be able to help."

"Christopher is a good man. When he told me about your mission..." Imran leaned closer to the screen. "Though

I confess, I feel I already know you. Your father spoke of you constantly in his letters."

Joseph's hand moved to the silver cross beneath his collar—his mother's last gift, pressed into his palm moments before Hassan led him into the escape tunnel. Fifteen years he'd worn it, and still it brought her voice back.

"He wrote to you?" Joseph managed.

"Every month, until..." Imran's smile faded. "Until the attack. We were corresponding about expansion plans for the mission. He had such vision for what could be built there."

"That's why I'm calling. Christopher said you knew my parents, understood the region."

"I did more than know them—I learned from them." Imran held Joseph's gaze through the screen. "Your father taught me that ministry in hostile places requires more than conviction. It requires wisdom. Strategy. The willingness to adapt while remaining faithful to the calling."

"Mr. Mercer offered to fund the rebuilding," Joseph said. "But the terms are... complicated."

"They always are." Imran's face grew thoughtful. "Tell me what troubles you about his offer."

For the next twenty minutes, Joseph laid out everything —Mercer's conditions, Qadir's restrictions, his own uncertainty about accepting money with strings attached. Imran listened without interrupting, revealing nothing.

When Joseph finished, Imran was quiet.

"Your father faced similar choices," he finally said. "Donors who wanted influence over the mission's direction. Government officials who offered 'cooperation' in exchange for restrictions on our activities. He learned to discern between wisdom and compromise."

"How did he know the difference?"

"He asked a simple question—does this limitation prevent me from fulfilling God's calling, or does it merely change how I fulfill it?" Imran held Joseph's gaze through the screen. "The mission was never about buildings or visibility. It was about transformed lives. If Mercer's money enables that work, even with conditions, then perhaps the compromise is worth it."

Uncle David spoke for the first time. "But what about the withdrawal clause? If things get dangerous—"

"Then Joseph withdraws." Imran's tone was firm. "William and Lyla died because they refused to leave when they should have. Their sacrifice was noble, but it also left their work unfinished. Sometimes survival is the wiser choice."

The words landed like a benediction and a rebuke. Joseph had spent years seeing his parents as martyrs. Imran saw them as fallible people who'd made a fatal miscalculation.

"I don't want to repeat their mistakes." Joseph's voice was quiet.

"Then don't." Imran's voice gentled. "Honor their vision, but learn from their errors. Your father's greatest strength was also his greatest weakness—he couldn't imagine abandoning the people he served. That loyalty was beautiful. It was also deadly."

Not doubt about the calling, but clarity about the cost. His parents' example was worth following, but not imitating.

"I wish I could talk to you more about this," Joseph said. "There's so much I don't know about what they built there, how they navigated—"

"Then come to Oxford," Imran interrupted. "You're

flying to Pakistan soon, yes? Route through London. Spend a day or two here. I'll tell you everything I remember about your parents' work. And..." he paused, "there's someone else you should meet. Someone whose experience in hostile regions could prove invaluable."

Joseph glanced at Uncle David, who nodded.

"When?"

"As soon as you can arrange it." Imran's smile returned. "The past holds wisdom for the future, Joseph. But only if we're willing to learn from it."

After the call ended, Joseph sat staring at the blank screen. Uncle David's hand rested on his shoulder.

"You're going to accept Mercer's offer," David said.

"Yes." Joseph closed the laptop. "And then I'm going to Oxford."

———

*Oxford, England—Three Days Later*

Joseph paused at the entrance to Wycliffe Hall, the ancient stones of Oxford rising around him like monuments to centuries of faith and scholarship. Students in academic gowns swept past, their conversations creating a low murmur that reminded him how far he was from Mississippi. From Pakistan. From everything familiar.

Uncle David had returned to Biloxi—pastoral duties couldn't wait indefinitely. Joseph had made this pilgrimage alone, carrying his father's Bible and questions that had haunted him since childhood.

A receptionist directed him through wood-paneled corridors lined with portraits of stern theologians. Finally, he arrived at a heavy oak door with a simple brass nameplate—*Rev. Imran Ashraf, Research Fellow.*

Joseph knocked.

"Come in, please."

The study was exactly as it had appeared on video, but somehow more substantial in person. Dust motes danced in afternoon sunlight. The smell of old books and sandalwood incense created an atmosphere of quiet contemplation.

Imran rose from behind his desk—a compact man in his early sixties, silver threading through his neatly trimmed beard. He wore a simple charcoal cardigan over a white shirt, the informal academic dress somehow lending him more authority than any clerical collar could. He moved with surprising vitality, crossing the room with quick, purposeful steps to embrace Joseph like family. "Welcome," he said warmly. "I've been counting the days."

Joseph found himself returning the embrace, feeling the sting of unexpected tears. This man had known his parents. Had worked alongside them. Had survived when they hadn't.

"Thank you for seeing me," Joseph managed.

"Seeing you?" Imran stepped back, hands still on Joseph's shoulders. "My dear boy, I've been praying for this moment since I heard you planned to return. Your father would be so proud." He gestured toward a sitting area near the window where a silver tea service waited. "Come. I've prepared chai the way your mother used to make it."

They eased into worn leather chairs. Imran poured tea with practiced grace, the familiar aroma of cardamom and cinnamon triggering a cascade of memories. Joseph's mother at the mission stove, steam rising from the pot, her soft humming as she stirred.

"I can see her in your face," Imran said, watching Joseph. "The same determination. The same fire barely contained beneath a gentle exterior."

Joseph sipped the chai. Perfect. Exactly as he remembered.

"Christopher said you maintained connections with underground churches in Pakistan," Joseph said. "That you could help me understand what I'm walking into."

"I can try." Imran leaned back. "Though understand that Pakistan today is not the Pakistan you left. The TLP has grown more organized, more politically connected. The blasphemy laws are weaponized with increasing frequency. And the bureaucratic obstacles—well, you've already experienced those with Qadir's restrictions."

"You know about Qadir?"

"I know he's dangerous precisely because he appears reasonable." Imran's face darkened. "Men like him have learned that overt persecution draws international attention. So they use regulations, permits, administrative delays. They strangle ministries with paperwork rather than violence. It's more effective and far less visible."

Joseph's hand drifted to his bag where the permit approval lay folded between his father's notes—60% size reduction, the prohibition on visible religious symbols—compromises disguised as accommodation. "My father dealt with similar officials. How did he manage?"

"By being simultaneously visible and invisible." Imran smiled at Joseph's confusion. "He built relationships openly —with village leaders, local businessmen, even some sympathetic officials. But the actual discipleship, the conversions, the baptisms—those happened quietly, in homes and hidden places. The mission compound was a community center that happened to have a chapel. Most people saw the medical care and education. Only those ready to see it understood the spiritual transformation occurring beneath the surface."

Joseph gripped his mother's cross at his neck, pulled out his father's Bible, flipped to margins dense with notes. "He wrote something here about the mission being bigger than any building. I'm trying to understand what he meant."

Imran leaned forward, reading the familiar handwriting with evident emotion. "He wrote that after the first major persecution—about a year before the final attack. The TLP burned down a small worship hall we'd built in a neighboring village. Killed three believers. Your father was devastated. But then he saw something remarkable."

"What?"

"The church didn't disappear. It scattered into homes, into market stalls, into fields where believers worked side by side. Persecution had destroyed the building but strengthened the bonds between people." Imran's eyes grew distant. "That's when William understood—we were never building a mission. We were building a movement. The structures were just tools, not the goal itself."

The words resonated deep in Joseph's chest. All his planning had focused on physical reconstruction—blueprints, materials, timelines. But his father had been thinking about something more organic, more resilient.

"The people I'm going back to," Joseph said. "They've been meeting in secret for fifteen years. What if rebuilding a visible mission actually endangers them more than it helps?"

"That's the right question to ask," Imran replied. "Though I think you'll find the answer isn't either-or. They need both—the underground network that's kept them alive, and a visible presence that reminds them they haven't been forgotten. The key is building in a way that serves both purposes."

A knock interrupted them. Imran glanced at his watch, then smiled.

"Ah. Perfect timing." He rose. "There's someone I'd like you to meet. Someone whose experience in hostile environments could prove invaluable to your mission."

Joseph stood as Imran moved to the door. "Who?"

"A man who has walked the path you're about to take." Imran opened the door. "Joseph Freeman, meet Darius Karimi."

# FIVE

## Darius Awan

*OXFORD, ENGLAND*

Joseph had expected an academic—someone like Imran, comfortable in libraries and lecture halls. Darius Karimi looked like a man who'd seen war. Silver hair and a neatly trimmed beard framed a face weathered by sun and hardship. But it was his eyes that caught Joseph—dark, penetrating, holding depths of experience that no amount of study could replicate.

"Mr. Freeman." Darius's voice carried the melodic accent of Farsi, though his English was flawless. He didn't offer his hand immediately, instead studying Joseph with an intensity that made him want to look away.

"Please, call me Joseph."

"Very well." Darius finally extended his hand. His grip was firm, calloused. "Imran tells me you plan to rebuild your parents' mission in Pakistan."

"That's right."

"Then you're either very brave or very foolish." Darius

moved past him into the study, lowering himself into the chair Joseph had vacated. "Forgive my bluntness, but the Northwest Frontier Province is no place for optimistic Americans who think good intentions will protect them."

Heat rose in Joseph's chest. "I'm not—"

"You're young," Darius continued, as if Joseph hadn't spoken. "Educated. You've spent most of your life in safety. What do you actually know about surviving in a place where your faith makes you a target?"

Darius waited for his answer.

"My parents died there," Joseph said, forcing his voice to remain level. "I was ten years old when I escaped through a tunnel while the TLP burned everything around me. So don't tell me I don't understand danger."

Darius's face didn't change. "Understanding danger and knowing how to navigate it are different things. You witnessed tragedy. That doesn't qualify you to prevent it from happening again."

"Then help me learn." Joseph leaned forward. "Imran said you've established churches in Iran, Afghanistan, Central Asia. That you've worked in places even more hostile than Pakistan. I'm not asking you to believe in me— I'm asking you to believe in what my parents started and what the people there have kept alive for fifteen years."

"Why?" Darius's question was sharp. "Why should I risk my networks, my contacts, my credibility to support a mission that's already failed once?"

Joseph clenched his fists. "Because it didn't fail. My parents built something that transformed lives. The TLP destroyed buildings, but they didn't destroy faith. Hassan and his group have been meeting in secret all this time, waiting for someone to come back. That's not failure—that's resilience."

"Resilience that could be undone by one careless mistake from an inexperienced missionary who thinks passion is enough." Darius moved to the window. "I've seen it before. Well-meaning Westerners arrive in hostile regions with noble plans. They don't understand the culture, don't speak the language fluently, don't recognize threats until it's too late. Then they retreat to safety while locals pay the price for their naiveté."

"I speak Urdu. I understand the culture—I was born to a Pakistani mother. And I'm not naive about the risks. That's exactly why I'm here—to learn from people like you who've succeeded where others failed."

Darius turned from the window. "What makes you think I've succeeded?"

"Because you're still alive. Because you've planted churches that are still growing thirty years after you started. Because Imran trusts you enough to introduce us."

Darius's expression changed to something like respect.

Joseph continued. "You're right that I've lived in safety. But I'm also right that I'm called to this work. God doesn't always call the qualified—sometimes He qualifies the called. I can't do this alone. I need wisdom from people who've walked this path before me."

Neither spoke for a moment. Imran remained by the window, letting the conversation unfold without interference.

Finally, Darius returned to his chair. "Tell me about your preparation. What have you actually done to equip yourself for this mission?"

For the next hour, Joseph laid out everything—the fundraising, the permit negotiations, the team he hoped to assemble, the restrictions he'd have to work within. Darius asked pointed questions, probing for weaknesses in Joseph's planning. Each question revealed another gap in his knowledge, another risk he hadn't fully considered.

But Joseph didn't deflect or make excuses. He acknowledged the gaps, admitted his inexperience, and asked how to address each vulnerability. Slowly, almost imperceptibly, Darius's interrogation became a conversation. His challenges became advice. His skepticism became cautious engagement.

"The people who've survived there," Darius said finally, "what do you know about them? Their names, their stories, their current situation?"

Joseph reached for his bag, pulling out his mother's diary. "My mother documented testimonies. Dozens of them." He opened to a marked page. "Tariq—my childhood friend. Son of a tanner. Baptized at twelve, memorized the entire Book of John. His father was martyred in a second raid for refusing to deny Christ."

He turned pages. "Samina—Hassan's wife. She leads a women's group. At least she did fifteen years ago. I don't know if she's still..." His voice trailed off.

Darius took the diary, reading with careful attention. His face softened as he absorbed the words.

"These are real people," Darius said quietly. "Not abstractions. Not projects. People with families, histories, faith that has cost them everything."

"That's why I have to go back," Joseph said. "Not because I think I can save them—they've saved themselves by staying faithful. But because they shouldn't have to hide forever. Because they deserve to know they haven't been forgotten."

Darius closed the diary, handing it back with obvious respect for what it contained. "Your mother was a remarkable woman. This documentation..." He shook his head.

"Most missionaries don't think to preserve these stories. They're too focused on their own accomplishments."

"She wanted to remember every person touched by the Gospel," Joseph said. "She said each testimony was a thread in a larger tapestry that God was weaving."

"And now you want to continue that weaving." Darius studied Joseph with new focus. "Even knowing it might cost you what it cost your parents?"

Joseph met his gaze without flinching. "Especially knowing that."

Darius was quiet for a long moment. Then he stood, extending his hand across the space between them. "I'll help you. Not because I think you're ready—you're not. But because those people deserve someone who cares enough to be this stubborn about returning."

Joseph rose, gripping Darius's hand. The older man's look remained serious, but something had changed—a door opening where there had been only wall.

"I'll need you to understand something," Darius said. "When I agree to help, I don't halfway commit. I'll go with you to Pakistan. I'll use my contacts to help establish your mission. But in return, you must listen when I tell you something is too dangerous. You must trust my judgment even when it contradicts your passion. Can you accept that?"

"Yes."

"We'll see." Darius released his hand. "Imran, do you have that list I sent you?"

Imran moved to his desk, retrieving a folder. "Right here. Eight names—people with specific skills relevant to Joseph's mission. All experienced in hostile environments."

"We'll need to assemble a team," Darius explained. "You can't do this with just local believers and good intentions. You need engineers who understand building in conflict zones. Medical professionals experienced with limited resources. Security experts who know how to assess and mitigate threats."

Joseph's head spun with the sudden shift from skepticism to strategic planning. "When would we start?"

"Immediately," Darius said. "If you're serious about this, we begin building your team now. Some of these people might be available within weeks. Others might take months to recruit. But by the time you're ready to break ground in Pakistan, you'll have a foundation of experienced professionals around you."

He glanced at Imran. "Can we use your college for a planning session? Gather the candidates who are local, do video calls with the others?"

"Of course," Imran replied. "I'll arrange space and send out invitations."

The speed of it all left Joseph breathless. An hour ago, Darius had been challenging his competence. Now they were planning recruitment sessions and discussing logistics.

"Why?" Joseph asked. "What changed your mind?"

Darius's look softened—barely perceptible, but genuine. "Because you didn't try to convince me you were ready. You admitted you weren't and asked for help anyway." He moved toward the door, then paused. "And because your mother's diary reminded me why I do this work. Those testimonies— those are real victories in a war most people don't even know is being fought. If there's a chance to protect those victories, to help them grow..." He shrugged. "Then I can't walk away."

———

Joseph walked Oxford's ancient streets as afternoon faded to evening. The meeting with Darius had left him strangely energized. He'd been tested, challenged, pushed to his limits—and somehow earned the respect of a man who didn't give it easily.

His phone buzzed. A text from Uncle David: "*How did it go?*"

Joseph smiled as he typed: "*I found my mentors. And they're terrifying.*"

David's response came quickly: "*Good. You need people who'll tell you the truth.*"

Joseph pocketed his phone and continued walking, letting Oxford's atmosphere sink into his bones. Students hurried past in their gowns. Bells tolled from a nearby chapel. The ancient university had trained missionaries and theologians for centuries—men and women who'd carried the Gospel into hostile territories, who'd paid the cost that his parents had paid.

He thought about Darius's final words. *Your mother's diary reminded me why I do this work.* The testimonies his mother had carefully documented weren't just history—they were fuel for the next generation. Proof that the work mattered. Evidence that transformed lives were worth any price.

Joseph paused at the edge of a courtyard, watching light fade from Gothic spires. In two days, the team would gather. People with skills he didn't have, experience he couldn't replicate, wisdom he desperately needed. Darius and Imran had opened doors he didn't know existed.

The question that had haunted him since accepting Mercer's offer—was he compromising too much?—felt less urgent now. Compromise was part of wisdom. His parents had compromised on dozens of issues to maintain their presence in Pakistan. What they'd never compromised was their core calling: to serve people and share Christ's love.

Darius and Imran would help him navigate the difference. Mercer's money would provide resources. Hassan and the local believers would provide knowledge of the current situation. And somewhere in the balance of all those elements, Joseph would find the path forward.

He wasn't following a unique path. He was joining centuries of faithful people who'd carried the Gospel into hostile territories, who'd paid the cost that his parents had paid.

And for the first time since that fundraiser in Biloxi, Joseph felt something that might have been readiness.

Not the reckless confidence of youth, but the sober awareness that he was surrounded by people who wouldn't let him fail alone.

# SIX

**The Assembly**

Darius Karimi had assembled teams for impossible missions before. Tehran, after the revolution. Kabul, during the Soviet occupation. Mazar-i-Sharif, when the Taliban controlled everything north of the Hindu Kush. Each time, he'd looked at eager faces and wondered which ones wouldn't make it home.

He adjusted the last chair in the semicircle at St. Michael's Church, then stepped back to assess his work. Eight chairs facing a simple podium where Joseph would stand. The conference room smelled of coffee and damp wool, rain streaking the windows behind them.

Sixty-three years old now. How many more missions did he have left in him? The question surfaced more frequently these days, usually late at night when old injuries ached and older memories refused to sleep.

The door opened. A petite woman stepped in first, dark

hair in a neat bun, tailored coat despite the rain. She carried a leather portfolio and moved with the precision of someone who measured every action.

"Reverend Karimi?" Her accent was educated British, but something underneath spoke of South Asia. "I'm Maya Chaudhry. Imran said three o'clock?"

"Please, just Darius." He gestured to the chairs. "You're early. That's good."

She smiled, choosing a seat near the center. "Hazard of the profession. Lawyers learn to arrive before the judge."

Behind her came a tall Asian man carrying a blueprint tube, pausing in the doorway as if calculating the room's dimensions. Then a younger woman in a vibrant hijab, eyes bright with curiosity. Others followed—eight in total, each one hand-selected from a network of people who understood what it meant to serve in hostile places.

Eliza Cohen arrived next—thirties, laptop bag slung over one shoulder, the practiced efficiency of someone who'd documented crises worldwide. Rebecca Miller, a nurse practitioner with steady hands and gray-streaked auburn hair. Manny Hernandez, fresh from seminary, twenty-five and earnest, carrying both a Bible and a tablet.

The last to arrive was Ian Daniels. Former SAS, now training NGOs in crisis zones. He entered with the bearing of a soldier even in civilian clothes, scanning the room's exits before taking the seat nearest the door. Their eyes met briefly. Ian's expression said he knew exactly what this was about, and he wasn't sure he approved.

"Thank you all for coming," Darius began, remaining standing while they settled. "Some of you know me. Others know only what Imran told you. Before we start, I want to be clear—what I'm asking you to consider is dangerous. Not hypothetically dangerous. Actually dangerous."

He let that settle before continuing.

"A young man named Joseph Freeman plans to rebuild his parents' Christian mission in Northwest Pakistan. The same mission that was destroyed by militants fifteen years ago. The same region where persecution has intensified, not diminished. Where blasphemy laws are weaponized, where government officials actively work to prevent Christian ministry, where the TLP operates with near impunity."

Maya's pen moved across her notepad. Samuel Wong—the engineer—adjusted his glasses. Leila Nassar, the linguist, and a Muslim, leaned forward with interest.

"Joseph has secured funding from an American tech company. He has preliminary permits from Pakistani authorities, though with severe restrictions. What he doesn't have is experience, expertise, or a realistic understanding of what he's walking into." Darius paused. "That's where you come in."

"Why us?" The question came from Thomas Okafor, the agricultural specialist. His Nigerian accent was thick, his expression skeptical. "There are organizations with resources, with infrastructure already in place. Why assemble a team from scratch?"

"Because organizations have protocols, committees, liability concerns," Darius replied. "They move slowly and avoid risk. Joseph needs people who can act quickly, adapt constantly, and work in gray areas where official channels fail."

"You mean people who don't mind bending rules," Ian said flatly.

"I mean people who understand that serving in hostile places requires wisdom, not just compliance." Darius met Ian's gaze directly. "You've worked Somalia, Yemen,

Afghanistan. You know the difference between reckless risk and calculated necessity."

Ian's expression didn't soften, but he didn't argue.

"Joseph Freeman." Maya looked up from her notes. "The missionary's son who escaped the original attack?"

"The same."

"I've heard of him," she said thoughtfully. "There was an incident in America several years ago. A football game. Someone was injured, and Freeman..." She trailed off, glancing around as if unsure how to continue.

"Healed him," Leila finished, her tone matter-of-fact. " The video went viral. People claimed it was fake, staged, but the player later said his heart had stopped on the field."

The room shifted. Some faces registered interest, others skepticism.

"I'm not here to debate miracles," Darius said. "What matters is that Joseph has a gift that draws attention— wanted or not. That makes him both an asset and a liability."

"What's your connection to this?" Samuel asked. "Why are you involved?"

Darius considered how much to reveal. These people deserved honesty, but not all wounds needed to be exposed.

"Thirty years ago, I helped establish underground churches in Iran," he said. "Many thrived. Some were discovered. People I trained, people I cared about..." He stopped, collecting himself. "They paid prices I couldn't pay for them. I've spent three decades trying to get it right— teaching others to build ministries that can survive persecution."

He gestured toward the empty podium. "Joseph reminds me of myself at twenty-five. Passionate, deter- mined, dangerously naive. He'll get himself killed, and everyone who follows him, unless someone teaches him how to survive."

"So we're not just rebuilding a mission," Maya said. " We're trying to keep an idealistic American from becoming another martyr statistic."

"Essentially."

The room absorbed this. Rain continued its percussion against the windows.

"Tell us about the team structure," Samuel said, pulling out his own notebook. "What roles need filling?"

For the next twenty minutes, Darius outlined the framework. Samuel would handle structural engineering and construction management. Maya would navigate legal challenges and advocacy. Leila would provide linguistic and cultural interpretation—and as a Muslim committed to religious freedom, her perspective would bridge communities in ways a Christian team alone could not. Thomas would develop sustainable agriculture and food security. Ian —if he agreed—would design security protocols and threat assessment.

Eliza would document their work while protecting identities. Rebecca would provide medical care with limited resources. Manny would handle communications technology and coordinate with supporters.

Each person asked pointed questions. What was the budget? What were the permit restrictions? How would they coordinate with local believers? What happened if Pakistani authorities shut them down?

Darius answered everything he could, admitting freely when he didn't know. Joseph would arrive soon to provide specifics. For now, Darius wanted to gauge their interest, their concerns, their commitment levels.

"Which tech company is funding this?" Maya asked.

"Stellarion."

Her eyebrows rose. "Alexander Mercer is funding this? That's... unexpected."

"And complicated," Darius acknowledged. "He has business interests in Pakistan—wants to expand satellite internet infrastructure there. The mission serves multiple purposes for him."

"So we're helping a billionaire access emerging markets," Thomas said. "Why not work with established organizations instead? Groups with resources, infrastructure already in place?"

"Because established organizations wouldn't touch this," Ian said, speaking for the first time since his earlier comment. "Too risky, too politically complicated, too likely to end in casualties. Am I right?"

Darius nodded. "Which is why we need people willing to work outside traditional structures. People who understand that the most important work often happens where institutions fear to go."

"I have a question." Ian's voice cut through the discussion like a blade. "What's the extraction plan?"

The room quieted.

"If things go sideways—when things go sideways—how do we get out?" Ian sat straighter. "I've seen enough operations in hostile zones to know that good intentions don't stop bullets. If the TLP targets the mission, if local authorities turn against us, if political winds shift—what's our exit strategy?"

"Stellarion requires a withdrawal clause," Darius said. "If security conditions deteriorate beyond acceptable levels, the mission suspends operations and personnel evacuate."

"Who determines 'acceptable levels'?"

"Their security director, in consultation with us."

"And the local believers who can't evacuate? The Pakistani Christians who don't have foreign passports?" Ian's tone sharpened. "What happens to them when we pull out and leave them exposed?"

Several team members shifted uncomfortably.

"That," Darius said quietly, "is the moral complexity we'll live with. We can't save everyone. We can only create opportunities and hope local leadership can sustain what we start."

"That's not good enough." Ian stood. "I've participated in too many operations where Westerners arrive with noble plans, stir things up, then retreat to safety when consequences arrive. The locals always pay the highest price."

"You're right," Darius agreed, not trying to argue. "They do. They always have. That's why we need people like you— to minimize that risk, to plan for worst-case scenarios, to build something resilient enough to survive our eventual departure."

Ian moved toward the door. "With respect, Darius, I don't think Joseph Freeman understands what he's asking people to risk. And I'm not sure you do either, if you're willing to put a team in that environment without ironclad security guarantees."

"There are no ironclad guarantees," Darius replied. "There never are. Only calculated risks and faithful obedience to callings we can't ignore."

Ian paused at the door, his hand on the frame. "My younger brother went to Afghanistan with an NGO eight years ago. Passionate, committed, certain God would protect him." His voice dropped. "He was killed in a Taliban ambush three months into his deployment. Twenty-six years old."

Silence filled the space. Rain drummed against windows.

"I'm sorry," Darius said.

"So am I." Ian turned back to face the room. "Which is why I need more than passion and faith before I commit to something that could get more good people killed."

"What would you need?"

The voice came from the doorway.

# SEVEN

## The Commitment

Darius hadn't heard him arrive. None of them had. Joseph Freeman stood at the threshold, his face set with determination but his eyes holding something else—understanding, perhaps. Or pain.

He stepped into the room, and Darius noticed details he'd missed during their first meeting. The way Joseph's hand moved unconsciously to a silver cross beneath his collar. The slight tension in his shoulders that suggested he'd heard more of Ian's objection than just the last statement. The worn messenger bag that likely contained his father's Bible.

"I heard what you said about your brother," Joseph continued, moving toward Ian. "I'm sorry for your loss. And you're right to question whether I understand what I'm asking people to risk."

Ian's posture remained rigid, defensive.

"My parents died in Pakistan," Joseph said. "I was ten years old, hiding in a tunnel while militants burned every-

thing above me. My mother pressed this cross into my hand
—" he pulled it out from beneath his collar, "—seconds
before I ran. I heard her screaming. I heard my father's
voice. Then I heard nothing."

The raw honesty stopped everyone. Even Ian's hard
expression softened slightly.

"For fifteen years, I lived with guilt that I survived when
they didn't. That I was safe in America while believers in
Pakistan suffered the consequences of my parents' work."
Joseph's voice steadied. "I'm not naive enough to think this
mission will be safe. I know people might die—might die
because of choices I make. That terrifies me."

He looked around the room, meeting each person's gaze.
"But those people are already dying. Already suffering.
Already hiding their faith because there's no one willing to
stand with them. My parents started something that
mattered. Hassan and the local believers kept it alive for
fifteen years. I can't guarantee your safety if you help me. I
can't promise everything will work out. All I can promise is
that what we're building matters enough to risk everything
for."

Ian remained by the door, his face unreadable.

"I need you," Joseph said directly to him. "Not just your
skills, but your skepticism. Your experience. Your understanding of how things go wrong. Because you're right—I
don't fully grasp what I'm asking people to risk. But I'm
willing to learn. And I need teachers who won't let me make
fatal mistakes."

The room held its breath. Rain continued its steady
rhythm.

The silence stretched.

Ian moved back to his chair and sat. "I'll help you plan
the security infrastructure. Threat assessment, emergency

protocols, evacuation routes." His voice carried a warning. "But I won't sugarcoat the dangers. And if I say something is too risky, you listen. Deal?"

"Deal."

Maya spoke next. "My father was a lawyer in Lahore who represented Christians in blasphemy cases. We fled to London when I was fourteen because the threats became too dangerous." She rolled up her sleeve, revealing a jagged scar. "This is from the last attack before we left. They broke into our home and found both of us. My father tried to protect me, but..."

Joseph's expression tightened with recognition—shared trauma.

"I became a civil rights attorney because of what happened to my family," Maya continued. "If I can help create legal protection for believers in Pakistan, help prevent what happened to us from happening to others..." She let the sentence hang. "Count me in."

One by one, the others committed. Samuel with his structural engineering expertise. Thomas with his agricultural knowledge. Eliza, Rebecca, Manny—each bringing specific skills, each accepting the risks. Leila, who saw the mission as a chance to use her linguistic gifts for something meaningful.

"I'm not a Christian," she said shyly. "But I've documented the erasure of minority faiths across three continents. The Baha'i in Iran. Rohingya Muslims in Myanmar. Uyghurs in China." Her voice strengthened. "Your community deserves to have its story preserved, its resilience documented. I can help ensure the world knows you exist—that you refuse to disappear."

The room absorbed this—a Muslim woman committing to help build a Christian mission. Joseph tempered his surprise, but didn't hate the fact. He had many Muslim friends growing up in Pakistan.

When the last person had spoken, Darius allowed himself cautious hope—not the reckless optimism of youth, but the hard-won certainty of someone who'd seen both success and failure. This team might actually succeed. Not because they were naive about the dangers, but because they understood them and chose to proceed anyway.

"We start immediately," Darius said. "Samuel, I need preliminary assessments of building in that region—materials, labor, timelines. Maya, begin researching legal frameworks and potential advocacy channels. Ian, develop our security protocols. Everyone else, coordinate with Imran to establish communication systems and logistics."

He glanced at Joseph. "You'll work with each team member individually over the next few weeks. Learn from them. Let them learn from you. By the time we're ready to break ground in Pakistan, we need to function as a unit, not a collection of individuals."

"When do we leave?" Joseph asked.

"Three months, maybe four," Darius replied. "Enough time to plan properly, to build relationships, to prepare for what we'll face." He looked around the room. "And enough time to back out if anyone changes their mind. This commitment is serious, but it's not final until we're on the ground."

"I won't change my mind."

"We'll see," Darius replied, not unkindly. "Conviction is easy in Oxford's conference rooms. It's harder when you're looking at actual threat reports or dealing with casualties."

———

Joseph watched the team disperse into Oxford's rainy afternoon, their voices fading down St. Michael's corridors. Relief should have followed—Darius had assembled experienced professionals willing to risk their lives for a mission most would call foolish. But instead, their trust pressed against Joseph.

Darius began stacking chairs, restoring the room to its original configuration.

"Thank you," Joseph said. "For believing in this. For bringing them together."

"They committed because you were honest about your limitations," Darius replied, folding the last chair. "Don't lose that honesty when the real pressure starts."

Joseph absorbed this. "What's the hardest part? Of leading in hostile places?"

Darius paused, his hands resting on the chair back. "Knowing when to push forward and when to pull back. Your parents never learned that balance."

The observation stung because it was true. His mother's final scream still echoed in nightmares—her refusal to leave even when Hassan begged them to flee.

"They believed staying was faithfulness."

"And it was," Darius moved toward the door. "But faithfulness without wisdom is just stubbornness wearing a religious disguise. Learn the difference, or you'll repeat their mistakes."

They walked together through the corridors, past portraits of theologians who'd faced their own impossible callings. Outside, rain had gentled to mist, softening Oxford's ancient stones.

"In three days, we meet again," Darius said. "You'll present your vision in detail—budget, timeline, strategic priorities. The team will tear it apart, and you'll rebuild it based on their input. Then we'll do it again. And again. Until the plan is strong enough to survive contact with reality."

"And then?"

"Then we pray." Darius's smile was brief but genuine. "Because even the best plans require divine intervention in that part of the world."

Joseph watched Darius disappear into the mist, his silhouette fading among Oxford's spires. The team was assembled. The planning would begin. In three months— maybe four—they would board planes for Pakistan, carrying skills, experience, and faith that they could go to his childhood home and make a difference.

———

Back in his hotel room that night, Joseph sat on the edge of the bed, his father's Bible open beside him, his mother's diary in his lap. Two sacred texts. Two parents' legacies. Both pointing him toward the same impossible calling.

The day's events replayed in his mind. Ian's challenge. The team's commitments. Darius's warning about knowing when to retreat. His mother's prayer echoed from the diary's pages: *The wisdom to know when to stay and when to leave.*

She'd prayed for wisdom she knew she lacked, trusting that her son might learn what she couldn't teach. The burden of that prayer—the hope she'd placed in him—felt almost too heavy to carry.

He pulled out his phone and opened the message thread with Hassan. For the past three years, their communication had been brief, coded, cautious—a few words every few months, never enough to draw attention. Now he typed without hesitation:

*"I'm coming home. Team assembled. Funding secured. Three months. Tell no one until I arrive."*

His thumb hovered over the send button. Once he pressed it, there was no taking it back. Hassan would tell the believers. They would wait, hope, prepare. If Joseph failed them now...

He thought of Tariq's childhood drawing that his mother had described in the diary. Of Miriam's imprisoned husband. Of Fatima wanting to worship openly once more before she died. Of Hassan, who'd tended a scattered flock for fifteen years, waiting for someone to return.

He thought of Ian's brother, dead in Afghanistan at twenty-six. Of Maya's scar. Of Darius's lost students in Iran. Of the cost that faithfulness demanded.

And he thought of his mother pressing the silver cross into his palm, choosing to save him even as she stayed behind to die.

Joseph hit send.

The message delivered. Three dots appeared immediately—Hassan, awake in Pakistan despite the late hour, probably never far from his phone.

*"We've been waiting. God be with you, beta."*

Joseph set the phone down and looked around the hotel room. This was still the West—safe, comfortable, familiar. In three months, he would cross a threshold he couldn't uncross. He would enter the world where his faith made him a target, where his calling might cost him everything.

Where his parents had paid the ultimate price.

Where others might pay it again because of choices he would make.

But he wouldn't cross that threshold alone. Darius would go with him. Ian would plan for worst-case scenarios.

Maya would fight legal battles. His team was as committed as he was.

And in Pakistan, Hassan was waiting. Old friends were waiting. People who'd kept faith alive through fifteen years of darkness, hoping someone would remember them.

Joseph closed his mother's diary and set it beside his father's Bible. Two legacies. Two callings. One path forward.

He knelt beside the bed and prayed—not for safety, not for success, but for the wisdom his mother had asked God to grant him. The wisdom to know when to stay and when to leave. The wisdom to lead without getting people killed. The wisdom to build something that would outlast his inevitable mistakes.

Outside, Oxford slept beneath its ancient spires. Inside, Joseph made peace with what was coming.

The mission would rise again.

And this time, God willing, it would be built on faith as much as stone.

# EIGHT

## The Gathering

*SHINGLI PAYEEN VILLAGE, PAKISTAN*

Hassan shifted on his thin cushion, feeling the ache in his knees. The bitter aroma of over-steeped tea filled the cramped living room. Shadows of dusk stretched across the worn carpet. A single bulb hung from the ceiling, its light too weak to push back the encroaching darkness. Outside, the muezzin's call to prayer floated through the neighborhood—the familiar, haunting melody that had been the soundtrack to both peace and persecution in their lives.

At fifty-three, Hassan's body carried years spent in vigilant service. His calloused hands—once those of William Freeman's assistant at the mission, now those of a day laborer—cradled a chipped teacup as he studied those with him in the room.

Six faces turned toward him, expressions ranging from hopeful to hostile. Nadir, the quiet merchant—fifty-something, with the cautious bearing of someone who'd lost much—who'd lost his shop to a suspicious fire last year.

Amir, a thin man in his thirties with nervous energy, and his wife Samina, quieter, with careful eyes. Fatima, the eldest at seventy-two. Miriam, whose husband had been imprisoned for three years. And Tariq, whose bitterness cut deepest because he and Joseph had once been inseparable.

Seven believers total—all that remained of a vibrant congregation of over a hundred. Seven who had answered his urgent summons after Amir brought the news that had changed everything.

The metal box sat on the low table between them, its surface pitted and weathered by years. Hassan had kept it hidden for years, moving it from location to location, never leaving it in one place long enough for curious eyes to wonder about its contents. Inside lay their history— evidence that a church had once thrived here, and that a remnant still survived.

"Beta, tell them again what you heard," Hassan said to Amir, who sat nervously beside his wife Samina.

Amir cleared his throat, glancing through the thin curtained windows as if expecting to be overheard. "Sahib, my cousin Nadeem—he works as a clerk in Deputy Commissioner Qadir's office. Three days ago, an application came across his desk requesting to rebuild the old mission compound." His voice dropped even lower. "It was filed on behalf of an American named Joseph Freeman."

"Ai hai, is it true?" Fatima whispered, her weathered hands clutching a frayed dupatta around shoulders bent by decades of hardship. "Is the son of William Freeman truly returning?"

Hassan must rally these scattered believers without igniting false hope or dangerous expectations. More than that, he needed their trust. For fifteen years, he had been their quiet shepherd, keeping the flame of faith alive while remaining invisible to those who had destroyed the mission.

"I believe so, ji." Hassan set down his cup on the low table. The soft clink seemed unnaturally loud in the tense room. "Nadeem wouldn't have risked telling Amir unless he was certain. The application even included architectural plans for rebuilding."

Miriam leaned forward. "But why now, Hassan? After all these years?" Her voice held no accusation, only genuine confusion. "The laws are even harsher now. The blasphemy statutes can put us in prison for life just for having a Bible. The local authorities don't look for evidence anymore—just an allegation from any Muslim citizen is enough."

"And the international organizations that once protected us have mostly withdrawn," added Amir. "Since the new religious protection amendments, we exist in a legal gray zone at best. We're tolerated as long as we're invisible. Any public expression of faith—"

"Is considered provocation," Hassan finished grimly. "I know the risks. But perhaps that's exactly why Joseph is returning now—when we need him most."

"An American who abandoned us." Tariq's voice cut through the room from his corner. At twenty-seven, he had been only twelve when the mission burned, Joseph's constant companion. His angular face, handsome despite the permanent furrow between his brows, twisted with bitterness. "Why should we risk everything again for someone who fled while we suffered like dogs?"

Amir and Samina exchanged glances, their hands finding each other's in silent communication. Fatima's lips pressed into a thin line of disapproval at Tariq's words.

Hassan studied the floor. The others had gone completely still. This was what he had feared—the wounds were still raw, the trust shattered. How could he make them understand that night? The screams. The flames licking at the mission walls. The impossible choices forced upon a child.

"You don't know what happened, beta." The ceiling fan creaked above them, pushing around the warm air. "I was there during the attack. I was the one who helped Joseph escape."

"Then you're as guilty as he is," Tariq shot back, his dark eyes flashing. "My father died because he wouldn't deny Christ after the mission was destroyed. Where was the church when they came for the rest of us?"

Hassan had asked himself the same question in his darkest moments.

"Tariq," Fatima admonished, "show respect to your elder."

Hassan raised a hand. "Nahi, let him speak. These questions deserve answers."

The young man's chest heaved. "They hunted us like animals. Those of us who survived—we lived in fear, meeting in cellars, whispering our prayers. Some of us still bear the scars."

Seconds stretched in the stillness. Sidelong glances were exchanged among the group.

Hassan reached into his leather satchel, the same one he had carried for decades. From it, he withdrew the metal box, unwinding the thread wound around two makeshift clasps.

"Before you judge, there are things you should know."

The room fell silent as he placed the box on the low table. Even Tariq leaned in despite himself. Hassan lifted the lid, revealing yellowed papers with fading ink, a thumb drive wrapped in cloth, and a small notebook bound in cracked leather.

Miriam leaned forward. "What is it?" Her headscarf slipped back, revealing streaks of gray in her dark hair.

"Our history." Hassan's voice caught. "The record of our community until that night. Every baptism with full names and addresses, every testimony that identifies converts by family lineage, photographs that show faces of believers long scattered." He looked around the circle. "Proof that we existed. That we mattered. That we weren't erased."

He gestured to the other contents. "And the names of Muslims who believed in what William Freeman was doing —who helped us even though it put them at risk."

*If Faraz ever found this box, he could dismantle what remained of the church in a single week. Every believer's name would become a target. Every address, a raid waiting to happen. And the Muslims who'd risked everything to help us—they would face the harshest punishment of all.*

"You've kept this hidden all these years?" Amir's voice held both wonder and fear.

"Someone had to preserve the truth," Hassan said. "Someone had to bear witness that we existed, that we mattered. But it must never fall into the wrong hands."

Yusuf spoke for the first time, his shopkeeper's instincts alert. "If authorities found those records..."

"They would have everything they needed to destroy us completely," Hassan finished. "Which is why this box stays hidden until Joseph returns. Then we'll decide together what to do with it."

From beneath the papers, Hassan withdrew a faded photograph and passed it to Fatima. The image showed the compound—simple buildings surrounded by flowering gardens, a cross rising proudly from the chapel roof. Smiling faces—Pakistani and American—gathered on the steps, arms linked in fellowship. In the foreground stood

William Freeman and his wife, a young Joseph between them.

"The mission as it once was. As it could be again."

Fatima touched the photo with reverence. "I remember," she whispered, her voice thick with emotion. "My eldest son was married at the mission—thirty years ago, when William Freeman first arrived. I watched that compound grow from a single tent." Her weathered fingers traced the image. "Now I've watched it burn. I want to see it rise once more before I die."

She passed the photograph to Miriam.

The photo made its way around the circle, each person holding it like a sacred relic. When it reached Tariq, he stared at it for a long moment, his expression unreadable.

"And this," Hassan continued, revealing a handwritten ledger bound in faded blue cloth, "contains the names and locations of every believer who scattered after the fire. Sixty-seven families at first. Now forty-three." Some had scattered across borders with nothing but the clothes they wore. Others had whispered denials of Christ with trembling lips, choosing survival over martyrdom. And then there were the graves—shallow ones dug in haste, and the unmarked places where bodies were never found.

"I've visited each one, at great risk, to maintain our connection. Some monthly, others when possible. I've baptized their children, prayed over their sick, buried their dead." Hassan kept his voice steady. "Always in secret, always careful."

Samina's voice, rarely heard in these gatherings, cut through the tension. "You've been our pastor all these years." Her fingers clutched the edge of her dupatta.

Hassan shook his head. "Nah. Never a pastor. Just an old

gardener tending what remained until the true shepherd returned."

The hard lines around Tariq's mouth relaxed. He glanced between Hassan and the documents. "You've been planning this since Joseph left?"

"Because he made me a promise," Hassan replied. The memory surfaced with painful clarity—the boy's face streaked with ash and tears. "The night I helped him escape, he promised he would return one day and rebuild the mission." He took the photo from Tariq and looked at young Joseph's image. "When he returns, he'll have a flock to lead."

"If he truly cared, why didn't he come sooner?" Tariqpressed, but the edge had gone from his tone.

A dog barked in the distance. The call to prayer had ended, and the neighborhood had fallen into the quiet of evening devotions.

"You don't understand what his escape cost him," Hassan said, rising to his feet with unexpected force. He kept his volume low. "I was there when they came for his family."

The memory crashed over him in vivid detail—the rush to the trap door, the shouts of the mob, the desperate scramble through the tunnel.

"He refused to leave at first," Hassan continued, the words thick with emotion. "Joseph—only ten years old then —begged them to let him stay. I can still hear him crying as the trucks sped toward the schoolhouse."

The room was utterly still now. Even the ceiling fan seemed to pause in its creaking rotation.

"I took him to my cousin's in the hills. Then on to Islamabadwith nothing but the clothes on his back." Hassan's voice broke. "So before you question his courage, remember he was just a child who lost everything in one night."

Hassan looked around the room, meeting each gaze directly. The single bulb illuminated their faces.

"Now we must decide—do we remain scattered, or do we help Joseph rebuild what was destroyed? Not just walls and roofs, but a community of faith in this place that has forgotten God's name."

The silence stretched, broken only by the distant sounds of life continuing outside—a child's laugh, a motorcycle engine, the clatter of dishes.

Fatima spoke first. "I will help him." Her voice quavered but held firm. "I am old. What more can they take from me? I want to worship in a proper church once more before I die."

"It will be dangerous," Amir said. "But we've lived in danger so long, perhaps it's time to risk for something greater than mere survival."

Nadir was next. "My shop burned because someone accused me of selling Christian materials. I lost everything already. What more can they take?"

One by one, they agreed—all except Tariq, who stared at the photograph in Hassan's hands. "My father died in the second raid." The anger in his tone faded. "Three months after the mission burned, when they discovered some of us were still meeting in secret for prayer. The TLP militants went house to house." His voice dropped to a whisper. "They gave my father one chance to deny Christ. He refused. They executed him in our courtyard as an example to others."

Hassan understood the question beneath Tariq's words —*Will he be worthy of my father's sacrifice? Will he be worthy of ours?*

"That..." Hassan reached to place a hand on the young man's shoulder, "is something he must learn from us."

Tariq gave him a single, sharp nod. "Then I will see what Joseph has become. Whether the boy I knew grew into a man worthy of my father's sacrifice."

"That's all I ask," Hassan replied, relief coursing through him. He had not realized how tightly his muscles had been clenched until they released.

Miriam pulled a worn envelope from inside her dress. "There's something you should know, Hassan. I received another letter from my husband yesterday." Her hands trembled as she unfolded the paper. "The prison doctor says his lungs are failing. They refuse to release him or provide proper medicine."

She read aloud, her voice breaking: "'Tell Hassan I pray for the mission's return. Tell him I dream of worshiping there once more. Even if I cannot see it with my eyes, I will see it with faith.'"

Tears tracked down her cheeks. "He's dying, Hassan. He won't live to see what we're building."

Hassan sat beside her. "Then we will take pictures for him," Hassan said gently. "We will document every step, every stone laid. And we will pray without ceasing for his release."

"I've been praying for fifteen years," Miriam whispered. "Sometimes I wonder if God has forgotten us."

"He hasn't," Fatima said firmly, moving to Miriam's other side. "But He asks us to be faithful even when we cannot see His hand at work."

Hassan looked at the photograph again—William and Lyla Freeman, arms around their young son, standing before the mission they'd built with their own hands. They hadn't lived to see what would grow from their sacrifice. But Tariq was here because of them. Miriam's faith had survived because of them. This small gathering of believers existed because two Americans had believed their calling mattered more than their safety.

"We should pray," Fatima suggested, already shifting to kneel on the carpet despite her arthritic knees. "Allah humein himmat day."

One by one, they rose and moved toward Hassan—first Miriam with her dignified limp, then Samina wiping flour from her palms, Nadir with his careful merchant's steps, and finally Tariq, hesitant but drawn by something stronger than his doubt. They formed a circle in the center of the cramped room, beneath the single bulb.

Hassan closed his eyes as their hands linked together. "Jesus. You who sees all things, who has preserved us through fire and persecution—"

Three quick raps at the door froze them in place.

Hassan opened his eyes to find six startled faces staring back at him.

No one had been expected. No one should know they were gathering.

Hassan placed a finger over his lips, quickly placing the materials back into the metal box. Tariq moved to the window, edging the curtain aside to peer out.

The knock came again, more insistent.

"Open up, Hassan," came a voice from outside that sent a chill through the room. "Or I'll break the door down."

# NINE

**The Threat**

"Hide everything," Hassan whispered urgently, closing the lid of the box. "Now."

Nadir slid the box beneath a loose floorboard while Samina gathered the teacups, arranging them as if they'd been sharing a casual meal. Miriam produced a Quran, placing it prominently on the table and opening it to a random page.

"Federal Investigation Agency," Faraz called through the door. "Open up. I know you're in there."

Hassan exchanged a final glance with his followers, seeing their fear reflected back at him. He straightened his shoulders, smoothed his kurta, and moved to the door. Each step felt like walking through waist-high water.

He opened the door, forcing his features into a neutral expression.

Faraz Qureshi stood on the threshold, his lean frame silhouetted against the evening sky. The scar across his left cheek looked silver in the fading light. He held up an official identification card with the FIA emblem clearly visible.

"Salaam alaikum," Hassan said, his tone steadier than he felt.

"Walaikum salaam." Faraz tucked his credentials into his breast pocket, his attention moving past Hassan, scanning the room behind him. "I've been conducting inquiries in the neighborhood. I need to ask you some questions."

Hassan stepped aside and Faraz entered, and the small living room shrank—ceiling too low, walls too close, nowhere to look but at one another.

"Just friends sharing a meal," Hassan replied, gesturing to the cushions beside the low table. "Would you care for some tea, brother?"

Samina was already in the kitchen, her hands fumbling with the kettle. Nadir adjusted his position, casually draping his arm over the edge of the cushion that concealed the loose floorboard.

Faraz lowered himself onto a cushion, smoothing his uniform as he sat. "The Agency has been monitoring certain activities in this district. How long have you all been friends?"

"Many years," Tariq answered quickly. "We grew up in the same neighborhood."

Faraz accepted the tea Samina offered but didn't drink. Across from him, Hassan eased onto his cushion, fighting to keep his breathing even. "How may I help you this evening?"

A smile crossed Faraz's face, but his eyes remained flat as stone. "We've been tracking unusual communications coming into our region. Foreign interests showing a renewed concern for our community."

Hassan kept his expression neutral. "What sort of foreign interests?"

"Western. Christian." Faraz said with a scowl. "That American family—the Freemans—their compound was quite the problem before it was...resolved." He locked eyes with Hassan. "The FIA has flagged similar patterns emerging. Strange how these infidels never learn their lesson."

Sweat gathered at the small of Hassan's back as the temperature in the room seemed to rise. "The Freemans are dead," he said. "Their mission destroyed. What concern could the government possibly have now?"

Faraz set his teacup down with a soft click. "You've been seen there recently." The words fell like stones into still water. "You were in the garden." His tone hardened. "Examining the foundation. Curious place to spend your time. Do you have attachments that should be of concern to national security?"

Six pairs of eyes turned to Hassan, silently pleading for him to say the right thing.

"William Freeman's clinic treated my mother when no one else would," he said simply, drawing on the truth to make his story believable. "When the fever came through our village, he was the only one who didn't turn us away." He met Faraz's stare directly. "Is it so strange that I would remember kindness?"

"Kindness," Faraz repeated, as if testing the word. "Or perhaps blasphemous loyalty? My position forces me to take such matters very seriously."

Hassan shrugged. "Loyalty to whom? A dead man."

Faraz rose suddenly and walked around the small room like a predator drawn to fear. He examined a book-shelf, ran his finger along a windowsill. "The FIA can dig deeper into all of your associations, Hassan. See if there's anything that can put you on the wrong side of the Quran."

Tariq sat rigid. Faraz focused on the young man, something calculating in his look.

"You," Faraz said, approaching Tariq. "I recognize you. Your father was Ibrahim the tanner, yes?"

Tariq's jaw tightened. "Yes."

"A good Muslim man who made an unfortunate choice." Faraz's manner carried false sympathy. "Refusing to renounce his association with the Christian missionaries. Such loyalty cost him everything."

"My father was a man of principle," Tariq said, barely controlling himself.

"Principle." Faraz nodded slowly. "Is that what you call it? I call it foolishness. A man who abandons his true faith for foreign lies deserves whatever fate befalls him."

Tariq's hands clenched into fists. Hassan caught his eye, shaking his head slightly. *Don't give him what he wants.*

Faraz turned his attention to Miriam. "And you—your husband is in prison, is he not? For distributing...what was it? Religious materials?"

Miriam's face went pale. "My husband is innocent."

"The courts determined otherwise." Faraz's smile was cruel. "Though I understand he's not well. Prison conditions can be quite harsh, especially for those who persist in their delusions. Perhaps if his family were more cooperative with authorities, his situation might improve."

The threat was clear. Hassan placed himself between Faraz and Miriam. "We are all cooperative citizens, Director. We obey the laws, pay our taxes, mind our own business."

"Do you?" Faraz's attention swept the room again. "Then perhaps you can explain why a group of known Christian sympathizers is meeting here, after hours, with the curtains drawn and the door locked?"

"We are friends sharing a meal," Hassan repeated. "Nothing more."

"Friends." Faraz approached the table, his hand hovering over the prominently displayed Quran. "Then you won't mind if I look around? Ensure there's nothing here that violates our laws?"

Hassan's blood ran cold. The metal box was barely hidden beneath the floorboard. One thorough search and Faraz would find everything—the names, the addresses, the photographs that could destroy what remained of their church.

"Do you have a warrant?" Fatima spoke with surprising strength for a woman her age.

Faraz turned to her, eyebrows raised. "A warrant? Dear grandmother, the FIA doesn't need warrants for routine security checks. Especially when there are concerns about national interests."

"Then we have nothing to hide," Hassan said, praying his words didn't betray the lie. "Look wherever you wish."

Faraz studied him for a long moment. Then he approached the bookshelf, running his fingers along the spines. He pulled out a few books, flipped through them, replaced them.

Hassan's heart hammered. The loose floorboard was only three meters away. If Faraz noticed it, if Nadir's arm moved at the wrong moment...

"Your wife," Faraz said suddenly, not looking at Hassan. "She used to lead women's gatherings, didn't she? Bible studies, I believe they were called."

"My wife is dead," Hassan said.

"Yes." Faraz turned, his look almost sympathetic. "Seven years now, isn't it? Such a tragic accident. A fire, they said. Started while she was sleeping." He approached Hassan.

"Though some suggested it was no accident at all. That perhaps someone wanted to send a message about the dangers of... persistent evangelism."

The memory came flooding back—the charred remains of their small home, the neighbors who'd seen men running from the scene, the authorities who'd declared it an accident and closed the investigation within hours. "You know who killed her," Hassan said.

"I know many things," Faraz replied. "I know that your wife refused multiple warnings to stop her activities. I know that she believed her foreign God would protect her." His smile was vicious. "I know she was wrong."

Tariq stood abruptly, but Amir grabbed his arm, holding him back.

Faraz's hand went to his side near the bulge of a weapon. "Careful, young man. Assaulting an FIA officer carries severe penalties."

"Tariq, sit down," Hassan commanded, his words hard. The young man hesitated, then slowly lowered himself back to his cushion.

Faraz's attention went to the photographs on the wall—family pictures, neighborhood scenes. He paused at one, then pulled it down. Hassan's stomach dropped. It was a group photo from fifteen years ago, taken at a neighborhood celebration. In the background, barely visible, stood the Freeman mission compound.

"Interesting," Faraz murmured, tucking the photo inside his jacket. "A nice memory of better times, yes?"

"That's my property," Hassan protested.

"Consider it borrowed. For my files." Faraz headed toward the door, then paused. "I should mention—there was a merchant in the bazaar. Khalid, his name was. He also had fond memories of the foreigners who used to live here."

His words grew colder. "Last month, his shop burned down. The FIA classified it as an unfortunate accident. Such accidents happen to those with misplaced loyalties."

He opened the door, letting in the cool evening air. "We remember those who stand with Pakistan—and those who don't." He looked at each face in turn. "Choose wisely which side of that memory you wish to occupy."

The door closed behind him with terrible finality.

For three heartbeats, no one moved. Then Samina released a shuddering breath, and Yusuf whispered a prayer. The tension that had held them rigid broke, replaced by a flood of fear.

"He knows!" Tariq's voice cracked. "He knows Joseph is coming back!" He stood and paced the small room like a caged animal. "He must stay away—this is too dangerous for us now."

"Tariq is right," Miriam agreed, her fingers pleating the silk edge of her headscarf. "You saw his eyes when he looked at us. The hate he possesses for Christians."

"My children," Samina whispered. "If they discover I'm involved..."

"He has more power now than when he was with the TLP," Nadir said quietly. "Back then, he was just a religious zealot. Now he has the full authority of the FIA behind him."

Hassan went to the window, watching Faraz's retreating figure disappear into the gathering darkness—confident, unhurried, certain of his power. The scar on his left cheek had been clearly visible, a permanent reminder of the night he'd helped destroy the mission.

"Everyone knows he led the compound raid," Tariq added. "Many say he pulled the trigger that killed the Freemans."

Faraz's car pulled away, red taillights fading into the night.

"No." Hassan retrieved the hidden box from beneath the floorboard. "This is why Joseph must return."

"Have you lost your mind?" Tariq demanded. "That man will kill him—kill all of us! He was ruthless with the TLP, and now he has FIA resources..."

Hassan placed the box on the table and opened it. "If we abandon our faith now, everything the Freemans sacrificed was for nothing."

He looked at each of them in turn. "Faraz suspects, but he doesn't know. If he knew for certain, he'd have been here with a full FIA team, warrants, arrests."

"What are you saying?"

"That we must be smarter, more careful." Hassan's words grew stronger. "From now on, we meet only in pairs. Never the same location twice. We use different routes to gather. We tell no one—not even family—about Joseph's return until he's here and we can assess the situation."

He straightened his shoulders. "Samina, you'll be our messenger to the Christian community in Peshawar. Your position at the hospital gives you reason to travel without suspicion."

She nodded, though her hands still trembled.

"Nadir, prepare the back room of your new location as a safe house. Stock it with emergency supplies—water, food, medical items. A place where people can hide if needed."

Miriam leaned forward. "What about Joseph? Will we help him rebuild the mission when he returns?"

"We'll do what God instructs us," Hassan answered. "If that means following Joseph's lead, then so be it."

"It's too dangerous," Tariq insisted, but some certainty had left his features. Despite his anger, there was hurt beneath his words—the pain of abandonment never fully healed.

"Joseph Freeman is coming home," Hassan said, his words quiet but firm. "And regardless of Faraz Qureshi's threats and his government authority, we will be ready. Not because we are brave, but because we serve a God who has preserved us through fifteen years of persecution. He won't abandon us now."

They slipped out in pairs, taking different routes home. Faraz knew the purpose of their meeting. He knew about Joseph's application. The only question was how long before the Director acted instead of merely watching.

Hassan returned the metal box to its hiding place— proof that the church had survived, that faith had persisted, that God's work continued even in the darkest places.

His wife had died for that faith. His friends had suffered for it. Joseph's parents had been martyred for it as well.

Did Hassan have the courage to continue what they'd started, knowing it might cost him everything he had left?

Outside, the night air held its chill. Inside, Hassan knelt and prayed for wisdom and strength. And to not lead his people to slaughter.

The mission would rise again, God willing.

But the cost could be overwhelming.

# TEN

## The Arrival

*BENAZIR BHUTTO INTERNATIONAL AIRPORT, ISLAMABAD*

The immigration officer's eyes moved between Joseph's passport and his face with methodical skepticism. Behind the glass partition, fluorescent lights hummed and flickered. The officer's finger tapped the photo page—once, twice—as if the rhythm might reveal some hidden truth.

"Purpose of visit?" His English carried the precise diction of Pakistani civil servants, each syllable measured.

"Religious work." Joseph kept his voice steady, despite the flutter in his chest. The line behind him stretched long —businessmen checking watches, families corralling restless children, tourists wiping sweat from their necks in the airport's inadequate air conditioning.

The officer's eyebrow lifted fractionally. "Religious work." He typed something into his computer, waited. The screen's glow reflected in his reading glasses. "What sort of religious work?"

"Humanitarian mission. Medical care, education, agricultural development." Joseph had rehearsed this. Ian Daniels had drilled him on what to say, what to omit, how to frame his purpose in language that wouldn't trigger immediate rejection.

"You are Christian?"

"Yes."

More typing. More waiting. The officer pulled out a phone, spoke rapid Urdu that Joseph's rudimentary understanding couldn't fully parse. He caught fragments—"American," "religious worker," "Freeman."

That last word sent ice through his veins. They knew his name. Of course, they knew his name—it was on the visa application, on every document filed with Deputy Commissioner Qadir's office. But hearing it spoken with such familiarity suggested surveillance beyond routine.

The officer set down his phone. "You will wait here, please." He gestured to a row of plastic chairs against the wall.

"Is there a problem?"

"Please. Wait." The officer waved the next person forward, effectively dismissing him.

Joseph gathered his carry-on and moved to the chairs. Around him, the airport continued its perpetual motion—announcements in Urdu and English, the squeal of luggage carts, the smell of cardamom chai from a nearby vendor mixing with jet fuel and human exhaustion.

Fifteen minutes passed. Then thirty. Joseph pulled out his phone—no signal yet. Uncle David would be waiting for an update. Darius would want to know he'd arrived safely. The team they'd so carefully assembled would be monitoring his progress.

But Joseph sat alone in a Pakistani airport, watched by security cameras and suspicious officials, waiting for permission to enter a country that had already killed his parents.

A man in a dark suit approached, his FIA badge visible on his belt. "Mr. Freeman. Come with me, please."

———

The interrogation room was small and windowless, smelling of stale cigarettes and industrial cleaner. A metal table bolted to the floor. Two chairs. A mirror that was certainly one-way glass.

A middle-aged officer with tired eyes and a bureaucrat's patience settled into the chair opposite Joseph, opening a manila folder. "I am Inspector Hamza Malik." He spoke without looking up. "Your visa application has raised some concerns."

"What concerns?"

"You plan to establish a religious facility in Shingli Payeen district." Malik scanned the document. "This is a sensitive area. We have had... problems with unauthorized religious activities."

Joseph chose his words carefully. "My application went through proper channels. Deputy Commissioner Qadir approved it."

"Yes." Malik finally looked up. "With significant restrictions. Tell me, Mr. Freeman, are you aware of Pakistan's blasphemy laws?"

"I am."

"And you understand that proselytizing to Muslims is illegal? That distribution of Christian materials outside designated worship spaces is illegal? That any action perceived as disrespecting Islam can result in imprisonment or death?"

The litany was familiar—Ian had briefed him extensively. But hearing it delivered in this sterile room by a man with the authority to enforce those laws made Joseph's mouth go dry.

"I understand," Joseph said. "My mission will focus on humanitarian work. We'll operate within all legal restrictions."

"Will you?" Malik leaned back, studying Joseph with unsettling focus. "Your parents operated a similar mission fifteen years ago. They, too, claimed to focus on humanitarian work. Yet they were found to be actively converting Muslims, distributing prohibited materials, encouraging apostasy."

"That's not—" Joseph stopped himself. Arguing would accomplish nothing. "My parents provided medical care and education to people who had nowhere else to turn. If some of those people chose to embrace Christianity, that was their decision."

"A decision that violated Pakistani law," Malik said. "A decision that led to violence, death, destruction. Are you prepared to repeat your parents' mistakes?"

Joseph thought of Hassan's text messages over the years, brief and coded, describing believers who met in secret, who risked everything to maintain their faith. He thought of Tariq, Miriam, Fatima—people who'd survived fifteen years of persecution because his parents had shown them something worth dying for.

"I'm prepared to serve people who need help," Joseph said finally. "Within the bounds of Pakistani law."

Malik closed the folder. "We will be watching your activities very closely, Mr. Freeman. The FIA takes national security seriously. Any violation—any suggestion that you are engaging in illegal religious activities—will result in immediate arrest and deportation. Do you understand?"

"I understand."

"Good." Malik stood, collecting his folder. "Your passport will be returned at the exit. Welcome to Pakistan."

The words carried no warmth, no genuine hospitality. Only warning.

———

Joseph emerged from the secured area two hours after landing, his legs unsteady and his mind reeling from the interrogation. The arrivals hall swarmed with people— families embracing, drivers scanning the crowd, vendors hawking SIM cards and currency exchange.

And there, standing near a support pillar with his hands in his pockets, was Hassan.

Joseph recognized him instantly. Fifteen years had etched lines into his face and threaded silver through his dark hair, but that expression—warm, steady, unchanged— belonged to the man who'd guided a terrified ten-year-old through smoke and flames.

Their eyes met across the crowded terminal.

Hassan's face transformed. Without a word, without a sign, he crossed the distance between them and pulled Joseph into an embrace that felt like coming home.

"Khush amdeed," Hassan whispered, his voice thick with emotion. "Welcome home, beta."

Joseph buried his face in Hassan's shoulder and wept— for his parents, for the years lost, for the fear that had followed him across an ocean. Hassan held him, one hand cupping the back of Joseph's head, murmuring words of comfort in Urdu that Joseph only half understood but felt in his bones.

When Joseph finally pulled back, wiping his eyes, Hassan kept both hands on his shoulders. "Let me look at you." His gaze traveled over Joseph's face, searching. "You have your father's eyes. Your mother's jaw. But something else—something new."

"I'm not the boy you saved," Joseph managed.

"No." Hassan's smile carried both sadness and pride. "You are the man who came back. That takes different courage."

They stood in the middle of the arrivals hall, oblivious to the crowd flowing around them, two men separated by culture and age but connected by bonds forged in fire.

"Come," Hassan said finally, picking up Joseph's luggage. "We have much to discuss. And I have people waiting to meet you."

As they walked toward the exit, eyes followed them. Security personnel. Other travelers. The surveillance that Inspector Malik had promised. Pakistan welcomed him the way it had always welcomed his kind—with suspicion, scrutiny, and the ever-present threat of violence.

But Hassan walked beside him, steady and certain, and for the first time since accepting Mercer's offer, Joseph's shoulders relaxed.

# PART II

# ELEVEN

## The Homecoming

"The FIA questioned you?"

Joseph turned from the window where the Margalla Hills rose to the north. Hassan's Toyota rattled over another pothole as they left Islamabad behind.

"For two hours," Joseph confirmed. "Inspector Malik. He made it very clear I'm being watched."

Hassan nodded, unsurprised. "Faraz Qureshi leads the local FIA office. He was with the TLP during the raid."

Joseph's hands clenched in his lap. "The man who…"

"Maybe," Hassan said with a sigh. "No witnesses to confirm except for the militants. Qureshi has more power now. Government authority instead of mob violence. He visited us three days ago."

"Us?"

"Those who I wrote you about, mostly." Hassan glanced at Joseph. "There are seven of us who meet regularly. Maybe forty more scattered in the region. All living in fear, all hoping your return means something will change."

Joseph's stomach tightened. "Hassan, I don't know if I can—"

"I know." Hassan's voice was gentle. "You're not your father, Joseph. You don't have to be. But you're here. That matters more than you realize."

They drove through villages where children played cricket in the streets and old men sat in tea shops watching the world pass. Women in bright dupattas walked with water jugs balanced on their heads. The call to prayer echoed from mosques, that haunting sound that Joseph remembered from childhood—beautiful and terrifying in equal measure.

"Your parents," Hassan said as they neared their destination, "they knew the risks. Your mother especially. She understood what it meant to be Pakistani and Christian. But your father..." He paused, searching for words. "William believed love could overcome hate. That service could soften hard hearts. He was wrong about many things, but right about what mattered most."

"Did they suffer?" The question had haunted Joseph for fifteen years.

"It was quick," Hassan said, though his tone suggested he was choosing mercy over truth. "The mob was large, angry. Your parents didn't run. They stood together at the mission entrance, trying to reason with them. When the shooting started..." He swallowed hard. "I was already in the tunnel with you. I heard it but didn't see. Perhaps that's God's mercy."

Joseph's hand went to the silver cross beneath his shirt. His mother's last gift, pressed into his palm as flames consumed their world.

"I should have stayed," Joseph whispered. "I should have fought—"

"You were ten years old. There was no fighting to be done. Your parents sent you away because they loved you more than their own lives. Don't dishonor that sacrifice by wishing you'd died with them."

The words were harsh but necessary. Joseph had carried survivor's guilt for so long it had become part of his identity. Hassan's blunt dismissal of it felt like surgery without anesthesia—painful but potentially healing.

They turned onto a narrow dirt road, leaving the main route behind. The sun was setting now, painting the sky in shades of orange and pink. In the distance, Joseph could see the outline of structures he didn't recognize—newer buildings, expanded development. His childhood landscape transformed by years he'd spent in exile.

"We're almost there," Hassan said. "I've prepared a room in my home. It's not much, but it's safe. Tonight, you'll rest. Tomorrow..." He smiled slightly. "Tomorrow you'll see what remains. And what we might build."

———

Hassan's home was a modest structure at the edge of the village—mud brick walls, a corrugated metal roof, a small courtyard with a hand pump for water. Chickens scattered as they pulled up, and a neighbor's goat bleated in protest at the disturbance.

Inside, the main room was simple but clean. Cushions were arranged around the perimeter, a low table in the center, a cooking area separated by a curtain. The walls were bare except for a single piece of Arabic calligraphy—a verse from the Quran that allowed Hassan to appear Muslim to casual observers.

"Please, sit," Hassan said, gesturing to the cushions. He moved to the kitchen area. "I'll make tea."

Joseph lowered himself onto a cushion, his body suddenly aware of exhaustion. The flight, the interrogation, the emotional reunion—it all crashed over him at once.

Hassan returned with two cups of chai, the familiar cardamom and cinnamon scent filling the small space. He sat across from Joseph, and for a moment they simply sipped tea in comfortable silence as the light faded outside.

"Tell me about your life," Hassan said finally. "After you left. I know some from our messages, but there's much I don't know."

So Joseph told him. About Uncle David taking him in, about the small Mississippi church that became his refuge. About seminary—three wonderful years in New Orleans, studying missions and practical theology and utilizing his gift. About working alongside Uncle David in Biloxi as assistant pastor, learning to preach, to counsel, to lead a youth group.

About the football injury that had exposed his gift to the world, the accusations and skepticism that followed. About how the viral video complicated his ministry work—some churches wouldn't invite him, fearing controversy. Others sought him out for the wrong reasons, wanting spectacle instead of service.

About the years spent raising funds, dealing with bureaucracy, assembling a team. About Mercer's offer with its complicated strings attached.

Hassan listened without interrupting, his face impassive, though Joseph caught glimpses of pride, concern, understanding.

"You've become what your parents hoped," Hassan's

voice was warm. "Not a copy of them, but your own man with your own calling."

"I don't feel ready," Joseph admitted. "Especially after seeing this place again, after hearing about Faraz and the FIA watching. I keep thinking I've made a terrible mistake."

"Perhaps you have," Hassan said, and Joseph looked up in surprise. "Or perhaps God uses our mistakes to accomplish His purposes. Your parents made mistakes too. They stayed when they should have fled. They were stubborn when they should have been flexible. But their mistakes created space for something to grow."

He stood and moved to a small trunk in the corner, returning with a bundle wrapped in faded cloth. "I've kept this safe for you. I didn't know if you'd return, but I prayed you would."

Joseph unwrapped the cloth with trembling hands. Inside was a worn journal with a cracked leather cover, its pages yellowed and fragile. On the first page, in his mother's familiar handwriting: *Lyla Freeman - Mission Journal.*

"Your mother's diary," Hassan said softly. "She documented everything—testimonies of believers, daily struggles, prayers, doubts. The last entry was written a week before the attack." He paused. "I saved it from the fire. I've kept it hidden all these years, waiting for you."

Joseph opened to a random page, seeing his mother's script flowing across the paper. A testimony from someone named Amina, converted at twenty-three, now leading a women's Bible study. His mother's note beneath: *Her faith reminds me why we're here. When I'm discouraged, I think of her courage and find my own renewed.*

He turned more pages, finding entries about his childhood, about the mission's challenges, about threats that grew more frequent each year. And then, near the end, an entry dated one week before the attack:

*The warnings are becoming more direct. William believes we should stay, that running would abandon those who depend on us. I'm torn. My faith says stay. My mother's heart says protect Joseph at any cost. Tonight I watched him sleep and prayed God would give us wisdom. If we leave, the believers are exposed. If we stay... God help us, if we stay.*

Joseph's vision blurred. His mother's fears, her love, her impossible choice—all preserved in fading ink.

"She was afraid," he whispered.

"Yes," Hassan said softly. "Terrified. But she stayed."

Joseph thought of Darius's words in Oxford, of the team assembled despite their fears. "Faith isn't the absence of fear," he said quietly. "It's action despite it."

Hassan's expression softened with recognition. "Your mother understood that better than anyone. So did your father. Now you must learn it for yourself."

Joseph held the diary against his chest, feeling his mother's presence in a way he hadn't since childhood. This was better than any letter could have been—weeks and months and years of her thoughts, her prayers, her daily walk with God documented in her own hand.

"Thank you," Joseph managed. "For saving this. For keeping it safe."

Hassan nodded. "There's more inside—testimonies from people still living here. Tariq's father. Miriam before her husband was imprisoned. Fatima when she was younger and still had hope." He paused. "Your mother documented their stories so they wouldn't be forgotten. Now you can return those stories to them—show them they matter enough to be remembered."

The idea took root. His mother's diary wasn't just

personal history—it was a bridge between past and present, between the mission that was and the one that might be.

Hassan gave him space to process, busying himself with preparations for dinner. After several minutes, Joseph composed himself enough to inquire. "The believers who remain—can I meet them?"

"Not yet. It's too dangerous to gather openly so soon after your arrival. Give it a few days. Let the FIA get bored watching you. Then I'll arrange something."

"And the mission site?"

"Tomorrow, if you're ready. I'll take you at dawn, before the village wakes. You should see it alone first, before we make plans."

Joseph nodded. Tomorrow he would face the ruins of his childhood home, the place where his parents had died and his calling had been born. Tonight, he simply needed to be present with the man who'd saved his life, in a country that might yet claim it.

"Hassan," Joseph said, his voice rough with emotion. "Thank you. For everything you've done. For keeping the faith alive, for preserving their memory, for not giving up."

Hassan's voice caught. "Your parents gave me more than I could ever repay. A faith worth living for, a purpose beyond survival, a family when I had none." He reached across the table and gripped Joseph's hand. "I would have waited another fifteen years if that's what it took. Some debts can never be repaid—only honored."

They sat together as darkness fell outside, two men bound by tragedy and hope, preparing to attempt what might be either redemption or another catastrophe.

But for tonight, it was enough to simply be home.

———

Sleep came in fragments. Joseph lay on a thin mattress in Hassan's guest room, listening to unfamiliar sounds—dogs barking in the distance, the rustle of wind through trees, the occasional rumble of a distant truck. His body ached with jet lag and emotional exhaustion, but his mind refused to settle.

He pulled out his mother's diary again, unable to resist reading more. He found an entry from when he was seven years old:

*Joseph asked me today why some people hate us. I didn't know how to explain persecution to a seven-year-old. I told him that sometimes people are afraid of things they don't understand, and fear makes them do terrible things. He thought about this for a long time, then said, "We should teach them not to be afraid." Such simple wisdom from a child. If only it were that easy.*

Joseph smiled through tears. He remembered that conversation now, remembered his childish certainty that fear could be reasoned away. How naive he'd been.

He turned to another entry, this one from two years before the attack:

*We had eighteen baptisms this month. Eighteen souls who chose Christ despite knowing the cost. Hassan organized the ceremony in a cave outside the village—hidden from prying eyes but open to heaven. I watched their faces as they emerged from the water, pure joy radiating from them—though we all knew what that joy might cost. This is why we're here. This is what makes the danger worth it.*

Eighteen baptisms. Joseph wondered how many of those eighteen still lived, still believed, still gathered in secret to worship.

He found more testimonies as he read—men and women who'd found faith through the mission's work. Some he recognized from Hassan's earlier descriptions: Miriam, whose husband now rotted in prison. Tariq's father, martyred for refusing to recant. Others were unfamiliar, their fates unknown.

Near the very end, he found the final entry. The one written a week before everything ended:

*I'm writing this by candlelight while William sleeps. The latest threat came today—a letter nailed to our door warning us to leave or face consequences. William wants to stay. He believes abandoning the believers now would be cowardice. Part of me agrees. Part of me wants to pack Joseph up tonight and run as far as we can.*

*I've been reading Nehemiah again. "Those who were building the wall...did their work with one hand and held a weapon in the other." That's what we've become—builders who must be ready to fight, or at least to flee.*

*If something happens to us, I pray Hassan will get Joseph to safety. I pray my son will grow up knowing his parents died doing something that mattered. And I pray—God forgive me— that he'll have the wisdom to know when to stay and when to leave. That's a wisdom William and I have never quite mastered.*

*Whatever comes, I trust God's purposes are larger than our understanding. Even if we can't see how this story ends, I believe it ends well. Not for us, perhaps, but for the kingdom we serve.*

The entry ended there. One week later, his parents were dead.

Joseph pressed the diary to his chest, his mother's final prayer echoing in his mind. *The wisdom to know when to stay and when to leave.* She'd prayed for wisdom she knew she lacked, trusting that her son might learn what she couldn't teach. The burden of that prayer—the hope she'd placed in him—felt almost too heavy to carry.

Joseph closed the diary carefully and set it on the small table beside his mattress, next to his father's Bible—the one he'd discovered in Uncle David's attic and carried back across an ocean. Two sacred texts. Two parents' legacy. Both speaking to him across fifteen years of loss.

His mother had prayed he would know when to stay and when to leave. That wisdom still eluded him. But he was here. That had to count for something.

Tomorrow he would see the ruins. Tomorrow he would begin to understand what rebuilding actually meant. Tomorrow the real work would start.

# TWELVE

## The Ruins

*THE NEXT MORNING*

Dawn came with the muezzin's call, that haunting melody drifting through the pre-dawn darkness. Joseph woke disoriented, forgetting for a moment where he was. Then memory crashed back—Pakistan, Hassan's home, his mother's diary on the table beside him.

He dressed quietly and found Hassan already awake in the main room, two cups of tea steaming on the low table.

"You're ready?" Hassan asked.

Joseph nodded, though his stomach churned with apprehension. For fifteen years, he'd carried images of the mission in his mind—the way it looked before, the way Hassan described it after. Now he would see the reality.

They drove through empty streets as the village slowly stirred to life. A few early risers headed toward the mosque. A shopkeeper rolled up his metal shutters. Dogs trotted along the roadside, searching for scraps.

Hassan turned down a road Joseph didn't recognize—

newer asphalt over what had once been dirt. Development had reached even this rural area, transforming the landscape of his childhood. But then they rounded a bend, and Joseph saw it.

Or what remained of it.

Hassan pulled to the side of the road and cut the engine. Neither man moved for a long moment.

"Take your time," Hassan said quietly. "I'll wait here."

Joseph stepped out of the car, his legs unsteady. The morning air was cool, carrying the scent of earth and distant cooking fires. Birds sang from nearby trees—the same birds, perhaps, that had sung fifteen years ago when this place was alive.

He walked toward the entrance, his feet finding the path automatically despite the years. The metal gate hung crooked on its hinges, rust eating through the decorative scrollwork his father had commissioned from a local craftsman. Beyond it, the compound stretched out like a war zone frozen in time.

The chapel stood skeletal against the lightening sky, its roof completely gone, walls blackened by fire and pocked with bullet holes. Joseph moved closer, his hand reaching out to touch the scorched brick. His fingers came away gray with soot.

He stepped through what had once been the entrance— the double doors long since stolen or burned. Inside, the space was open to the elements, weeds growing through cracks in the concrete floor. The pulpit was gone. The pews were gone. Even the cross that had hung behind the altar was gone, leaving only a rectangular shadow on the wall where soot hadn't quite reached.

Joseph stood where his father used to preach, turning slowly to take in the destruction. He could see it as it had been—wooden pews filled with believers, his mother at the piano in the corner, sunlight streaming through windows that depicted scenes from Christ's life. He could hear his father's voice echoing off these walls, passionate and certain, believing that love and service could overcome hatred.

Joseph knelt where the altar had been, his knees pressing into the weed-choked concrete. Tears came, streaming down his face as fifteen years of grief finally found release. He wept for his parents, for the believers who'd died or scattered, for the dream that had burned. For his own failures—the years spent in safety while others suffered. The guilt that had paralyzed him. The fear that still threatened to overwhelm him.

"I'm sorry," he whispered to the empty chapel. "I'm so sorry I took so long."

The ruins offered no response. Only the wind moving through burned timbers, the distant call of a rooster, the slow brightening of dawn.

Joseph stood and moved outside. The clinic building stood adjacent to the chapel—or what remained of it. The structure was more intact than the chapel, though the windows were broken and the door hung off its hinges. Joseph stepped inside carefully, watching for unstable flooring.

The examination room where his mother had treated patients was stripped bare. Cabinets hung open, their contents long since looted or destroyed. Medical equipment was gone. Even the examination table had been taken, leaving only metal brackets where it had been bolted to the floor.

But on one wall, faded and peeling, remained a poster his mother had made—a chart showing proper hand-washing technique, illustrated with simple drawings. Beneath it, in English and Urdu: *Clean hands save lives.*

Such a simple message that basic care could change the world.

Joseph traced the faded letters with his finger, remembering his mother in her white coat, always ready to serve whoever came through those doors. Muslim, Christian, Hindu—she'd treated them all with the same gentle competence, the same conviction that every person mattered to God.

He found more remnants as he explored—a rusted sign indicating the women's health office, a broken chair in what had been the waiting room, shards of glass from medicine bottles. Each piece a fragment of the life that had thrived here.

The school building was in the worst condition, its roof partially collapsed and one wall completely gone. Joseph approached carefully, testing each step. Inside, he found desks overturned and broken, their wood splintered by years of weather and neglect. Chalkboards were cracked. Books had long since rotted into pulp.

His parents had stood here on that final day, trying to reason with the mob. They'd believed until the very end that dialogue, faith, and humanity would prevail.

They'd been wrong.

Joseph knelt by the fireplace, its stones blackened but intact. He ran his fingers along the bottom edge of the mantle, searching. There—barely visible, carved in letters no bigger than his thumbnail: JF. TM.

He'd been eight. Tariq ten. They'd used a nail, working carefully so no one would notice. Their initials, their friendship, etched into stone.

His throat tightened. Tariq probably didn't even remember.

Tariq. His childhood friend. The angry young man Hassan described, scarred by loss and betrayal. This graffiti carved before the fire, before the violence, before faith became something to hide.

Joseph ran a finger across the worn initials, a fading mark that whispered this place had once been home.

He continued through the compound, cataloging the destruction and the occasional miracle of survival. The water pump still stood, though rusted. The garden where his mother had grown herbs for medicine was overgrown with weeds, but here and there Joseph spotted familiar plants—mint, basil, chamomile—that had survived and spread.

The residential building where his family had lived was nothing but a foundation and one partial wall. Joseph stood where his bedroom had been, trying to remember. The window that overlooked the garden. The shelf where he'd kept his collection of rocks. The prayer his mother said with him every night before sleep.

"You kept your promise."

Joseph turned to find Hassan standing behind him.

"You said you'd come back," Hassan continued, moving to stand beside Joseph at the tunnel entrance. "I wasn't sure you would. Or could. But you're here."

"I don't know if I can do this," Joseph admitted. "Build something new on top of this much death."

Hassan lowered himself to sit on a chunk of collapsed wall, gesturing for Joseph to join him. "Your parents built the original mission on top of centuries of persecution. Christians have been dying in this region since the first century. This ground is soaked with martyrs' blood going back to the apostles."

He gestured to the ruins around them. "Every generation faces the same choice—abandon the calling because it's dangerous, or continue the work because it matters. Your parents chose to continue. I chose to continue. Now you must choose."

Joseph looked at the devastation surrounding them— the burned chapel, the gutted clinic, the collapsed school. "What if I choose wrong? What if I get more people killed?"

"You will," Hassan said simply. "Not because you're incompetent or faithless, but because this work is dangerous. People die in wars, Joseph. And make no mistake— this is a war. Not with guns and bombs, but with ideas and faith and the stubborn insistence that love is stronger than hate."

A rooster crowed in the distance. The sun had risen fully now, bathing the ruins in golden light.

"The question isn't whether people will die," Hassan continued. "The question is whether their sacrifice advances the kingdom of God or simply adds to the tally of meaningless violence."

"Can we create a place where our people can worship without watching the door?" Joseph asked.

"No," Hassan said. "Not completely. Not in Pakistan, perhaps for generations. But we can create moments of it. Pockets of safety. Communities where faith is stronger than fear, even if just for a season."

He stood, offering Joseph his hand. "Your mother's diary —you read the final entry?"

Joseph nodded.

"Then you know she prayed you would learn what she and your father never mastered—knowing when to stay and when to leave. That wisdom will be tested, Joseph. Probably sooner than you hope."

———

They walked through the compound together, Hassan pointing out where things had been. "The community garden here. The playground over there. The small library where women learned to read."

Joseph tried to imagine it coming alive again. Construction crews clearing the rubble. New walls rising where old ones had fallen. The sound of children playing, of women gathering for Bible study, of his father's voice preaching hope to people who desperately needed it.

But he also imagined other things. Mobs and raids. Fire and bullets. Screams in the night. The pattern repeating because they'd believed it could be different.

"I've been afraid my whole life," Joseph said, stopping near the burned chapel. "Since the night we escaped, I've been afraid. In America, I feared not fitting in. Then, of failing, not living up to my parents' legacy. Now I'm afraid of getting it wrong. Fear never leaves, does it? You just learn to function despite it."

Hassan stretched his arm across Joseph's shoulders. "The Bible teaches that 'fear of the Lord is the beginning of wisdom.' The people most dangerous in this work are those who follow their own heart, not Christ's call."

Joseph thought of his team assembled in Oxford. Ian with his security protocols. Maya with her legal expertise. Darius with his decades of experience in hostile places. Fear hadn't stopped them. They would be in Pakistan within hours. "What do you think? Honestly. Can we rebuild this?"

Hassan was quiet for a long moment, scanning the ruins.

"Yes," he said finally. "Not what it was—that's gone forever. But something new. Something that learns from past mistakes while honoring past sacrifices."

He turned to face Joseph. "But it requires you to stop trying to resurrect your parents' dream. You must build your own. Smaller, perhaps. More hidden. More strategic. But yours."

The words settled over Joseph. He wasn't here to copy his father. He was here to continue the work in his own way, with his own gifts, informed by his own experiences.

"Your permits restrict the compound size," Hassan continued. "Sixty percent reduction?"

"Yes."

"Then we don't fight that. We build smaller, more integrated with the village. Not a foreign compound separated by walls, but a community center that happens to have a chapel. Medical care without the Christian branding. Education without the missionary school label."

Joseph began to see it—not a fortress of faith but a network of service. "We don't need to be loud. We just need to serve."

"A place where people can gather naturally," Hassan finished. "Where believers can hide in plain sight. A place where we help them and disciple them to help others."

It wasn't the grand vision Joseph had carried for fifteen years. It was smaller, subtler, more vulnerable. But as he stood in the ruins of his parents' bold experiment, he realized that might be exactly what this place needed.

"When can we start?" Joseph asked.

Hassan's smile was tired but genuine. "We already have. The moment you stepped off that plane, we started. Everything from here is continuation."

———

Back at Hassan's home, Joseph pulled out his phone and composed a message to Darius, to Uncle David, to the team in Oxford:

*I've seen what remains. It's worse than I imagined and better than I feared. The buildings are gone, but the people survived. Starting over with new plans. More details soon. Pray for wisdom.*

He hit send, then turned to Hassan. "I need to meet them. The seven believers. I need to hear their stories, understand what they've survived, learn what they need."

"I'll arrange it," Hassan said. "Faraz is watching, but he's only one man. We can be smarter than his surveillance."

"And the compound? When do we break ground?"

Hassan poured fresh tea, sitting cross-legged. "Not yet. First, we build trust. You meet the believers. You listen to their needs. You establish relationships in the village—not as an American bringing solutions, but as William and Lyla's son coming home."

It went against every instinct Joseph had developed over three years of fundraising and planning. He'd assembled a team, secured millions in funding, navigated bureaucracy and permits. His plan had timelines, milestones, measurable objectives.

But Hassan was right. None of that mattered if he couldn't win the trust of the people he'd come to serve.

"How long?" Joseph asked.

"As long as it takes," Hassan replied. "Weeks, maybe months. This isn't a construction project, Joseph. It's a restoration—not of buildings, but of hope. That takes time."

Joseph thought about Mercer's expectations, about the

team waiting in Oxford, about the milestone-based funding that required visible progress. Then he thought about his mother's diary entry: *Love the people more than the mission.*

# THIRTEEN

## The Surveillance

*KHYBER PAKHTUNKHWA PROVINCE, PAKISTAN*

Faraz Qureshi's fingers drummed against the polished metal desk in his office at the FIA regional headquarters. Islamic calligraphy adorned the walls. Service commendations lined up in identical black frames. A Pakistani flag stood in the corner. On the shelf, law volumes progressed from thinnest to thickest, spines aligned to the millimeter.

A manila folder lay open before him. Flight manifests. Customs declarations. Surveillance photos in plastic sleeves, stacked by timestamp.

His eyes lingered on one particular image—a tall young man with dark hair exiting the international terminal at Islamabad Airport. Nothing remarkable about him at first glance. No outward sign of the threat he represented. But Faraz knew better.

The secure phone beside his hand vibrated, screen illuminating with a message from his contact at immigration:

*Freeman has landed.*

Three simple words that sent electricity through Faraz's system. His hand rose instinctively to his left cheek, fingers tracing the raised scar that ran from temple to jaw—fifteen years old but burning as if fresh.

"So you've returned," he whispered.

The memories surfaced unbidden—his days as a mid-level TLP commander, the raid he'd personally led, screams piercing the night air, the acrid smell of accelerant, flames dancing across the mission compound. The burning beam striking his cheek during the chaos. That night had marked him physically, but it had also been the catalyst that transformed him from zealous militant to determined bureaucrat.

He'd spent years cultivating the right relationships, leveraging his "patriotic actions" while concealing brutal details. His rise had been calculated—police force to counterterrorism to the Federal Investigation Agency—positioning him to suppress Christian activities with the state's full authority.

Faraz gathered the documents and slid them back into the folder. This wasn't just another Western intruder to harass. This was Joseph Freeman, son of the missionary Faraz had destroyed. This was personal—unfinished business.

But it went beyond vendetta. The Freeman mission had been a cancer in the region—offering medical care and education laced with spiritual poison. He'd seen how villagers began questioning traditions, how women spoke more boldly, how children sang foreign songs. The unity of faith that kept Pakistan strong had frayed wherever William Freeman's influence spread. Joseph's return threatened to renew that corruption, undermining the Islamic principles Faraz had sworn to uphold.

He checked his watch. Rahman would be in his study now.

His reflection stared back from the window—the scar creating a permanent sneer on his otherwise handsome face. A small price for purpose.

No—Rahman would say he was exactly where Allah intended. Personal feelings were irrelevant when defending the faith against those who would corrupt it with tolerance and equality.

Faraz tucked the folder under his arm and moved to the door, pausing only to straighten the framed calligraphy from Qur'an 8:30 on his wall—*And they planned, but Allah also planned. And Allah is the best of planners.*

———

The afternoon sun illuminated the courtyard of Masjid Al-Taqwa as Faraz entered through its ornate gates. The mosque stood as a testament to the community's devotion—its white marble dome gleaming against the azure sky, minarets reaching heavenward. Several men nodded as he passed, respecting his rank.

Behind the main prayer hall, down a narrow corridor lined with intricate tilework, lay the private study of Maulana Hafiz Rahman—scholar, preacher, and the most influential religious voice in the district. Faraz paused outside the carved wooden door, hearing the soft cadence of Rahman reciting Quranic verses. He hesitated, knowing the impropriety of interrupting prayers, but the urgency of his news outweighed protocol.

He knocked firmly.

"Enter," Rahman's voice carried irritation.

Faraz stepped inside. The room smelled of aged leather, sandalwood, and the faint musk of incense. Bookshelves lined three walls, each shelf bowing under Islamic texts, commentaries, and historical volumes. Rahman sat cross-legged on a mat, his white beard neatly trimmed, eyes sharp beneath bushy eyebrows. The prayer beads in his hands stilled.

"Faraz." The edge vanished from Rahman's voice. "What brings my most diligent student at this hour?"

Faraz lowered his head in respect. "Forgive the intrusion, Hafiz sahib. A matter has arisen that requires your guidance."

Rahman gestured to the cushion across from him. "Sit. Allah's work does not adhere to our schedules."

Faraz settled onto the cushion, placing his folder between them. "After fifteen years, William Freeman's son has returned to Pakistan."

Rahman's fingers paused on his prayer beads. "The missionary's boy? The one who escaped that night?"

"Joseph," Faraz confirmed, his scar seeming to tighten with the memory. "He's come to rebuild what his father started."

Rahman leaned forward. "Show me what you've learned."

Faraz opened the folder methodically, laying out surveillance photos in chronological order. "He arrived from England yesterday. Traveled alone, but I suspect others will follow." He pointed to an official document. "He's already secured property permits for the old mission land."

"Your position at the FIA continues to serve Allah's

purpose," Rahman observed, studying the documents. "Few could assemble this information so quickly."

"Allah has placed me where I can be most useful," Faraz replied. "My office gives me access to intelligence networks that most cannot reach." He continued his report. "Financial records show over three hundred thousand dollars transferred in the past month alone from a foundation with ties to Stellarion."

"Alexander Mercer?" Rahman's eyebrows rose.

"The same. He's funding the mission rebuild, Hafiz sahib." Faraz's jaw tightened. If Freeman accomplished what Faraz had spent fifteen years trying to prevent—establishing Christian influence—his credibility with both the government and the religious council would be destroyed. Everything he'd built since that night—his position, his authority, his reputation as defender of the faith—would crumble. He couldn't allow that.

Rahman's fingers worked his prayer beads, his eyes distant. "What else have you discovered about this Joseph Freeman?"

Faraz produced another file. "After escaping Pakistan, he was raised by his uncle—a Christian pastor in America. There are accounts of unexplained healings attributed to him." He handed over a photograph showing Joseph bending over a padded person on a sports field.

Rahman examined the image with a critical eye. "Claims of miracles are powerful recruitment tools."

"Which is why we must respond strategically," Faraz said. "My position allows me to monitor his activities through official channels. I can track his meetings, his contacts, document any violations of visa restrictions or propagation laws."

"And what approach do you recommend?" Rahman

asked, though his tone suggested he already knew Faraz's answer.

"Patience and precision," Faraz replied. "When we destroyed the mission, we acted with righteous anger. This time, we build a case methodically. We work through the government and legal system whenever possible."

Rahman nodded approvingly. "You've learned much since those days of impetuous action."

"Your guidance has been invaluable, Hafiz sahib," Faraz acknowledged. "You taught me that true jihad requires wisdom as well as conviction."

"And what of the community?"

"I implement subtle influence." Faraz folded his hands. "My office gives me legitimacy when addressing our concerns."

The first notes of the adhan began to sound outside, calling the faithful to prayer. Rahman listened for a moment before returning his attention to Faraz. "Your position in government is Allah's blessing to our cause," he said, rising to his feet. "You serve as our eyes and hands where we cannot reach."

Faraz stood as well, gathering his documents. "What are your instructions, Hafiz sahib?"

"Continue your surveillance. Document everything methodically." Rahman moved to his desk and wrote a brief note. "I'll arrange a meeting with Asim Qadir. He's a bureaucrat, but his position may prove necessary."

He handed the folded paper to Faraz. "Introduce yourself."

"And the mission property?"

"We observe and wait," Rahman said, his voice calm but resolute. "Allah has placed you in the FIA for this purpose, Faraz. Use your position wisely."

As they walked through the corridor, the call to prayer filling the air, Rahman placed his hand on Faraz's shoulder. "Remember, you serve a higher authority even as you wear the government's badge. Balance them with wisdom."

Faraz unconsciously traced the scar on his cheek. "Inshallah. I won't fail."

"I know," Rahman said simply, before turning toward the prayer hall. "Now come, let us pray."

————

Rahman's note secure in his pocket, Faraz emerged from the mosque in the early evening. A game of street cricket froze mid-bowl. Boys melted into doorways, abandoning makeshift wickets and a ball that rolled to a stop.

Their fear triggered a memory—the screaming of Joseph's mother as Faraz set the schoolhouse ablaze. The sounds had never left him—crackling flames, shattering glass, and William Freeman's final words before the bullet had silenced him.

*"God forgive you, for you know not what you do."*

Faraz's jaw tightened. He knew what he was doing—then and now. The TLP militant and the FIA director were not separate men, but two faces of the same purpose. What he had begun with fire, he would finish with the full weight of his authority.

This time, there would be no escape. This time, Joseph Freeman would never succeed in rebuilding what Faraz had torn down fifteen years ago. Not the buildings. Not the mission. Not the legacy.

This time, the Freeman name would be erased from Pakistan forever—by the law, by the faith, by whatever means necessary.

He pulled out his phone and opened the surveillance photos from the airport—Joseph's face clear in the frame, unsuspecting, vulnerable. Faraz's thumb hovered over the image for a moment before he forwarded it to three contacts with a single word.

*Watch.*

# FOURTEEN

**The Journey**

"Stay close," Hassan murmured, his sandals scuffing against packed earth as they moved through the twisting maze of alleys. "We've doubled back twice already."

Joseph's legs moved mechanically behind him, hyper-aware of the phone's absence. Hassan had insisted they leave their devices at the house to avoid being tracked, and Joseph had reluctantly complied.

That doorway—hadn't he hidden there once during a game of hide-and-seek? The cracked wall to his left bore the same jagged lightning pattern he'd seen as a boy. Fifteen years of American concrete and steel fell away with each footfall on ancient stones, and suddenly he was eight again, his friends frantically trying to find him.

The last echoes of the evening call to prayer brought him back to the present. Hassan's sandals scuffed against packed earth, unnaturally loud in the hush that had settled over the mud-brick walls. Somewhere in the distance, a woman's voice called to her child, and Joseph's throat tightened—how many times had he heard his mother calling across these same narrow spaces when he was late coming home?

"Not much farther," Hassan murmured, his weathered face glancing back.

Joseph breathed in the aromas of cumin and wood smoke. Suddenly he was eight years old again, hiding behind his mother's skirts as she stirred the evening meal, listening to his father's voice carry across the compound as he read scripture by lamplight.

Hassan slowed his pace, head swiveling left and right before approaching a weathered wooden door, unremarkable among dozens of others. He rapped his knuckles against it in a distinct pattern—three quick taps, pause, two more. Joseph's pulse hammered in his throat as they waited.

A moment passed. Then another. Joseph drew breath to speak when the sound of a bolt sliding free cut through the silence. The door creaked open just wide enough to reveal a sliver of light and a single cautious eye.

"Salaam," Hassan whispered.

The door swung inward, and Joseph stepped into a small, sparsely furnished room lit by a pair of battery-powered lanterns.

Hassan quickly scanned the alley behind them before shutting the door and locking three separate bolts with soft metallic clicks. Six people stood frozen in the warm pools of light, their faces turning toward him like flowers following the sun. His chest expanded with recognition—Nadir, silver threading his temples now. Fatima, whose gentle smile hadn't changed, carrying more years and more peace than Joseph remembered.

Then his gaze caught on a tall figure standing apart from the others, arms crossed, brow furrowed, lips pressed together. Fifteen years had carved away the boy's softness, leaving sharp angles and guarded eyes, but Joseph would have known him anywhere.

"Tariq," he breathed.

The room fell quiet.

Fatima's fragile frame rushed to him with a cry. "Joseph! Praise God! We never thought—" Her voice cracked as she pulled back, hands clinging to his shoulders as if testing his solidity.

"The son returns to us." Nadir clasped Joseph's hand between both of his own, his face creasing with emotion.

The others followed—Samina with tears streaming, Miriam embracing him wordlessly—all except Tariq, who remained motionless in the shadowed corner. Joseph's heart lifted with each embrace, each tearful welcome. During those long sleepless nights in his Biloxi apartment, he had imagined exactly this moment.

"Please, sit," Hassan gestured to the thin cushions arranged in a circle on the floor. "We have much to discuss."

Joseph settled down with his bag beside him, aware of Tariq's eyes tracking his every movement. The warm embraces still tingled on his skin, but a chill climbed his spine. He forced a smile, drinking in those around him. These were his people—the remnant who had kept faith alive in the shadow of persecution.

"I can hardly believe I'm sitting here with you all," Joseph began, fighting back tears. "Seeing your faces. It's like coming home."

"Is it?" Tariq stepped into the dim light, revealing hard features. "So the shepherd returns after the wolves have feasted."

Joseph's smile faltered. The warmth in his chest curdled

into something cold and uncertain. He had anticipated hostility—but not from his childhood friend.

"Tariq—" Hassan began.

But Tariq raised an open hand. "Fifteen years, Joseph. Fifteen years we've endured while you were safe in America." His eyes glittered in the lamplight. "Do you know what happened after you left? After Hassan smuggled you away and the rest of us remained?"

Joseph's mouth went dry. "I—"

"They came back," Tariq said. "Three days after the first attack. They wanted to be sure nothing survived. My father refused to deny Christ." His mouth set in a hard line. "They made an example of him."

Tariq took another step, his voice dropping to a harsh whisper. "Do you remember what we promised each other, Joseph? The summer before you left? We knelt in the chapel together and prayed that God would use us to serve this community. You said we would be partners in your father's ministry someday."

His eyes darkened. "I kept that promise. When the authorities closed our school, I taught the children in secret for years—in corners of the marketplace, abandoned buildings, anywhere we could gather safely. I was fourteen when they arrested me the first time. While you were in American schools, I spent three months in a cell learning what happens to Christian teachers in Pakistan."

Tariq's admonishment settled in Joseph's chest like a lead weight. The memory flooded back with painful clarity—two boys with earnest hearts, believing God had called them to serve together.

He gestured at the others in the room. "After the attack, these people looked to me—a child—for guidance I wasn't prepared to give. Hassan did what he could, but he was watched too closely. I had to grow up overnight, helping families who lost everything, moving our meetings constantly to avoid detection." He shook his head. "So forgive me if I don't welcome your return as if you didn't abandon us."

The silence that followed pressed against Joseph's eardrums. Every eye in the room seemed to bore into him, some sympathetic, others questioning. During the flight to Pakistan, he had rehearsed this moment countless times, imagining joyful reunions, planning how he would explain his vision for rebuilding. But he hadn't prepared for this—for the raw wound of abandonment still festering after fifteen years.

"I learned about your father from Hassan's letters," Joseph managed, his throat constricting. "I'm so sorry, Tariq."

"Sorry doesn't rebuild what was destroyed," Tariq replied. "Sorry didn't protect those you left behind."

Nadir leaned forward, his gentle voice a contrast to Tariq's edge. "We've survived, Joseph. But it hasn't been easy. The authorities watch us. Neighbors report us. We meet in different homes each week, never in the same one twice."

Fatima nodded. "My son was denied entry to university when they discovered our faith. Nadir lost his shop in the marketplace."

"And now you return," Tariq said, "expecting what exactly? That we'll celebrate? That we'll follow you back to the place where our friends died?"

Emptiness yawned in Joseph's chest. He had come with certainty—conviction that he followed God's will. But now that conviction was being rejected.

Hassan moved to stand between Joseph and Tariq. "I helped Joseph escape because he was a child. Would you have had him stay to die? And I told you all that night he had vowed to return one day."

"Children make many promises," Tariq scoffed.

Joseph reached for his bag, needing something solid to anchor him. "I understand your anger, Tariq. I can't imagine what you've all endured." He withdrew his father's Bible, its cover cracked and blackened along one edge. "But I never forgot any of you."

Joseph cradled the Bible in his palms and swept his thumb across a charred corner. Tiny flakes of scorched leather drifted to the floor like black snow. A trace of burned wood—somehow preserved in the pages after fifteen years—drifted up to his nose.

Fatima's eyes widened. Her hand rose to her throat. Even Tariq's steady glare faltered for a heartbeat.

"Every night before bedtime, my father would read to me from this Bible." Joseph turned to the page in Isaiah and read, "The desert and the parched land will be glad; the wilderness will rejoice and blossom." He looked around the circle, meeting each person's gaze. "I've assembled a team to help us rebuild—professionals with experience in construction, medicine, education. They'll be arriving over the next two days."

Fatima glanced nervously at the covered window. "Whisper when you mention foreigners. The walls in this village have ears."

Tariq laughed, a harsh, bitter sound. "Foreigners. What do they know of surviving here? Of building something that won't just be torn down again?"

"They know their crafts," Joseph countered, finding his voice again. "And they're committed to our cause."

"Your cause," Tariq corrected. "Not ours. We've learned to live in the shadows, Joseph. To worship in whispers. Your father's mission was beautiful, but it made us targets. Visible. Vulnerable."

Heat flared in Joseph's chest, and he bit back his first response. He needed to listen—truly listen—to their concerns.

The room fell silent. Amir exchanged concerned glances with Nadir.

"The chapel will be our first priority," Joseph said. "A place where we can worship openly again."

"A chapel?" Nadir said. "Joseph, we've survived by being invisible. Our gathering places look like everyone else's homes. No crosses, no Christian symbols visible from outside."

"The authorities monitor construction permits closely," Fatima added. "They'll know what you're building and why."

"Especially with Faraz Qureshi," Raheel said with visible unease. "He won't take rebuilding the chapel lightly."

"I understand your concerns," Joseph said. "But there's a difference between wisdom and fear. My father built that chapel as a declaration—that we have nothing to hide, that our faith deserves its place in this country too."

"And they burned it to the ground," Tariq countered, his voice sharp but no longer hostile. "Your American perspective makes you think visibility brings protection. Here, it brings scrutiny, then accusations, then violence."

"We have international backing this time," Joseph insisted. "Support from organizations that can bring pressure if we're targeted."

"Foreigners won't stop a local mob with gasoline," Tariq said. "And your friends will eventually leave. We'll be the ones who remain to face the consequences."

Hassan, who had been quiet until now, cleared his

throat. "Perhaps there is wisdom on both sides. Joseph, these people have survived persecution you cannot imagine. But Tariq, sometimes hiding our light can become a habit of fear rather than purpose."

He turned to the others. "What Joseph hasn't mentioned is that he's already faced resistance. Just yesterday, Joseph was detained for hours at the airport, his belongings searched, his purpose questioned. The authorities are already watching his every move."

"The mission will have measures your father never had," Joseph said, addressing Tariq directly. "Samuel Wong, our engineer, has designed the compound with multiple exits, reinforced walls, and discreet surveillance systems. We have Ian Daniels, a security expert who's worked in hostile environments worldwide."

Joseph pulled out a folded paper from his pocket and spread it on the floor. "We'll build in phases. First a chapel and a deep well. Then a community center complete with a medical clinic. Worship, healthcare, and clean water. But I won't rebuild in the shadows. That would mean they've already won."

Nadir cleared his throat. "Perhaps we should hear more about this plan before judging it."

"Thank you," Joseph said, grateful for the lifeline. "The William Freeman Foundation has secured funding and permits to build on the original land, though with significant restrictions. The government requires a 60% reduction in size, no visible religious symbols outside, and regular inspections. Regardless, we start with the chapel. A place to worship and invite God's presence, even if more discreetly than before."

"And when they come to burn it down again?" Tariq challenged.

"We have political support this time," Joseph replied. "International backing."

"Papers and promises won't stop a mob," Tariq said.

Someone's breath hitched in the corner. Joseph looked from face to face, seeing doubt, fear, and— most painful of all—hope fading like sunlight at dusk. His plans were crumbling before they began.

His prepared speech died in his throat. This wasn't about blueprints or funding or assurances. It was about trust broken and the cost of faith.

He turned to face Tariq directly. "I can't understand what you were forced to endure." His voice cracked mid-sentence, brittle as if the words themselves might shatter. " I've lived with the privilege of safety while you risked everything to keep your spirit alive." Joseph looked down at his hands, remembering the countless nights he'd lain awake in his American bedroom. The guilt had been a constant companion, as familiar as his own heartbeat. "Not a day passed that I didn't question why I survived when others didn't. Why I was safe when you were suffering. I can't undo that, Tariq. But I'm here now, not to replace what was lost, but to honor it by continuing forward together."

Joseph flipped through the pages of his father's Bible. " But I've carried the vow I made to Hassan before God the night I left." His fingers hesitated. "This isn't just my plan. I believe with everything in me that God has prepared all of us for this moment."

His voice broke. "I can't do this without you—any of you. This is your mission as much as mine."

His heartbeat thumped in the silence that followed. Tariq stared at the burned Bible in Joseph's hands, his expression shifting almost imperceptibly.

Fatima straightened her slight frame. "Tariq speaks hard

truths we all feel. But Joseph, your father once told me that God's timing is perfect, even when it seems late to us. Perhaps you couldn't have returned before now—perhaps you needed to become the man who could help us rebuild, not just with bricks but with discernment."

Amir nodded. "We've worshiped in whispers. Maybe it's time our whispers become songs again."

Tariq's jaw tightened, but he remained silent, his eyes never leaving the Bible. "My father taught me that faith without action is dead," his tone grew softer. "But action without wisdom is just as fatal."

Joseph answered with a quiet nod.

"If we help you," Tariq continued, "it must be different this time. Not just a compound built by foreigners, but something that grows from within our community. Something that can withstand the storms that will come."

Joseph's chest loosened. "That's exactly what I want," he said earnestly. "A mission that belongs to all of us."

Fatima smiled, the first genuine smile Joseph had seen from her. "Then perhaps God has indeed brought you back to us, Joseph Freeman."

One by one, the others nodded, some with reservation. Even Tariq gave a single, curt nod—not friendship, but acknowledgment.

Hassan stood. "There is something you must know. We're being watched. Faraz Qureshi—the man who led the raid that killed your parents—knows you've returned."

The room tilted. Joseph's hand found the wall, fingers splaying against the rough mud brick as his father's Bible slipped from his other palm and thudded to the floor. *Faraz Qureshi. The man who led the raid.* The name carved itself into his consciousness like a blade.

Joseph's gaze drifted to the small window where darkness pressed against the glass like a living thing. Somewhere beyond that fragile barrier, in the labyrinth of alleys they'd just navigated, predatory eyes were surely watching.

Waiting for Joseph to make a mistake.

# FIFTEEN

## The Bridge

*THE NEXT EVENING*

Joseph stood at the edge of Malik's farmyard as head-lights cut through the mountain darkness. The Land Cruis-er's engine groaned up the final switchback, dust billowing in its wake. His team—finally here.

The vehicle lurched to a stop near the natural outcrop-ping where Joseph had parked the night before. Doors opened, and figures emerged, stretching after the three-hour drive from Islamabad. Darius first, his silver beard catching the moonlight. Then Maya, adjusting her head-scarf. Samuel with his ever-present notebook. Ian scanning the ridgeline out of habit.

"Joseph!" Darius called, his voice warm despite the late hour. "God is faithful."

Joseph crossed the yard to meet them, clasping hands, embracing shoulders. Behind him, Hassan emerged from the house, followed by Malik.

"Welcome, friends," Malik said in careful English. "You honor my home."

More vehicles arrived—Thomas and Leila in a rented sedan, Eliza and Manny following in a battered pickup they'd borrowed from a contact in Peshawar. The team assembled in the yard, their faces drawn from travel but expectant.

"Everyone is inside," Joseph said, keeping his voice low. "They've been waiting. But I need to warn you—there's tension. Skepticism. Years of suffering have made them cautious."

"As they should be," Maya replied. "We're strangers claiming to help. They have every right to question us."

Ian nodded. "What's the security situation?"

"Malik has lookouts posted on the ridge," Joseph said. "No one followed us last night. But if Faraz Qureshi knows I'm here, I should expect him keeping an eye on me eventually."

"Then we proceed carefully," Darius said. "But we proceed."

———

The farmhouse felt smaller with fifteen people inside—the local believers seated along one wall, the international team arranged opposite them. Oil lamps cast dancing shadows. The smell of chai mingled with kerosene and nervous sweat.

Joseph stood between the two groups. The divide between them felt wide as a canyon.

"Thank you all for taking this risk," he began, switching between English and Urdu as needed. "I've told our team about your courage, your faithfulness through fifteen years of persecution. Now I'd like them to hear your stories directly."

Silence stretched. Then Fatima rose, her aged frame somehow commanding despite her years.

"I am Fatima," she said in halting English. "Seventy-two years. My husband died in the first raid. My son cannot find work because we are Christian. My grandson was beaten last month for refusing to convert." Her voice strengthened. "But I still believe. Still pray. Still hope."

She looked directly at the international team. "You come with your skills and your money. This is good. But can you stay when the authorities come? When the mobs form? When your safety is threatened?"

The question hung like smoke.

Maya stood. "May I respond?"

Fatima nodded.

Maya rolled up her sleeve, revealing the jagged scar Joseph had seen once before. The lamplight caught the raised tissue, making it seem to pulse.

"I was ten years old," Maya began, her words unwavering. "My father was a lawyer in Lahore who represented Christians in blasphemy cases. He said every person deserves justice, regardless of their faith." She traced the scar with her other hand. "Militants broke into our home one night looking for my father."

The room went silent.

"They said my father was a traitor to Islam. That anyone who helps Christians deserves punishment." Maya's jaw tightened. "They broke his hands with a hammer. Told him he'd never defend infidels again. Then they turned to me."

Miriam's hand rose to her throat. Tariq stood straighter.

"My father threw himself between us. The knife meant for my heart caught my arm instead." Maya's eyes glistened, but her voice remained firm. "We fled to London the next day with nothing but the clothes we wore. My father never practiced law again—his hands healed wrong. But he taught me something more valuable than any case he ever won."

Her eyes swept the room, pausing on each face. "He taught me that defending the persecuted isn't just a job. It's a calling. One that requires sacrifice." She lowered her sleeve. "So when you ask if I'll stay when danger comes—the answer is yes. Because I've already faced that danger. And I know what it costs to run."

No one spoke for a long moment. Then Fatima crossed the room and embraced Maya, her weathered hands patting the younger woman's back.

"You understand," Fatima whispered. "You truly understand."

Ian cleared his throat. "My younger brother went to Afghanistan with an NGO eight years ago." His Yorkshire accent thickened with emotion. "James. Twenty-six years old. Passionate, committed, certain God would protect him."

He stared at his hands. "Taliban ambush killed him three months into his deployment. They found his body two days later, dumped on a roadside with a note: 'This is what happens to Christian crusaders.'"

The stark words fell like stones.

"I spent years angry at God, at James, at everyone involved in his mission." Ian looked up, his eyes hard but honest. "I blamed idealistic Westerners who think passion is enough. Who rush into hostile places without proper security, without understanding real threats."

Tariq shifted, his expression unreadable.

"That's why I'm here," Ian continued. "Not to repeat James's mistakes. But to honor his conviction by doing this work right. With proper planning. With security protocols that actually protect people instead of getting them killed."

He turned to Tariq directly. "You challenged Joseph yesterday about having an extraction plan. You were right to challenge him. I won't support any operation that treats local believers as expendable. So if we rebuild this mission, we do it with systems in place to protect everyone—not just the foreigners who can leave when things get difficult."

Tariq held Ian's gaze for a long moment before giving a slight nod of acknowledgment.

"My village was destroyed when I was seven." Thomas Okafor's deep voice cut through the silence before anyone else could speak. He pulled out his phone, showing a worn photograph. "Government soldiers during the Biafran War. They burned our crops, killed our livestock, poisoned our well."

He passed the phone to Nadir, who studied the image before handing it to Fatima.

"My mother died of starvation that winter. My father survived but never recovered. He taught me that the most effective weapon against oppression isn't violence—it's self-sufficiency."

Thomas gestured toward the window, though darkness hid the landscape beyond. "Food security means freedom. When you can feed yourselves, you're not dependent on those who would control you. When your well provides clean water, you're not vulnerable to those who would poison it." His eyes found Nadir. "Your father's notes show the mission once grew enough food to support forty people. We can do that again. Better than before. And that means this community won't just survive—it'll thrive."

Nadir, who'd lost his shop to a suspicious fire, leaned forward. "How long will you stay? These projects—they take months, years. Will you still be here when Faraz Qureshi decides we're too visible?"

Before anyone could answer, a woman's voice filled the room—speaking Pashto. Heads turned. Leila Nassar had risen, her words flowing in perfect mountain dialect. "I am not a Christian," she said, causing murmurs among the locals.

She switched to Urdu. "But I believe every person has the right to worship according to their conscience. I've spent five years documenting how minority faiths are systematically erased. In Iran, Baha'i communities disappear overnight. In Myanmar, Rohingya Muslims are slaughtered. In China, Uyghurs vanish into camps." Her voice grew passionate. "Your story deserves to be preserved, not forgotten. I'm here to document your resilience, to record your testimonies, to ensure the world knows you exist."

Miriam leaned forward. "But you're Muslim. Working with Christians—doesn't that create problems for you?"

"Yes," Leila admitted. "My family disowned me. Friends from university stopped speaking to me. Some call me a traitor to Islam." She pulled out a small notebook. "But my faith teaches me that Allah is merciful and just. How can I honor those attributes by remaining silent while others suffer?"

Darius stood. "I cannot promise we'll never leave. I've worked in Iran, Afghanistan, Central Asia for thirty years. Sometimes I've been forced out. Sometimes I've had to retreat to protect those I served." He moved to the center of the room. "But I've learned that the strongest ministries aren't built by foreigners who never leave. They're built by foreigners who train locals to lead—so the work continues regardless of who's present."

He looked at Hassan, then at Tariq. "We're not here to be

heroes. We're here to be servants. To build something with you, not for you. And when the day comes that we must leave—whether by choice or force—the mission will remain because it's yours, not ours."

A nervous cough drew attention to the corner. Samuel Wong pushed his glasses up, his engineer's hands fidgeting with his tablet. "I'm just an engineer. I don't have dramatic stories of persecution or family tragedy. I grew up in a comfortable home in Singapore. Went to good schools. Had opportunities many never get."

He pulled up architectural drawings on his tablet. "But my grandfather was a pastor in China during the Cultural Revolution. The Red Guards destroyed his church, burned his Bibles, sent him to a labor camp for ten years." Samuel's words grew firmer. "When he finally returned home, he spent the rest of his life rebuilding churches. Not the same churches—those were gone forever. But new ones. Smaller, hidden, adaptable."

He turned the tablet to show the group. "These designs incorporate everything he taught me. The chapel is central to the design—the first building, as Joseph wants. But it's integrated with other structures that will follow. Multiple exits throughout. Reinforced walls that look ordinary but can withstand assault."

Tariq rose and approached Samuel, studying the drawings. "This entrance—it has multiple paths?"

"Three," Samuel confirmed. "One through the main doors, two concealed routes that connect to the future clinic and community center. The chapel stands alone initially, but the foundation is designed so we can expand around it —creating a compound where the chapel is the heart, but not the only structure."

"My grandfather used to say the strongest structures are

the ones that bend without breaking," Samuel continued. "That's what we're building. The chapel comes first, visible and declaring our presence. Then we add the community center, the clinic, the school—each building reinforcing the others, creating something that can adapt, survive, endure."

Tariq studied the designs, his expression shifting. Something like interest flickered across his face—not full acceptance, but possibility.

The soft whir of a camera shutter broke the moment. Eliza Cohen lowered her lens, her expression apologetic. "Sorry. Force of habit." She set the camera aside. "I know what it's like to have your story erased. My grandmother survived Auschwitz. After the war, she spent fifty years telling anyone who would listen what happened there. Not for revenge. Not for pity. But because she believed that the dead deserved to be remembered."

Eliza gestured to the believers. "Before she died, she told me: 'The world forgets quickly. Document everything. Make sure the truth survives even when the witnesses don't.'" Her voice caught. "That's why I'm here. To document your faith, your courage, your refusal to disappear. So that even if this mission is destroyed again, your story survives."

The youngest team member had been silent until now. Manny Hernandez stood, his hands trembling. "I don't have the experience these others have. I just graduated seminary last year. I grew up in California, going to church without fear, taking my freedom for granted."

He pulled out his phone, showing a message thread. "But six months ago, I read about a pastor in Sudan who was imprisoned for baptizing converts. His wife wrote online asking for prayer support. I couldn't stop thinking about her —about their family suffering while I lived in comfort."

Manny's Spanish accent thickened. "I have no special

skills. No dramatic testimony. But I believe God doesn't always call the equipped—sometimes He equips the called. So I'm here to serve however you need. To carry supplies, to dig foundations, to fetch water. Whatever it takes."

His honesty seemed to resonate more than any dramatic story could have. Fatima smiled at him, the expression grandmotherly and warm.

Hassan rose, his weathered face reflecting years of keeping these believers together. "For fifteen years, I've held this community through storms. We've met in homes, in cellars, in caves. We've baptized in secret, shared communion in darkness, prayed with hands over mouths to muffle our voices."

He gestured to both groups. "But we were never meant to live this way. The church thrives in light, not shadow. In community, not isolation." His voice grew stronger. "These people—" he indicated the international team, "—they come with resources we lack. But more than that, they come with shared understanding of what it costs to follow Christ in hostile places."

Hassan moved to stand beside Joseph. "I've known Joseph since he was born. I carried him through the tunnel the night his parents died. I made him a promise—that we would keep the faith alive until he could return." He placed a hand on Joseph's shoulder. "He's kept his promise. Now we must decide if we'll keep ours."

The room fell silent. Oil lamps flickered, casting shifting shadows across faces—some still skeptical, others softening, all caught between fear and hope.

Tariq stood. Every eye turned to him.

"My father died believing in William Freeman's vision," he said, his voice steady but edged with pain. "He refused to deny Christ even when they put a gun to his head. His last words were 'Jesus is Lord.'" Tariq's jaw worked. "For fifteen years, I've asked myself if his death meant anything. If our suffering served any purpose."

He looked at Joseph, then at the international team. "I still don't fully trust you. You can leave when danger comes—we cannot. But..." He paused, something shifting behind his eyes. "But maybe that's the point. Maybe faith means trusting anyway. Building anyway. Hoping anyway."

Tariq extended his hand to Joseph. "For my father's sake. For all who died believing this mission mattered. I'll work with you."

Joseph gripped Tariq's hand, feeling the calluses of years of manual labor. "Thank you."

"Don't thank me yet," Tariq replied, but something like a smile ghosted across his face. "Wait until you see how demanding I am about security protocols."

Ian laughed—a short, sharp sound that broke the tension. "Good. I need someone who'll actually follow them."

The room exhaled. Conversations began—quiet at first, then building. Maya sat with Miriam, discussing advocacy strategies for her imprisoned husband. Samuel spread architectural drawings on the wooden table, surrounded by curious locals pointing and suggesting modifications. Thomas pulled out seed catalogs, showing Nadir drought-resistant crop varieties.

Joseph stepped outside into the cool mountain air, breathing deeply. Through the farmhouse window, he watched his two worlds merge—international experts and local believers, finding common ground in shared purpose.

Hassan joined him, two cups of chai in hand. He offered one to Joseph.

"Your father would be proud," Hassan said quietly.

"Or terrified," Joseph replied, accepting the tea. "We're about to rebuild everything that got him killed."

"Yes." Hassan sipped his chai. "But this time, with wisdom he never had. With preparation. With people who understand the cost." He gestured toward the window. "That's the difference. Your father charged forward with passion but little strategy. You're building with both."

Inside, Darius's distinctive laugh rose above other voices. Tariq was demonstrating something with his hands—probably explaining local building techniques. Maya had her iPad out, showing Miriam something that made the older woman's face light with hope.

"They're not separate anymore," Joseph observed. "International and local. They're becoming one team."

"That," Hassan said, "is how you build something that lasts. Not with foreign money or local knowledge alone. But with both, woven together until you can't tell where one ends and the other begins."

A cold breeze swept through the yard, carrying the scent of sage and distant snow. Joseph pulled his jacket tighter, thinking about Faraz Qureshi somewhere in the valley below, watching, planning, building his case.

"Faraz won't ignore this," Joseph said. "Once we break ground, once construction begins—"

"Then we'll face that when it comes," Hassan interrupted. "Tonight, we've accomplished something more important than avoiding danger. We've created unity. That's the foundation everything else builds on."

Through the window, Leila showed Fatima how to use a smartphone to record testimonies. The old woman's face glowed with wonder as she saw her own voice captured on the screen.

"Tomorrow we return to the mission site," Hassan said.

"All of us together. We'll walk the land, pray over it, begin clearing rubble. The real work starts then."

"And the real danger," Joseph added.

"Yes." Hassan finished his chai. "But we don't face it alone anymore."

Inside, someone—Manny, probably—had started singing. A hymn in Spanish that Joseph didn't recognize, but the melody was achingly beautiful. Other voices joined— English, Urdu, Pashto—creating harmony from different languages, different experiences, united in shared faith.

Hassan set down his empty cup and placed a hand on Joseph's shoulder. "That is how you build something that lasts. Not with foreign money or local knowledge alone. But with both, woven together until you can't tell where one ends and the other begins."

# SIXTEEN

**Pressure**

Faraz brushed past Qadir's secretary, ignoring the man's protest. "Sir, you cannot—"

He pushed through the office door without knocking. A whiff of stale air hit his face. He tossed the folder of surveillance photos onto Qadir's desk, scattering the documents beneath it.

"He's here." Faraz planted his palms on the edge of the desk and leaned forward. "Joseph Freeman landed in Islamabad six days ago. We need to shut him down before he gets started."

Qadir looked up, then straightened. He reached for the scattered pictures. "Director Qureshi. I wasn't expecting you."

Faraz ignored the comment. As if Qadir deserved such courtesy. The ceiling fan wobbled overhead, its uneven rhythm matching the throbbing in his temples.

He flipped open the folder, revealing surveillance

photos. "Hassan—William Freeman's former assistant—has been holding secret Christian gatherings." He pointed to seven separate photos of seven separate people entering a village home. "These men and women went underground after we burned the mission years ago."

He slid another photo across the desk. "Joseph Freeman at Islamabad International Airport. The missionary's son who escaped the fire." He tapped a customs report. "He cleared immigration six days ago. According to this, he's back to rebuild the mission. Your office issued the preliminary permits, didn't you?"

Qadir examined the evidence, his brow furrowing. "You've been thorough, Director. I'm impressed by your intelligence network."

Faraz replied with a half smile. "I've already activated surveillance protocols typically reserved for suspected terrorists."

"We have legal grounds to stop this." Qadir looked up. "Foreign religious interference. National security concerns. I could revoke the permits immediately."

Faraz circled behind Qadir's desk, examining the wall map of the district. Qadir stirred. "The situation is more complicated than a simple permit revocation."

He returned to his seat and pulled the chair closer, positioning it higher than Qadir's. Qadir swallowed as Faraz extracted a thick report bound in blue from his briefcase and slid it across the desk.

"Alexander Mercer, CEO of Stellarion and tech billionaire. His company has substantial investments planned for our technology sector. The Prime Minister's office has taken a personal interest."

Qadir flipped through the pages—investment projections, technology transfer agreements, employment figures.

Billions in potential capital. Thousands of jobs. "What does this have to do with Freeman?"

"Everything." Faraz turned to a specific page. "The William Freeman Foundation is listed here, under Mercer's philanthropic initiatives. He's funding the mission through Stellarion's charitable donations."

Qadir's eyes widened. "Mercer is bankrolling the missionary's son?"

"Generously—hundreds of thousands in transfers over the past month alone." Faraz closed the report. "And therein lies our complication."

"So we let them build their Christian fortress because some American businessman offers the internet?"

"Pakistan needs American trade agreements to counter Indian influence." Faraz lowered his voice. "And Mercer has the ear of the United States President."

Faraz stood and paced between the desk and the door, the worn carpet muffling his steps. Photographs of government officials lined the walls. Framed certificates. A Pakistani flag in its stand.

"Direct action would create an international incident," Faraz continued, moving to straighten a photograph on Qadir's wall. "One that would cost this country billions in aid and investment. Is that what you want?"

"Of course not, Director. What approach would you recommend?"

Faraz extracted another file from his briefcase, thinner than the first, stamped red with CONFIDENTIAL. He opened it. Alexander Mercer's profile—business holdings, political connections, personal history.

"If Freeman is the heart of this mission, then Mercer is its lifeblood," Faraz said, tapping the file. "Without his funding and political protection, Freeman has nothing."

Qadir leaned over images of Mercer at technology summits, charity galas, political fundraisers. Reports on his company, his competitors, his controversies. The overhead light flickered once, twice, as if struggling to illuminate the scheme taking shape.

"We don't stop Freeman directly..." Qadir began.

"We convince Mercer to withdraw his support," Faraz finished, the corner of his mouth lifting. "And then Freeman's mission collapses on its own."

The elegance of the approach was undeniable. No international incidents. No diplomatic complications. No direct confrontation that could be traced back to the government. Simply remove the foundation, and watch the structure crumble.

"How will we proceed?" Qadir asked.

"I'll build a case against Freeman—make him appear a liability to Mercer's broader interests. Maulana Rahman has already primed his followers. Any Christian mission is a threat to our Islamic values. He's prepared to mobilize protests the moment we give him evidence." Faraz tapped the desk. "My position gives me access to immigration records, financial transactions, communication monitoring. Everything we need."

He returned to his seat, playing the role of composed federal director. "You will find a way to separate Freeman from Mercer's money through bureaucratic channels. I need you to buy me time by slowing down the construction through every regulatory obstacle you can create."

"I'll need political cover," Qadir said, a calculating look replacing his earlier deference. "I've spent years navigating these waters, building relationships with the right people. My position here is valuable to more than just myself."

Faraz studied him with new interest. "Your family's

textile business has flourished under your... regulatory oversight. I've seen the permits you've expedited for your brother's factory."

Qadir stiffened. "I serve Pakistan by promoting economic development."

"As do I," Faraz nodded. "You'll have the cover you need." He grabbed a pen and wrote down a number. "Use this discreetly."

"What is it?"

"The interior minister's contact information. If you must call him, tell him you're working with me."

Qadir took the note, his posture straightening as he examined the writing.

Faraz stood and adjusted his jacket. "One more thing, Qadir. This operation has my personal attention. I expect daily updates on your progress."

"Of course, Director Qureshi," Qadir said. "And if we encounter... complications?"

"The Interior Minister is watching this situation closely. Your promotion to Commissioner has been under consideration, hasn't it? Success here would ensure it happens." Faraz set his palms on the desk and leaned into Qadir's space. "Failure means reassignment to some remote outpost where careers go to die. Your family would find Quetta quite challenging."

Qadir went pale. "I understand completely."

"Good. Just remember, I have the power to put someone else in your position." As Faraz stepped into the hallway, civil servants scurried past with averted eyes. The customs report crinkled in his breast pocket—Joseph Freeman's immigration photo, his declared address, his stated purpose of visit. All the intelligence he needed to begin his work.

Joseph had his father's green eyes and the same quiet

conviction that had made William Freeman so dangerous. For a moment—a flicker of doubt.

Was Faraz still serving Pakistan, or had this become something more personal? The two were inseparable now. Joseph Freeman represented everything that threatened the Pakistan he had sworn to protect—foreign influence disguised as charity, Western values undermining local traditions.

Yet the face in that passport photo haunted him. Those green eyes—so like his father's when he looked up at Faraz from the burning mission floor. "I forgive you," he'd said, even as Faraz raised his weapon. The words had meant nothing then. Fifteen years later, they still echoed in his nightmares, along with the screams that followed.

Faraz's fingers pressed harder against his scar. No, this wasn't personal vengeance—it was justice delayed. His history with the family only strengthened his resolve. This time, there would be no escape for the Freeman legacy.

Faraz continued to the exit, glaring at a pencil-neck bureaucrat who dared meet his gaze. The man looked away first.

It was time to use the full power of his office to welcome Joseph Freeman to Pakistan.

# SEVENTEEN

## The Foundation

*THE MISSION COMPOUND*

Joseph killed the engine and sat for a moment, still gripping the wheel. Through the windshield, the ruins waited—charred walls, scattered stones, fifteen years of abandonment.

"Ready?" Darius asked from the passenger seat.

Joseph nodded and stepped out.

The convoy had brought everyone—the international team in their Land Cruisers, local believers packed into Hassan's borrowed bus. Doors opened. Boots hit packed earth. Voices murmured in half a dozen languages as people emerged into the morning sun.

Joseph walked toward the chapel ruins, his father's Bible and a trowel in his backpack. Behind him, footsteps crunched on gravel. The two groups—international and local—moved separately at first, maintaining their invisible divide.

Hassan joined him at the chapel's foundation. "Your

father laid the cornerstone himself. Right there." He pointed to a weathered block, its inscription still visible: *Freeman Mission, Est. 1995.*

Joseph knelt to run his fingers over the carved letters. Solid. Permanent. His father had built to last.

"We're really doing this."

"We are." Hassan's hand rested on Joseph's shoulder. "Together."

The others gathered in a loose semicircle around the chapel's footprint. Joseph stood, turning to face the group. The gap between the two sides was still there—international team on one side, local believers on the other. But it was smaller than before. Narrowing.

"Thank you for coming," Joseph began. "What we do today isn't just about clearing rubble or organizing material. It's about reclaiming what was taken. About declaring that faith survives, even when everything else burns."

He pulled his father's Bible from his backpack—leather darkened by smoke, edges charred. Several of the local believers leaned forward, recognizing it.

"This survived the fire," Joseph continued. "Hidden in my uncle's attic for fifteen years. My father's Bible, with his notes in the margins, his prayers written on the pages." He opened it to Ezra 3, where his father had underlined verses about rebuilding the temple after exile.

"When the Israelites returned from Babylon to rebuild," Joseph read, "some wept because the Israelites remembered the former temple. Others shouted with joy at the new foundation being laid. Both responses were right—grief for what was lost, hope for what would be built."

He looked around the circle. Some faces showed grief—Tariq, Miriam, Fatima, those who remembered. Others showed hope—his team, eager to begin.

"Today we examine our foundation and what we plan to build," Joseph said. "Not the same as my parents' mission. Something new. Something that honors their sacrifice while learning from their mistakes."

He set the Bible on the cornerstone and pulled out the trowel.

"I'd like us to break ground together. Each person adding their mark. Committing this place and our work to God."

Silence held for a moment. Then Darius stepped forward.

"In Iran, we built in secret," Darius said, kneeling beside Joseph. "Underground churches that met in homes and basements. But always we dreamed of the day we could build openly." He took the trowel and drove it into the earth beside the cornerstone. "This is that day. Not for Iran, but for Pakistan. For these people who've waited fifteen years."

He handed the trowel to Hassan.

Hassan took it, turning it over. "I've tended this ground for fifteen years. Kept the believers together. Prayed for this moment." He dug the trowel in, lifting soil that hadn't been touched since the fire. "William and Lyla Freeman, this is for you. We remember. We continue."

Fatima's arthritic hands shook as she took the trowel. "My husband died believing in this place. My children grew up here. My grandchildren have never known a church building." She pressed it down, her weathered face set with determination. "Let them know. Let them see what their grandfather died for."

Tariq stared at the trowel before taking it. "My father's blood soaked this ground. The TLP executed him in our courtyard for refusing to deny Christ. For fifteen years, I've asked if his death meant anything." He looked at Joseph.

"Today, I choose to believe it did." The trowel bit into the earth.

One by one, the locals came forward. Miriam, praying for her imprisoned husband. Nadir, who'd lost his shop. Fatima, who had been with Joseph's parents from the beginning. Each adding their mark, their prayer, their commitment.

Then the international team. Maya spoke about justice. Samuel about building wisely. Ian about protecting what the team would build. Thomas about making the land fruitful again. Leila about preserving their story. Each person knelt, each hand on the trowel, each prayer rising into the clear morning air.

When Joseph's turn came again, he knelt where the altar had once stood. Fifteen years of guilt, fear, and doubt pressed down on him. But also fifteen years of calling, of preparation, of being shaped for this moment.

He drove the trowel deep.

"Lord," he prayed aloud, "this ground has known fire and blood. It's tasted martyrdom. Now let it witness resurrection. Let what rises here be more than buildings—let it be a community that can't be destroyed by flames or fear. Let it be a light that persecution can't extinguish."

"Amen," voices echoed—English, Urdu, Pashto, blending together.

Joseph stood. Around him, the two groups were no longer separate. The international team had shifted closer to the locals. The locals had stepped toward the internationals. The gap had closed.

Hassan moved to the center, addressing everyone. "Tomorrow we begin clearing rubble. Next week, we pour the new foundation. In three months, God willing, these walls will rise again." He gestured to the ruins around them.

"But today, we've laid the real foundation—not of stone and mortar, but of unity. Of shared purpose. Of faith that refuses to stay buried."

Samuel spread his architectural drawings on a flat stone, and immediately people clustered around—pointing, suggesting, debating modifications. Thomas led a group to the old garden plot, already planning what to plant. Maya pulled out her tablet, documenting everything for their legal records.

Joseph stepped back, watching his two worlds merge.

Hassan joined him, two cups of chai somehow manifested from someone's supply bag. "Your father would be proud," Hassan said, offering a cup.

"Or terrified," Joseph replied, accepting it. "We're painting a target on our backs."

"Yes." Hassan sipped his tea. "But this time, the target is surrounded by people who know how to aim back. Not with violence but with the kind of strength that survives persecution."

Through the ruins, Joseph could see both groups working together now. Ian showed Tariq the security plans. Maya interviewed Fatima, recording her testimony. Darius prayed with Miriam. Samuel explained load-bearing calculations to local craftsmen who'd never used such terms but understood the principles.

The foundation was laid. Not perfect. Not safe. But real.

And that was enough for today.

———

From his rocky perch above the compound, Faraz pressed the binoculars to his eyes, metal warming against his palms. His worst fears unfolded below. Fifteen years of vigilance, and now—not just Hassan, but a crowd. More than a dozen figures gathered where only desolation had existed.

He adjusted the focus on the tall figure beside Hassan. The man's bearing, the way others deferred to him—the missionary's son. Joseph Freeman. Grown into a man and now here.

Warm wind carried dust and distant voices up the hillside, words too scattered to catch but unmistakably prayer. The TLP leadership had dismissed his warnings as a personal vendetta. This gathering was proof of an organized Christian resurgence.

The crowd formed a circle around Joseph and Hassan before the chapel's skeletal remains. Joseph raised a trowel. The gathering fell silent. With ceremonial solemnity, Joseph drove the tool into the earth where his father once preached his blasphemy.

"An inauguration," he whispered. Not just of a building, but of resistance. Defiance cloaked in hymn and heritage. He'd spent years dismantling such illusions, brick by brick. But he'd been too patient. Mercy had been mistaken for weakness. Never again.

One by one, others stepped forward. Young, old, men, women—each taking their turn, participating in symbolic rebirth. The trowel passed hand to hand like some sacred relic.

Cold calculation replaced shock. This wasn't a nostalgic pilgrimage—this was a declaration. The mission would rise again unless he acted.

Joseph spoke to his followers, hands moving like his father's. Their faces tilted upward—hope, determination, that sickening devotion Faraz had seen fifteen years ago.

The crowd shifted. A figure near the edge caught his attention—standing apart from the others, posture hesitant, as if unsure whether to participate. When the person looked up, Faraz adjusted the focus. Recognition struck like lightning.

A face from the files. One of Hassan's faithful from the original mission. The file was extensive—family connections, vulnerabilities, pressure points. Everything Faraz needed.

Adrenaline spiked. How convenient.

The believer moved through the ceremony mechanically, accepting the trowel when the turn came, but the expression carried no joy. Only desperate hope. The kind of hope that could be exploited.

Perfect.

Faraz lowered his binoculars, pulse racing. This file contained leverage—the kind that bound tighter than faith. Obligations that couldn't be ignored. Choices that could tear a person apart.

Strings he could pull.

"Welcome back," he murmured, easing away from his position. Stones shifted beneath his boots. He steadied himself and erased his presence.

The binoculars slid into their case with a satisfying click. His truck waited a quarter-kilometer down the hidden path —enough distance to avoid detection. Each step sharpened his focus, scenarios building and collapsing until one crystallized.

*Let Freeman lay his foundation. I'll ensure nothing rises from it.*

# EIGHTEEN

## Progress

*Two Days After Groundbreaking*

"Careful—those stones are original. We'll build on them."

Hassan's voice carried across the compound. Two young men paused in their work, nodding before continuing to clear debris from the foundation. The noon sun beat down on what had once been the mission chapel.

A low rumble echoed in the distance. Hassan glanced toward the road and the faint sound of an engine. Just a truck, probably farmers. But his muscles tensed nonetheless.

The volunteers moved through the rubble like ants reclaiming a destroyed hill. Hassan ran his fingers along a blackened beam—scorched wood still solid beneath the soot. Freeman had built to last.

A shout from the north corner. Someone had uncovered intact flooring, stone tiles arranged in a cross pattern.

Hassan's throat tightened. How many prayers had been offered there?

"We should document this. Joseph will want to incorporate it into the new design."

Government patrols had been seen twice this week on nearby roads. Too close.

Hassan checked his watch. Nearly noon. "Let's break for food and water. An hour to rest, then we continue."

The men set down their tools and gathered in the shade. Plates of chapli kebab appeared, cups of cool water. Hassan poured himself a cup, his attention moving across the horizon, the road, the faces of his people.

Near the eastern wall, Tariq gestured to five young volunteers. None older than twenty. Something in their posture—tense shoulders, furtive glances—sent warnings through Hassan's mind.

Children of persecuted families. Young believers who'd watched parents lose jobs, siblings denied education, relatives imprisoned.

Tariq had been twelve when the mission burned. Old enough to understand, too young to act. That helplessness had hardened.

Hassan moved in their direction.

"The authorities imprison our brothers for owning a Bible. My father died rather than deny Christ. And what do we do? Hide and whisper while our oppressors crush us!"

The younger believers nodded. One exchanged a glance with another—eyes hard.

"Now that we're rebuilding this mission, perhaps it's time we stopped cowering—"

"Enough, Tariq."

Hassan's shadow fell across the circle.

Tariq's head snapped up. "These brothers deserve to know what we've endured."

"The believers should also live to see the mission rebuilt." Hassan kept his voice low. "There are ears everywhere."

"We were just talking," one of the young men said.

"Talk against the government is dangerous."

Tariq's jaw tightened. "So we pretend everything is fine? My father didn't die so we could hide forever."

Every word had truth behind it. But truth delivered in anger could burn.

"Your father died so our faith would continue. Not so we could throw our lives away."

Other workers had stopped. This was attention the group couldn't afford.

"There is a time to tear down and a time to build."

"My father didn't die for us to rebuild walls. He died for truth."

The workers stood frozen.

Tariq pulled away from Hassan's attempted grip. "We'll talk more later." He walked to the water containers.

The group dispersed. Hassan released a held breath. Crisis averted—for now. But the younger believers returned to work with sharper movements, more animated conversations.

The engine noise had faded. Hassan couldn't shake the unease it left.

A solitary figure perched on a fallen column. Miriam, head bowed over worn paper. Hands trembling. Tear tracks through the dust on her cheeks.

Hassan approached quietly.

"May I join you?"

Miriam looked up, wiping her face. "Of course."

Hassan settled beside her. Workers gradually returned to tasks. They sat in silence.

"From your husband?"

Miriam tucked the letter into a pocket. "It came yesterday."

Hassan waited.

"He's not well, Hassan. The prison doctor says his lungs are failing from the damp. The officials refuse to release him or provide proper medicine."

Hassan looked down. What could he offer? No medicine. No legal recourse. Only prayers—and even those felt worn thin.

"What does he say about his spirit?"

A ghost of a smile. "Strong as ever. He writes that he's sharing Christ with his cellmates. Two have already believed." The smile faded. "But he doesn't think he'll live much longer. He wants me to describe our rebuilding in my letters, every detail as the chapel rises."

Hassan took her hand. Calluses of hard work.

"We will take pictures for him. And pray for his release."

"I've been praying for fifteen years, Hassan. But there are times I wonder if God has forgotten us."

Raw honesty struck deep. He had no platitudes.

"I don't believe He has forgotten. But I do think He weeps with us."

Miriam nodded. "Tariq is angry. I understand his anger. I feel it too—this desire for action, for change."

Hassan followed her gaze. Tariq attacked a pile of debris with contained fury. The younger believers kept glancing his direction. "Look at them. The way the others watch him now. It's different."

The subtle shift. The way volunteers worked more as a

unit. One caught Tariq's attention, nodded. Another had stopped work entirely, staring at the road.

"Determination can destroy or build," Hassan said. "The question is which path the team will choose."

"And how much time before that choice is made for them." Miriam added.

The rumble came again—closer now. Hassan straightened. Still nothing visible, but the sound was building.

"We should get back."

Hassan offered his hand.

Miriam stood. "You carry too much, my friend. This burden isn't yours alone."

Hassan managed a tired smile. "Nor yours." The foundation where the chapel was beginning to emerge. "We carry it together."

Near the supply tent, whispered fragments between two younger believers—"can't keep waiting—" and "—time for action—"

Hassan called out instructions. His voice carried authority that had held their community together through fifteen years.

Then the sound—undeniable now. Engines, maybe three, churning dust on the road. Heading their way.

———

Three vehicles emerged from the dust cloud. The lead SUV was black and official. Behind it were two trucks loaded with building materials.

Workers stopped. Tools were lowered. All eyes turned.

"Everyone keep working."

Hassan forced calm into his voice, but his pulse

hammered. Official vehicles meant government. Government meant trouble.

The SUV rolled to a stop. The door opened. Faraz Qureshi stepped out, his crisp uniform stark against the dust and rubble. Four local policemen emerged from the other vehicles.

Hassan's stomach dropped. Their last encounter—the gathering at his home, the interrogation, threats about Khalid's shop burning—Faraz had made it clear he was watching.

And now he was here.

"Brother!" Faraz's voice carried false warmth across the clearing. He approached, hand outstretched. "I'm pleased to see you again, under better circumstances than our last meeting."

Hassan's hand found the wall. Workers had gone silent. Tariq stood near the foundation, jaw tight, hands clenched.

Hassan forced himself forward and accepted the handshake. Faraz's palm was smooth against his calloused one.

"Director Qureshi. This is unexpected."

"I represent governmental interests in the development council now." Faraz gestured to his men, who began unloading supplies from the trucks. "We've come to offer assistance. Lumber, cement, nails. Word has reached us about your efforts here."

An older worker whispered to his companion. Hassan caught the words 'burned' and 'attack.' Yes, workers remembered who Faraz was. What he'd done.

"We understand Alexander Mercer's company is funding this project." Faraz smiled, but his eyes remained cold. "His investments are vital to Pakistan's technology sector. Our government wishes to ensure his interests are well supported."

Hassan's eyes narrowed. "That's very generous. But I will need to discuss this with the leader of this enterprise. Until then, I cannot accept your offer."

"Would that be Joseph Freeman?" Disappointment crossed Faraz's face. "I would be honored to meet him personally."

"He's not here today. Your arrival was unexpected."

Tension crackled between them. Faraz drew closer, dropping his voice so only Hassan could hear.

"Between us, certain officials are concerned about potential delays in your project. Delays that might be interpreted as... lack of local support for Mr. Mercer's broader investments." There was an edge beneath his diplomatic words. "We wouldn't want him to feel unwelcome."

Hassan's shoulders tensed despite his effort to remain calm. "We appreciate your concern. But all decisions go through Mr. Freeman."

"Of course." Faraz conceded with a slight bow. "Protocol must be respected."

His gaze drifted beyond Hassan toward the village volunteers. Then his attention focused on the chapel's foundation, where Tariq stood with a defiant gaze.

Faraz's eyes lingered before returning to Hassan. "I understand you're rebuilding exactly as it was before? The same layout, same purpose?"

Hassan hesitated. "We are adapting to current needs."

"Of course, of course." Faraz allowed his gaze to drift back to Tariq. When their eyes met, Faraz offered the subtlest nod—an acknowledgment, an invitation. "Adaptation is necessary for survival, isn't it?"

Around them, Faraz's men moved through the compound, offering help while their eyes swept across every detail. One entered the chapel ruins.

"Your men seem eager to help."

"They understand the importance of community relations. Especially with foreign investors watching our region so closely."

A worker approached Hassan, murmuring about needing help with excavation. Hassan nodded, relieved.

"If you'll excuse me. Duty calls."

"Of course." Faraz extracted another file from his briefcase—thinner, bound in blue. He opened it briefly, just long enough for Hassan to glimpse Alexander Mercer's photograph. "Please convey my offer to Mr. Freeman. I'll return next week to check on his response. Deputy Commissioner Qadir would be pleased if we could help."

Hassan's brow lifted at Qadir's name. The connection between the government official and Faraz added another layer of threat.

"I will tell him of your visit."

Faraz nodded, looking satisfied. He gestured to his men, who disengaged and returned to their vehicles. As the officers walked away, their eyes swept across the compound. Hassan recognized the look—cataloging weaknesses, gathering intelligence.

Faraz climbed into the SUV.

Hassan held his ground, gazing at the departing convoy and wondering what this visit was really about.

———

Dust settled slowly after the convoy disappeared. Hassan stood motionless, the road empty long after the vehicles were gone.

"What did he want?"

Tariq approached, his voice hard.

"To offer help." Hassan turned back to the compound. "And to remind us we're being watched."

"Help." Tariq spat the word. "From the man who burned this place down. Who killed my father."

"I know who he is."

"Then why didn't you refuse him outright? Tell him we want nothing from murderers?"

Hassan met Tariq's angry gaze. "Because refusing would give him an excuse to shut us down. We're building with government permits, on government-watched land, with foreign funding under monitoring. We can't afford to provoke them openly."

"So we smile and accept help from the man who destroyed everything?" Tariq's fists clenched. "That's cowardice."

"That's wisdom." Hassan kept his voice even. "Your father's courage was real. His sacrifice matters. But open confrontation gave Faraz exactly what he wanted—an excuse to destroy us completely. We survived because we learned to be strategic about when to fight and when to build."

Tariq's face flushed. "My father died with honor."

"Your father died heroically." Hassan's voice carried conviction now. "He chose faithfulness over safety. That's why we remember him. Why we're rebuilding what he helped protect." He paused. "But we also learned from his sacrifice. We learned that sometimes the most faithful thing is to survive—to outlast our enemies rather than giving them martyrs."

The words hung between them. Tariq looked away, working his jaw.

"You want me to bow to the man who murdered my father."

"I want you to outlive him. To build something that survives his hatred. Your father's blood is in this ground. The question is whether we honor that by dying like he did, or by building something that makes his death mean something."

Other workers had resumed their tasks. Hassan knew most were listening. This conversation would spread through the community.

"I need to know you're with us. Not just in body, but in spirit. Can you work within the constraints we face? Or will your anger destroy what we're trying to build?"

Tariq stared at the foundation, the partially cleared rubble, workers moving through ruins his father had once loved. Something shifted in his expression—not acceptance, but consideration.

"I'll work with you. But if Faraz crosses the line—if he threatens us directly—I won't stand by."

"If he threatens us directly, we respond. Together. With wisdom." Hassan placed a hand on Tariq's shoulder. "Your father's courage, but with strategy he didn't have time to learn."

Tariq didn't pull away. After a moment, he nodded and returned to work.

Hassan turned his attention to the road. Faraz would return. This visit had been reconnaissance, not confrontation.

He walked to where Miriam had returned to sorting stones, her movements mechanical, her expression distant.

"He recognized me."

Hassan's chest tightened. "You don't know that."

"I saw his eyes. He knows who I am. What leverage he has."

"Then we protect you. We—"

"You can't protect me from this, Hassan." Miriam finally met his gaze. "He holds my husband's life in his hands. If he threatens to..." She couldn't finish.

Hassan had no answer. No reassurance that wouldn't be a lie.

"We should tell Joseph when he returns. He needs to know what we're facing."

"What we've always faced." Miriam returned to her work. "Nothing has changed except the face of our oppressor wears a government badge now."

Hassan looked out over the compound—workers clearing rubble, laying foundation, building something that might be destroyed before completion. But building nonetheless.

The sun was setting. Time to send workers home, to disperse before drawing more attention. Tomorrow the team would return and continue.

If Faraz allowed them.

# NINETEEN

**Leverage**

The door opened.

Faraz looked up from the file spread across his desk. "Thank you for coming. Please, sit."

The visitor hesitated at the threshold. The door closed with a click. Footsteps crossed the tile floor—measured, reluctant. The chair opposite his desk scraped as weight settled into it.

Faraz closed the file and set it aside, hands folding atop the polished mahogany. His office was designed to intimidate—Islamic calligraphy on the walls, service commendations in black frames, law volumes arranged by thickness on the shelves. The Pakistani flag stood in the corner. Everything precisely placed. Everything communicating authority.

"I appreciate your cooperation in coming here." His voice carried warmth. "I know this isn't easy. Being summoned to the FIA creates anxiety. Especially for people in your position."

Silence answered him. He let it stretch, watching hands grip the armrests of the chair. White knuckles. Tension in the shoulders.

"I've been reviewing your file," Faraz continued. "Quite thoroughly, actually. Your situation is complicated. Difficult. Fifteen years is a long time to endure hardship. Most people would have broken by now. But you haven't. That shows remarkable strength."

He paused, allowing the words to settle.

"Someone you care about deeply—their situation concerns me. The medical reports are troubling. Health failing. Without proper intervention, without the right care..." He trailed off, shaking his head. "The prognosis isn't good. Months, perhaps. Maybe less."

A sharp intake of breath across the desk. *Good. The information was landing.*

"But it doesn't have to end that way." Faraz leaned forward, elbows on the desk, expression earnest. "I have connections. Influence in places that matter."

He let that word hang in the air—outcomes. Vague enough to mean everything.

"These connections aren't easy to leverage. They require capital. Not money—I'm not asking for a bribe. No, they require a different currency. Information. Cooperation. Small gestures that demonstrate goodwill between parties."

The visitor shifted. Hands released their grip on the armrests slightly, then tightened again.

"The compound where you've been working—the Freeman mission." Faraz's voice remained pleasant, as if discussing the weather. "It's a project of significant interest to my department. Foreign funding. International workers.

Religious activities in a sensitive region. My job is to monitor these situations. To ensure they don't create complications."

He stood, moving to the window. Outside, Peshawar's afternoon traffic crawled past. Horns blared. Dust swirled.

"I'm not asking you to betray anyone. I'm not asking you to harm your community." He clasped his hands behind him. "I simply need awareness. Who comes to the compound. What they discuss. Their plans for construction, for expansion, for whatever activities they're planning."

Faraz returned to his desk, settling into his chair. He pulled the file closer, opening it to a specific page. Medical documentation. Diagnoses. Prognoses. All carefully arranged to maximize impact.

"Nothing you tell me would endanger your friends. I'm not interested in persecution. I simply need to know what's happening so I can do my job properly. Ensure compliance with regulations. Maintain security. Protect Pakistani interests."

His finger traced a line on the medical report.

"In exchange, I could ensure proper medical attention. Transfer to a better facility. Access to specialists. Medications that aren't currently available. Perhaps even..." He paused, letting hope build. "Perhaps even early consideration for clemency. Medical grounds. Humanitarian reasons."

The visitor's breathing had grown shallow. Faraz could sense the war happening behind that silence—desperation fighting against loyalty, hope battling with principle.

"Fifteen years you've endured." His voice softened, almost gentle. "Fifteen years of sacrifice. Of hardship. Of waiting for something that may never come. Unless someone with influence intervenes. Unless circumstances change."

He closed the file.

"I'm offering you that change. A way to end the suffering. To bring resolution after all this time. Not through violence or dramatic intervention—simply through proper channels, properly applied."

Faraz leaned back, giving space for the proposal to breathe.

"Think of it practically. What I'm asking doesn't harm anyone. Joseph Freeman's mission will proceed—I can't stop it, wouldn't try. But knowing their activities helps me manage expectations with my superiors. Helps me protect the project from those who want to shut it down violently. In a sense, your cooperation protects the mission as much as it helps me."

The lie was smooth. He'd used variations of it before.

"The information would be simple. 'Today they poured foundation for the north wall.' 'A delivery of lumber arrived Tuesday.' 'The international team held a meeting about security protocols.' Nothing classified. Nothing that compromises anyone. Just...awareness."

His voice took on an edge, subtle but present.

"Of course, these arrangements require actual cooperation. Verbal agreement means nothing without follow-through. I would expect regular reports. Weekly, perhaps. A phone call. A brief meeting. Nothing elaborate."

The visitor's hands trembled slightly on the armrests now.

"And if information proves inaccurate, or if I discover you've warned the mission about our arrangement..." He let the sentence dangle unfinished. "Well. That would demonstrate a lack of good faith. Would complicate my ability to help with the medical situation. Would, in fact, make intervention impossible."

He stood again, moving to the bookshelf. His fingers traced the spines of law volumes—penal codes, administrative regulations, precedents.

"Pakistani law is complex. Prison administration more so. The bureaucracy surrounding medical care in correctional facilities is deliberately opaque. Without someone navigating that system on your behalf, nothing changes. The medical reports continue their decline. The condition worsens. Eventually..."

Faraz turned back, expression grave.

"Eventually, you receive notification. Not a release. Not a transfer. Just...notification. That's how these situations end when no one with authority intervenes."

He returned to his desk, settling into the chair with deliberate slowness.

"I'm offering intervention. A way forward after fifteen years of waiting. The question is whether you're willing to accept the terms."

Silence stretched. Outside, a car horn blared.

"You might think loyalty to the mission matters more. That refusing to cooperate shows integrity." Faraz's voice grew colder now, the pretense of warmth falling away. "But loyalty to whom? To Joseph Freeman, who abandoned Pakistan for fifteen years while you suffered? To his international team, who will leave when difficulties arise? Or loyalty to the person whose fate actually depends on your choice?"

He leaned forward, elbows on the desk again.

"Think carefully about priorities. About what—and who —truly matters. The mission will survive or fail regardless of what you tell me. But the person in that facility won't survive without intervention. That's certain. That's documented."

Faraz tapped the medical file.

"I'm not asking you to make this decision now. Take time. Consider your options. Weigh what's being asked against what's being offered. But don't take too much time."

His expression hardened.

"Medical conditions don't wait for moral deliberation. They progress. They worsen. They reach points beyond intervention. The window for help isn't infinite. It's closing. Weeks, perhaps. Maybe less."

The visitor remained frozen. Silent.

"You've survived fifteen years of hardship. Endured more than most people could bear. Maintained faith under circumstances that would break anyone else. I respect that. Truly." Faraz's voice carried sincerity now—perhaps the only genuine emotion he'd expressed. "But survival for what? For continued suffering? For watching someone you love fade because you chose principles over practical action?"

He stood, walking around the desk. Stopped beside the chair. Looked down.

"I'm offering you a way out. A path forward. Not through miracles or divine intervention—through simple cooperation. Through information that doesn't harm anyone but helps ensure proper care for someone who desperately needs it."

Faraz returned to his seat. He pulled out a business card, writing a number on the back. Slid it across the desk.

"My private line. When you're ready to discuss this further. When you've made your decision."

The card sat untouched between them.

"I'll expect to hear from you within the week. That gives you time to consider, to pray if that helps, to weigh your options. But after a week, I'll assume you've chosen continued suffering over accepting help. And at that point, my ability to intervene ends."

He opened a different file on his desk, signaling the meeting's conclusion.

"I'm a government official, not a missionary. I can't force you to cooperate. Can't compel you to accept assistance. All I can do is make the offer. The choice is entirely yours."

Faraz looked up one final time.

"But make no mistake—it is a choice. Between intervention and decline. Between hope and resignation. Between doing what's necessary to save someone, or maintaining principles while waiting for them to die."

The silence in the office was absolute now. Even the fan seemed to pause.

Finally, movement. The visitor stood. Chair scraping against tile.

No words. Just a slow turn toward the door.

Faraz called after the retreating figure, voice following across the office. "Consider carefully. And remember—this conversation remains between us. Sharing it with anyone at the mission would demonstrate precisely the kind of disloyalty that makes cooperation impossible."

The door opened. Hesitation at the threshold.

Then footsteps in the hall. Receding. The door shut, muting the footfalls.

Faraz remained at his desk, satisfaction settling over him. The meeting had gone exactly as planned. The leverage was clear. The terms were explicit. The pressure was applied.

Now came the waiting.

He returned his attention to the file, reviewing details one more time. Fifteen years of documentation. Medical reports tracking decline. Petitions for clemency, all denied. A case with no hope—except through his intervention.

A knock at his door. His assistant.

"Director Qureshi? Your next appointment is waiting."

"Give me five minutes."

The door closed. Faraz stood, moving to the window again. Somewhere in the city, his visitor was processing the meeting. Weighing options. Wrestling with impossible choices.

They always chose survival. Always chose the person they loved over abstract principles. It was human nature. Predictable. Exploitable.

This believer would be no different.

A week. Maybe less. Then the phone would ring. The voice would be quiet, defeated, compliant. And through that compliance, Faraz would gain access to everything happening at the mission. Every plan. Every weakness. Every person worth targeting next.

He smiled, turning from the window.

Let Freeman build his chapel. Let the international team work their construction. Let Joseph think his mission was succeeding.

Faraz would tear it down from the inside. Not with fire this time, but with betrayal. With the slow rot of compromised loyalty. With the unbearable weight of impossible choices forced on desperate people.

Much more effective than burning.

Much more permanent than violence.

He returned to his desk. Checked his calendar. Next week would be busy—meetings with Qadir, reports to Rahman, continued surveillance of the compound.

But he'd find time for the phone call when it came. The

quiet voice admitting defeat. Agreeing to cooperate. Accepting the terms.

The creaked open. Slow. Hesitant.

Then a broken voice—a whisper. "And if I refuse?" His visitor had returned.

Faraz leaned back in his chair. Satisfaction warmed his chest. There it was. The question that meant she was already considering cooperation. Already calculating whether resistance was possible.

"Then your husband dies in that cell, Miriam."

# TWENTY

## The Suspension

"What do you think?" Joseph asked, standing on makeshift scaffolding at the chapel's eastern wall.

Sunlight pierced through gaps in the half-completed roof trusses, dappling the stone floor where his father's church once stood.

Darius smiled. "The foundation is strong."

"I keep thinking about my father standing right here. Building something that wasn't supposed to be destroyed." Joseph pulled out his phone. His frown deepened. "Still no response from Mercer about yesterday's update. That's unusual."

"He'll respond." Darius's hand settled on Joseph's shoulder. "In the meantime, we rebuild what was lost. That says something about God—and about you."

Below them, Leila Nassar—their Muslim linguist—worked alongside Tariq, measuring and marking the doorframe.

"Halfway done." Joseph descended the wooden ladder. His boots hit the ground, puffing up dust.

"God has been faithful," Darius said.

"With our current balance, we can complete the chapel. With Mercer's next installment, we start on the clinic." Joseph checked his messages again—still nothing.

"One step at a time. Today we celebrate how far we've come."

Joseph walked to the entrance where Samuel and Eliza studied blueprints spread over a folding table.

"Simple, but meaningful. When we finish, I think we should have a proper dedication. Sunset worship, testimonies, prayers. Maybe communion."

Samuel's face brightened. "A worship service?"

"We could document parts of it," Eliza suggested. "Share with the underground churches throughout Pakistan."

Leila paused in her work nearby.

"This service—is it important beyond the building itself?"

Joseph met her gaze. "In Christianity, the church isn't about the building. It's about the people—the community of believers. These walls and this roof, they're just a gathering place. The true church is the people who will worship here."

Leila tilted her head. "That is different from my understanding of a mosque. For us, the masjid itself holds great significance—its orientation toward Mecca, its architecture, its very presence in the community. The physical structure itself is sacred."

"That's an interesting difference. For us, this building could burn again tomorrow, and the church would still exist —because the church is the people, not the building."

"Yet you still rebuild. You risk much for walls that you say are not essential."

Joseph smiled. "Because while the building isn't the church, it serves the church. It provides a visible presence, a place of safety, a symbol of hope." He ran his hand along a freshly laid stone. "And sometimes, people need symbols they can see."

"I understand. In my faith, the mosque serves as both physical and spiritual center—a place where the community gathers, learns, and worships together." Leila glanced around at the rising walls. "I have watched all of you work—Christians from different countries, different backgrounds—with such joy. It is as if the structure itself matters less than what you are building together."

"Would you come?" Joseph asked. "To the service?"

She hesitated. "I would not want to intrude on your ritual. Our faiths have different understandings of worship."

"Not an intrusion," Darius said. "An honor. You've helped build these walls—you should see what they're meant for."

Leila adjusted her headscarf. "Perhaps I could observe, from the back. I would be interested to see how Christians dedicate a sacred space, even if you view its sacredness differently than we do."

Across the compound, Thomas Okafor knelt in the mission's long-neglected garden—the same spot where Joseph's mother had explained which seeds needed planting.

"Excuse me." Joseph walked toward the garden plot.

Thomas looked up, wiping sweat from his brow. "Ah, Joseph! Perfect timing. This soil has remarkable potential despite years of neglect. This garden must have been exceptional once."

Joseph knelt beside him, taking a handful of dark soil and letting it sift through his fingers. "It was. We grew everything—cardamom, mint, herbs for medicinal purposes. My mother called it God's superstore." The memory stung. "Every morning before sunrise, she'd be out here tending to something or another."

Thomas nodded. "She knew what she was doing. There's still evidence of proper crop rotation, companion planting." He pointed to different sections. "When we finish the chapel, we should restore this too."

"I agree. Let's do it."

Tariq approached. His wariness had softened, but skepticism remained.

"Thomas, the irrigation junction needs your expertise." Tariq turned to Joseph. "Darius mentioned you're planning some kind of service when the chapel is finished?"

Joseph stood, brushing soil from his hands. "Yes. A dedication. Nothing elaborate, but meaningful."

"A public Christian worship service? With people coming from other villages?" Tariq crossed his arms. "You might as well send the TLP a personal invitation."

"We can't hide forever, Tariq. This mission—this chapel —it exists to be a light. My father understood the risks of visibility."

"And he died for it."

Thomas became suddenly interested in his gardening tools.

"Yes. He did. But not before touching countless lives— including yours."

Pain crossed Tariq's face.

"I'm not suggesting we broadcast it on loudspeakers. But we need to claim this space for its purpose. Otherwise, what are we building?"

Darius approached. "Perhaps we can find middle

ground. Security precautions without compromising the spiritual significance."

Tariq's shoulders relaxed. "I'm not against worship. I'm against making targets of people who've already suffered enough." He gestured toward Fatima, who was cleaning smoke damage from the original cornerstone. "Ask her what happened after your family left. Ask about the raids, the interrogations, the years of looking over their shoulders."

"I understand your concern—and I value your perspective, Tariq. You've kept faith alive here when many would have abandoned it. But this mission—this chapel—it represents something more than safety. It represents hope. Resilience."

"Hope won't stop bullets."

"No—but without it, what are we protecting?"

Tariq held Joseph's gaze before sighing. "I'll help plan security. Small groups arriving at different times. Lookouts posted. No vehicles that could be traced." He turned to leave, then paused. "Your father would have insisted on the same precautions."

Relief and sorrow mixed in Joseph's chest.

"He'll come around," Darius said. "His caution comes from care, not opposition."

"I know. And he's right about the security. We must be careful."

Hassan appeared, troubled expression clear.

"Joseph, a word?"

Hassan stepped away from the others, glancing around before speaking in low tones.

"I've heard disturbing news—Faraz Qureshi met with government officials yesterday morning. A long meeting, many papers exchanged."

Cold weight settled in Joseph's stomach. "What kind of meeting?"

"The kind that precedes bad news for people like us. My friend thinks Qureshi is positioning himself for something. Using his connections to cause problems."

"For the mission?"

"Or for anyone supporting it." Hassan's expression darkened. "I thought you should know, especially with your American benefactor being so generous. Rich Americans make easy targets for political accusations."

"Thank you for telling me. I'll keep it in mind."

His phone buzzed. A new email from Stellarion. "It's from Mercer's chief legal counsel."

Eliza and Samuel approached.

"About time," Samuel said. "We sent those progress photos two days ago."

The subject line read **"Project Funding Update."** Joseph opened it. The first sentence was enough.

The words detonated. His vision blurred. Compound sounds—hammering, voices, the cement mixer—became distant static.

"Joseph?" Eliza's voice seemed underwater. "What is it?"

He couldn't speak.

Darius took the phone and read aloud:

"'Mr. Freeman—After careful review of current geopolitical considerations and following consultations with Pakistani government representatives, Stellarion has made the difficult decision to suspend funding for your mission reconstruction project, effective immediately. The political climate has become complex, and continuing our support could jeopardize other critical initiatives in the region. The final transfer made last week will be the last. We wish you success in finding alternative funding sources. Regards, Victoria Harlow, Chief Legal Counsel.'"

Silence fell over the group. Around them, construction continued—hammers, voices, the cement mixer. The sounds felt like mockery.

"Qureshi," Hassan said. "This is his doing."

The sunlight that had seemed promising earlier was now harsh and accusing. Every incomplete detail stood exposed—the missing roof sections, the unfinished electrical conduits, the gaps that would remain unfilled.

Was this God's will? Had Joseph misread everything? The calling that had pulled him back from America, the sense of divine purpose—had it all been self-deception?

"They can't do this," Eliza whispered.

"They can," Samuel said. "And they have."

Joseph turned to Darius. "What if I was wrong? What if this whole thing—coming back, rebuilding—what if it was just my idea, not God's?"

Darius studied Joseph's face. "Do you remember what you told me when you first arrived? That you felt called not just to rebuild walls, but to restore hope."

"And look where that's led us." Joseph gestured at the incomplete structure. "Halfway finished means halfway failed. These people trusted me."

"Get Maya. She needs to see this."

Darius nodded and hurried toward the administrative tent. Minutes later, Maya arrived, iPad under one arm. She looked from face to face. "What happened?"

Joseph handed her his phone.

Maya read in silence with a tight jaw. She handed the phone back and opened her tablet. "Give me a moment."

The group waited.

"Can we sue them for breach of contract?" Samuel asked.

Maya shook her head. "Their contract will have contingency clauses. Even if we filed in US courts, Stellarion could tie us up for years in discovery and legal challenges."

Joseph's shoulders slumped. "So there's nothing we can do?"

"I didn't say that. What we need right now is to document everything—our current state of completion, all communications with Stellarion, photographs of progress. This creates a record of actual conditions versus whatever concerns they're citing."

Eliza nodded, pulling out her camera. "I'll start photographing everything."

"The question isn't just legal, it's strategic," Maya continued. "Why terminate so abruptly?"

Joseph looked at the unfinished structure. "We could probably finish the chapel, but without Mercer's money, nothing else."

"I'll draft a formal response requesting clarification and transitional funding. But we should prepare for the likelihood that this decision is final."

"And if they refuse?" Darius asked.

"Let me review the full contract tonight. The involvement of both legal and security departments suggests navigating around some contractual obligation. There might be a vulnerability there, or at least a basis for negotiation."

"So we're just stuck."

Maya's expression softened. "Joseph, my job is to be honest about our legal position. And the truth is, we have minimal leverage here. But that doesn't mean we're without options."

Joseph looked at the chapel—at the walls that stood. Halfway complete. So close, yet impossibly far.

"Maybe this is the answer I've been afraid to hear. Maybe God's will isn't always what we want it to be."

Darius's eyes narrowed. "Joseph. God's timing isn't always our timing. But His purposes don't change because of obstacles."

"Maya, draft that response. But in the meantime, let's see what resources we have left. How far they'll take us. And then we'll figure out the rest."

The weight remained, but something else stirred alongside it—not the confident determination from before, but something quieter.

"One stone at a time." Joseph said as if praying. "Just like when we started."

# PART III

# TWENTY-ONE

## The Source

*TEHSIL MUNICIPAL ADMINISTRATION—PESHAWAR CITY*

The whiskey was forbidden—haram under Sharia law
—but Faraz savored it anyway, rolling the crystal tumbler
between his palms as he stood at Deputy Commissioner
Qadir's office window. The amber liquid caught the dying
sunlight.

Below, the city darkened. Minarets stood silhouetted
against the sunset.

Fire had marked the beginning of his battle with the
Freeman father. Now his cunning would mark victory over
the son.

The call to evening prayer filtered through the city. Faraz
didn't respond. Allah would understand his delay. This
moment—this victory—had been fifteen years in the
making.

"The view from your office continues to improve,
Commissioner." Faraz turned to face the Deputy
Commissioner.

Qadir cleared his throat. "Progress marches forward." His leather chair creaked as he leaned back, mustache trimmed in geometric precision. "Though some try to drag us backward."

"A toast, Commissioner." Faraz raised his glass. "To bureaucracy—more effective than bullets when wielded correctly."

Qadir's mustache twitched. He lifted his own tumbler with careful deference. "Indeed. Alexander Mercer's chief financial officer was most cooperative once we presented your concerns about his investment."

The crystal clinked softly.

"'Effective immediately' rings quite well." Qadir slid a document across the desk.

Faraz set his tumbler down and picked up the paper. Stellarion Technologies letterhead topped the page.

*After careful review of current geopolitical considerations and risk assessment protocols, Stellarion Technologies has determined it necessary to suspend all non-essential philanthropic disbursements in the northwestern region, effective immediately...*

Beautiful. No mention of Christianity, no reference to the mission specifically—just clinical corporate language that amounted to a death sentence for Joseph Freeman's dreams.

"Mercer is a businessman first. His charity extends only as far as his profit margin."

Qadir steepled his fingers. "The strategy you outlined worked perfectly, Director. Though I confess, I was skeptical at first. Mercer doesn't strike me as a man easily manipulated." His dark eyes carried genuine curiosity. "How exactly did you gather such accurate intelligence?"

The question was predictable. Information was currency

in their world, and Qadir wanted to understand the source of Faraz's advantage.

Faraz replaced the document on the desk, aligning it with the corner, then returned to his whiskey.

"Information is a commodity like any other, Commissioner. It simply requires the right source."

"And what source might that be?" Qadir pressed, then added quickly, "If you're able to share, of course."

Faraz paused, weighing his options. Too much information would give Qadir leverage. Too little would diminish his own value in this partnership. He ran his thumb along his jawline, briefly touching the edge of the scar.

"Let's just say Joseph Freeman believes everyone in his circle shares his dedication." Faraz took a measured sip.

Qadir's eyebrows rose. "You have someone inside his organization?"

"Faith is a curious thing. Sometimes it's outweighed by more earthly concerns—family safety, financial security, old grudges. The right pressure applied to the right person yields remarkable results."

"Impressive. Very impressive." Qadir took another sip, then ventured, "And this source—they'll continue providing intelligence now that the funding has been cut?"

"Everything necessary flows through proper channels." Faraz straightened his jacket. "But the operational details remain with the FIA, Commissioner."

The subtle reminder of jurisdictional hierarchy made Qadir shift in his seat. "Of course, Director. I didn't mean to overstep. I merely thought—"

"Your cooperation has been valuable." Faraz's tone softened slightly, the way a teacher might acknowledge a promising student. "The regulatory pressure from your office provided the perfect complement to our intelligence work."

Understanding flickered across Qadir's face—gratitude mixed with the awareness that he'd been gently put in his place. He nodded slowly. "I'm pleased the partnership has proven effective. My office remains ready to assist however needed."

"Which is why I wanted to meet here rather than summon you to regional headquarters." Faraz gestured to the opulent office. "What we're doing requires discretion. The fewer people who see us meeting, the better."

Qadir straightened slightly, clearly pleased to be included in Faraz's confidence. "Of course. And speaking of discretion—Sheik Hafiz Rahman will be pleased with our progress. He specifically mentioned the Freeman situation in our last conversation."

Faraz set down his glass. "Rahman understands the threat these foreign influences pose."

"His approval carries significant weight," Qadir added carefully. "Not just religiously, but politically. With elections approaching, his sermons at Masjid Al-Taqwa reach thousands every Friday. His endorsement can make or break careers in this province." He adjusted his tie. "The Council of Islamic Ideology consults him on matters of religious interpretation. If he declares something un-Islamic..."

"The people listen," Faraz finished. "And the politicians follow. Precisely why opposing this mission serves all our interests."

"Precisely." Qadir stood as Faraz moved toward the door, then hesitated. "Director, if I may—this source of yours. If you need any local resources to help maintain the flow of information..."

Faraz stopped, turning back. His voice dropped to a

temperature that made Qadir take a half-step back. "I don't require instruction on source management, Commissioner. The FIA has been running intelligence operations since before you held your current position."

A flush crept up Qadir's neck. "Of course, Director. I merely meant—"

"I know what you meant." Faraz's tone remained cool but not hostile. "Your concern is noted. The source will continue to produce. What matters now is that you're ready to act when I provide the intelligence. Can you do that?"

"Absolutely." Qadir nodded quickly. "My office stands ready."

"Good." Faraz moved to the door. "I'll be in touch when the next phase begins. Until then, maintain your routine. No unusual attention on the mission. Let them think the funding cut has ended our interest."

"Understood."

Faraz paused at the threshold. "The Freeman mission may seem small, but these infections spread if not treated completely. We've cut off the money. Next, we isolate them. Then we eliminate the threat entirely."

"I have full confidence in your strategy, Director."

Faraz gave a curt nod and stepped into the outer office where Qadir's assistant was preparing to leave. The young man's eyes widened at seeing the FIA Regional Director, and he quickly gathered his things and hurried out.

The government building was mostly empty as Faraz made his way down the marble corridors. A few late-working bureaucrats shuffled papers under harsh fluorescent lights, not looking up as he passed. The security guard at the entrance nodded respectfully and stepped aside.

Outside, Peshawar had settled into evening. Street vendors were closing their stalls, scents of cardamom and grilled meat lingering in the cooling air. Headlights cut through gathering darkness as evening traffic navigated the ancient streets.

His phone vibrated in his pocket. Stepping away from the building's entrance, Faraz checked the message—

*Freeman just received notice. "Funding suspended. He looks devastated. Meeting called for tomorrow morning."*

Satisfaction surged through him. Faraz imagined Joseph Freeman reading the letter—the same corporate language destroying his dreams. Just as Faraz had destroyed his father.

His fingers moved quickly across the screen—*"Watch him closely. Report any plans they make."*

Slipping the phone back into his pocket, Faraz walked toward the parking area. Fifteen years ago, he had stood amid the flames of the burning mission, believing he had erased the Freeman legacy forever.

He wouldn't fail again.

Joseph Freeman might have his father's determination, but Faraz had something more valuable—someone inside Freeman's inner circle, feeding him every plan, every hope, every vulnerability.

This time, when the Freeman mission fell, it would stay buried.

# TWENTY-TWO

## The Valley

*THE MISSION COMPOUND*

Joseph sat on the wooden chair, elbows on his knees, the revised plans spread across his makeshift desk. His pen had crossed through half his father's vision—the clinic, the school, the community center. Red lines through dreams that had felt so certain.

Although the chapel would be finished in six weeks. It would only be the chapel.

Through the tent flap, workers navigated the construction site. Hammers rang against stone as the chapel's eastern wall rose. But beyond it, empty foundations marked where the clinic was meant to stand. Stakes and string outlined a medical facility destined to remain unfinished.

What should have been.

The mission garden flourished in the foreground. The plants Thomas had helped establish pushed through the soil in neat rows—growth that required no permits, no funding, no official approval. The cardamom his mother had once tended still grew.

Joseph's shoulders slumped. He ran his fingers through his tangled, unwashed hair. How long had it been since he'd properly slept? The days had blurred together after the meeting where he'd conveyed the inevitable—"We can complete the chapel. Nothing else."

"I don't understand," he whispered. "I was so certain."

His mother's silver cross caught the fading light on his desk. His chest tightened. All those prayers about a comprehensive mission. A medical clinic serving villages with no healthcare. A school offering education to children who had none. A community center where Muslims and Christians could find common ground.

Now? A chapel. Beautiful, solid, faithful—but alone.

His team members had followed him here—from England, from Iran, from different corners of the world. Lives disrupted, careers paused, homes left behind for a vision that had been cut by two-thirds. Several local volunteers had gone home. Had the believers given up on the reduced mission? On him?

Joseph slid from the chair to his knees. The hard-packed earth was rough beneath him. He clasped his hands together and pressed his forehead against his thumbs.

"Father." The words caught in his throat. "I don't know if I've failed You or if You're testing me. I don't know if I misunderstood Your calling or if this is part of Your plan." His voice cracked. "The people who trusted me—donors who sacrificed, churches that believed, workers who came—are all waiting for direction I don't have."

His mind filled with images of local children who had watched construction with wide, hopeful eyes. The villagers who had cautiously approached, asking when the medical clinic would open. The women who had inquired about literacy classes.

"And now the vision is reduced. A chapel rising while the clinic and school remain nothing but stakes in the ground. How do I tell people who came to serve in a clinic that all we can offer them is manual labor?"

Joseph's shoulders began to shake. The enormity of his situation threatened to drown him. Hundreds of thousands in donations. Countless prayers and hopes and dreams—all stalled when Mercer's funding was cut.

"I can't do this anymore. Not without the resources. Not like this."

A sudden gust of wind rustled through the garden, carrying the scent of mint and growing things. The sound transported him to earlier that week, when similar sounds had meant progress. Hammers striking stone, workers calling to each other, the steady percussion of construction.

He remembered standing beside Darius that morning, watching the foundation work. The older missionary's weathered face had been contemplative as he observed the activity.

"You remind me of myself thirty years ago," Darius had said, his Iranian accent giving weight to his words. "So determined to carry everything on your own shoulders. The Western model of the heroic solo leader is not biblical, Joseph. Moses had Aaron and Hur. David had his mighty men. Paul had Timothy, Silas, Luke. The strength of God's work is found in shared leadership."

Joseph had nodded politely at the time, eager to return to supervise. Now, kneeling alone in his tent with the reduced mission spread before him, the words returned with troubling clarity.

"But what good is shared leadership without shared

resources?" he asked aloud. "Even Moses needed Pharaoh to let the people go. Even Nehemiah needed the king's letters and timber."

His team, those local Christians who risked everything, looking to him for direction when he had none to give. A community waiting for a medical clinic the mission couldn't build.

"Father," he prayed, his voice hoarse, "I don't know how to lead when I can only offer a fraction of what I promised. When the vision has been cut down from what You called me to build."

Joseph reached for his father's Bible on the nightstand. It fell open to Nehemiah chapter 4. His eyes caught the familiar passage where Nehemiah faced opposition to rebuilding Jerusalem's walls—

*When our enemies heard that we were aware of their plot and that God had frustrated it, we all returned to the wall, each to our own work.*

Joseph sat on his cot, reading. "Those builders faced opposition too." He flipped back to Ezra, reading about the temple reconstruction that was halted for years before resuming. The pattern was there, written across scripture— great works for God often faced interruptions, opposition, and setbacks. But the builders had divine provision. Where was his?

The garden caught his eye again—those plants, requiring no funding, no permits, yet still fulfilling their purpose. Hadn't Jesus himself spoken of mustard seeds? Hadn't the early church spread across continents with barely more than sandals and walking sticks?

"Maybe I've misunderstood what success looks like," Joseph whispered. "But these people came to build something tangible. How do I tell them that spiritual work is enough when I promised them buildings?"

A tear slipped down his cheek. He wiped his face with the back of his hand and moved to the tent opening.

The garden's steady growth continued against the backdrop of the chapel walls. The mint and cardamom might flourish, but medical clinics needed equipment, schools needed supplies.

"I don't need to have all the answers. But I need something I can tell them tomorrow."

Many team members had taken on reduced roles. Some remained on site, overseeing the scaled-back work, but the uncertainty weighed on everyone. Each had skills and perspectives they valued. Samuel with his engineering background. Leila with her fluency in local dialects. Darius with his decades of experience. Maya with her legal expertise.

But skills without funding were unrealized potential.

Joseph closed his eyes and took a deep breath of the cool night air. "Father, if this is Your will, show me the way forward. If I've misunderstood Your calling, make that clear too. But don't leave me paralyzed in the middle, not knowing whether to press forward or call it finished."

The stars were emerging overhead. Joseph stood there for a long moment, watching their steady glow.

Buildings might be cancelled, but growth continued.

Ministry happened with or without buildings.

*"The mission was the people, not the structures."* That's what Joseph had told others, but did he believe it himself?

Joseph stood at the threshold between despair and something else. Not hope, exactly. Not yet. But perhaps the beginning of a different understanding. The buildings mattered, yes. But the people mattered more. And the team was still here.

What could the mission do with what remained?

Joseph stepped back into his tent and reached for his notebook. Tomorrow, he wouldn't just face his team—he would gather them.

He stared at the crossed-out plans on his desk. The clinic. The school. The community center. All gone. But the chapel—his father's chapel—would stand in six weeks.

Maybe that was enough to start with.

Not the full vision. Not yet. But a beginning.

As he continued writing, the first genuine sense of peace in days settled over him. Perhaps this pause wasn't an ending but a redirection—a divine nudge toward something he couldn't see yet.

He closed the notebook and stood. Through the tent opening, the chapel walls caught the first light of dawn. Incomplete. Waiting.

Joseph stepped outside and walked to the foundation. He knelt and placed both palms flat against the stone—still cool from the night, solid despite everything.

"One stone at a time," he whispered, then stood and called across the compound, "Everyone up! We have work to do!"

# TWENTY-THREE

## The Balance

Joseph lingered in the shadows beneath the workers' meal station's corrugated roof, observing calloused hands reaching for bowls of rice and lentils as men took their midday break from rebuilding the chapel. A few children—laborers' sons and daughters—hovered near, their dark eyes fixed on the food with quiet anticipation. Cardamom and cumin mingled with dust and the metallic rasp of the tin roof above.

Fatima directed the distribution with gentle efficiency, her voice carrying across the space in soft Urdu as she counted out portions. Each worker approached with dignity intact despite their circumstances—shoulders straight, heads held high, grateful but not servile. Joseph recognized the faces of men who had been laying bricks and setting beams with cautious hope. Now they came for sustenance while the skeletal walls behind them stood as a monument to interrupted dreams.

The weight pressed against Joseph's chest like a physical

thing. Three days since Mercer's funding evaporated. Three days of watching his team's faces shift from shock to resignation to quiet desperation. Three days of having no answers to offer when people asked what came next.

He leaned against the support beam, the rough wood catching on his shirt. Every interaction here highlighted what they might lose—not just the chapel construction, but the ability to expand their reach. The medical clinic they wouldn't be able to build. The school they couldn't establish. The completed chapel that would never provide a permanent place of worship.

"You carry the weight of the world on your shoulders this morning."

Joseph turned to find Darius approaching, two steaming cups in his work-worn hands. The Iranian missionary's silver hair caught the filtered light, and his dark eyes held the kind of steady calm that came from decades of navigating impossible circumstances.

"Coffee for you," Darius said simply, offering one of the cups. "Fatima insisted I bring you the American brew. Chai for me, of course."

Joseph accepted the coffee gratefully, wrapping his fingers around the warm ceramic. The first sip brought familiar comfort—strong and bitter, just enough to cut through the morning's despondent haze.

"I've been watching you watch them," Darius continued, settling beside Joseph against the support beam. "What do you see?"

Joseph's gaze swept across the distribution again. A young laborer wolfed down his meal before returning to work. An elderly craftsman's lips moved in silent devotion. Teenagers helped carry tools back to the worksite, their respect for the older workers evident in every gesture.

"I see people who trusted us to do more than this," Joseph said finally. "I see promises we can't keep."

"Mmm." Darius sipped his chai thoughtfully. "I see something different."

Joseph waited, but the older man didn't elaborate immediately. Instead, Darius watched Fatima hand a bowl of rice to a mason whose bandaged hand spoke of a recent injury.

"That man injured his hand in a construction accident two weeks ago," Darius said quietly. "Can't work at full capacity. His family depends on his wages, but he still shows up every day to do what he can. That bowl of rice—it represents commitment continuing when everything seemed finished."

The coffee warmed Joseph's throat, but it couldn't touch the cold knot in his stomach. "But it's temporary relief, Darius. Band-aids on hemorrhaging wounds. The clinic would have provided real healing. The school would have offered genuine hope for the children. Now…"

"Now you sound like a man who believes God's work depends entirely on human funding."

The gentle rebuke stung because it carried truth. Joseph stared into his coffee, watching steam rise in the still air.

"Doesn't it?" The words came out more bitter than he'd intended. "We can't order the medical equipment because we can't finish the building. We can't purchase textbooks because we can't construct classrooms. The chapel walls stand incomplete because we can't pay for materials. Good intentions don't cure diseases or educate children or provide worship space."

Darius shifted beside him. "You know," he said, his accent adding weight to each word, "when the Revolutionary Guard shut down our church in Tehran, I had similar thoughts. We'd just purchased new sound equipment, renovated the basement for children's ministry, ordered Bibles in Farsi. Thousands of dollars—a fortune for us then—invested in what seemed like God's clear direction."

Joseph looked up, drawn into the story despite his despair.

"The authorities came on a Tuesday morning. Confiscated everything. Arrested half the leadership team. Sealed the building permanently." Darius took another sip of tea. "I stood across the street that night, watching soldiers nail boards over our doors, and I asked God the same question you're asking now—why let us invest everything in dreams You wouldn't allow us to complete?"

"What did you learn?" Joseph's voice came out rougher than intended.

"That God's definition of completion often looks different from ours." Darius gestured toward the distribution area. "Within six months, that single sealed church had become twelve house churches scattered across Tehran. Now the Iranian church is the fastest growing per capita in the world, despite—or perhaps because of—the persecution. The equipment we'd lost? Families opened their homes and praised God with their voices alone. The children's ministry we'd planned? Parents began teaching their own children and their neighbors' children too. The Bibles they confiscated? We memorized scripture and shared it mouth to mouth, heart to heart."

A child's laughter punctuated the air as one of the younger boys discovered a piece of candy tucked into his father's meal bag. The sound seemed incongruous against Joseph's internal turmoil.

"But that's different," Joseph protested. "You were dealing with persecution, not financial betrayal. You were building something spiritual, not trying to provide concrete medical care and education."

"Was I?" Darius set down his tea cup and turned to face Joseph fully. "Joseph, tell me what you see when you look at Fatima organizing this distribution."

Joseph followed his gaze. The elderly woman moved with purpose, greeting each worker by name, remembering specific needs—asking about someone's back pain, inquiring whether a child's cough had improved, slipping extra portions to laborers with particular struggles.

"I see someone doing what she can with what she has."

"I see pastoral care," Darius said firmly. "I see medical follow-up. I see education about nutrition and dignity and hope. I see ministry happening without buildings or equipment or official funding."

The words landed like stones dropped into still water, creating ripples Joseph hadn't expected. He watched Fatima hand a bowl to an elderly craftsman, her voice gentle as she reminded him about the prayer meeting happening in her home tomorrow evening.

"The walls aren't the church, Joseph. The equipment isn't the ministry. The funding isn't God's provision." Darius's voice carried the authority of someone who'd learned these truths through fire. "Those things can enhance our work, certainly. But when they become prerequisites for faithful service, we've confused means with ends."

Joseph felt something shift in his chest, a loosening of the tight knot that had taken residence there since reading Mercer's withdrawal letter. But doubt crept in immediately behind it.

"Easy to say," he murmured. "Harder to believe when

you're responsible for forty-three people who followed you across the world based on promises you can't keep."

"Ah." Darius nodded knowingly. "Now we reach the heart of it. This isn't about the mission failing—it's about you failing as a leader."

The directness of it stole Joseph's breath. He started to deny it, but the words stuck in his throat.

"You feel responsible for everyone's sacrifices," Darius continued. "Their career disruptions, their financial investments, their emotional commitment. You're carrying guilt that belongs to God alone."

"Because I am responsible." Joseph's voice cracked with the admission. "I'm the one who cast the vision. I'm the one who said God was calling us here. I'm the one who convinced them to come."

"And you believe God's call was false because human funding was withdrawn?"

The question filled the space between them with heavy implication.

Joseph stared at his hands wrapped around the coffee cup. "I don't know anymore," he whispered. "I was so certain. The doors opened so clearly, the resources came together so providentially. How do I know the difference between God's leading and my own ambition?"

Darius was quiet for so long that Joseph looked up to see if he'd somehow given offense. But the older man's face held compassion rather than judgment.

"Joseph, do you know the book of Job?"

"Of course."

"What did Job understand about suffering that his friends missed?"

Joseph searched his memory, feeling like he was being

tested but unsure of the right answer. "That suffering isn't always punishment for sin?"

"Deeper than that." Darius leaned forward slightly. "Job understood that faith isn't contingent on favorable circumstances. His friends kept insisting that right living guaranteed blessing, that suffering meant hidden sin. But Job recognized something more profound—that loving God isn't a transaction based on what we receive in return."

Around them, the meal distribution continued its quiet rhythm. Joseph watched a young worker help an older craftsman navigate the uneven ground, their conversation animated despite the modest nature of their circumstances.

"Job said something that revolutionized my understanding during those dark months in Tehran," Darius continued. "'Though he slay me, yet will I hope in him.' Not 'If He blesses me, I'll serve Him' or 'When He provides, I'll follow Him.' Though he slay me—even if following God leads to loss, disappointment, suffering—yet will I hope."

The words settled into Joseph's consciousness like seeds finding soil. He'd read that passage dozens of times, but never while sitting in the wreckage of his own certainties.

"You think this funding loss is God slaying my dreams?"

"I think this funding loss is an opportunity to discover whether your faith is rooted in God's character or God's provision." Darius's voice gentled. "Whether you'll serve Him for who He is or only for what He gives."

Joseph closed his eyes, feeling the truth of it penetrate defenses he hadn't realized he'd built. Had his certainty about God's calling been tied too closely to the apparent ease with which resources had appeared? Had he confused blessing with validation?

"The team needs leadership," he said quietly. "They

need direction and hope and practical answers. How do I give them what I don't have?"

"By giving them what you do have." Darius gestured toward the distribution again. "Look around you, Joseph. This meal service—it wasn't in your original plans, was it?"

Joseph shook his head.

"Yet it's feeding workers. Providing strength. Creating connections between your team and the laborers. Ministry is happening, even though your blueprint was interrupted." Darius paused. "Perhaps especially because your blueprint was interrupted."

Joseph opened his eyes and really looked at the scene before him. Samuel Wong knelt beside a worker's son, showing him how to fold paper airplanes while his father ate. Leila helped translate technical instructions for an elderly craftsman with decades of experience. Thomas discussed building techniques with a local mason whose knowledge complemented his engineering training.

Ministry was happening. Not the ministry he'd planned, but ministry nonetheless.

"The chapel will get built eventually," Darius said softly. "Maybe not the way we originally envisioned, maybe not on our preferred timeline. But God's work doesn't wait for perfect circumstances."

"Though he slay me, yet will I hope in him," Joseph murmured, testing how the words felt in his mouth.

"Though he slay me, yet will I serve him," Darius corrected gently. "Hope is important, but service—continuing to love and care for His people regardless of personal cost—that's where faith becomes tangible."

Something loosened in Joseph's chest, a knot of fear and responsibility that had been choking him for days. The weight didn't disappear entirely, but it redistributed itself across broader shoulders—not just his own, but the community's. Not just human shoulders, but divine ones.

"I need to call the team together," Joseph said, surprising himself with the steadiness in his voice.

"Yes, you do." Darius smiled, the expression transforming his weathered features. "But first, let me pray with you."

Joseph nodded, setting down his coffee cup and bowing his head. Around them, the meal service continued its gentle rhythm, a backdrop of quiet service and persistent hope.

"Father," Darius began, his accented English lending formality to the prayer, "You see this young man wrestling with questions that have plagued Your servants throughout history. Give him wisdom beyond his years, strength beyond his natural capacity, and faith that transcends circumstances. Help him lead not from his own understanding, but from Your heart for these people."

Joseph felt the words settle over him like a blessing, each phrase addressing fears he hadn't articulated even to himself.

"And God," Darius continued, "transform this interruption into invitation. This setback into setup. This crisis into opportunity. Show us how to serve You not in spite of our limitations, but through them."

"Amen," Joseph whispered, and meant it.

When he raised his head, Darius was watching him with eyes that held decades of tested faith. "Better?"

Joseph tested his breathing, his posture, the weight in his chest. "Different," he said honestly. "Still uncertain about the practical details, but..." He searched for words. "Less afraid of the uncertainty."

"Good." Darius stood and collected their empty cups.

"Because the team is waiting for direction, and you now have something to offer them."

"What's that?"

"A leader who's learned to trust God's character rather than God's provision. A leader who'll serve faithfully through setbacks. A leader who understands that ministry happens in the midst of interrupted plans, not despite them."

Joseph stood as well, his legs steady beneath him for the first time in days. Through the open doorway, he could see his team members scattered throughout the compound—some helping with the meal distribution, others sitting in quiet conversation, a few staring at the incomplete chapel walls with expressions he now recognized as mirrors of his own recent despair.

They needed what Darius had just given him—not answers to all their questions, but permission to serve faithfully amid uncertainty.

"Though he slay me, yet will I serve him," Joseph repeated quietly, the words feeling like both declaration and invitation.

Darius clasped his shoulder briefly. "Now go lead them. Not because you have all the answers, but because you're willing to seek them together."

Joseph nodded and stepped away from the meal station's shade into the bright Pakistani morning. The chapel walls still stood incomplete, but they no longer looked like monuments to failure. They looked like labor in progress, like promises deferred but not abandoned.

He picked up a hammer and marched to the work.

# TWENTY-FOUR

**Sabatoge**

"Your father had that same look before I killed him."

Faraz Qureshi whispered the words to the surveillance photo on his laptop screen—Joseph Freeman's face, so like William's it could have been a ghost. The same defiance. The same fire.

His mobile phone buzzed against the scarred desk. A text from his informant. Then another. Then photos loading slowly in the encrypted app.

*Funding cut backfired. Workers staying. Unpaid.*

*Locals bringing tools, food, cement. Won't stop now.*

*Freeman more determined. Leading prayer meetings on site.*

The photos finished loading—grainy but clear enough. Freeman lifting his hands before the chapel's skeletal walls. Villagers unloading supplies. Laborers praying together.

Faraz slammed his fist into the desk. A photograph of himself shaking hands with the Interior Minister shifted on its stand.

His scar burned. Unacceptable. Qadir must learn of this.

He dialed the secure government line, dabbing sweat from his neck.

"Qadir. It's Director Qureshi. The Freeman situation has escalated. I'm sending you surveillance photos now."

A sigh. "I'm in a budget meeting. This can't wait?"

"No! The funding cut failed. Construction continues with community backing. Freeman's using the setback as inspiration." Faraz attached the photos through the encrypted government channel, watching the upload bar crawl. "They're continuing with unpaid labor."

Qadir paused. "How is this possible? Mercer withdrew his support."

"Freeman leads prayer meetings. Villagers are rallying. Check the images."

"They're coming through now." A beat. "I see them. This is unexpected."

"If they continue at this pace, they'll finish within a month or two."

"Without legal permits, they gain nothing. Without Mercer's support we can revoke permissions, confiscate the land."

"By then they'll have finished. They'll celebrate."

"Then we dismantle what they've built. Publicly. Legally."

"This was supposed to break him. Instead, he's inspiring others. This setback is becoming their rally cry."

"Director." Qadir's voice weakened. "Your personal investment in this matter is showing."

"This isn't personal. It's about precedent. About control."

"Which we can maintain through proper channels. I'm meeting the Interior Minister next week. I recommend no direct action until then."

"The bureaucratic approach is too slow."

"It's the legal approach. We don't want to draw attention in Islamabad."

Faraz slammed the receiver into its cradle. Peshawar's late afternoon heat suffocated his office—the air conditioner struggling, walls adorned with official certificates and the Prime Minister's framed photograph pressing in. The distant drone of traffic hummed below. His watch ticked.

He glanced at Joseph's surveillance image.

Qadir was wrong. Freeman wasn't surviving—he was becoming a symbol. By the time the permits were pulled, it would be too late. The story would spread underground, a tale of faith tested and triumphant.

He pulled out his mobile phone and opened the encrypted messaging app.

*Need more than surveillance now. Time to create division from within.*

The reply came within seconds.

*What do you need me to do?*

Faraz smiled coldly as he typed.

*Find the cracks. Widen them. Make them doubt each other. Report back through this channel only.*

Outside, the city blared into dusk, unaware of the quiet war unfolding in its midst.

The son would not be martyred. He would be dismantled—from the inside out.

———

Joseph scrolled through Hassan's phone, each social media post hitting like a fist. Poorly cropped photos surrounded by inflammatory captions in both English and Urdu, the images clearly taken from within the mission compound.

The latest showed him addressing the team the previous afternoon, moments after they'd learned about the funding loss. The caption burned into his vision—*American missionary loses funding but continues endangering locals. How many Pakistani Christians will suffer for his arrogance?*

Two hundred shares. Dozens of comments from faces he'd seen in neighboring villages.

"When did these start appearing?"

"Right after we learned Mercer pulled funding," Hassan said grimly. "These posts have been appearing almost daily for the past week, but they've intensified in the last three days. Yesterday the police questioned one of our laborers about why his family associates with 'foreign agitators.'"

Joseph's stomach dropped. He scrolled to another post—an image of the incomplete chapel with text overlaid—*Freeman builds monuments to his ego. Followers will pay the price when he leaves.* Four hundred shares. Comments about illegal construction and foreign missionaries never learning.

"Families are starting to pull back from our community meetings," Hassan said. "People are afraid, Joseph."

Joseph's composure cracked after reading the comment —*Freeman's father got Pakistani Christians killed 15 years ago. Now the son returns to finish the job, even after Alexander Mercer abandoned his foolish mission.*

His breathing turned shallow. "Who's behind these accounts?"

"Anonymous. But they know details only someone close would know—exactly when Mercer pulled funding, Rebecca's medical shipment before she even unpacked it." Hassan paused. "Someone is feeding them information."

Joseph looked up sharply. "Someone like Tariq?"

Hassan shook his head slowly. "Tariq brought these

posts to my attention. He's the one who insisted we show you. But Joseph, you need to understand what these posts are doing to our community."

"Tell me."

"They're weaponizing real concerns. Look at this one." Hassan pointed to a post showing Maya explaining legal options for Christians, captioned—*Western missionaries believe Sharia law is primitive. First they change our laws, then our faith.*

"The imam shared this during Friday prayers. Nearly a thousand people heard his commentary about foreign influences. Even some of your international team are questioning your leadership now—Thomas asked me about evacuation plans, Rebecca is inquiring about flights back to England."

The betrayal cut deep. "They came to you instead of me?"

Hassan's voice carried the weight of holding the community together. "Joseph, I've spent fifteen years rebuilding what was destroyed after we sent you to America. I kept believers together when they had nothing. I know how quickly fear can fracture everything we've built."

Joseph moved to the tent opening, legs unsteady. Below, Samuel showed a local teenager how to mix mortar, both laughing despite the language barrier. But now Joseph noticed the teenager's nervous glances toward the compound entrance.

"When you came back," Hassan said, "you brought architectural plans already drawn, medical protocols already established. You consulted with us, yes, but…" He spread his hands. "These posts work because they're twisting something real."

The words stung. Joseph wanted to argue, but the truth took root. The plans he'd insisted on despite suggestions for modifications. The timeline that prioritized progress over community readiness.

"I never claimed to have suffered what you've all endured."

"But you did claim the authority to lead us through decisions that affect our safety. To continue building when wisdom might suggest pausing to reassess."

Through the tent opening, hammering from the chapel site continued—but now Joseph heard it differently. Not as a testament to faith, but potentially as provocation.

"What would you have me do? Abandon everything?"

Hassan studied Joseph's face with the patience of someone who'd weathered many storms. "I would have you recognize that these attacks aren't random. Look at the precision, the timing, the inside knowledge." He gestured toward the phone. "Someone is using our legitimate growing pains as cover for sabotage."

Clarity cut through Joseph's confusion. "You think this is coordinated?"

"I think whoever's behind this waited for us to be vulnerable—waited for the funding crisis—and then amplified every natural tension. The question is whether they're trying to drive us out entirely, or if they have some other purpose."

Joseph pressed his palms against his temples. "The details they know, the private conversations, the internal schedules—either we have a security problem, or someone very close to us has divided loyalties."

"That's what concerns me most. I've been watching, listening. Some of these posts appeared within hours of private meetings. Someone is documenting our every move."

The possibility settled between them.

"I've been so focused on addressing community concerns that I missed the real threat. Someone's using our adjustment period as cover for something more sinister."

Hassan nodded. "Which is why we need to act carefully. If we have a betrayer in our midst, we can't let them know we suspect."

"Then what do you recommend?"

"We call a meeting. Everyone—team members, local believers, even those who've been staying away because of these attacks. But we do it strategically. I'll share different information with key individuals beforehand—different schedules, different plans for security measures. Then we watch to see which version appears in the next round of posts. Whoever received that specific information is our betrayer."

Joseph felt purpose returning. The attacks had been meant to isolate him, to fracture their unity. Instead, they were revealing the true nature of the opposition they faced.

"And if we discover the source is someone we trusted?"

Hassan's expression grew resolute. "Then we deal with betrayal as a community. United. These attacks want to divide us—we respond by becoming stronger together."

As Hassan prepared to leave, he paused at the tent opening. "Joseph, the posts aren't going to stop just because we've identified the pattern. Whoever's behind them wants to see this mission destroyed completely. Tonight we decide if we give them what they want, or if we show them what happens when they attack a community that refuses to be broken."

After Hassan left, Joseph remained at the tent opening. Every relationship, every interaction carried weight in this conflict. The social media attacks had made the battle lines visible, but the war had been going on much longer than he'd realized.

The question was no longer whether Joseph Freeman belonged here. It was whether they could unmask their betrayer before the sabotage defeated them completely.

# TWENTY-FIVE

## The Confession

Joseph's grip tightened on the printouts. His pulse thundered in his ears—loud enough to drown out the crinkling of the pages between his fingers. He faced the gathered group—twenty faces, some tense, some tired. His international team and the local believers stood shoulder to shoulder—men and women who had risked danger to rebuild.

Some met his eyes. Others looked away. Miriam lingered at the edge, her hand buried in her pocket.

He held up the screenshots. "Someone here has been sharing images and information about our meetings with those who want us to fail."

A few gasps broke the stillness. Others traded uneasy glances.

"These photos were taken from inside these walls. The posts include details only someone in this room would know." Joseph steadied his voice. "This puts all our lives at risk."

Tariq stepped forward immediately, his jaw set. "Whoever did this should be sent away immediately."

"Find them now!" someone called from the back.

"It has to be one of the new workers," another voice added.

Agreement rippled through the group as accusations flew. Joseph caught Miriam's slight movement—just a half-step backward, her hand still buried deep in her pocket as the room erupted with suspicion.

"Maybe someone's phone was hacked—"

"We should check everyone's devices—"

"Or someone was threatened..."

Suspicion bloomed like smoke. Joseph felt it stinging his throat. *Was this how it began? A small crack, a slow crumble?*

His gaze returned to Miriam. She'd edged farther back now, her face pale beneath the dust.

Tariq's voice cut through the rising murmurs. "Whoever you are, you're a coward. My father—he stood before the militants, refused to deny Christ, and they shot him while I watched. He gave his life for the truth. And you feed our enemies?"

Miriam stepped forward.

The room fell still.

"It was me."

The words struck like a blow. She pulled a folded letter from her pocket, her fingers trembling.

"Faraz Qureshi approached me three weeks ago," she said. "He knew about Amir. About the prison." Her voice broke. "He promised medical care. Maybe even a reduced sentence."

Joseph's mind reeled. Amir—imprisoned fifteen years after the persecution. His name had faded from conversation, but never from Miriam's eyes.

"He's dying," she whispered. "The last letter said the infection spread through both legs. When Faraz offered help... I was weak."

The room exploded.

"How could you?"

"After everything—"

"She has to leave!"

Tariq stormed forward, face inches from hers. "My father chose death over betrayal. And you—what? Sold us out for comfort?"

Miriam flinched but didn't retreat. "I was desperate—"

"Desperation isn't an excuse! It's cowardice!"

Joseph watched her shoulders curve inward under the weight. His own shame surged—*he'd seen her shrinking, sensed something, and did nothing.*

He stepped forward and placed himself between them.

"Enough."

His voice wasn't loud, but it stopped them.

Joseph knelt, grounding himself in the dust at Miriam's level. His own fear—of failure, of being unworthy of this calling—pressed on his ribs like a weight. But here, now, mercy felt like the only solid ground.

"She was used," he said. "Faraz didn't force her to betray us—he found what she loved most and twisted it. What wouldn't any of us do, if it meant saving the person we couldn't bear to lose?"

No one replied. Miriam wept quietly.

Dr. Maya, the team's medic, was the first to move. She stepped forward, laying a gentle hand on Miriam's shoulder. "I'm sorry about Amir."

Thomas, their logistics coordinator, followed. "I've never had my faith tested like that."

One by one, they came. Some spoke. Others simply

stood beside her. Even Tariq, though still tense, held back, struggling with his war of grief and conviction.

Joseph rose slowly, watching it happen—the anger unraveling, the fragile threads of forgiveness knitting themselves through the space.

He caught Hassan's eye and nodded toward the construction office. The older man followed.

"They listened," Joseph murmured.

Hassan's lined face softened. "They follow your lead."

Joseph exhaled, a dry sound more exhaustion than relief. "The funds are almost gone. The chapel isn't finished. If Mercer pulls out..."

He let the rest hang in the dust-laced air.

Hassan laid a hand on his shoulder. "You're afraid."

Joseph nodded. "Of failing all of them. Of failing my father's legacy."

"Today," Hassan said, "you led with mercy, not fear. That legacy is intact."

"Be patient." Darius, their field coordinator, stepped into the doorway. "God's timing isn't ours. But this moment? This forgiveness? Heaven celebrates it."

Joseph turned back toward the group. Miriam was still surrounded—not cast out but drawn in.

*Lord,* he prayed, *You've carried us this far. Keep carrying us.*

He didn't know how long the work would last. Or when Faraz would strike again. But for now, the people were together. They would build—stone by stone.

And when the money ran out?

They'd keep building anyway.

———

Faraz stood motionless on the rocky outcrop above the mission compound, body rigid, muscles locked like the stone beneath him. Through his binoculars, he had watched it all—Miriam's trembling confession, the flare of outrage, the impossible turn to forgiveness.

The binoculars dug into his eye sockets as he pressed them harder against his face. The scar tissue tightened, pulling his cheeks into a half-grimace. "Impossible," he whispered, the word evaporating in the dry wind.

He had calculated everything. The woman's guilt should have shattered the fragile unity Joseph had built. Instead, the missionary's son knelt beside Faraz's informant. Watched others follow. It was like watching William Freeman all over again—the same infuriating capacity for forgiveness that had made the father dangerous was now revealed in the son. As FIA Regional Director, Faraz had observed dozens of organizations fracture under pressure— this resilience was not normal and concerning.

He lowered the binoculars. Crimson blurs floated across his vision. His mouth turned to sandpaper. He couldn't swallow. "Like father, like son," he murmured as pressure gathered behind his eyes like a storm front. His teeth welded together.

Below, the group was breaking apart. Joseph and his father's old assistant, Hassan, headed to the construction tent. Miriam remained surrounded, not accused but embraced.

Faraz stalked away from his vantage point, kicking loose stones that clattered down the hillside, betraying his position. He didn't care. His fingertips tingled with a distant numbness that spread to his wrists. His focus sharpened to a needle point. Good. The situation grew clearer with his discomfort.

His radio crackled—one of half-dozen operatives he had positioned around the compound perimeter. "Sir? We have three teams in position. Alpha team at the north access road, Bravo covering the village approach, Charlie monitoring communications. Awaiting your command."

He pressed the transmitter. "Maintain position."

"Any developments?"

"The informant is compromised."

"Shall we proceed with detention under the blasphemy code?"

Faraz hesitated. Detaining Miriam now would be satisfying—but not effective. Not anymore. "Negative."

He clicked off and started down the slope, boots grinding against the gravel. His satellite phone gave him direct line access to military intelligence, provincial police, and border patrol. Another tactic failed, but he had dozens more. Delays, funding blockades, psychological warfare—these were merely the gentlest tools in the FIA's arsenal, the warning shots before the artillery. Yet Freeman only grew stronger with each pressure point—more than routine. A possible professional embarrassment.

*What breaks a man like that?*

Then it came—not the man. The people around him. Break *them*, and Joseph would slowly and completely fall. This effective approach wouldn't appear in any official FIA playbook. He could construct separate investigations for each of Freeman's associates, finding or fabricating evidence as needed. Official harassment disguised as routine enforcement.

He reached his unmarked government SUV and turned the ignition. At the fork, one road curved left toward the regional FIA headquarters where his staff waited for his instructions moving forward. The other veered right toward a place where Faraz could speak freely without the constraints of his official position.

His phone buzzed. A message from Rahman—*"What news of the infidels?"*

Faraz didn't reply. He pulled out a prepaid phone, impossible to trace, instead. He dialed a number memorized but never saved. As he waited, his fingers brushed against his Glock that had ended four investigations permanently. In his glove compartment sat a stack of blank arrest warrants, pre-signed by a friendly judge.

"Peace be upon you," a gruff voice answered.

"And upon you, peace. This is Faraz."

A pause, then warmth—"Brother. Too long," said the gravelly voice of the former TPL associate. Such connections were technically prohibited for FIA personnel, but this one proved invaluable for operations requiring deniability.

"The mission is being rebuilt. The same one. The Freeman boy is leading it." He kept his voice steady, but the personal hatred seeped through.

"He returns to his father's ashes."

"He thinks he can redeem what was lost."

"He'll learn otherwise," said the voice. "What do you need?"

"Men who remember why we began. Quiet ones."

"This sanctioned?"

"No."

"You risk exposure."

"There are no American dollars left to protect. That has been addressed. As of now, the government will not intervene."

A beat of silence. "What do you require of my men?"

"To surveil Freeman's inner circle."

"How many?"

"Three, for now," Faraz said, mentally reviewing the dossiers his intelligence unit had compiled. "Hassan Awan who helped the boy escape fifteen years ago. We have his family tree mapped to third cousins. The Iranian apostate, Darius Karimi—whose visa status I can revoke with one signature. And the attorney, Maya Chaudhry—whose license to practice is tenuous at best." Meanwhile, Joseph Freeman stood below with nothing but donated lumber and borrowed faith—a paper shield against an approaching storm.

"When do we start?"

"Immediately if possible. But no martyrs. No bodies. Just fear."

"It will be done. And the son?"

"When he's alone," Faraz said, turning to the TPL compounds, "he will break. No blood. No fire. Just silence and abandonment—until even his God seems to have forgotten him."

"A quiet ending."

"The kind no one writes songs about." Faraz ended the call. Dust rose behind his speeding vehicle as it vanished into the hills.

# TWENTY-SIX

## The Poison Shadow

Darius Karimi adjusted the woven bag on his shoulder, the canvas strap digging into his skin. The marketplace of Peshawar's outskirts sprawled in an open tapestry of colors. Bartering voices and sharp scents of cinnamon and lemon reminded him of the bazaars in Tehran from his youth. Vendors called out prices beneath flapping canvas awnings while women in vibrant headscarves examined produce with practiced eyes.

"The rice prices have doubled since last month," Tariq's dark eyes narrowed at the burlap sacks displayed. "This is robbery."

The young man's jaw tightened—the same tension Darius observed whenever Tariq felt the world was conspiring against them, which was often. At twenty-seven, Tariq carried himself with the wary defensiveness of someone who'd learned early that life took more than it gave.

"Good morning, brother," Darius greeted the vendor, a

thin man with an untrimmed beard. "Your rice looks excellent."

The man nodded. "Best in the market. From the Punjab fields."

Tariq stepped forward. "Eight hundred rupees for five kilos? Last month it was four hundred."

"Prices change. Fuel costs. Taxes." The vendor shrugged. "Seven-fifty, for you."

"Five hundred," Tariq countered sharply.

Darius placed a gentle hand on Tariq's shoulder, remembering the spice merchant in Tehran who'd hidden Bibles beneath cumin sacks for three years. "My young friend is concerned about feeding many people. We run the new community center near Shingli Payeen."

The vendor's expression shifted subtly. "The old Freeman mission?"

"The very same," Darius confirmed, noting a flicker of recognition.

"Six hundred. And I'll add some cardamom."

Tariq opened his mouth to push further, but Darius squeezed his shoulder. "We accept your generosity. Thank you."

As they moved to the next stall, Tariq's frustration bubbled over. "We could have gotten it for five-fifty."

Darius selected a tomato, testing its ripeness. "Perhaps. But he'll remember us as reasonable people, not difficult customers. Next time, that matters more than fifty rupees."

"Every rupee counts here."

"In Isfahan, I knew a church elder who was imprisoned for hosting meetings." Darius chose his words carefully. "His daughter is now leading three house churches —not because we protested his arrest, but because we helped his family survive. Anger makes us feel powerful when we are powerless, but it rarely changes what made us angry."

A man in his periphery caught his attention. He wore a gray kurta and watched them too intently. He looked away when Darius turned. The man spoke briefly into what appeared to be a mobile phone. Across the marketplace, another man mirrored the same behavior. The familiar prickle of surveillance crawled up his spine.

The men exchanged subtle hand signals—coordinated movements that spoke more of professional training than casual observation.

"We need to be efficient today," Darius said, keeping his voice casual. "Joseph mentioned the flour supply is nearly gone."

Tariq nodded as if still unconvinced about the rice transaction but willing to move on. "Flour, lentils, oil, and tea. Maya also requested office supplies—printer, generators for power backup, secure data storage for confidential information."

They moved methodically through the market, their bags growing heavier. Darius found himself glancing frequently at the two patient watchers, noting how they maintained distance while staying within sight.

A commotion erupted near the market's western edge. Darius heard fragments: "Tirah Valley" and—"children killed" and "government lies."

"What's happening?" Tariq asked.

A young man rushing past answered breathlessly—"The military killed seven protesters in Tirah Valley yesterday—claimed it was Taliban, but everyone knows it was them. There's video proof!"

The atmosphere transformed within minutes. Vendors began packing goods, conversations grew heated, and more people streamed toward the gathering crowd. The two men who had been watching them were now positioned near different exits.

Men with faces partially covered by scarves now appeared at the crowd's edges, their movements too coordinated, too purposeful.

"We should finish quickly." Darius navigated through congested pathways, scanning for the last items. The two men followed. Panic began to rise. "We must leave. Now."

"But we still need—"

"We'll come back another day."

Darius guided them to a narrow side street, away from the main demonstration. The weight of their purchases slowed their progress as they pushed against the flow of people moving toward the commotion.

A voice rose above the others, amplified somehow. "Brothers! Sisters! Our children die while we remain silent!"

The crowd's energy shifted from agitation to something more volatile. The change hit him like a pressure drop before a storm. He quickened their pace, but spotted three men blocking the narrow exit he'd targeted, pretending to argue among themselves.

"This way," he redirected, pulling Tariq toward another pathway.

They reached a choke point where the market narrowed between two buildings. Behind them, a new wave of shouting propelled the crowd forward suddenly. Bodies pressed between them, and Darius lost his grip on Tariq's sleeve.

"Tariq!" he called, struggling to maintain his footing.

A man collided with him, hard enough to knock him against a wooden stall. "Forgive me, brother." He steadied Darius with one hand. The man's eyes met his, neither apologetic nor angry. A sharp prick bit through Darius' kurta.

Before Darius could react, the man vanished into the crowd.

A burning sensation spread like a drop of oil on water from the small puncture. He had heard about similar attacks—a missionary colleague in Mashhad, a church elder in Shiraz. His heart rate quickened, partly from the substance now entering his bloodstream, partly from grim recognition.

*Focus. Find Tariq. Get to safety.*

Darius pushed forward, scanning every face while fighting the fire spreading through his veins. His vision remained clear, but he knew that wouldn't last. Whatever they'd used, he had hours, perhaps minutes if he was less fortunate.

"Tariq!" he called again, louder this time.

He spotted the young man ten meters ahead, looking back frantically. When their eyes met, Tariq fought his way back through the press of bodies.

"We got separated—"

"Listen carefully," Darius interrupted, his voice steady despite the burning sensation. "I've been poisoned. We need shelter, somewhere quiet. Now."

Tariq's eyes widened. "What? How—"

Behind them, someone screamed. The distinct crack of a gunshot echoed from the demonstration's center.

Tariq grabbed Darius' arm, pulling him to a narrow alley. "This way. My cousin's shop is close."

Darius focused on each step as the poison progressed. His decades of emergency medical training from underground church work told him what was happening—

increased heart rate, the beginning of muscle tremors, soon he would find breathing difficult.

Tariq pounded on a metal door halfway down the alley. "Wasim! Open up!"

The door swung inward, revealing a stocky man with a worried expression. "Tariq? What's happening out there?"

"My friend needs help," Tariq said, supporting Darius, who now leaned heavily against his right shoulder.

Inside the small storeroom stacked with fabric bolts, Darius lowered himself onto a wooden crate as Wasim locked the door behind them, muffling the chaos outside.

"He needs a doctor," Tariq explained.

"No," Darius managed, his breathing becoming labored. "No doctor. They'll be watching hospitals."

Confusion crossed Wasim's face, but Tariq understood. "Someone did this deliberately? During the protest?"

Darius winced. "To make it appear like a natural death." A new wave of burning surged through his chest.

"If they're watching this closely," he added, each word deliberate, "they still see our efforts as a threat."

"I'll call Joseph," Tariq said, reaching for his phone.

"Wait." Darius gripped Tariq's wrist with surprising strength. "This was coordinated. Professional. They knew who I was, targeted me specifically." He fought to keep his thoughts clear as numbness crept into his extremities. "Our enemies are more dangerous than we thought."

Tariq knelt beside him. "What do you mean?" The hardness in Tariq's voice had vanished, replaced by vulnerability Darius hadn't heard before. "What can I do?"

"Get back to the compound. Tell Joseph..." Darius' vision blurred momentarily. He blinked hard, forcing clarity. "Whoever did this isn't just attacking me—they're targeting Joseph's support structure..." He struggled for air. "First me, then who? They're trying to isolate him, make him vulnerable."

Tariq's expression hardened with understanding. "Faraz Qureshi. The same pattern as before—eliminating everyone around a target before striking the final blow."

The unspoken question hung between them—Would he survive this attack?

Wasim brought water, which Darius sipped. The cool liquid offered momentary relief from the burning that had spread throughout his chest.

"In my experience," Darius said, "they either want quick death or slow suffering. This feels like the second. Meant to incapacitate, create fear."

Tariq's hands clenched into fists. "The same people who killed my father? Who burned the mission?"

"Perhaps." Darius closed his eyes briefly, gathering strength. "But more sophisticated now. More patient."

Outside, sirens wailed. He could hear the marketplace chaos expanding—perfect distraction for what had just happened to him. Real grievances exploited for other purposes.

His vision darkened at the edges. The poison's progression was accelerating. Darius had witnessed enough death in his decades of ministry to recognize its approach, but he couldn't tell if this darkness was terminal or merely the prelude to prolonged suffering.

"Tariq," he managed, "whatever happens, remember what I told you about anger."

The young man nodded, tears threatening despite his obvious attempt to maintain composure.

"And tell Joseph this proves we're on the right path." Darius gripped Tariq's arm with surprising strength. "Go now. Joseph is their real target—they'll try to isolate him completely before they strike. Every hour matters."

As consciousness slipped away, Darius's final thought was urgency—Joseph needed to be warned.

Tariq stood, resolve hardening his features. "I'll warn Joseph." "Tell him..." Darius forced the words through the fog. "Tell him this proves we're on the right path. They only attack... what threatens them."

"I will." Tariq moved toward the door, then paused. "And Darius? You're not dying today. I won't let you."

"Go," Darius whispered. "Joseph first."

The door closed. Wasim's hand pressed a cool cloth to his forehead. And Darius surrendered to the darkness, trusting that Tariq would reach Joseph in time.

———

Faraz Qureshi paced his office beneath the ceiling fan's persistent whir, checking his phone with each turn. No calls. No messages. The fan's rotating blades marked time like a metronome—each sweep another second of waiting. His fingers twitched as he moved from window to desk to door and back again.

He glanced at the wall where surveillance photos created a mosaic of his obsession.

*It should be done by now.*

Joseph Freeman's face dominated the collection—emerging from Islamabad International Airport, inspecting the mission ruins, conferring with his team. Surrounding Joseph's images were photographs of his inner circle—Hassan, his father's former assistant; the attorney Maya Chaudhry; and Darius Karimi, the Iranian missionary whose extensive experience made him dangerous.

Faraz tapped the image of Karimi taken at the airport, the man's silver hair and penetrating eyes betraying nothing. "By now you should be feeling it," he whispered to the photograph. "The burning. The weakness. The fear." Faraz touched the scar across his cheek. Allah had marked him that night at the Freeman mission—not a punishment—a consecration. Where Joseph Freeman built, Faraz would tear down. Where the missionary sought to convert, Faraz would preserve.

His phone remained silent.

The market operation had been meticulously planned. The Tirah Valley protests provided perfect cover—legitimate outrage exploited for his purposes. His men had been in position. The specialist briefed. Everything should have proceeded as planned.

So why hadn't they called?

The secure line on his desk rang. The screen displayed no name, only a number he recognized. He drew a steadying breath before answering.

"Yes?"

"It's done." The voice was flat, emotionless—the same voice that had promised results when Faraz had called in the favor three days ago.

Faraz's shoulders loosened marginally. "Tell me."

"The Iranian was at the marketplace with the young one —Tariq. We tracked them through four stalls before the demonstration provided the opportunity."

"And?"

"Contact was made precisely as planned. The poison was delivered during the initial surge."

Faraz moved to his desk, where a small notebook lay open. He made a precise check mark beside the first name on a short list. "Any complications?"

"None. The operative who made contact escaped successfully. He's already across the district border."

"Witnesses?"

"Impossible to identify anyone specific in the chaos. The local authorities are blaming the violence on TTP militants. Seven confirmed dead in the protest, sixteen injured. Your man will simply be another casualty, a heart attack resulting from the chaos of civil unrest."

Faraz's gaze returned to Karimi's photograph. "And his condition?"

"He recognized what was happening immediately. More experienced than we anticipated. He and the young man sought shelter in a fabric shop off the main square."

A flicker of annoyance tightened Faraz's jaw. "That was unexpected."

"It changes nothing," the voice replied. "The compound is already circulating. The effects are progressive and irreversible without specific intervention. Death is inevitable within six hours."

"And if they get him to a hospital?"

"Local facilities lack the capability to identify the compound, let alone treat it. By the time they could transfer him to Islamabad, organ failure will be complete."

Faraz rubbed his chin. "And there's no connection to me?"

"None. The operative who made contact disappeared. He's already across the district border. The authorities have their narrative—TTP extremists causing chaos. No one will look further."

"What about Freeman? Has there been any reaction from the compound?"

"We have men watching. No unusual movement yet. They likely don't know what's happened."

Satisfaction bloomed in Faraz's chest. "Good. Very good."

"Will there be anything else?"

Faraz hesitated, considering. "No. But remain available. We'll proceed with the next phase soon."

The line went dead without a farewell.

He set down the phone and walked to the window. He closed his eyes.

Below, the city pulsed with its usual rhythm—cars honking, vendors calling, children playing in narrow streets. They moved through their lives unaware of what had begun today. None of them could grasp the necessity of what he'd done, the sacred obligation that drove him. Protecting Pakistan's soul from corruption wasn't a choice—it was Allah's command.

William Freeman had been the beginning. Now Freeman's son threatened to unravel Faraz's work. Work sanctioned by the Quran, honoring Allah and the prophet Mohammad, peace be upon him.

He returned to the wall of photographs, studying them with renewed purpose. Karimi had been the logical first target—the spiritual mentor, the experienced guide who had navigated persecution before. Without him, Joseph Freeman would lose not just wisdom but confidence.

"First the foundation, then the pillar," Faraz murmured. The Quranic verse that had guided him since youth whispered through his mind—*And never will the Jews or the Christians approve of you until you follow their religion.*

The Christians always sought the same thing—to reshape Pakistan, to erode its Islamic foundation stone by stone. Joseph Freeman called it healing. Faraz recognized it for what it truly was: invasion disguised as compassion, poison masked as medicine.

Allah had placed him exactly where he needed to be—a guardian embedded within the system, a defender with both the insight to see and the power to act.

He studied the photographs, focusing on Maya Chaudhry. Unlike the others, she was Pakistani by birth—but her Western education and years in London had transformed her into something else. Her legal skills and local heritage made her valuable to Joseph's team, providing legitimacy and access.

He moved to his desk and flipped open his laptop, accessing the file on Maya Chaudhry—immigration records, legal licensing documentation, and travel history that ordinary citizens couldn't access.

Faraz tapped her image, then pressed his finger hard enough to tear the paper.

# TWENTY-SEVEN

### The Awakening

*Darius poisoned? No. That can't be.*

The Land Cruiser's tires bit into loose gravel as Joseph accelerated through another pothole, sending a jolt through the vehicle's frame. His fingers gripped the steering wheel until they went numb—a hollowness spreading through his chest.

"Slow down at this junction," Rebecca Miller said, her voice measured despite the urgency. The nurse practitioner braced one hand against the dashboard while the other clutched her phone. "Left here—this route avoids the main protest areas."

Joseph eased off the accelerator just enough to make the turn without skidding. Tariq's panicked voice echoed in his mind—"Darius is dying."

Rebecca studied the unfamiliar streets ahead. "These back alleys all look the same to me. How close are we?"

"Three minutes if we don't hit roadblocks." Joseph

weaved around a donkey cart, earning angry shouts from its driver.

As he navigated around a cluster of men gesturing angrily at a television displayed in a shop window, his mind raced through the implications. News footage showed protesters clashing with police in Tirah Valley—the same valley where their construction project had faced serious opposition three weeks ago when religious leaders had organized demonstrations against the chapel rebuild.

The timing, the location, the specific targeting of Darius. Someone who knew where Darius would be and when he'd be vulnerable.

*Why Darius specifically?* If they wanted to hurt the mission, there were more obvious targets.

"Joseph?" Rebecca's voice pulled him from his thoughts. "You're going too fast. We need to get there alive if we want to help Darius."

They turned onto a narrow side street where buildings pressed close on either side, blocking the afternoon sun. Children scattered from their path, a deflated soccer ball forgotten in their wake. A fabric shop stood between a mobile repair stall and a spice vendor, its metal shutters partially lowered. Tariq waited outside, pacing. His face, normally set in lines of perpetual skepticism, now showed naked fear.

Joseph engaged the parking brake and leapt from the vehicle. "How is he?"

"Conscious, but fading." Tariq's voice cracked. "He's asking for you."

Rebecca rushed with her medical bag in hand. "Any changes since your call? Has a doctor seen him?"

"No doctor yet. My cousin Wasim has been helping—it's his shop."

Joseph followed them through the narrow doorway into a space that smelled of new fabric and old dust. Bolts of colorful textiles lined the walls, incongruously bright against the grim tableau at the room's center. Darius lay on a makeshift bed of fabric rolls, his silver hair damp with sweat, skin ashen beneath his natural olive complexion.

His chest rose and fell—shallow, irregular. Wasim knelt beside him, supporting his head with a folded cloth.

Rebecca assessed the situation. "We need a doctor here now."

"I've made some calls," Tariq said. "But no one wants to face the consequences of helping an infidel."

Wasim created more space while Tariq adjusted the shop's single overhead bulb.

Joseph approached slowly, cold dread settling in his stomach as he took in Darius's condition. The older man's eyes were half-closed, lips tinged with blue.

"Darius," he said, kneeling opposite Rebecca.

The missionary's eyelids fluttered. Recognition sparked in his gaze. "Joseph." The word emerged as barely more than a whisper.

"Save your strength," Joseph urged, reaching for his hand.

Darius's fingers felt cool and damp, but his grip remained surprisingly firm. "Listen to me." Each word seemed to cost him tremendous effort. "This was...coordinated. Professional."

"Who would orchestrate something like this?" Joseph asked, leaning closer.

A spasm of pain crossed Darius's face. Rebecca moved to his side. "He needs to be in a hospital."

A weight pressed against Joseph's chest. Every person on

his team faced dangers he hadn't fully grasped. Every local believer who associated with them risked similar targeting.

"This is my fault," he whispered.

Darius's grip suddenly tightened on Joseph's hand. "No." The word emerged weakly. "They don't waste this kind of precision on irrelevant threats."

Joseph stared at him.

"Opposition this organized means we're threatening something important," Darius continued, each phrase punctuated by labored breathing. "Remember Stephen's martyrdom in the book of Acts. The church didn't retreat. It exploded across the known world."

The reference struck Joseph with terrible clarity, but he wasn't ready to think of Darius in terms of martyrdom—the very idea made his throat constrict.

"You're not Stephen," Joseph insisted. "We're getting you through this."

"Same enemy. Different methods." Darius's voice grew fainter.

Rebecca looked up from her phone. "We need to move him to a safer location."

Joseph nodded, turning to Tariq and Wasim. "Can you help us carry him to the vehicle?"

As they prepared to lift Darius onto an improvised stretcher of fabric bolts, Joseph's phone vibrated in his pocket. He pulled it out, expecting a message from Hassan or one of the team members back at the compound.

Instead, an unknown number displayed on the screen with a single message: "The Iranian was first. The lawyer will be next."

Joseph's head snapped up. *Maya.*

"Joseph?" Rebecca's voice pulled him back to the moment. "We need to move."

He pocketed his phone without showing her the message. There would be time for warnings and security protocols once they reached the compound.

As they lifted Darius and prepared to carry him to the vehicle, something stirred deep inside Joseph—a familiar warmth that began as a small ember and expanded outward. It traveled to his shoulders, down his arms, and settled in his hands as a white-hot intensity that made him clench his fists.

The healing gift—awakening after months of dormancy like a battle horn sounding across a valley. He didn't know if it would be enough to save Darius. But it was no longer silent.

———

Darius's eyelids fluttered open. He slammed them shut as the room spun. His chest rose in shallow, stuttering gasps—each inhale a mountain to climb, each exhale a small victory. His fingers twitched. His nails bit into his palms. Heat pulsed from his core outward, setting his nerves ablaze. His scholarly mind measured the progression of his final hours. He had fought the good fight; now he was ready for his crown of righteousness.

Through half-closed eyes, he watched shadows move around him—Joseph, Rebecca, Tariq—their voices distant and distorted as they prepared to transport him from Wasim's fabric shop. Even as consciousness slipped away, Darius remembered the story Reverend Masih had told him —how Joseph had healed a woman whose body had been ravaged by lupus for decades, then had raised a twelve-year-old girl from the dead.

The vibrant bolts of cloth that had surrounded him for

the past hour blurred into watercolor smears of emerald, sapphire, and crimson. The sharp scent of dye and incense now barely registered as his senses dulled.

"We need to move him now," Rebecca's voice cut through the fog. "His condition is deteriorating rapidly."

The cool press of her fingers against his wrist seemed to come from miles away. Darius tried to focus on her face— the determination in her eyes, the tightness around her mouth betraying her concern.

"Careful with his head," Joseph instructed. "Tariq, take that end."

The shop's ceiling fan spun lazily above, its wooden blades creating hypnotic patterns that threatened to lull him into darkness. Darius fought it. He needed to stay conscious long enough to warn Joseph about the pattern of attacks. In Iran, in Syria, in every closed country where he'd worked, Darius had witnessed the same methodical dismantling of Christian leadership. First the foreign advisors, then the local leaders, then the infrastructure.

Each word required monumental effort, but he must make Joseph understand this was only the beginning. His tongue stuck to the roof of his mouth, the words coming out thick and slurred despite his concentration.

"The blanket—wrap it around him," Rebecca directed. "We need to keep him warm until we can get him to medical help."

Rough fabric smelling of wool and cardamom settled over him. Hands slid beneath his shoulders and knees, preparing to lift him. He caught glimpses of wooden poles and a tablecloth stretched between them.

"On three," Joseph said. "One, two—"

"Stop."

The same voice that had just been counting now cut

through the fog in Darius's mind. Movement halted abruptly.

"Joseph, we don't have time," Rebecca protested. "The poison is spreading. If we don't get him proper medical attention soon—"

"I know," Joseph interrupted, his voice carrying a strange certainty that hadn't been there moments before. "That's why we need to stop."

Darius felt the fabric beneath him shift as someone knelt beside the stretcher. Joseph's face appeared above him, features tense with unfamiliar determination. His eyes—usually gentle, sometimes uncertain—now burned with a fiery purpose.

"I can't let you die," Joseph whispered, low enough that perhaps only Darius could hear. "Not when God has given me the means to prevent it."

Darius tried to speak, to tell Joseph to save himself, that martyrdom was sometimes God's plan, that his own death might serve a greater purpose than his life. The poison had progressed too far—organs shutting down—unless...

"What are you doing?" Tariq's voice cut in.

"Something I haven't done in several months," Joseph answered.

Through Darius' haze of pain, Joseph stretched out his hands like a conductor before an orchestra. His lips moved silently.

"Joseph, this isn't the time for—" Rebecca began.

"Please," Joseph said without opening his eyes. "Trust me."

Wasim, the shop owner, backed away, pressing himself against shelves stacked with fabric bolts. "What is happening?" he whispered in Urdu.

"I don't know," Tariq answered in the same language.

The room fell silent except for Darius's labored breathing. He felt himself slipping further away, darkness encroaching from the edges of his vision. An irregular flutter grew in his chest.

In his sixty-two years, Darius had faced death many times. He'd prepared himself for martyrdom decades ago, surrendering his life to whatever purpose God intended. But was this his time? Was his work really finished?

Joseph opened his eyes. Darius saw something achingly familiar—a look he'd witnessed throughout his decades of ministry. The look of surrender. The look that comes when someone steps aside and lets God work through them.

"Darius," Joseph said. "God's not ready to take you."

Joseph placed his palm firmly over Darius's heart. The contact brought an immediate sensation—warmth, impossibly deep and flowing, like liquid sunlight pouring into Darius's body. It spread outward from Joseph's hand, like the poison but with the opposite effect.

Where there had been pain, now came relief. Where there had been distorted vision, now came clarity.

Darius gasped, drawing in a full breath for the first time since the attack. His back arched involuntarily as the warmth surged through him, reaching into every muscle, bone, and sinew. The pain vanished so completely it left him disoriented, like stepping from a roaring factory into sudden silence.

"Ya Masih," Darius whispered in Persian. "Oh Christ."

The room around him came into sharp focus—the vibrant fabrics no longer blurry smears but intricate patterns of thread and color. The scents of the shop returned in full force—sandalwood incense, tea brewing somewhere in the back, the faint tang of dye. He could hear the street sounds outside—bicycle bells, children's voices—with perfect clarity.

Joseph's eyes were wide with wonder, as though he himself couldn't fully comprehend the gift flowing through his hands. Sweat beaded on his forehead, and his face had gone pale with exertion, but his hand remained steady on Darius's chest. The healing warmth continued for several more seconds before gradually subsiding, leaving Darius completely restored.

Rebecca rushed forward, pressing her fingers to Darius's wrist, then his neck, counting silently. "Impossible," she whispered, touching various points on his chest as if searching for evidence the poison remained. "Your color is returning. Your breathing is normal." She shook her head in disbelief.

Tariq stood frozen, his skepticism shattered by undeniable evidence. The cynical mask he wore had slipped, revealing the face of the twelve-year-old boy who had once believed in miracles before watching his father die for his faith. "I saw it," he murmured, more to himself than anyone else. "With my own eyes, I saw it."

Wasim fell to his knees, prayers of thanksgiving tumbling from his lips. "Allah hu akbar," he repeated, though his eyes remained fixed on Joseph with a new understanding.

Darius sat up, strength returning to his limbs. The poison that should have killed him within hours had vanished. He flexed his fingers, feeling the blood flow freely through veins that moments ago had been constricting with toxins.

"How do you feel?" Joseph asked.

"Like I've been reborn," Darius answered. He placed his

hand over Joseph's, still resting on his chest. "This gift you failed to tell us about—it's real."

Joseph nodded, a complex emotion crossing his face. "It comes when needed, not when wanted. I can't control it, only surrender to it."

Rebecca interrupted, "Joseph, I've seen many things as a nurse—but nothing like this. What happened was beyond explanation."

"There doesn't need to be—" Darius replied before Joseph could answer. "Some things transcend explanation."

He swung his legs over the side of the makeshift stretcher, testing his balance. His muscles responded perfectly, as though the attack had never happened. The fabric shop spun briefly around him, then steadied.

"Joseph," Darius said, gripping the younger man's arm as Joseph swayed slightly, drained by whatever power had flowed through him. "This gift—it's why evil fears you. It's why they're trying to isolate you."

Joseph looked down at his hands.

Darius pressed his hand against his heart where moments ago death tried to take him. "I can still feel it—this warmth flowing through me." He shook his head. "After decades of ministry, to experience this myself..."

He reached for Joseph's shoulder. "There's a reason..." he collected himself, "'Plans fail for lack of counsel, but with many advisers they succeed.'"

Darius took a deep breath, savoring the very act of breathing. "What you carry is too precious to navigate alone. I understand now why God brought me to Pakistan." His eyes moistened. "Not just to help rebuild the chapel, but to walk beside you as you surrender to God's will—for the mission, just as you did for my healing."

"We need to move," Tariq urged, peering through the

shop's curtains at the street outside. "Word of this will spread, and Faraz will come for all of us now." His voice had changed—the bitterness that had colored it since Joseph's arrival had softened, replaced by something approaching respect.

Rebecca packed her bag quickly. "We should get back to the compound." She paused, looking at Darius with fascination. "I still can't believe it."

Darius stood fully, surprised at the complete absence of weakness or pain. It was as though the last few hours had been erased from his body, though not from his memory. He'd experienced many miracles in his decades of ministry, but never one so personal, so complete.

"Wasim," he said to the shop owner, who was still kneeling on the floor. "What you've seen today—"

"I will tell no one," the man interrupted, crossing his heart. "But I will never forget."

"No," Darius responded. "Tell everyone you can. God's work should never be hidden."

As they helped Darius gather his things, the shop door flew open—the bell above it jerking violently on its mount. Hassan filled the doorway, breathless and ashen. One arm hung limp at his side, his head was bloodied, and the calm he usually wore like armor had cracked open.

"What is it?" Joseph asked.

"Someone just tried to kill me."

# TWENTY-EIGHT

**Salted Ground**

The government complex stood like a fortress of bureaucratic power, its marble halls and thick walls insulating occupants from the chaos of Peshawar's streets. Faraz Qureshi straightened his collar as he approached the heavy wooden door.

Through the frosted glass panel, he glimpsed two silhouettes. His pulse quickened. Maulana Hafiz Rahman's distinctive profile was unmistakable. The religious leader's presence here, unannounced and urgent, meant something had gone wrong.

Faraz knocked twice, crisp and confident.

"Enter."

The door swung open, revealing Qadir behind his desk and Rahman seated in the adjacent leather chair. The maulana's fingers worked through his prayer beads.

"As-salaam alaikum, Deputy Commissioner. Maulana sahib." Faraz inclined his head, noting the untouched tea service on the side table. They'd been waiting for him.

"Wa alaikum as-salaam, Director Qureshi." Qadir stood quickly, his deference apparent as he gestured to the empty chair beside Rahman. "Please, sit."

The leather creaked as Faraz settled into it, maintaining a straight-backed posture. Qadir's nervous glance toward Rahman confirmed what Faraz already knew—this meeting had been arranged at the maulana's request.

"I assume you've called me here regarding the developments at the mission site," Faraz began, his tone carrying the authority of someone accustomed to subordinates. "Hassan's attackers encountered complications, but the old man's survival is inconsequential. He's merely a relic from the previous generation. Without Karimi—"

"The Iranian advisor." Rahman's calm voice cut through. His prayer beads stopped clicking. "Yes, we should discuss Darius Karimi."

The maulana's tone made Faraz reassess the situation. Rahman might not have official government authority, but his religious influence extended far beyond Faraz's bureaucratic reach—a reality that had served Faraz well throughout his career, provided he maintained the delicate balance between his official position and his allegiance to Rahman's cause.

"My operative confirmed the delivery," Faraz said, his hand moving involuntarily to his scar. "Clean injection during the market chaos. The poison was specially procured—untraceable, fatal within twelve hours. Witnesses saw him being helped into that fabric shop, barely able to walk."

Wood scraped against wood as Qadir opened his desk drawer. He withdrew a manila folder, aligned it with the desktop's edge, and slid it across to Faraz. "Director, you should see this."

Inside, a single photograph, time-stamped from late the previous afternoon.

Faraz's breath caught.

Darius Karimi stood in the mission compound's courtyard, his arm around Joseph Freeman's shoulders. Not hunched in pain. Not pale from poison. The Iranian's face was animated in conversation, his free hand gesturing as he pointed to something off-camera.

Faraz's scarred cheek began to burn.

"That's..." The word *impossible* died on his tongue. His operative had never failed. The poison had been administered. He'd seen the preliminary reports of Karimi visibly dying.

"My people observed him late yesterday afternoon," Rahman said, his voice carrying a frustrated edge that made Faraz's chest constrict. "Walking. Talking. Counseling Freeman as if he'd spent the day in pleasant contemplation rather than fighting for his life." The maulana leaned forward, his prayer beads swinging like a pendulum. "You are not the only one with eyes in the field."

The implication was unmistakable. Rahman had been watching—not just the mission, but Faraz's operations.

A bead of sweat traced down Faraz's temple despite the room's cool interior. His mind raced through possibilities. Body double? Misidentification? But no—he knew Karimi's face, had studied it for weeks. The man in the photograph was undeniably the Iranian advisor who should be cooling in a morgue.

"There are..." Rahman continued, his fingers resuming their journey across the prayer beads, "disturbing reports from my observers. Workers arriving at odd hours, speaking in hushed tones about witnessing something extraordinary. About Freeman possessing abilities that defy explanation."

"Propaganda," Faraz managed, though his voice sounded hollow even to himself. "Christian lies to—"

"To what? Inspire their workers to continue without pay?" Qadir interjected, then quickly modulated his tone when Faraz's eyes narrowed. "Forgive me, Director, but whatever happened in that fabric shop, the result is clear—Karimi lives, and the mission's construction continues."

Faraz forced his fingers to relax, placing the photograph back inside the folder. Blood pulsed through his temples.

"Deputy Commissioner," Faraz said, his voice level, "the situation requires adaptation, not panic. Hassan's survival is irrelevant—he's an old man with no influence. And if Karimi somehow recovered, it changes nothing about our fundamental position."

"Doesn't it?" Rahman's question hung in the air like incense smoke.

Qadir stood, moving to the window that overlooked the city. The late afternoon sun painted everything in shades of amber and shadow. "With Alexander Mercer's funding terminated, certain...constraints have been lifted. The Interior Ministry no longer concerns itself with diplomatic ramifications." He turned, backlit by the dying light. "Your office could authorize the revocation of their construction permits. Structural violations, unauthorized religious assembly, employment of foreign nationals without proper documentation."

Faraz nodded slowly. "The law is indeed our weapon. But perhaps for this case, we need something more...immediate."

"What are you suggesting, Director?" Qadir asked.

"I'll authorize three trucks. Armed officers for a routine inspection."

"A routine inspection?" Qadir raised an eyebrow.

"That uncovers security concerns. Foreign agitators. Suspicious materials." Faraz's hands had curled into fists without his conscious thought. "We'll handle this properly."

The two other men exchanged glances. The maulana's fingers moved across three beads in quick succession.

"The compound has volunteers," Rahman observed. "Witnesses. International team members with cameras and satellite phones."

"Then they'll document a legal inspection that discovered violations requiring immediate action." The rage in Faraz's chest had condensed into something cold and precise. "No martyrs. No headlines. Just bureaucratic efficiency."

"Your position at the FIA grants you considerable power, Faraz," Rahman said, studying him. "But it also requires discretion. We don't want an international incident."

Faraz nodded, understanding the subtext. His rise through government ranks had always served two masters— the state and the faith. "My official reports will reflect regulatory violations only. What happens beyond the paperwork..." He let the implication hang.

Qadir pulled out his official letterhead with the Interior Ministry seal. "I'll prepare the local authorization, though with your position, Director, I assume you have the necessary federal clearances already."

"I do," Faraz confirmed. "But your documentation will maintain the appearance of proper protocol."

The pen's scratching filled the silence. Rahman watched Faraz with those penetrating eyes, seeing too much, understanding more than he should.

"The Freeman family..." the maulana said, "seems remarkably difficult to eradicate."

Heat crawled up Faraz's neck. "The father is dead. The mother is dead. The mission burned."

"And yet here we sit, discussing their son's reconstruction efforts." Rahman rose, his robes rustling like wind through dry leaves. "Perhaps certain seeds are meant to grow regardless of the fire."

"Or perhaps," Faraz said, standing as well, "the fire simply wasn't hot enough."

Qadir blotted the ink and presented the document with both hands. Faraz took it with the casual ease of a superior accepting a subordinate's work.

"One more thing," the maulana said as Faraz turned toward the door. "If this 'routine inspection' fails to stop Freeman..." The pause stretched like a blade being drawn from its sheath. "Perhaps I'll need to share with our brothers the full account of what happened that night. The...personal choices you made at the Freeman compound." Rahman's eyes flicked briefly toward Qadir, whose brow creased before he caught himself and looked away. "Some actions—even in service to our cause— might be difficult for your superiors to understand."

Faraz's fingers tightened on the door handle until his knuckles went white. But he knew what Rahman meant. One more failure, and his standing with the religious authorities would crumble, regardless of his government position.

"I've always been in service to our cause," Faraz said. "The authority I've cultivated, the networks I've built—they exist to protect our faith and our way of life."

"Then prove it," Rahman replied. "Not with words, but with results."

"The inspection will not fail," Faraz said, his voice steady as stone. "Freeman's blasphemy ends tonight."

He pulled the door open and entered the hallway, leaving behind the wood-paneled sanctuary and Rahman's doubt. The document in his hand was more than permission—it was vindication. Three trucks. Armed officers. Legal authority.

As he strode to the elevator, Faraz's phone buzzed. A message from his operative at the compound—*"Movement at the site. They're gathering in the main building. All of them."*

Perfect. They'd be contained, controllable. No scattered targets, no confusion. Just Freeman and his followers, caught in one neat package.

Rahman was wrong. Some seeds weren't meant to grow. Some ground was meant to remain salted, barren, a testament to the price of defiance.

Tonight, he would prove it.

———

The portable lamp threw amber light across Joseph's cramped tent, illuminating the faces gathered around his collapsible table. Ian Daniels leaned forward, arms crossed. Maya sat with her notebook ready. Hassan shifted uncomfortably in a makeshift sling, fresh bruises marking his face. Darius nursed a cup of tea. A dog-eared map lay stretched across the table's surface.

"We need better coverage here," Ian said, pointing to the northern approach.

"Tell us exactly what happened," Joseph said to Hassan. "Every detail."

Hassan straightened. "I was returning from devotionals in the hills. The street was nearly empty." His good hand gripped the table edge. "A black van appeared—no markings, tinted windows. A man asked for directions. His Pashto was perfect, but something felt wrong."

Darius nodded from near the tent entrance.

"While I was speaking, two others emerged from the rear. They flanked me, grabbed my arm, opened the side door." Hassan paused. "They called me 'the missionary's dog' and said I would answer for my betrayal."

Maya looked up. "They knew who you were?"

"Yes." Hassan touched his bruised cheek. "If my neighbor Abdul hadn't started shouting, roused the street..." He gestured to his injuries.

The pattern was escalating—Darius poisoned in the market, Hassan ambushed near his home. The same day.

"This wasn't random," Ian said. "And we have more that concerns me."

"Go on," Joseph said.

Ian placed both palms flat on the map. "We're completely exposed." No preamble, no softening the blow. "I have four trained men. Need twelve minimum. No 24-hour coverage possible. Local volunteers are untrained—well-meaning, but they'll get people killed in a crisis."

He pulled a pen from his pocket and marked the map with quick strokes. "Darius's poisoning and Hassan's assault tell us this is coordinated. But we have no protection protocols for off-compound movement." He looked up, eyes hard. "We need security escorts for all key personnel. But we don't have the manpower."

Hassan shifted abruptly. "What if we rotate the volunteers? Double up?"

Ian shook his head. "They'll collapse in a week. It's denial, not a plan."

Heavy silence.

"The compound itself?" Joseph asked.

Ian circled three sections of their perimeter. "Blind spots. Sentries struggle to cover 60%. Anyone with basic training could exploit these. The ruins provide perfect cover."

"What are our options?" Maya asked.

"Few," Ian replied. "We consolidate, tighten shifts, but it's not enough. If Faraz launches anything coordinated, we'd be overwhelmed in minutes."

Joseph's eyes fell on the chapel at the map's center. He reached for his Bible, then set it back down without opening it.

"So we evacuate?" Maya said.

Ian didn't answer.

Joseph thought of the children playing among the tents each morning, the quiet prayers over bread, the volunteers who had risked everything.

The tent flap snapped open. One of Ian's security men stood breathless, dust coating his boots.

"Sir," he addressed Ian, then turned to Joseph. "Government trucks approaching. Three vehicles. Moving fast."

Joseph's pulse quickened.

"Officials or military?" Ian demanded.

"No markings. Could be officials. Could be military. Hard to tell."

"How long?" Darius asked.

"Five minutes. Maybe less."

Ian issued rapid orders. "Move women and children to the rear compound. Alert perimeter guards—no visible weapons. No provocations."

The sentry disappeared. Outside, tent flaps opened. Mothers swept children up. Volunteers kicked dirt over cooking fires. Others huddled in prayer circles. Their movements carried a rhythm of experience—people who'd been attacked before.

"I should speak with them," Hassan said, rising slowly. "They know me."

"They tried to abduct you yesterday," Maya snapped. "And possibly kill you!"

Hassan looked at Joseph. "If I can calm them—"

"If this is what we think it is," Joseph said, "there will be no calming."

Darius moved beside him. "This is coordinated. Everything leads here. The poisoning, the threats. This is the move."

Joseph turned to Maya. "Take stock. Account for everyone. Get Rebecca ready—if this goes badly, we'll need her medical skills."

He moved toward the entrance. The canvas parted. Fading light revealed the clustered tents, the rising dust on the horizon.

Three trucks barreling from the mountains. Just like the day his parents died.

He stepped toward the main gate. A scripture flickered in his memory—*When you pass through the waters, I will be with you.*

He gripped the tent pole, steadying himself against the weight of that promise and the memory it couldn't erase.

*Where were you, Lord, when they attacked the compound fifteen years ago?*

# TWENTY-NINE

**Marigolds**

The diesel growl reached Joseph before the dust cloud did
—three engines harmonizing in a predator's chorus that
dragged him back fifteen years, to tending the garden with
his mother just before she and his father were killed. Joseph
stepped forward, his mother's scream fresh in his ears, his
pulse frantically beating.

"Everyone stay calm," Joseph called to the workers scattered across the half-built chapel. Hammers stilled mid-
swing. The scrape of trowels against mortar ceased. Even
the morning birds fell silent, as if the entire valley held its
breath.

Ian Daniels materialized at Joseph's left shoulder. "My
scout reports three vehicles, government plates," he
murmured. "A fourth one hanging back on the access road."

The lead truck entered the compound and stopped. The
two others took positions behind and on each side—a
perfect V. The passenger door opened with deliberate slowness. A man emerged, savoring his entrance, dust swirling

around his polished boots. As he turned toward them, Joseph noticed a jagged scar across his left cheek, and something in the man's posture—a strange blend of authority and anticipation—sent a chill down Joseph's spine.

"Mr. Freeman." The stranger's voice carried across the compound, smooth as oil on water. "How fortunate to find you here."

The familiarity in the man's tone made Joseph's stomach drop. This wasn't a chance encounter. Though they'd never met, something about this man felt like a ghost stepping out of his nightmares.

Behind him, uniformed officers fanned out, their rifles held at the ready. Not quite pointing at anyone. Not quite safe. An officer in a crisp uniform stepped forward, unfolding documents with theatrical flair.

"By order of the Federal Investigation Agency," the officer announced, his voice pitched to carry, "and in accordance with national security protocols, this facility is under investigation for potential violations of the Foreign NGO Registration Act, Section 38-B regarding undisclosed foreign funding sources, and Regulation 247-B regarding unauthorized construction beyond permitted specifications."

Joseph forced his shoulders to relax, his voice to remain steady. "Our permits are in order. We've stayed within every guideline—"

"Have you?" the stranger interrupted, strolling forward with his hands clasped behind his back like a teacher disappointed in a student. "Shall we examine that claim?"

The official continued reading, each word falling like a stone. "All construction activity must cease pending full inspection. All personnel will step away from their work stations and remain in designated areas for documentation."

Tariq started forward, his face flushed with anger, but Hassan caught his arm.

"Put down your tools," Joseph called to his workers, keeping his voice level. "Step back from the construction. Comply with everything they ask." He glanced at the stranger. "May I ask who you are?"

The stranger's smile widened a fraction. "Director Faraz Qureshi, Regional Director of the Federal Investigation Agency." He flashed his credentials. His eyes swept the compound with unsettling familiarity, pausing briefly at the western corner. "You've made changes. The old generator shed used to be over there, behind those tamarind trees. Interesting choice to move it."

Joseph's breath caught. The generator shed had indeed been there when he lived here as a boy, but it had been destroyed in the attack and never documented in any of the rebuilding plans they'd filed. There was no way this man should know that detail. Unless.

Faraz's gaze found Joseph's again, studying his reaction with cold satisfaction. "One must understand a property's history before assessing its present state, wouldn't you agree, Mr. Freeman?"

"Inspector," Faraz commanded an officer behind him, "begin recording. We'll want complete documentation of all violations." He pulled out his own phone, the camera's red recording light blooming to life. "For transparency, of course. The Deputy Commissioner requires thorough evidence."

They moved through the compound with systematic thoroughness. Faraz led, his phone sweeping across every corner. At the chapel's walls, he examined the mortar joints with professional interest before shaking his head with apparent regret.

"Substandard work," he announced to his recording, his voice carrying genuine disappointment. "These joints won't hold through the winter rains—a clear safety hazard." He kicked at a perfectly sound foundation stone. "Amateur foundation work. The whole structure risks collapse."

Maya Chaudhry appeared at Joseph's elbow, her voice barely a whisper. "Document everything. Get our own video. This is theater for a legal case."

Joseph nodded to Leila, who quietly raised her phone, keeping it partially concealed behind Nadir's broad shoulders.

The inspection continued its destructive path. In the tool shed, Faraz "accidentally" spilled a can of nails, the metallic cascade ringing across the compound. At the water station, his excessive tug on the tap made the fixture groan —a perfect excuse to note "inadequate sanitation" with feigned concern.

But it was in his mother's garden that Faraz's mask finally slipped. The small plot had been lovingly restored, the first green shoots of vegetables emerging alongside marigolds planted in her honor. Faraz stood at its edge, studying the flowers with an expression that might have been nostalgia.

"Marigolds," he said almost to himself. "Once planted in rows of seven."

Joseph froze, the blood draining from his face. His mother's peculiar habit of planting in rows of seven—her "perfect biblical number"—had been a private tradition. The unease that had been building since Faraz arrived crystallized into sharp, terrible suspicion.

Faraz's boot came down on a young marigold, grinding it into the earth as his eyes found Joseph's. "Foreign flowers die here."

Joseph's vision blurred red at the edges.

Ian's hand found his arm, a subtle restraint. "He wants you to react. Don't give in to it."

Through the roar of blood in his ears, Joseph heard another engine approaching. The fourth vehicle pulled through the gates with two uniformed officers in front and two young men in the back.

The young men emerged first—street vendors from the bazaar who sometimes loitered near the compound hoping for work. They kept their eyes fixed on the ground, avoiding everyone's gaze, especially Hassan's.

"Ah," Faraz announced, "our witnesses have arrived."

The FIA officer, a thin man with nervous hands, pulled out a folder. "Hassan Awan, under the authority of the Federal Investigation Agency, you are being detained for questioning regarding suspected foreign intelligence connections and dissemination of anti-state propaganda."

The compound fell silent. Even the wind seemed to stop.

Hassan stood perfectly still, his weathered face revealing nothing. "What evidence?"

The first young man spoke, his voice mechanical, rehearsed. "For three months, we have heard him recruiting people near the marketplace. He speaks of American interests and distributes materials from foreign sources."

"What materials?" Hassan asked.

The second young man picked up the script, his words tumbling out too fast, too practiced. "Literature from American organizations. Maps of sensitive locations. Information about government officials. You showed these things many times, every week at the market."

"Every Tuesday and Thursday," the first one added, then looked confused, as if unsure whether that detail was part of what he was supposed to say.

"We have told our families," the second continued, finding his rhythm again. "Many people know but were too afraid to speak. But we cannot stay silent when our country's security is threatened."

Joseph's stomach knotted. The accusation landed like a stone through stained glass.

"These are lies," Tariq exploded, unable to contain himself any longer. "Hassan doesn't speak much at the market. He buys supplies and leaves. Everyone knows—"

Hassan's expression shifted—not surprised, but deep, resigned sad. As if he'd been expecting this moment for a long time.

"Everyone knows," Faraz interrupted smoothly, "that national security is the FIA's highest priority. These brave young men have come forward despite the danger to themselves." He gestured to a junior officer who produced several pamphlets. "And we found these American missionary materials in Mr. Awan's home during our preliminary search earlier this morning. Unless..." He paused, looking directly at Joseph. "Unless someone has been pressuring witnesses to stay silent? Obstruction of an FIA investigation is also a serious offense."

The trap was elegant in its simplicity. Defend Hassan too vigorously, and they'd be accused of obstruction. Stay silent, and Hassan would be taken.

The officer stepped forward, producing handcuffs that caught the morning sun like silver flames. "Hassan Awan, you are under detention for questioning under the National Security Act, Section 9-F regarding foreign intelligence activities."

Hassan moved then, but not to run or resist. He walked forward with a dignity that made the armed men around him look small, their weapons suddenly ridiculous in the face of his calm. As he passed Joseph, their eyes met.

"Keep building," Hassan said clearly, loud enough for everyone to hear. Then, softer, his lips barely moving, words meant only for Joseph—"Build."

The handcuffs clicked closed with a sound like breaking bones. Hassan didn't flinch as they led him to the FIA vehicle, his steps measured, unhurried, as if he were walking to morning prayers rather than to interrogation.

Faraz followed, pausing beside Joseph. Joseph could smell expensive cologne that couldn't quite mask the underlying scent of ambition and hatred.

"Faith is a beautiful thing," Faraz said conversationally, as if discussing weather. "The stubborn belief that God will intervene." His eyes flickered with dark memory. "But sometimes He doesn't, does He?" He leaned closer, his breath hot against Joseph's ear. "Sometimes He just watches."

The convoy began to move, engines roaring back to life. Dust rose in brown clouds, obscuring the vehicles as they pulled away. Joseph stood frozen, watching Hassan's gray head through the FIA car's rear window until even that disappeared into the haze.

The compound remained silent for long moments after the last engine faded. Workers stood in shocked clusters. Maya had her hand over her mouth. Even Ian looked shaken.

Then Tariq was there, grabbing Joseph's hand, pressing something small and cool into his palm. Joseph looked down at a key, worn smooth in places, attached to a small tag with numbers written in Hassan's careful script.

"Last week," Tariq said, his voice cracking, "Hassan gave this to me. Said if anything happened to him, you'd need what's in the safety deposit box at the village bank." Tariq's eyes, still red with unshed tears, bored into Joseph's. "He said you should go alone. That you'd understand when you saw it."

Joseph closed his fingers around the key. Through the space where his mother's crushed flower lay, he could see the chapel's unfinished walls reaching toward heaven. He set his jaw.

"The enemy thinks he's won. Let's prove him wrong."

# THIRTY

**Protective Custody**

The morning air still held diesel fumes and broken promises from yesterday's raid. Joseph pushed away the metal cup of cooling coffee across the scarred wooden table in the compound's dining area. He rubbed his thumb across Hassan's key at the bottom of his jacket pocket, certain that government eyes were cataloging his every move.

Across from him, Darius Karimi stirred sugar into his tea, the spoon clinking gently against the cup's edges. Ian Daniels sat to Joseph's right, his coffee untouched, his eyes scanning the compound's perimeter where his security team patrolled as Faraz's armed guards chatted and smoked cigarettes.

"Hassan knew." Darius set down his spoon with deliberate care. "Men like him always know when the net is closing."

The key in Joseph's pocket pressed against his leg. He'd carried it through a sleepless night, tracing its edges, wondering what Hassan had hidden.

"The charges won't hold," Joseph said, though the words tasted hollow. "Those boys' testimony was obviously rehearsed. Any honest court—"

"There are no honest courts for blasphemy cases." Darius's face carried years of missionary experience. "The accusation itself becomes the verdict."

Ian's chair creaked as he changed positions. "My sources in Islamabad sent word an hour ago." He lowered his voice, though the nearest guard was fifty meters away. "This isn't local anymore. Deputy Commissioner Qadir is taking direct orders from the Interior Ministry. Someone very high up wants this mission closed."

"Because of the chapel construction?" Joseph asked.

"Because of you." Ian's pale eyes met his. "You healing Darius got the attention of the local Muslims—it threatens the narrative the government needs to maintain. A Christian performing miracles in an Islamic republic?" He shook his head. "That's not just a religious issue. It's political dynamite."

Darius sighed. "In Tehran, before the Revolution, we thought we could work within the system. We had permits, government connections, even friends in high places. Then overnight, those friends became strangers, and those permits became evidence against us."

"This is different," Joseph insisted. "We're not trying to overthrow anything. We're just building."

"Yes," Darius said, his dark eyes holding infinite sadness. "But sometimes, Joseph, building something new is seen as tearing down what exists. Your very presence here challenges their world order."

The morning sun climbed higher, casting sharp shadows across the compound. The volunteer workers began their day with quick glances over shoulders, hushed conversations that died when anyone approached.

"What does Hassan's key open?" Ian asked.

Joseph pulled it from his pocket, the brass warm from his body heat. The tag bore only numbers—347-B. "A safety deposit box at the village bank. Tariq said Hassan told him I'd understand when I saw what's inside."

"You can't go." Ian's tone brooked no argument. "If they're watching—and they are—you'll be arrested the moment you leave the compound."

"Unless they want you to go," Darius suggested. "To see where you lead them."

Before Joseph could respond, engines hummed. Three late-model Mercedes sedans rolled through the gates, black paint gleaming like oil, windows tinted dark, license plates bearing government seals.

Ian stood smoothly, his hand moving to his hip where he kept a concealed radio. "Stay seated," he murmured. "Let them come to us."

The lead vehicle's door opened, and an official emerged —uniform pressed to knife edges, shoes reflecting the morning sun, leather portfolio under his arm. Two assistants flanked him, one carrying a camera, the other a stack of documents.

"Mr. Freeman." The official's voice carried the dispassionate tone of someone delivering weather reports. "I am Director Mahmood from the Regional Administration Office. I have documentation requiring your immediate attention."

He placed the portfolio on the wooden table with ceremonial efficiency, extracting papers covered in official seals and dense Urdu text. The camera assistant began recording, the red light a silent witness.

"Tariq!" Joseph called.

Tariq appeared almost immediately. His face darkened at the sight of the officials.

"I need you to translate," Joseph said. "Every word. Exactly."

Tariq took the documents with trembling hands. His eyes scanned the text, his expression growing more grave with each line.

"By order of the Provincial Government," Tariq began, his voice steady despite the tremor in his hands, "in accordance with Section 144 of the Criminal Procedure Code regarding unlawful assembly and potential public disorder..." He paused, swallowing hard. "All foreign nationals associated with the Freeman Mission are hereby placed under protective custody within the compound boundaries."

Director Mahmood nodded approvingly at the translation's accuracy. "Continue."

"Movement beyond the compound perimeter is forbidden except when summoned to appear for the muqadma..." Tariq's voice caught. "Seven days from today, your case will be heard before the civil court in Peshawar."

Joseph's lungs emptied. A public trial—not a closed court, but a spectacle for the entire region to witness.

"Furthermore," Tariq continued, "all local citizens who have associated with the mission must present themselves for registration. Names, addresses, family members, and nature of involvement will be documented for public safety."

The compound had gone silent. Workers stood frozen at their posts. Maya appeared from her tent, her face pale.

"And," Tariq's voice dropped, "any local citizen found in violation of this order, maintaining contact with foreign agitators, will be subject to investigation under Sections 295 and 298 of the Pakistan Penal Code."

The same blasphemy laws they'd used against Hassan.

"This isn't legal," Maya said with a scowl. "You cannot restrict movement without formal charges."

"We can and we are," Director Mahmood interrupted smoothly. "This is a matter of civil administration. For your own protection, of course. Emotions are running high in the village. We wouldn't want any unfortunate incidents."

Ian positioned himself between Joseph and the nearest assistant. "And if we refuse to comply?"

The Director's smile was razor-thin. "Deportation proceedings will begin for all foreign nationals. As for local citizens..." He shrugged with elaborate unconcern. "They would be free to make their own choices, knowing the full consequences of association with individuals under government investigation."

Joseph watched as understanding dawned on the faces around him. Accept house arrest, or abandon every local believer to persecution. The elegance of the trap turned his stomach.

"The registration," Joseph said. "What happens to those names?"

"Public record," the Director replied. "Posted in the village square, published in the district newspaper. Transparency in all things, Mr. Freeman. The people have a right to know who among them associates with foreign influences."

A public enemies list. Every local believer marked, their families exposed, their employers pressured. Heat flushed Joseph's face.

Movement near the compound entrance caught his eye. Miriam had arrived for morning prayers, her worn purple dupatta bright against the dust, its frayed edges trembling with each step. Two policemen intercepted her, their voices carrying across the compound.

"Name and address," one demanded, hand on his baton.

Miriam stood straighter, though her hands shook. "I am here to pray."

"Name and address, or you will be arrested for obstruction."

"Miriam Shahid," she said clearly, her voice carrying defiance.

The policeman began writing, his partner photographing her face. "You are forbidden from entering these premises. Any further contact with the foreign agitators will result in your immediate arrest."

"These are my people," Miriam protested, trying to step past them. "My church family—"

The first policeman grabbed her arm, not violently but firmly enough to stop her progress. "Your church is closed. Go home."

Joseph started to rise, but Darius's hand on his wrist stopped him. "Don't," the older man whispered. "This is what they want—you interfering with lawful orders."

Miriam's eyes found Joseph across the distance. In them, he saw not accusation but understanding, and somehow that was worse. She adjusted her dupatta with dignity, then turned away. But as the police escorted her toward the gate, she called out in English, loud enough for everyone to hear:

"The church is not a building! You cannot close what lives in our hearts!"

The policeman pushed her away from the gate.

Director Mahmood cleared his throat. "Mr. Freeman, I require your signature acknowledging receipt of these orders."

The pen he offered looked ordinary enough—a simple ballpoint. But Joseph understood that taking it meant accepting the cage they'd constructed, becoming complicit in his own imprisonment.

"What about medical emergencies?" Maya asked, still fighting on legal grounds. "What about food supplies? What about—"

"All necessities will be provided through official channels," the Director replied. "We are not barbarians, Dr. Chaudhry. Though I should note—your visa status is also under review. It would be unfortunate if procedural irregularities were discovered."

The threat unspoken but clear—everyone's visa, everyone's permits, everyone's legal right to exist here rested on Joseph's compliance.

Joseph took the pen. As he wrote his name on the document, he heard more voices at the gate—other local believers arriving for morning prayers, each one being turned away, registered, photographed, cataloged.

"Guards will remain at all exits," Director Mahmood announced, collecting the signed papers with satisfaction. "For your protection, of course. Any attempt to leave without authorization will be considered a violation of public safety orders."

He turned to go, then paused, as if remembering something trivial. "Oh, and Mr. Freeman? The muqadma—the trial, as you would say in English—will be public. Very public. The entire district has been invited to attend. Justice must not only be done—it must be seen by all."

The convoy departed with the same ceremony with which it had arrived, leaving guards stationed at the compound's exits.

"Only God can change this course now," Darius said.

"When human systems align against us this completely, divine intervention becomes our only option."

Joseph's fingers found the key again, its edges sharp with possibility and danger. Whatever Hassan had hidden, whatever he'd deemed worth protecting even as he saw his own arrest approaching—it waited behind the walls of a bank Joseph could no longer reach.

The morning sun climbed higher, beating down on the compound that had become their prison—where choosing faith meant choosing danger, where names on a list could destroy families, where building God's house had become an act of sedition.

"We start morning prayers," Joseph announced to the shell-shocked compound. "We continue our work. We continue to build."

The armed guards at the gate shifted their weapons, a casual reminder of the cage bars that now surrounded them. Seven days until their case would be heard. Seven days to understand Hassan's secret. Seven days to find God's intervention in a situation beyond human hope.

Joseph looked at the unfinished chapel, its walls reaching toward heaven like hands in prayer. Seven days until the trial. Seven days to understand Hassan's secret.

He pulled the key from his pocket and held it up to catch the morning light. The numbers on the tag—347-B—seemed to shimmer.

"Ian," he called across the compound. The security chief looked up from his post. "I need to see you. Now."

Joseph turned the key over in his palm one more time, then closed his fist around it.

# THIRTY-ONE

**Messages**

The first stone struck the fence just before sunrise, its impact ringing through the chain-link like a broken bell. Joseph pressed his fingers against the wire, watching six women in black approach through the morning mist, their faces half-hidden by dupattas pulled low. Miriam led them, her hands clutching more stones—each one wrapped in paper, tied with string.

"Please," she called in Urdu, then English. "Please, Joseph sahib."

Another stone cleared the fence, thudding into the dust at Joseph's feet. Then another. And another. The women fanned out along the chain-link, their hands moving in rhythm—stones wrapped in paper, each one landing like a prayer that refused to stay silent.

A guard jogged from the gate, rifle in hand, face hidden behind a mask. "Aray, ruko!" His voice carried weariness more than fury, but the authority in it made the women scatter like startled birds.

Except Miriam.

She stood twenty feet away, eyes locked on Joseph's. She reached beneath her dupatta and drew out a stone, holding it in both hands as if it were an offering. The guard stopped in front of her, gesturing with his rifle still slung, his Urdu too quick for Joseph to catch. He took the stone, turned it over, frowned at the wrapping, then returned it. A curt point toward the village. Go.

Miriam didn't go.

She drew her arm back and hurled the stone high, the arc clean and deliberate. It puffed a cloud of dust three feet from Joseph.

The guard's voice snapped now, angry, but Miriam finally turned away—only after pressing her hand to her heart and extending it toward Joseph. His throat ached.

Behind her, the guard's masked eyes tracked her all the way to the mist's edge.

The paper was rough, torn from a school notebook. The writing cramped, as if the words themselves were painful:

*My husband died alone in his cell yesterday. They would not let me see him. No doctor. No medicine. No last words.*

Joseph's knees weakened. He gripped the fence to stay upright, fingers wrapped tight around the links.

"Joseph?" Ian's voice came from behind. "You need to step back from the fence. You're too exposed there."

Joseph couldn't move. The paper trembled in his hand. "Miriam's husband is dead."

Ian's footsteps approached, crunching on the packed earth. "What?" Genuine shock sharpened his voice. "When? How?"

"Heart failure, according to this." Joseph handed him the paper. "A forty-three-year-old man with no history of heart problems."

Ian read quickly, his face darkening. "Hassan's been in custody for three days." His pale eyes reflected the same calculation Joseph was making. "If they let Amir die rather than appear weak by providing medical care…"

"Which is why you cannot go to the village." Ian's tone shifted from gentle to firm. "I know what you're thinking. That key in your pocket has been burning a hole in your mind since Tariq gave it to you. But Joseph, this is what Faraz wants. You, isolated, vulnerable, away from witnesses."

Joseph pulled out the brass key, its weight familiar now from constant handling. 347-B. Whatever Hassan had hidden, he'd deemed it worth protecting even as he saw his arrest approaching.

"Three of our local workers have already agreed to register," Ian continued, his voice dropping. "They'll testify at the court proceedings about the 'foreign corruption' of Pakistani citizens. The prosecutor is building a case that you're not here for religious freedom but for cultural colonization."

The morning sun climbed higher, burning off the mist. Around them, the compound stirred to life—the small group of international staff who'd come with Joseph from other countries. Their movements were subdued, conversations whispered. The energy that had driven the construction had turned to desperation.

"Maya needs to speak with you," Ian added. "She's in her tent."

Joseph found Maya sitting on her cot, her usually perfect hijab slightly askew, hands wrapped around a cup of tea. Her laptop sat open beside her, the screen showing an email inbox. She looked up as he entered, and he saw she'd been crying.

"They sent another message," she said without

preamble, gesturing at the screen. "The Pakistani Bar Association. If I leave now, voluntarily, I keep my visa status for future entry. If I stay through the muqadma and get deported..." She set down the cup with shaking hands. "I can never practice law in Pakistan again. Never."

Joseph sank onto the cot beside her. "Maya, you should—"

"Don't." Her voice cracked. "Don't tell me to go. Don't make this noble." She pressed her palms against her eyes. "If I leave now, abandon you all when it matters most, what kind of lawyer am I? What kind of Christian?"

Joseph had no answer. The mathematics of suffering didn't balance—stay and lose her life's work, leave and lose her integrity.

"Pray about it." The words cracked in his throat. "God will—"

"Will what?" Maya's laugh was bitter. "Show me a sign? Open a door? Joseph, all the doors are closing. Every single one."

She left him sitting there, staring at the legal files she'd organized so carefully—visa applications, asylum petitions, defense documents for a community that might not exist in four days.

The unfinished chapel drew him like gravity. Its exterior walls were complete, the roof secured, but the interior remained raw—bare studs where wood panels would be installed, empty window frames awaiting glass, the space echoing without furnishings. Inside, the air was cooler, filtered through the open window frames. Joseph sank to his knees on the concrete floor they'd poured just two weeks ago, when the volunteers had stayed past sunset, reluctant to leave.

"Where are You?" The words scraped his throat. "We're

doing everything right. Building Your house. Serving Your people. Where are You?" His voice broke. "Where are You, God. I need You."

The silence was absolute. No whisper of comfort. No sense of presence. Just the distant sound of guards talking at the gate, the occasional hammer strike from workers maintaining equipment they might never use again.

"They killed him." Joseph pressed his fingers against the concrete until they went numb. "They're going to kill Hassan. Faraz—the same man who murdered my parents—he's winning. And You're silent."

His father's Bible lay in his tent, but Joseph couldn't bear to open it. What would be the point? Every promise broken. Every assurance of God's protection rang hollow against Miriam's message, against Hassan in a cell somewhere, against Maya's impossible choice.

"Your parents thought the same thing."

Joseph's head snapped up. Darius stood in the chapel's doorway, his weathered face etched with understanding.

"How long have you been here?" Joseph asked.

"Since before you arrived. I've been praying too." Darius moved into the chapel, his footsteps echoing. "In Tehran, when they arrested my wife, I stood in the ruins of our church and cursed God. She was pregnant." Darius settled beside Joseph on the floor. "Our first child. The guards knew this when they took her. I prayed every prayer I knew. Fasted until I collapsed. Made bargains with God—my life for hers, my freedom for hers." He paused. "She died in custody. The baby too."

"How? How did you keep believing?"

"I almost didn't." Darius's hand found Joseph's shoulder. "But in my lowest moment, when I'd decided God had abandoned us all, an old woman came to my door. She'd walked twelve miles from her village because she'd heard there was a Christian who might have a Bible. Her granddaughter was sick, and she wanted to read her the words of Jesus before she died."

Darius's grip tightened. "I gave her my last Bible. And as I watched her weep with joy over those pages, I understood something. God's silence isn't absence. Sometimes it's His way of asking if we truly believe when we cannot see, cannot hear, cannot feel His presence. Job knew this—'Though he slay me, yet will I hope in Him.' Faith when it costs us everything."

"But Hassan—"

"Is in God's hands. As are we all." Darius stood, offering Joseph a hand up. "Faith isn't the absence of doubt, Joseph. It's choosing to act despite it."

Before Joseph could respond, Tariq burst through the chapel entrance, breathing hard.

"Joseph, you need to see this." He held out a crumpled piece of paper. "I found this near the water station. Someone dropped it."

Joseph smoothed the paper, reading the message written in careful English:

*Meet me at the old water pump station at midnight. My daughter is dying. I spoke to Imran at the fabric shop. He told me what you did for Mr. Darius. What the poison couldn't kill. I know what they did to your parents. I was young, just recruited. I'm sorry. Please come. Please.*

Joseph's pulse quickened. A guard who'd been present during the attack on his parents. Who'd investigated Darius's healing. Who had a dying daughter.

"It's a trap," Tariq said immediately. "It has to be."

"Maybe." Joseph folded the paper. "Or maybe it's an answer to prayer we didn't know we were praying."

"You can't seriously be considering going."

"The drainage tunnel." The thought came suddenly, perfectly formed. "Nadir's team broke through to the old tunnel yesterday."

Tariq's eyes widened. "The tunnel Hassan used to escape when they raided the compound?"

"Yes." Joseph's thoughts raced. "It connects to the original water system. Emerges near the pump station."

"Joseph, this is madness."

But Joseph was already moving, purpose flooding back into his limbs. "Find Marcus. Tell him I need to know the exact route. And Tariq?" He paused at the chapel entrance. "Tell no one else. Not even Ian."

The hours until midnight crawled. Joseph made a show of normalcy—reviewing court documents with Darius, checking on the workers, eating dinner. But his thoughts stayed in that tunnel the day the mission burned, Hassan's hand pulling him through darkness while smoke and screams sounded above.

At 11:30, he slipped into the construction storage area where Marcus waited, visibly uncomfortable.

"The connection is here." Marcus pointed to a grate in the floor. "New drainage pipe runs forty meters, then breaks into the old tunnel. That runs another hundred meters to the original exit."

"You're sure it's clear?"

"We crawled it yesterday to check the connections." Marcus grabbed Joseph's arm. "But sir, this is—"

"Necessary." Joseph pulled free. "If I'm not back by dawn, tell Ian everything."

The grate lifted without a sound. Joseph slid into the pipe, shoulders scraping metal, the air instantly damp and cold. The smell struck like a memory—wet earth, rust, and something ancient, like the breath of a sealed grave.

He crawled on elbows and knees, every movement echoing back at him. His own breath was too loud in the confined space. The beam from the flashlight jittered with each push forward, shadows jumping with each movement.

The forty meters to the old connection stretched endlessly. When his palms finally hit rough stone instead of concrete, the air thickened. Here the tunnel widened enough to crouch, but the walls were grooved—marks left by a chisel. Hassan's chisel. Hassan's escape route.

And just like that, the years collapsed. The same walls. The same damp. Hassan's voice behind him: *Don't look back, young Joseph. Don't look back.*

But he had. He'd seen the orange bloom of fire at the mouth the tunnel. Heard the scream cut short. The heat had driven him deeper into the darkness, turning the stone walls into an oven.

He shook the memory off like smoke, forcing himself forward. The passage curved, dipped, rose. A steady drip of water marked the seconds. Then—cool air on his face. The exit. Freedom. Or so it should have been.

He emerged behind the abandoned pump station, gasping, his clothes soaked with sweat and groundwater. The night air filled his lungs completely for the first time in hours. He stood on shaking legs, orienting himself. The village lay two kilometers to the east, a scatter of lights below.

A flashlight beam hit him full in the face.

Joseph froze. The beam pinned him in place, erasing everything else.

"Don't run." The voice was male, accented English. A figure stepped closer, holding the beam steady.

The light lowered. Something metallic glinted in the man's hand—not a weapon. A radio.

The figure stepped forward into the moonlight.

The uniform registered first. Then the mask. Then the memory—Miriam's defiance, the puff of dust as her last stone landed, the masked eyes tracking her through the mist.

The same guard from this morning.

His rifle slung across his back. In his hand, the radio. His thumb rested on the call button.

"You came," he said flatly. "Good."

The tunnel entrance waited behind Joseph, three steps away. But between him and every other way out stood the guard, alone under the moon.

His thumb pressed. The radio clicked alive.

Static crackled across the night. A voice responded—distant, tinny, demanding a report.

# THIRTY-TWO

**The Torchbearer**

"Back quadrant clear. No movement," the guard said into the radio in rushed Urdu.

Joseph leaned toward the tunnel entrance, knees flexing, ready to slip back into the dark.

Then came a plea in broken English—"My daughter is dying."

He lowered the radio, then his mask. "The fever has taken her mind. She no longer knows her mother's voice." Raw desperation filled his words. Hollow cheeks, sunken eyes—sleepless nights carved into his face. "You healed the Iranian—poison meant to kill him within hours. Please...I need your help." He raised his left hand toward the tree line, two fingers extended. Joseph's chest constricted. This was it —the trap sprung.

But what emerged from the shadows wasn't soldiers.

A boy stepped into the moonlight, rail-thin and angular, all knees and elbows in the way of boys caught between adolescence and manhood. He led two mules by rope halters, their hooves wrapped in rags, almost silent against the rocky ground—the kind of detail that required planning.

"Please help us." The guard's voice cracked on the last word, his composure splintering. The radio trembled in his grip. His mask had slipped down around his neck, revealing a face younger than Joseph expected—maybe thirty-five, with worry carved into every line.

Joseph's mind reeled, trying to reconcile the authority in the uniform with the raw pleading in the man's voice. The rifle across his back caught moonlight as his shoulders shook.

"Baba, we need to go." The boy's voice carried that uncertain pitch between tenor and baritone. His Urdu came out precise but hurried. "Amna said if the fever breaks one more time without staying down—"

"I know what your mother said." The guard rubbed eyes that hadn't seen sleep in days. When he looked back at Joseph, something shifted in his expression. "There's something you need to know. Before you decide."

The night sounds of Pakistan pressed in—crickets, a distant dog, the whisper of wind through the abandoned pump station's rusted fixtures. Joseph waited, his weight balanced between fleeing back to the tunnel and stepping forward into whatever confession was coming.

"I was there." The words landed between them. "The night your parents died. I was there. Only eighteen, just recruited. Faraz Qureshi was our squad leader."

The world tilted. Joseph's breathing came short and sharp. The guard's face floated in the darkness—young, desperate, haunted. But all Joseph could see was fire. Orange flames climbing wooden walls. The crack of gunfire. His mother's scream cutting through smoke.

His knees buckled. He caught himself against the pump station's concrete wall, his palms scraping rough stone.

Fifteen years. Fifteen years of nightmares, of waking with the taste of smoke in his mouth, jumping at the sound of crackling wood. And this man—this father pleading for his daughter's life—had been there. Had watched it happen.

"I held the torch." The guard's voice. "Not the one that started the fire—but I held a torch. Watched the flames climb the schoolhouse. Heard the—" He stopped, swallowing hard. "Your father had no weapon. He looked right at me—at a boy with a torch—and he said, 'I forgive you.'"

Joseph's hands began to shake. The memory rushed back with devastating clarity—not the fire itself, he'd been pulled away too quickly—but the moment before. His father's face in the doorway, calm and resolved. His mother's warm tears running across his cheeks.

"No." The word tore from Joseph's throat. "No, you can't—"

The guard's voice rose, then dropped again as he glanced toward the distant lights of a patrol route. "You need to know who's asking for your help."

The mules shifted restlessly, one pawing at the ground despite its muffled hooves. The boy tugged the lead rope, his eyes darting between his father and Joseph.

"I see him," the guard continued, his hand moving unconsciously to his chest. "Every night. Your father. Standing there with flames behind him and forgiveness in his eyes. And then Faraz..." He made a sharp gesture. "The sound of the shot. Your father fell forward, his arms spread wide."

Joseph slid down the wall until he sat on the ground, his head in his hands. The compound. The upcoming trial. Hassan's imprisonment. All of it suddenly felt small compared to this moment—sitting in the darkness with the man who'd helped murder his parents.

"Baba, what are you talking about?" The boy's voice cracked. "What fire?"

His father kept his eyes locked on Joseph. "Please. I'm not asking for myself. I'm asking for my daughter. For her mother and brother."

A vehicle engine growled in the distance. The guard's head snapped toward the sound, his entire body shifting into professional alertness. "The patrol is early." He gestured sharply at his son. "Take him into the trees. Now."

The boy moved to Joseph, gently touching his shoulder. "Follow me."

Joseph looked up. The boy's face was pale, pleading. What was his crime? What was his sister's? They'd done nothing.

Joseph pushed himself to his feet.

The boy led Joseph and the mules into the shadows. The guard adjusted his rifle, becoming once again the competent security officer on his rounds.

Headlights swept across the ground. Joseph pressed against the cold concrete, the boy tense beside him. One of the mules snorted softly, and the boy's hand gently stroked its muzzle.

"Salaam, Naveed." A voice called from the vehicle. "Anything suspicious in this section."

"Rat droppings and tetanus waiting to happen," Naveed said. "Nothing worth reporting."

Laughter from the vehicle. Some joke in Pashto that Joseph couldn't follow. Then the engine revved, tires crunching gravel as the patrol moved on.

Naveed waited until the sound faded completely before calling softly, "They're gone."

Joseph and the boy emerged from shadow. The mules followed, restless. Naveed pulled his radio again, checking in with another sector, maintaining his cover. Every movement careful, calculated. A man walking a tightrope between duty and desperation.

"Your shift supervisor," Joseph said, surprised by how steady his voice was. "When does he check this sector?"

"Not until dawn prayer. Maybe five-thirty." Naveed glanced at his watch. "I volunteered for this section. Nobody wants it, so we're safe until my shift ends at noon."

Twelve hours to reach the village, heal a child if God granted it, and get to the bank when it opened. If this wasn't a trap. If Faraz wasn't waiting. If he could find the strength to help the daughter of the man who'd helped kill his parents.

"Baba." The boy's voice carried weight beyond his years. "Amna sent me with the mules because she said you'd know what to do. But I don't understand—"

"Later, Kamran." Naveed's voice softened. "Right now, your sister needs him."

Kamran stood holding the mules with the same steady competence Joseph remembered in Hassan. Hassan, who was probably dead by now. Hassan, whose final gift was a brass key and a desperate instruction: *Everything depends on it.*

"How do I know?" Joseph asked. "How do I know this isn't exactly what Faraz planned? Use a sick child to draw me out?"

Naveed's hand dropped to his sidearm. The leather holster creaked as he thumbed the release. Metal scraped against leather—slow, deliberate. The pistol came free.

Joseph's breath stopped. Here it was.

But Naveed reversed the weapon, extending it grip-first

across the space between them. His hand shook, not with fear but with something rawer.

"Take it." Naveed thrust the pistol closer, forcing Joseph to either accept or step back. "If this is a trap—if I'm lying about my daughter—you can kill my son before being taken." His eyes glinted wet in the moonlight. "But if I'm telling the truth, then for the love of God, go to my home with Kamran. My daughter won't last until sunrise."

"Take it!" Naveed's voice broke completely. "Take it and decide—am I a father or a liar? But decide now."

Joseph stared at the weapon. The pistol's weight would be heavier than expected, he knew. Like the brass key in his pocket. Like the choice he faced—help the child of one of his parents' killer, or let her die for her father's sins.

He heard his father's voice, impossibly clear across fifteen years—*I forgive you.*

"I won't need it." The certainty in Joseph's words surprised him. "It's in God's hands now."

Naveed's shoulders sagged with relief. He holstered the weapon, then looked directly at Joseph. "Your father—what he said to me—I've never forgotten. Not one night in fifteen years."

"Then help me understand," Joseph said. "When your daughter is well and I return with your son. Help me understand what happened that night."

Naveed nodded once, sharply.

Kamran led one of the mules closer. "This one's gentler," he said, his English careful and formal. "Her name is Gulnar. It means—"

"Pomegranate flower." The memory surfaced unexpectedly. His mother had taught him the names of flowers in four languages, preparation that fire had ended.

The boy's face brightened. "You speak Pashto?"

"Pieces. Fragments." Joseph approached the mule carefully. "From before."

Kamran's hand extended just as Hassan's had that fateful night. Joseph took it and let himself be helped onto the mule's back. The saddle was worn smooth by use, and Gulnar stood patiently as he settled himself.

"The paths we'll take," Kamran said, mounting his own mule with fluid ease, "they're not on maps. Smuggler routes, some of them. Others are just animal tracks the villages have used for generations."

"Your father taught you these?"

Something passed across the boy's face. "My uncle, actually. My father's brother. He was..." A pause. "He traded things. Before he died."

Naveed stepped closer, his hand going to his son's knee. "Kamran knows the way better than anyone. He'll get you there safely, Joseph." His voice dropped. "May I call you Joseph?"

Joseph nodded. "After your daughter, I need to get to the Bank of Khyber branch in the village. It opens at eight."

Naveed's eyes narrowed. He rubbed his chin. "Hassan's business?"

Joseph's hand instinctively went to his pocket, feeling the key's outline. "You know about Hassan?"

"Faraz has been very thorough in his briefings. He's mentioned your 'accomplice' several times." Naveed glanced at his son. "Take the back paths from our home to the village. Then once he's finished his business, bring him back here before noon."

"We must go," Kamran said. "We must go now."

Naveed stepped back, his hand falling to his radio. "Faraz Qureshi isn't the angry young man who burned your mission. He's methodical now. Patient. He's been waiting fifteen years to finish what he started."

The radio crackled—someone checking another sector. Naveed responded automatically in Urdu, his professional mask sliding back into place even as his eyes remained on his son.

"Go," he said. "Take the path behind the abandoned kiln first. And Kamran?" He switched to Pashto, the words rapid and urgent. The boy nodded, his jaw tightening.

"What did you tell him?" Joseph asked the boy as they began to move.

Kamran glanced back, his young face grave in the moonlight. "He said to remember that Allah sees all paths, even in darkness."

*The light shines in darkness,* Joseph thought. *Always had. Always would.*

The mules' cloth-wrapped hooves found purchase on the path Joseph could barely see. Behind them, the compound faded into shadow, and ahead, the path rose with the hills.

Somewhere ahead, a young girl burned with fever. Somewhere ahead, Hassan's safety deposit box waited with contents that might save them all. And somewhere in the darkness between here and the village, Faraz Qureshi's network watched and waited.

But for now, there was only the rhythm of the mules' gait, the breathing of the boy who guided them, and the fading sound of a father's radio check-ins—maintaining the illusion that nothing had changed, that no boundaries had been crossed, that salvation wasn't riding through the darkness on muffled hooves toward a dying child's bedside and Hassan's secrets.

# PART IV

# THIRTY-THREE

### The Torchbearer's Daughter

The mules found their rhythm on the narrow mountain path, hoofbeats muffled against stone, echoing Joseph's thundering heart. His mount swayed beneath him with each careful step, her breathing steady and warm in the pre-dawn cold. Beside him, Kamran rode in tense silence, guiding them through switchbacks that disappeared into shadow.

Joseph gripped the worn leather reins while his mind drifted fifteen years back. *I was there. I held the torch.* Naveed's words circled like vultures, picking at wounds Joseph thought had healed. The guard's face—young, desperate, haunted—overlaid every memory of that night. How many others had there been? How many boys with torches, following orders, watching Joseph's world burn?

The mountain air bit sharp and clean, but Joseph tasted phantom smoke. Not from Naveed's torch—that was fifteen years buried—but the memory of ash coating his throat as Hassan pulled him through the escape tunnel. His mother's scream cut through the chaos above.

*"Your father looked right at me—and said, 'I forgive you.'"*

Even facing death, even watching his life's work consumed by flames, his father had chosen forgiveness over hatred. But forgiveness didn't mean walking blindly into danger for those who had destroyed everything he loved.

His mule jerked on loose shale, bringing Joseph back to the present. The path had narrowed to single file along a ridge dropping away into blackness. Brilliant stars wheeled overhead.

"How much farther?" Joseph whispered.

Kamran glanced back, his face pale in starlight. "Through the hills and away from the main road where Faraz's men patrol, an hour." His eyes studied Joseph. "You're afraid."

Heat flushed Joseph's cheeks. Was he that transparent?

"Aren't you?" Joseph asked.

"Of getting caught? Surely." Kamran's shoulders lifted. "But that's not what I see in your face. You look like my mother when she prays for my sister and wonders if Allah is listening."

The observation struck home. Was his faith so shallow that a teenage boy could read his doubt so easily?

They rounded another switchback. Below, scattered lights marked the village—where Hassan's secrets waited in a safety deposit box, and where a dying child needed healing Joseph wasn't sure he could give.

"Your sister," Joseph said, grasping for safer ground. "How long has she been ill?"

"Three days." Kamran's voice dropped. "Fever started Tuesday. By Wednesday, she couldn't keep water down. Yesterday..." His hands tightened on the reins. "She stopped recognizing us. Looked right at me and asked who I was."

Joseph's breath caught. Seven years old. About the same

age as Lily Carter when diabetes took hold. The same desperate love he'd seen in her father Nathan now echoed in this Muslim boy's voice.

"You don't think God will heal her?"

Kamran's mule picked its way around a boulder. "My mother's prayers to Allah haven't helped—three days of begging Him to take the fever." Bitterness sharpened his words. "What makes your prayers different?"

The question that had haunted Joseph his entire ministry. What made his praying, his laying on of hands special? What gave him the right to claim God's power when so many faithful people prayed without effect?

"Nothing makes my prayers different," Joseph said. "It's who I'm praying to. Jesus Christ suffered and died so we could receive healing—body, soul, and spirit. The prophet Isaiah wrote, 'By His stripes we are healed.'"

Kamran's laugh was sharp. "Jesus. Always Jesus with you Christians." He guided his mule around fallen branches. "We've prayed to Allah for three days. If He wanted Ayesha healed, wouldn't He have done it already?"

Something stirred in Joseph—not the warmth of healing, but something deeper. The call to witness.

"What if Jesus was who He said He was?" Warmth entered Joseph's voice. "God in human flesh, come to bridge the gap between heaven and earth? When healing comes through my hands, it's His suffering at work."

Kamran stayed quiet as the path began descending toward the valley where Naveed's village nestled between protective hills. Silence stretched between them. The boy was obviously thinking.

"But why doesn't He heal everyone?" Kamran asked. "Why do children still die while others live?"

The eternal question. "I don't know," Joseph admitted.

"But I've learned that sometimes the greatest healing isn't physical at all."

"What do you mean?"

Joseph thought of Nathan Carter, whose daughter's healing had led him to faith. "Your father helped destroy everything I loved. I should hate him. But that's not what Jesus did—He forgave the soldiers crucifying Him. He chose love even when love meant death."

Village lights grew closer, individual windows glowing like earthbound stars. Somewhere in one of those houses, a mother sat beside her dying daughter.

"You really believe this," Kamran said.

"With everything I am."

"Even though you're afraid?"

Joseph's smile surprised him. "Faith isn't the absence of fear. It's choosing to trust God despite it."

They entered the village outskirts, mud-brick houses pressing close. Kamran raised his hand, signaling caution. "Faraz has informants here. If anyone sees us together..." He left the threat unfinished.

"What would happen?" Joseph needed to understand the stakes clearly.

"Best case? They drag us to the district office for questioning." Kamran's voice was grim. "Worst case? Faraz decides you're too dangerous to leave alive, and anyone who helped you was obviously a traitor to Islam."

Weight settled on Joseph's shoulders. "Your family—"

"I knew the risks when Baba sent me." Kamran guided them between two houses, mules' hooves silent on packed earth. "But people here see Christians as invaders. They remember the British, Americans in Afghanistan. They think you come to steal children's minds."

"And what do you think?"

Kamran was quiet as they navigated narrow alleyways, taking a circuitous route toward his home. When he spoke, his voice carried new possibility. "I think a man who risks his life to heal his enemy's daughter might be different than the stories say."

A single oil lamp appeared ahead, burning in a window. Kamran straightened, tension radiating through his frame.

"That's our house." His whisper was barely audible. "There's a back entrance through the courtyard—less visible from the street. If we need to run, the old goat path behind the house leads to the hills. Twenty minutes of hard climbing reaches a cave where we can hide."

Joseph's heart hammered. Minutes from now, he would face the test that defined his calling. Could he touch the fevered skin of his enemy's child and let compassion flow instead of judgment?

"Kamran," Joseph said as they approached. "Will you pray with me?"

The boy's surprise showed in his stiffened posture. "To your God?"

"To the God who loves your sister. You don't have to believe yet—but will you listen? Will you open your heart to possibility?"

Kamran sat frozen—torn, Joseph guessed, between ancestral faith and desperate hope. Then, slowly, he nodded.

They dismounted in shadow, tethering mules to a wooden post. Joseph heard movement inside—soft footsteps, a woman's murmured prayers. The lamp flickered.

Joseph placed his hand on Kamran's shoulder. "Father God, we come as Your children. You know the pain in this house, the fear in this mother's heart." Peace settled over him, and his voice strengthened. "Jesus, by Your stripes we are healed. Let Your power flow where death threatens, let victory reign where despair rules."

The words settled into the space between them like seeds finding soil, fragile but full of potential.

"Amen," Joseph whispered.

Kamran hesitated, then echoed softly, "Amen."

From inside came labored breathing punctuated by a mother's soft weeping.

"If your Jesus heals my sister," Kamran whispered, "what does that mean for me?"

Joseph saw the hunger in the boy's face—the same hunger he'd seen in Nathan Carter, in Darius, in every person who'd encountered the reality of Christ's power. "It means everything changes," Joseph said. "Your life. Your family. Your understanding of who God is."

The words hung between them. Joseph thought of his own life—how healing Lily Carter had changed everything, how returning to Pakistan had changed everything, how this moment would change everything.

The door creaked open, revealing a lamplit hallway. A mother's broken lullaby drifted toward them, a sound of love refusing to surrender even as hope died.

Joseph stepped across the threshold. The smell hit him first—fever sweat, sickness, desperation. The warmth of the house after the mountain cold. The golden light from oil lamps casting shadows that danced on mud-brick walls.

He was in the heart of his enemy's home.

Behind him, Kamran followed, his breathing quick and shallow.

A woman appeared in the hallway—Naveed's wife, her face drawn with sleepless nights, her dupatta slipping from hair that hadn't been combed in days. Her eyes met Joseph's, and in them he saw what every parent feels when their child is dying: terror, hope, and a willingness to try anything.

She didn't speak. Just stepped aside, gesturing toward a room where lamplight flickered.

Joseph walked forward, each step a choice. To heal or not to heal. To forgive or to hold onto righteous anger. To be his father's son, or to be something less.

From the room came the sound of labored breathing, a child's fever-ravaged body fighting a battle it was losing.

Joseph entered the room, and saw her.

# THIRTY-FOUR

### The Box

"Amma?"

The word—soft, confused, perfectly clear—shattered three days of vigil. Ayesha's mother gasped, her trembling hand flying to her daughter's forehead.

"The fever," she whispered in Pashto, tears already streaming. "Kamran, the fever—it's gone!"

Joseph lifted his palm from the child's forehead, fingers still tingling with the strange electricity that always followed these moments. Ayesha blinked up at him, no longer wild and unseeing, just a seven-year-old girl confused about why everyone was crying.

Her mother collapsed against her, sobbing into the thin blanket. Kamran stood frozen in the doorway, his young face caught between awe and terror.

"We should go," Joseph said, familiar urgency already building in his chest. Word of the healing would spread—it always did—and with it would come danger. In this part of Pakistan, miracles drew crowds, and crowds drew attention from the curious and those who wanted harm to come to him.

They moved swiftly through the pre-dawn darkness, and by the time dawn light colored the eastern sky, Kamran was guiding their mules through narrow back streets. Somewhere a rooster cried out, answered by the far-off bark of a stray dog. He hadn't spoken much since they'd left his home, his sister sitting up and sipping broth, his mother keeping watch from the doorway with tears tracking silent paths down her face.

Kamran broke the silence as they rounded a corner. "My sister. The fever left her the moment you touched her forehead." He glanced back at Joseph, wonder and unease shifting across his features. "What kind of power is this?"

Joseph flexed his fingers against the familiar tingling. How could he explain a gift he'd carried since childhood? "It wasn't my power. Jesus Christ healed your sister."

Kamran shook his head slowly, trying to dislodge a stubborn thought. "I have prayed for my sister for three days. My father has wept before Allah, begging for her healing." He whispered, "But when you touched her..." He trailed off, searching for words that didn't exist.

"Jesus Christ healed her," Joseph said with conviction. "Him and Him alone."

The boy fell silent again, but Joseph could see more questions building behind his eyes—questions about faith and power, about Jesus Christ. They were the same questions that had flooded his good friend Nathan Carter after the same healing power brought his daughter Lily back to life three years ago.

Kamran's gaze lingered, troubled, dealing with a truth that could split his world in two.

They turned another corner and the squat, concrete

structure of the Bank of Khyber came into view. The street was empty except for a shopkeeper rolling up metal shutters and a lone dog picking through yesterday's trash. The bank's heavy iron gate still hung with a padlock, but through the barred windows, Joseph saw movement—a man in a crisp white shalwar kameez unlocking cabinets.

"The manager," Kamran whispered. "He will open in ten minutes." He led their mules into a narrow alley beside the bank, tethering them to a drainpipe.

Joseph's hand went to his pocket, feeling Hassan's key through the fabric. From the mouth of the alley, he scanned the square. The shopkeeper now dragged a crate into place, its wooden base scraping against stone. A bicycle bell chimed somewhere behind him, followed by the soft patter of bare feet on dust. The air smelled faintly of diesel, probably from an unseen generator.

A man in a grey cap passed along the far side of the street, glancing toward the bank before disappearing around the corner. The hairs on Joseph's arms rose—the prickling sense of being watched.

Kamran shifted beside the mules, scanning the street with a boy's wide-eyed vigilance that tried hard to be a man's composure. Joseph nodded once, more to steady himself than to signal readiness.

"Joseph-sahib. He is opening the door now."

Through the alley's mouth, Joseph watched the manager throw back the iron gate with a clang that echoed in the empty street. He adjusted his glasses, checked his watch, then disappeared inside, leaving the door ajar.

"Now," Joseph said, pushing away from the wall. "Before others come."

Kamran nodded, his eyes darting up and down the street. "I will stand watch here. If anyone comes—"

"If anyone comes, you leave," Joseph interrupted. "Don't risk yourself."

Kamran's chin jutted forward. "My father trusts me to bring you back safely. I will not fail him."

The bank's interior smelled of floor polish and paper. The manager looked up from behind his desk, surprise registering on his face at the sight of a foreigner entering his bank so early.

"Salaam alaikum," Joseph greeted him, trying to keep his voice steady despite the urgency drumming through his veins.

"Waalaikum salaam." The manager's response was automatic, though his eyes narrowed. "The bank is not yet officially open, sir."

"I understand, and I apologize for the intrusion." Joseph approached the desk, withdrawing Hassan's key from his pocket. "I need to access a safety deposit box. It's urgent."

The manager studied the key, then Joseph's face. "Your identification papers, please."

Joseph produced his passport. The manager—his nameplate read "Saleem Khan"—compared the photo to Joseph's face, the wall clock's second hand crawling past the twelve, then the one, then the two. Joseph's shirt clung to his damp back.

"You are American?" the manager asked, looking up from the passport.

"Yes."

"And this key is registered to...?"

"Hassan Awan," Joseph replied, his mouth suddenly dry. "He entrusted it to me before his..." He hesitated, unsure how much to reveal. "Before he was detained."

Something passed across Saleem's face—recognition,

perhaps, or concern. He rose from his desk without further questions. "This way, please."

The vault room was small, its walls lined with metal boxes of varying sizes. Fluorescent bulbs hummed overhead. The manager inserted his master key first, then motioned for Joseph to use Hassan's. The lock turned with a solid click that seemed to echo in the small space.

"I will give you privacy," the manager said, stepping back. "Please return to the desk when you are finished."

Once alone, Joseph pulled out the heavy metal drawer labeled 347-B. Inside lay a leather portfolio, worn soft with age, secured with a simple string tie. His hands trembled slightly as he undid the binding. On top lay a handwritten note in Hassan's careful script:

*These papers belonged to William Freeman. He prepared them to present to the Pakistani Assembly the morning after that terrible day. I have kept them safe all these years, waiting for the right time to use them. What was silenced by violence must now be heard through you.*

Joseph's throat tightened. He lifted the note to find a formal petition beneath, the letterhead showing the official seal of the Pakistani government. The date in the corner read August 13, 2010—two days before his father died.

The petition was meticulous—page after page of evidence his father had compiled. Joseph's breath caught as he examined the detailed documentation:

First came a catalog of harassment incidents, including sworn eyewitness accounts from former militants who had converted to Christianity after encountering his father's work. Their testimonies named specific TLP members who had threatened the mission.

Next, he found several grainy photographs from 2010, showing a younger, unscarred Faraz directing men with torches outside the mission walls. Joseph's hands shook as he stared at the face of the man who would later kill his parents—the same man who now hunted him as an FIA director.

One section specifically documented "Faraz Qureshi, age 20, son of merchant Muhammad Qureshi" as organizing efforts to intimidate Christian converts. Police reports filed and officially acknowledged, yet never investigated. The photographs showed shattered glass, scrawl of hate-filled graffiti.

But his father had documented more than persecution. Medical records showed hundreds of Muslim patients treated at the clinic without charge, many with William Freeman's signature on their charts. School enrollment forms listed Muslim children learning alongside Christians, their parents' signatures attesting to trust that transcended religious boundaries. The petition painted a portrait not just of a man under threat, but of a community that had flourished under his care—a community someone was determined to destroy.

Joseph's vision blurred as he turned the pages. The final section bore the heading "Request for Immediate Protection" and detailed intelligence that an attack was imminent. His father had known. He had tried to prevent it through proper channels.

Behind the petition lay a folder labeled "Presentation Notes." Joseph opened it to find his father's handwriting, the same slanting script he remembered from childhood birthday cards. The notes were clearly meant for an oral presentation, with key points underlined and parenthetical reminders about pacing and emphasis.

One passage had been highlighted in yellow, set apart from the rest—

*"I stand before you not as a foreigner seeking special treatment, but as someone who believes in Pakistan's founding principles. As Muhammad Ali Jinnah himself declared in 1947—'You are free; you are free to go to your temples, you are free to go to your mosques or to any other place of worship in this State of Pakistan. You may belong to any religion or caste or creed — that has nothing to do with the business of the State.' I ask only that this promise be honored—not just for me and my family, but for all Pakistanis who wish to worship according to their conscience."*

Joseph's hands shook as he read his father's words—words that had never been spoken, arguments never presented, truth silenced by bullets and flame. The pain struck him like a physical blow, doubling him over the small table.

At the back of the portfolio, one final document made Joseph's breath catch: a confirmation letter on government stationery.

*Meeting with Assembly Committee for Minority Affairs*
*Date: August 15, 2010, 10:00 AM*
*Petitioner: William Freeman*
*Matter: Urgent Request for Protection Order*

His father had been killed the day before this meeting.

Then Joseph turned the page and found something that made his heart stutter. At the bottom of the petition, thirty-two signatures of Muslim neighbors who supported protection for the mission. Many names he recognized—people still living in the village. But one name stood out like a shout —"Attestation witnessed by Asim Qadir, Assistant Magistrate."

The same Asim Qadir who now served as Deputy Commissioner. The same man who had been working with Faraz against Joseph's mission. The same official who had signed Hassan's arrest order.

Beneath these documents lay a sealed envelope marked in his father's handwriting: "To be opened only if petition fails." Joseph's fingers traced the faded ink and the imprint of his father's pen. With reverent care, he broke the seal.

*If you are reading this, then my hopes for justice through proper channels have failed. I do not know who will find these words or when. Perhaps it will be Hassan, faithful friend that he is. Perhaps a stranger with courage enough to speak truth.*

*Know that I seek no revenge. But truth must survive even if we do not. I forgive those who harm us, but forgiveness does not mean silence. Speak truth. Demand justice. But always with love.*

*For whoever carries this burden forward—Pakistan was founded on principles of religious freedom and equality. Do not let the dream of Jinnah die with those who defend it. The mission is not about buildings but about hearts. Whatever structures fall, rebuild them. Whatever names are forgotten, remember them. Whatever lights are extinguished, rekindle them.*

*With abiding hope,*

*William Freeman*

The paper trembled in Joseph's hands. These weren't just documents—they were his father's last testament, his final sermon interrupted by violence but preserved by love.

The sudden pounding of footsteps broke the sacred moment. The door flew open, and Kamran burst into the vault room, his face flushed with panic.

"Joseph-sahib! We must go now!" He whispered urgently. "Three vehicles just entered the village square—they're asking about strangers at the bank!" He grabbed Joseph's arm. "One of Faraz's spies must have seen you come in. They know you're here!"

Joseph's mind raced. He had seconds to decide. The portfolio represented evidence that could change everything at the muqadma—proof that his father had followed every legal channel, that the authorities had been warned, that Faraz had been identified as a threat years before he murdered William Freeman.

But it was also dangerous. The Muslim neighbors who had signed in support could face retaliation. Qadir's signature proved he once stood for justice before turning against it—a revelation that would either shame him into helping or drive him to destroy all evidence.

"Joseph-sahib, please!" Kamran's voice broke with fear. "My father trusted me with your safety. If we don't leave now, they will kill us both."

# THIRTY-FIVE

## The Whirlwind

"Move! Now!"

Kamran's hiss cut through the morning air as the metal door clanged shut behind them. He seized Joseph's elbow, pulling him toward the waiting mules with desperate strength.

Joseph clutched the leather portfolio against his chest— thirty-two signatures that could either save his mission or sign their death warrants. His boots kicked loose gravel as he stumbled forward.

Behind them, the shouting swelled. Heavy boots hammered across marble.

"They're coming," Joseph whispered, mounting his mule with fumbling haste. The animal snorted, ears flicking back at the tension in his grip.

Kamran was already astride, reins tight. "Follow me. Stay low. Three blocks to the old market road, then we climb."

They plunged into a maze of alleys. The morning call to prayer rose over the rooftops. Kamran used the sound as cover—sliding forward during the louder phrases, freezing in shadow when the voice softened.

They wound between shuttered shops and homes. Joseph's mule stumbled on uneven stone, nearly pitching him sideways. Every doorway was a threat, every shadow a possible betrayal. Sweat trickled down Joseph's spine despite the morning chill.

"There," Kamran pointed as they emerged from a narrow passage. "The market road."

The dirt track stretched upward into the foothills. Between them and its beginning lay fifty bare yards of open ground under the morning light.

A truck engine roared behind them.

"We must hurry," Kamran said.

They broke from cover, mules kicking up dust. Joseph's breath came sharp and quick.

*How many will die if they find me here?*

They reached the market road as vehicles swung around the corner—three pickup trucks crammed with armed men.

"They've seen us!" Joseph shouted.

"The first ridge is two miles ahead—" A rifle cracked, cutting Kamran's words short. Dust exploded inches from Joseph's mule's hooves. She shrieked, lurching sideways.

They drove the animals harder. Engines growled below, the trucks eating distance on the easier ground. The trail steepened. Joseph's mount labored beneath him, sides heaving. More gunfire echoed, closer now. A bullet whined off rock to their left.

Joseph hunched lower in the saddle, making himself small. His hands ached from gripping the reins. The portfolio shifted against his chest—he pressed one hand against it, holding it secure.

"There," Kamran called over the wind. "The boulder field—it will hide our escape."

Massive stones rose ahead like sleeping giants, the trail snaking between them. Joseph didn't hesitate—capture meant death.

They plunged into the maze. Hoofbeats echoed strangely, sound bouncing off the stone. The shouts behind grew fainter, disoriented by the terrain. Hope flickered.

Then came the engines ahead.

"No," Kamran breathed, reining in hard.

Through the gaps Joseph saw another convoy climbing from the opposite side. The trucks had split.

"The pass," Kamran pointed toward a thin blade of rock high on the slope. "It's our only way out—but it's narrow, and if they get men above it…"

Joseph's mouth went dry. Staying meant certain capture.

Boots scraped on stone behind them. Radios crackled with voices calling coordinates. Ahead, the second convoy shifted into position to seal the exit.

They were caught between two forces.

"What now?" Joseph whispered, the sound swallowed by the rocks.

Kamran's gaze swept from the pass to the soldiers, then fixed on Joseph. His dark eyes burned—not just with fear, but with something raw and searching.

"When you healed my sister," he said, voice low, "you told me your Jesus has power over death."

The boots were closing in.

"Yes," Joseph said.

Kamran leaned closer, the words almost lost in the wind. "Then ask him to save us."

Joseph closed his eyes. "Father, if you're listening?"

———

A low rumble answered Joseph from beyond the thorny acacia branches overhead. It swelled into a moan. The scent of rain followed—impossible, after months without a drop in this canyon. Then the wind rose, scouring the dry earth and whipping dust into the air. Within moments, a massive whirlwind formed, twisting skyward, a churning column of grit and shadow that swallowed the sun.

Kamran pressed himself against the rock. "Subhan Allah!" he gasped.

The dust storm exploded outward, turning the narrow canyon into a chaotic brown swirl. Grit chafed Joseph's face. Shouts erupted from their pursuers as visibility dropped to zero. Engines revved frantically. Confusion grew in their voices. Orders were barked in multiple directions. Men called out that they couldn't see.

Joseph grabbed Kamran's arm. "Let's go."

They fought through the whirlwind. Sharp stones cut through the thin soles of Joseph's worn boots. The mules followed obediently, even as the world disappeared around them. Joseph's lungs burned with each breath of dust-laden air. But he pressed forward, one hand on his mule's rein, the other clutching the precious documents.

Behind them, the sounds of pursuit faded. Engines stalled. Men shouted in frustration and fury, their voices growing distant as Joseph and Kamran pushed deeper into the dust-shielded trail.

The storm lasted exactly long enough.

As they emerged onto a ridge overlooking the valley, the

whirlwind dissipated as suddenly as it had come. The dust settled in gentle spirals, revealing a landscape transformed. The scent of sun-baked earth mingled with sharp ozone. Below, pickup trucks lay scattered and disoriented, some coughing weak sputters as dust-choked carburetors starved their engines. Their occupants clambered out, shielding their eyes and gathering in small groups to assess the damage.

"The wind..." Kamran gestured toward the now-peaceful canyon where their pursuers struggled with mechanical problems. "It came from nowhere. And it lasted just long enough for us to escape."

"He always hears," Joseph said. "And He never fails."

They rode in silence for several minutes, the animals picking their way down the rocky slope. Pebbles scattered beneath hooves, tumbling into shadowed crevices. Joseph adjusted the portfolio, now tucked tightly between his belt and belly.

The truth from Hassan's box weighed on him. He'd been face-to-face with his parents' killer—or at least the man who'd directed their murder. Faraz Qureshi had organized the attack on the mission. The photographs proved it. This man now wore a government uniform and had the authority to shut Joseph down.

Had Faraz personally killed his parents? Or just ordered it done? Joseph's hand moved unconsciously to his chin, remembering Faraz's scar. Was that mark somehow connected to that night? A burn from the flames? Something else?

The photographs imposed themselves over recent memories. The youthful zealot in those grainy images and the composed Qureshi were the same man, separated only by time and calculation. Joseph had looked into those eyes without knowing they had watched his parents die.

His skin crawled. His father's final letter pressed against his stomach through the portfolio. *I forgive those who harm us, but forgiveness does not mean silence.* Could Joseph forgive the man who'd orchestrated his parents' deaths? Who now sought to destroy everything Joseph had rebuilt?

The evidence he carried could expose Faraz, reveal Qadir's hypocrisy, and potentially shift the court in his favor. But using it would put thirty-two Muslim supporters at risk —people who had stood with his father when it was dangerous.

Joseph's mind raced with possibilities. He could present everything at the muqadma, naming Faraz Qureshi as his parents' killer. Or approach Qadir privately, leverage the documents for protection. Release them to international media, creating outside pressure. Or follow his father's example—seeking justice through proper channels while preparing for failure.

These documents were more than evidence—they were a torch passed from father to son. But how could he carry it without being consumed by its fire?

Kamran's gaze rested on him. "The healing. What you did for my sister. I've never seen anything like it."

"It wasn't me. Jesus healed your sister. I was just available."

"But how?" Kamran's voice carried curiosity, not skepticism. "In Islam, we believe Allah can heal, but this was different. When you put your hands on her, I felt something in the room. Peace, but also—power."

Joseph's pulse quickened. "Tell me what you know about Jesus."

Kamran shifted in his saddle. His mule snorted and

shook its head. "He was a prophet. A good man who taught love and peace. Muslims honor him, but..." He trailed off.

"But?" Joseph prompted.

"But you pray to him. You ask him for things. And he answers." Kamran's brow furrowed. "How can a dead prophet heal my sister and send wind to save us?"

"That's the heart of everything that happened today, Kamran. Jesus isn't dead."

Pulling the reins, Kamran stopped his mule. "What do you mean?"

"Jesus died on a cross, yes. But three days later, he rose from the dead. He conquered death." Joseph watched Kamran's face. "That's why he has power to heal your sister, to answer prayers. He's alive."

"Alive?" Kamran's voice dropped.

"Alive and wanting a relationship with every person He created." Joseph pulled his mule to a stop beside a small stream winding between weathered boulders. Crystal-clear water bubbled over smooth stones.

"That's what separates Christianity from every other religion, Kamran. It's not about following rules or earning paradise. It's about knowing God personally."

Kamran dismounted and knelt by the stream. He cupped water, drank, then splashed his face, washing away dust and sweat. He looked up, water trembling on his chin, his eyes a mirror of longing—and fear. "But how? How does someone know God?"

Emotion swelled in Joseph's chest. The question every evangelist longed to hear. He dismounted slowly, kneeling beside Kamran at the water's edge. Coolness rose from the stream.

"One of Jesus's followers spoke to a crowd who had just

realized they needed forgiveness. They asked the same question you just did."

"What did he tell them?"

Joseph closed his eyes, recalling familiar words. "'Repent, and be baptized every one of you in the name of Jesus Christ for the remission of sins, and you shall receive the gift of the Holy Spirit.'"

Kamran's brow furrowed. "I don't understand."

"Repent means to turn away from your sins and move toward God."

"Like asking forgiveness?"

"More than that. It's a complete change of heart. It's living for God instead of living for yourself." Joseph picked up a smooth stone. "Baptism is being immersed in water to outwardly express you are living for Jesus."

Kamran's eyes widened. "You go under the water?"

"Completely. It represents dying to the old life and being born again."

"And then?"

"God forgives every sin. Jesus paid the price when he died on the cross. And God's Spirit—the Holy Spirit—lives inside you, guiding, comforting, empowering you."

Kamran stared at the water. "The same Spirit that healed my sister?"

"The very same. The same Spirit that sent that whirlwind to protect us." Joseph met Kamran's gaze. "That's what you felt in the room. God's presence."

They remounted and continued toward the compound. Kamran kept touching his chest, as if trying to hold onto that moment. His jaw moved constantly, chewing over words he couldn't say.

The path wound through wild pomegranates, their

twisted branches heavy with unripe fruit. The bitter, green scent filled the air.

Finally, Kamran spoke. "My father would disown me."

Joseph's chest tightened. "Possibly."

"My brothers would consider me dead. They might try to kill me—to restore family honor."

"That's happened to others who've made this choice."

Kamran gazed into the distance. A hawk circled overhead, its cry sharp and lonely. "I'd lose everything—my inheritance, place in the community, a respectable marriage."

Joseph steadied his breath. "Jesus said following him sometimes means losing what you value."

"Everything I am is being my father's son." Kamran gripped the reins. "If I'm not that—who am I?"

"You'd be God's son. He never rejects you, never casts you out, never stops loving you."

They crested a hill. The compound appeared, a cluster of ruins around the partially rebuilt chapel.

Kamran's mule halted abruptly. "The cross you worship —we're taught it's shirk. Idolatry."

"We don't worship the cross. It's a symbol reminding us what Jesus did—died for our sins. But we worship Him, not the symbol."

Kamran stared at the chapel, breath visible in the cool air. The sun was high, lighting the whitewashed walls.

"When you touched my sister," Kamran said, voice thick, "something happened to me. Something broke inside. Like a burden I didn't know I carried was gone."

Joseph's heart thundered. He remained silent, letting the Holy Spirit work.

"I've prayed five times a day since I was seven," Kamran continued, tears tracking dust on his cheeks. "Fasted. Given alms. Memorized half the Quran. But never—not once—felt Allah near like I felt Him when He healed my sister."

His shoulders sagged. "It was like He'd been waiting for me."

Joseph's eyes burned but he stayed silent.

"If I lost everything—family, inheritance, place—but felt that presence every day..." Kamran looked at Joseph, face streaked with tears and dust. "Would it be enough?"

"What does your heart say?"

Kamran closed his eyes, hand on his chest. When he opened them, fear had been overtaken by something stronger. "My heart tells me I've been empty my whole life and didn't know it until today." He wiped his face. "If your Jesus fills that emptiness, nothing else matters."

Joy rose in Joseph. "Kamran—"

"But I'm afraid." The words tumbled out. "What if I'm wrong? What if this fades? What if I can't lose everything?"

Joseph guided his mule closer. "Faith is trusting God despite your doubts. And remember, your mother experienced Jesus healing your sister, and your father will know soon. If they don't agree, at least they'll understand."

The trail narrowed, winding between sun-baked rocks as they descended toward the valley. Only leather creaks and soft hoof pads broke the silence. The sun had shifted noticeably before Kamran cleared his throat.

"When could you baptize me?"

Joseph gripped his saddle horn. "We need to talk more. To make sure you're ready."

Kamran's hand moved to his chest again, fingers spread wide. "I felt Him, Joseph—in that room, in my heart. I can't pretend I didn't."

"The cost—"

"Will be worth it." Kamran's voice grew certain. "I don't

know how I know that, but I do. Whatever I lose, whatever happens."

Joseph's vision blurred. In all his dreams of returning to Pakistan, he never dared hope for this—a young Muslim boy, son of a man who worked for his parents' killer, asking to be baptized into the Christian faith.

"We could do it tonight," Joseph said, his voice breaking. "I've never seen anyone more ready."

# THIRTY-SIX

## The Evidence

*Why did Freeman come here? How did he escape?*

The question had gnawed at Faraz since he got word, sharpening with each passing hour. He strode into the bank's security room, throwing the door open so forcefully it cracked against the wall and rebounded.

The afternoon sun streamed through the windows, casting accusatory light across every surface. Someone had helped the missionary. Someone always helped them.

"FIA investigation," he announced to the guard who jumped to attention. The guard at the surveillance screens jumped to attention, his chair tilting, almost overturning until he caught it.

"Sit," Faraz ordered, waving the man back into his seat. He leaned forward, bracing his hands on the back of the guard's chair. "Show me the footage from this morning. Main entrance."

"Yes, sir." The guard's fingers tapped the keyboard. "What time frame, sir?"

"Just before the bank opened."

The guard's Adam's apple bobbed as he swallowed. "Yes, sir."

The black and white footage flickered to life, the time stamp blinking 7:51 AM—the bank entry door ajar. The lobby remained empty for a moment, sunlight pouring across the polished floors. Then, a single figure slipped through the entrance—Joseph Freeman. He was the first to cross the threshold, his steps tentative, his shadow stretching ahead of him.

"Slow it down," Faraz snapped.

The guard complied. Joseph followed a bank officer to a corridor on the right side of the lobby.

"What's down that hallway?"

"That leads to our safety deposit box room, sir," the guard answered nervously.

"Get the bank manager," Faraz demanded. "Now."

The guard scrambled from his chair, nearly tripping in his haste to escape the room. Joseph Freeman remained frozen on the monitor. *How did he get out of the mission compound undetected?*

The door opened again, admitting a balding man in a Western-style business suit, followed by the nervous security guard.

"Director Qureshi," the manager said, extending his hand. "How may I be of service?"

Faraz ignored the outstretched hand. "I need to know why this man was here this morning."

The manager blinked rapidly. "I...I would need to check the logs, sir."

"Do it now. This is a matter of national security."

The manager moved to a terminal, typing in credentials as sweat beaded at his temples. The security guard hovered near the door, ready to bolt. No one questioned the FIA's authority, especially when invoked with such conviction.

"According to our records," the manager said, "a customer accessed safety deposit box 347-B at 8:05 AM. He presented the required key and proper identification."

"Whose name is on the box?" Faraz demanded.

The manager squinted at the screen. "The box is registered to Hassan Awan."

A jolt ran through Faraz's body. Hassan—the man he'd arrested on blasphemy charges days ago. The man now sitting in a holding cell awaiting questioning.

"Hassan Awan is in government custody," Faraz said. "How could Joseph Freeman access his box?"

The manager consulted the screen again. "It appears Mr. Freeman is listed as having secondary access authorization. The paperwork is in order."

"Continue the footage," Faraz ordered the security guard, who jumped back to his station.

The video resumed. Joseph disappeared down the corridor to the safety deposit area. The guard fast-forwarded. Fifteen minutes later, the footage showed a teenage boy in shalwar kameez suddenly bursting into the safety deposit room. There was no audio, but the urgency in his movements was clear. He spoke rapidly to someone off-camera—presumably Joseph.

"Zoom in," Faraz commanded.

The guard magnified the image, focusing on the portfolio in Joseph's hands. The envelope was sealed tight, giving no hint of its contents. But Joseph's body language—the way he held it like a sacred text, the intensity in his face—told Faraz whatever was inside was valuable.

Two minutes later, Joseph reappeared in the main corridor, clutching a manila envelope. The boy stayed close beside him, both moving with obvious haste.

"Show me what happened next," Faraz demanded.

The guard switched to another camera angle showing the back corridor. Joseph and the boy sprinted toward the emergency exit. Moments later, three of Faraz's men rushed into the frame, weapons drawn—too late.

"The exterior camera," Faraz ordered. The guard clicked his keyboard and nodded toward another screen. Grainy footage appeared showing Joseph and the boy rushing into the alley behind the bank. They quickly disappeared around the corner at the far end. Two minutes later, three of Faraz's men burst through the emergency door, weapons drawn. They paused, looking both directions, then pursued down the alley.

Faraz's radio crackled to life at his hip. He snatched it up. "Qureshi."

"Sir, this is checkpoint three at the compound. The missionary was just seen inside."

Faraz turned back to the security footage, studying the frozen image of Joseph clutching the envelope. What had Hassan hidden all these years? What secrets lay in that box? *Financial records? Missionary correspondence? Or something more damaging—evidence from the night of the fire?*

The sealed envelope's importance was clear from the way Freeman protected it. Whatever was inside could be dangerous to Faraz's plans for the muqadma. He must know what Freeman had discovered.

Faraz pulled out his phone, dialing Qadir's direct line. The call connected after two rings.

"Asim," Faraz said, dispensing with formalities. "Joseph Freeman accessed Hassan Awan's safety deposit box this morning. He has something—documents of some kind."

"How serious?" Qadir's voice was measured, cautious.

"Serious enough that I need to question Awan immediately. Off the record. Arrange for a private interrogation room at the detention facility. No cameras, no records."

"That's outside protocol, Director." Qadir's voice lowered. "The international observers—"

"Don't worry," Faraz cut him off. "I've done this before. Make it happen."

A pause. "Very well. When will you need it."

"One." Faraz countered, ending the call without waiting for a response.

———

Joseph and Kamran approached the compound's hidden entrance through the old tunnel system. Naveed stood guard at the concealed opening, his face tense as his son emerged first, followed by Joseph clutching Hassan's precious portfolio against his chest.

"Go quickly," Naveed whispered. "The main gate guards saw nothing, but you must hurry before the shift change."

They moved swiftly through the shadows, into the compound, where midday light spilled across the chapel walls. The team had assembled at the sight of Joseph's return.

"We have something that may be useful," Joseph announced, his lungs still burning from their journey. He placed a hand on Kamran's shoulder. "And something even more important is about to happen."

Darius's keen eyes moved from Joseph's face to Kamran's. "You found Hassan's documents?" he asked. "And this young man found something else?"

"Yes." Joseph patted the portfolio. "I brought the documents." Then he touched the boy's shoulder. "And Kamran has made a decision."

"I want to be baptized," Kamran said boldly. "Today. Now."

Murmurs spread through the group. Tariq's eyebrows shot up. Maya clasped her hands together. Ian and the others exchanged glances that ranged from joy to concern.

"Prepare the stone trough," Joseph said, scanning the faces of his team. "Fill it with water. This is what we're here for—the first new believer since we began rebuilding."

As the team dispersed to prepare, Joseph led Kamran inside the chapel walls. Nadir and Tariq carried in the old stone baptismal trough—miraculously untouched during the fire fifteen years ago.

"Are you sure about this?" Joseph lowered his words, the evening air carrying the scent of dust and distant cooking fires. "You understand what it means?"

"I do," Kamran said. "Something changed inside me when God healed my sister. I can't go back to how things were before."

Joseph squeezed the boy's shoulder, feeling the tension beneath his fingers. "Your life won't be easy. But you won't walk this path alone."

Water splashed into the ancient stone trough as the believers poured bucket after bucket from the well. Thirty minutes later, the assembly gathered in the half-finished chapel, anticipation hushing their voices.

Joseph opened his mouth to speak when heavy footsteps interrupted. Naveed, still in uniform, shouldered his way through the crowd, his face hardening as he spotted his son. "Kamran!" he barked, boots grinding against the stone floor.

All eyes fixed on father and son, standing on either side of the baptismal trough.

"What is this?" Naveed demanded, his eyes revealing he already knew.

Joseph stepped forward. "Your son has decided to follow Jesus."

Naveed gripped Joseph's arm, dropping to a ragged whisper. "You don't understand. In this country, leaving Islam can mean death—not just for him, but for all of us."

Joseph met his gaze. "I understand the risk better than most."

"No." Naveed's jaw clenched. "You can leave. We cannot."

"Baba," Kamran said softly. "I have seen Jesus heal Ayesha when Allah couldn't. The fever that was killing her vanished when Joseph touched her."

Each word strengthened. "For three days, she didn't recognize any of us. Mother had given up hope. You were preparing yourself for her funeral." Kamran's eyes glistened in the soft light. "But when Joseph placed his hands on her and prayed in Jesus's name, the fever broke instantly. She sat up and asked for water. Ask Mama. She saw it too."

Naveed's hands clenched and unclenched at his sides.

"And today," Kamran continued, "when men hunted us on the mountain, Joseph prayed down a whirlwind that blinded them and covered our escape. In both moments, I felt God's presence." Wonder entered his tone. "The dust swirled all around our pursuers, Father. Bullets fired blindly into the storm. Men shouted in confusion, stumbling into each other. But Joseph and I walked away from it all, safe and sound."

A tear traced down Kamran's cheek, catching the lantern glow. "How can I deny what my own eyes have witnessed? This Jesus is real—He has saved both of your children, all in one day."

Naveed's shoulders sagged. Conflict played across his

features as he stared at his son. The calls of distant birds filtered through the open chapel.

"You believe this Jesus healed your sister?" Naveed asked.

"I know He did," Kamran replied without hesitation. "And He protected us today. And now I must follow Him, whatever the cost."

Naveed closed his eyes briefly, his son's decision settling across his shoulders like a physical weight. When he opened them again, resignation mixed with a father's fierce love.

"You are my son." The words came thick. "But I cannot stop you. Not after a day like this."

He stepped back, creating space for the ceremony to continue. The gesture carried neither blessing nor opposition—perhaps it marked the beginning of acceptance, however reluctant.

Joseph moved to the edge of the stone trough, goosebumps rising on his arms as he motioned for Kamran to join him.

"Brothers and sisters," Joseph began, carrying his words across the hushed assembly. "We witness today an act of courage and faith. Kamran has seen God's power and has chosen to follow Jesus Christ."

He turned to the boy, whose face shone with nervous determination. "Kamran, do you believe that Jesus Christ is the Son of God, that He died for your sins and rose again?"

"I do," Kamran answered, steady now, stronger than before.

"And do you commit your life to serve Him, whatever He may ask?"

"I do."

Joseph smiled, placing his hand on the boy's shoulder. "Then it is my privilege to baptize you."

Kamran entered the baptismal, his body tensing against the chill. Joseph placed one hand on the boy's back and another across his chest, feeling the rapid heartbeat beneath his palm.

"I baptize you, Kamran, in the name of the Father, of His Son Jesus Christ, and of the Holy Spirit."

He lowered the boy, submerging him beneath the water in symbolic death. Then Joseph raised him up, water streaming from his hair and clothes, droplets scattering light like stars. The first new believer baptized at the mission since his parents' deaths.

Kamran's face glowed as he lifted his hands, water dripping from his elbows. The chapel erupted in joyful praises and prayers, voices blending in whispered thanksgiving. Someone began singing "Nothing but the Blood," the melody quickly taken up by others, the ancient hymn breathing life into the ruined walls.

Kamran stepped out of the trough, his wet footsteps echoing on the stone floor as he approached his father. Water pooled at his feet. For a moment, they stood facing each other in the lantern light, neither moving, the decision like a bridge neither knew how to cross.

Then Kamran embraced Naveed, not caring that he was soaking his father's guard uniform, his arms wrapping around the older man with desperate love.

Naveed stood rigid at first, arms at his sides, conflict holding him motionless. Then, slowly—so slowly—Naveed's arms rose to return the embrace, holding his dripping son tightly against his chest, his chin resting on Kamran's wet hair.

The celebration continued around them, voices soft but joyful in the cooling evening air. Joseph watched as the team approached Kamran one by one, welcoming him into the family of believers. Darius offered a prayer of blessing, his weathered hands gentle on the boy's shoulders. Maya presented him with a Bible. Even Tariq, usually reserved, clasped Kamran's hand warmly, whispering something that made the boy smile.

Joseph stepped back from the circle, absorbing the scene of new life amidst the ruins they were rebuilding. This was why they had come. This moment made all the risks worthwhile. One soul at a time, the true mission was being restored.

As the group gradually broke into smaller clusters, the aroma of spiced tea drifted through the chapel as someone brought out a thermos to celebrate. Joseph caught Darius's eye and nodded toward his tent, where Hassan's documents waited. The symbolism wasn't lost on him—a new believer baptized, and perhaps the means to protect their fragile community hidden in those papers.

In his tent, Joseph opened Hassan's portfolio on the makeshift desk, spreading the documents with deliberate care.

Within minutes, Maya, Darius, and Ian joined him, their faces reflecting the joy of the baptism but sobering as they saw the papers spread across the desk.

"Show us what you found," Maya said, leaning over the desk.

Joseph selected the most significant document and handed it to her. "This was my father's petition to the Pakistani Assembly, dated August 2010. He was killed before he could present it."

Maya took the papers, her brow furrowing as she scanned the contents. "He was requesting official protection for the mission," she murmured. Then her eyes widened. "Joseph, look at these signatures."

She turned the document so the others could see. "There are thirty-two Muslim signatures here—thirty-two people willing to support protection for Christians." Her finger stopped at one name. "Including Asim Qadir's signature—the same man now working against us."

Darius let out a low whistle. "That's significant."

"More than significant," Maya said, her mind processing the implications. "This could completely change our position at the tribunal."

Ian studied the document over her shoulder, frowning. "But wait—some of these people might not be alive. It's been fifteen years."

His words settled over them. Joseph watched as Maya's excitement tempered with realization.

"And those who are still alive," Darius said, tracing a weathered finger over the names, "could face serious consequences if we use these signatures. They could be accused of blasphemy themselves for supporting a Christian mission."

Maya set the document down carefully. "We'd be putting targets on their backs."

Joseph stared at his father's fifteen-year-old petition, the moral dilemma pressing on his chest. Outside, he could still hear the soft sounds of celebration as Kamran received congratulations from the believers, laughter mixing with evening prayers.

"So, we have five days to decide," he said, "whether we protect the mission by potentially endangering others."

Through the tent window, Joseph could see Kamran and his father walking to the gate together, the boy still damp from his baptism, the father's arm now resting protectively across his son's shoulders.

What happened in the chapel tonight and what lay

within these documents were connected by a single truth: in this place, every act of faith carried consequences that rippled far beyond any one person. Kamran's baptism and these signatures represented the same courage—people willing to stand for truth despite the cost. The question was whether Joseph had the right to determine that cost for others.

# THIRTY-SEVEN

## The Surrender

Cold water ran red between Faraz Qureshi's fingers beneath the fluorescent glare of the detention facility's interrogation wing. The pink-tinged water swirled down the drain as he scrubbed beneath his fingernails, careful to remove every trace. Hassan's defiance had been more resilient than anticipated—no amount of pressure or pain had broken the old man's resolve.

"Sir," one of his subordinates called from the doorway. "Maulana Rahman is waiting on the line. He's called three times in the past hour."

Faraz closed his eyes briefly, composing himself. Rahman had been following his operation with increasing scrutiny, expecting immediate results. He straightened his collar and smoothed his hair before following the officer to his makeshift office.

"Maulana," Faraz greeted, picking up the secure line. "I was just completing the interview with Hassan Awan."

"And?" Rahman's voice was calm. "What did the old man reveal about the contents of the deposit box?"

"He maintains there was nothing but personal documents," Faraz replied, keeping his voice steady. "Family photographs, an old deed, nothing of significance."

"Yet the infidel Freeman went to considerable risk to retrieve these 'insignificant' items." Rahman paused. "You have failed repeatedly with this mission, Qureshi. First the poison failed to kill Karimi, then Freeman escaped your men in the mountains, and now Hassan refuses to speak. I'm beginning to think that Allah has abandoned you."

Faraz pressed his lips together. "The situation is more complex than anticipated. This morning's incident in the mountains was unexpected."

"Ah yes, the dust storm." Rahman's words carried weight. "The drivers reported it appeared from nowhere, precisely when your men had Freeman cornered. No meteorological warnings, no precedent. The timing was...providential, wouldn't you say?"

Faraz hesitated. "Weather phenomena can be unpredictable in the mountains, Maulana. Nothing more."

"Are you certain?" Rahman pressed. "Some of your men are claiming Allah himself intervened to protect the missionary. Such talk is dangerous. It undermines everything we're working toward."

The reports disturbed Faraz—testimonies of dust appearing from nowhere, enveloping only the precise area where his men had cornered Joseph and the boy, moving against the wind with what his officers described as unnatural intent.

"I've spoken with the men," Faraz said. "It was merely coincidence. Nothing miraculous."

"Yet we hear reports of a healing as well. A Muslim child, whose identity remains hidden."

Faraz's hand tightened around the receiver. "Propaganda. I have investigators looking into this lie."

Rahman said nothing for three long beats. "The muqadma is in five days, Qureshi. We cannot afford any more failures. I'm concerned you may harbor some personal vendetta that's clouding your judgment."

"My judgment is clear," Faraz insisted, though doubt gnawed at him. "I will handle Joseph Freeman."

"See that you do. By any means necessary."

The line went dead. Faraz set down the receiver, considering Rahman's final words. Was "by any means necessary" permission or a threat? If he failed again, someone else would be assigned to finish what he started—and Faraz might find himself on the wrong side of the maulana's significant influence.

He studied Hassan Awan's dossier. The old man's resilience was remarkable, withstanding methods that had broken hardened militants. Whatever Hassan protected in that box, he valued it more than his own life.

Faraz touched his scar, remembering William Freeman's eyes as he'd pulled the trigger fifteen years ago. The missionary had looked at him not with hatred but with pity —as if Faraz were the one to be mourned, not himself.

The dust storm weighed on him more than he wanted to admit. Faraz had been raised to believe in Allah's sovereignty, yet what would it mean if Allah had indeed intervened—not for the faithful Muslims, but for the Christian missionary? Such thoughts bordered on apostasy.

He shook his head, banishing the doubt. Coincidence. Nothing more.

His phone vibrated with a message from one of his

surveillance teams at the mission compound. They reported another rumor—a Christian baptism of a Muslim boy. The same boy who helped Joseph Freeman escape?

Something broke inside Faraz. The Freeman legacy was spreading again, contaminating pure Pakistani faith just as it had before. He could not allow it to continue.

He made his decision, reaching for the secure phone once more. This time he dialed a number few knew existed —a contact from his days with the TLP, before he'd joined the government ranks.

"It's Qureshi," he said when the line connected. "The operation we discussed years ago. It's time."

"The compound?" The voice was cautious.

"No. Too much attention. The muqadma." Faraz's voice was cold, detached. "Freeman must never reach it. Arrange everything. No survivors, no witnesses, maximum casualties."

"That crosses the line we established."

"The line has moved," Faraz cut in. "This ends now. Everything we've worked for is at stake."

After receiving confirmation, Faraz ended the call and locked the office door. He unrolled his prayer mat, facing Mecca, and began his evening prayers. As he pressed his forehead to the ground, he asked Allah for forgiveness for what he was about to do—and for victory against those who threatened the true faith.

They would blame the attack on TTP militants—a tragedy of Pakistan's ongoing religious tensions. And in the chaos, Joseph Freeman would join his parents, the Freeman mission would end forever, and Faraz would finally complete the destruction he'd begun fifteen years ago.

Rising, Faraz stood motionless, staring at the prayer rug

beneath his feet. The path was set. The final phase had begun.

————

*Would God abandon me now, after bringing me this far?*

The question haunted Joseph as he moved through the skeletal chapel, his footsteps hollow against the packed earth. Dawn light filtered through the unfinished eastern wall, streaming between exposed rafters to cast shadows like ladder rungs across the dirt floor. He had come here to pray after another fitful night, his sleep fractured by worry, seeking solace in this half-built sanctuary that mirrored his own incomplete faith.

Joseph ran his fingers along the rough-hewn baptismal trough. The stone was cool against his skin, solid in a way little else felt these days. Last night, it still held the waters of Kamran's baptism, the boy's face radiant as he emerged from beneath the surface, reborn.

Inhaling deeply, Joseph drew in distant wood smoke from the village. They would leave for the Peshawar this morning, for the trial in mere days. And despite uncertainty about how to handle Hassan's documents, Joseph couldn't shake his anxiety for what would happen to his team and the local believers.

The half-built walls around him mirrored his fractured confidence—foundations laid, structure rising, but still perilously exposed to the elements. Joseph knelt in the dirt, dust clinging to his jeans.

"I thought I understood what would happen," he whispered to the empty room. "I thought I was prepared for the cost."

The cost haunted him now. Not his own safety—he'd

made peace with that risk when he decided to return—but the lives entangled with his. Maya could lose her legal credentials. Darius might never return to his ministry in England. And the local believers would remain here after the international team was deported, vulnerable to Faraz's vengeance.

Joseph pulled his father's worn Bible from his backpack and opened it to Luke 22. The passage struck him differently now—Jesus asking for the cup to pass from him, yet submitting to God's will regardless.

*"Father, if you are willing, take this cup from me; yet not my will, but yours be done."*

He closed his eyes. Instead of the traumatic flashbacks that had haunted him for fifteen years—fire and screams and chaos—gentler memories surfaced with unusual clarity.

His mother kneeling in rich brown soil, planting her marigolds along the mission perimeter, her voice lifting in hymns as she worked. Seven-year-old Joseph had asked why she bothered with flowers when they needed to grow food.

"Beauty matters, Joseph," she'd said, tucking a bloom behind his ear. "It reminds people that God cares about more than mere survival."

The memory shifted. His father teaching village children under the sprawling banyan tree, sitting cross-legged on a mat while children clustered around him.

"The best ministry happens outside the walls, son," he had said, pointing toward the mission chapel. "The building just reminds us who we serve when we leave it."

Joseph's grip tightened on the worn leather cover of his Bible.

"I'm afraid, Jesus," he admitted, his voice failing. "Not for myself, but for them. What if I've led them all into a trap?"

His whisper rose toward the open rafters. "If this all falls apart at the tribunal, was it worth the risk to everyone who followed me back here?"

Minutes passed. No heavenly voice. No sudden clarity.

"I know healing Naveed's daughter was right," he continued. "I know baptizing Kamran was right. But help me face what comes next." He swallowed hard. "Help me surrender control."

Joseph remained kneeling as morning light strengthened through the gaps in the walls. Suddenly, a cool breeze swept through the unfinished chapel, rustling the pages of his father's Bible. The passage before him drew his eyes: *"not my will, but yours be done."*

His breathing slowed, deepened. The tightness that had coiled in his chest for weeks began to unwind with each exhale. The dirt beneath his knees no longer felt like the dust of failure but the soil of possibility.

A songbird landed on the exposed rafter above, its morning call piercing the silence. Joseph looked up, watching as the creature tilted its head, regarding him with curious black eyes before taking flight again through the open roof.

He closed the Bible. The anxiety that had chased him from sleep before dawn had become something else—not confidence, but a quiet certainty that transcended his fears.

Footsteps approached from outside, and Darius appeared in the doorway, his weathered face haloed by the strengthening light. "The trucks have arrived. Government officials are here to take us to Peshawar."

Joseph nodded, rising to his feet. The world around him was sharper, clearer—the rough texture of the stone walls, the scent of earth and wood, the distant voices of his team preparing for departure.

"We're ready," Joseph said, surprised by the steadiness in his voice.

Outside, the rumble of engines and slamming doors would have once reminded Joseph of the chaos of the mission assault. Now, he heard only the present moment, anchored in an inexplicable peace.

"What do you think will happen in Peshawar?" Darius asked as they walked toward the door.

Joseph paused and placed his hand on the frame. "I don't know," he answered honestly. "But I know who goes with us."

Joseph stepped into the bright morning sunlight. He didn't shield his eyes but welcomed the warmth on his face as he walked toward whatever awaited him, no longer burdened by the need to control the outcome.

# THIRTY-EIGHT

## The Widow's Pass

*Time to leave for Peshawar. Time to leave for the trial.*

Joseph's hand tightened on the gate. Three FIA trucks sat inside the compound. The predawn horizon blazed crimson over the mountains, illuminating the unfinished chapel. Both achievement and target.

He inhaled deeply—cardamom from the garden, marigolds from the perimeter. Smells that had once more become home.

"Hard to believe we're leaving," he murmured to himself.

Beyond the chain-link fence, locals had been gathering since word of the evacuation spread. Their faces peered through the diamond-shaped openings, eyes reflecting the same sunrise that warmed Joseph's face. A young woman with a child on her hip pressed her palm against the metal. An elderly man with a weathered face nodded solemnly toward Joseph. Several wiped tears with the edges of head-scarves or sleeves, though they stood tall, shoulders squared.

The security team had been clear—no visitors during evacuation. The barrier between them was wrong, like a physical manifestation of abandonment.

Joseph turned as footsteps approached from behind.

"Everything's almost loaded," Maya said, clipboard pressed to her chest. Dark circles shadowed her eyes. "I have the documents secured for the trial. We've left behind what we discussed with clear instructions."

Joseph nodded, watching as two more families approached the fence line, greeting others with embraces. "They deserve more than this. More than a goodbye through a chain-link fence."

"Joseph," Maya's voice softened. "Let's see what God has in store for the courtroom before we start giving in to despair."

"I know," he said, regretting his doubt. "I'm sorry. It's just —this feels like failure."

Maya's hand found his shoulder, squeezed once. "God never fails."

Joseph refocused on the immediate goal—get everyone out safely, honor the work they'd done, somehow make this departure meaningful instead of devastating. He needed to give the people staying behind something to hold onto. Hope that wouldn't dissolve once the vehicles disappeared up the mountain road.

The compound buzzed with activity. Three trucks were positioned near the main building, the international team loading their belongings.

Ian spoke with his local security team, most young men under twenty-five. He noticed Joseph and approached. "We may have unexpected visitors before we get to Peshawar."

"What visitors?"

"Don't know exactly," Ian checked his watch. "But I'd

assume Faraz Qureshi has something to do with it. Which means we need to start moving now."

Joseph processed the information while giving the compound one last look. His gaze caught on an intense conversation happening near the final truck. Naveed was gesturing emphatically to the driver of the lead vehicle.

"What's with Naveed?" Joseph asked.

"I haven't a clue," Ian said.

Naveed approached Joseph and Ian with two men his age. "There's been a change. I'll be driving you to Peshawar."

"Any reason why?" Ian asked.

"I know these mountains—every path, every alternate route. My cousin Hamza and my friend Salman will drive the other vehicles. They know the passes as well as I do, and neither has much love for Faraz Qureshi."

"Alternate route?" Joseph studied the man. "We've heard there may be trouble on the trip to Peshawar."

Naveed nodded once, but said nothing.

A commotion near the fence caught their attention. The crowd had grown substantially, now stretching along the entire western perimeter. Some were singing softly—a Christian hymn in Pashto Joseph had learned as a boy.

"We need to leave as soon as possible," Naveed pressed.

Darius joined them, a duffel bag slung over his shoulder. "Everything is loaded and everyone is ready."

As the team loaded into the three SUVs, Joseph found himself drawn back to the fence line. The crowd had continued to grow—perhaps forty people now, faces he recognized from services, from the work site, from community outreach. They stood shoulder to shoulder, fingers hooked through the chain-link, watching silently as the team prepared to leave.

Joseph couldn't depart like this, separated by metal and

protocol. He crossed the compound, ignoring Ian's questioning look, and approached the fence.

Hands reached toward him—not grasping or desperate, but offering connection. Joseph raised his own, pressing his palms against the chain-link where theirs waited on the other side. The metal was warm from the morning sun and from their touch.

"I don't have the right words," he began. "What we've built here together—it was never meant to be temporary."

"God's work is never temporary," a woman replied, her eyes steady despite the tears on her cheeks.

Joseph swallowed hard. "We're leaving, but God's Spirit remains. Be bold in your faith and your love for one another."

A murmur passed through the gathered crowd. One by one, people stepped closer to the fence.

"I will continue teaching the children," said a young woman who had assisted in their makeshift school.

A man Joseph recognized as a mason who worked on the chapel grasped Joseph's fingers through the fence. "I will tell my story. How Jesus helped where Allah couldn't."

One after another, they gave their testimonies and made their pledges—to maintain the mission, to carry forward the work in whatever ways they could. Joseph stood motionless, overwhelmed by their courage and commitment.

A shadow fell across Joseph's shoulder. He turned to find Darius. "We need to move, Joseph." Darius rubbed his jaw. "Ian and Naveed are getting nervous."

Joseph nodded, then turned back to the fence. "Stay strong in the faith." He cleared his throat. "Pray God's will prevails."

"God willing," came the unified response.

A minute later, Joseph glanced in the side mirror as they

pulled away. The locals still lined the fence, hands raised now in blessing toward the departing vehicles. The image seared into his memory—not of abandonment, but of continuation.

They had traveled less than two miles when Naveed veered from the main road onto a rough track partially hidden by brush.

"This isn't the way to Peshawar," Joseph said, alarm rising as he braced himself against the dashboard.

Naveed's intense eyes focused on the rearview mirror. "Qureshi plans to attack the convoy." He shifted gears as the truck bounced over uneven terrain. "He means to make sure none of you make it to Peshawar alive."

———

The truck lurched over the hidden mountain path as Joseph steadied himself against the dashboard, gripping the door handle tighter with each jolt. Behind them, two vehicles carrying the rest of the team kicked up dust, masking their escape from the main road. In the side mirror, Joseph spotted black SUVs speeding down the highway they had just abandoned.

"They're still on the main route," he said. "They haven't spotted us."

Naveed's expression remained focused, his eyes scanning the terrain ahead. "They will. Faraz doesn't give up easily."

The road twisted sharply upward. Loose stones pinged against the undercarriage. Joseph braced as the truck tilted toward a ravine that dropped hundreds of feet below.

"You know these roads well." Joseph tried to keep his voice steady around another hairpin turn.

"I grew up here," Naveed said through a clenched jaw as he navigated around a fallen boulder. "Before everything went wrong."

Joseph's satellite phone buzzed. Darius was calling from the second vehicle.

"We're losing Maya's truck," Darius reported, tension in his voice. "The terrain is too rough."

Joseph twisted in his seat, seeing the third vehicle struggle up a steep incline, its tires spinning against loose gravel.

"Naveed, we need to wait for them."

"If we stop, we all die." Naveed didn't slow down. "Tell them to abandon that vehicle," he shouted at the phone, "and join yours. Quickly."

In the side mirrors, Maya, Thomas, Rebecca, and their driver Hamza scrambled from their disabled truck and crammed into Darius's vehicle. The overloaded SUV lurched forward, barely making it up the incline.

"Where are we going?" Joseph asked, running his sleeve across his sweaty forehead.

"There's an old route. It should bring us around the worst of it."

"Should?"

"Nothing's certain anymore." He downshifted as they climbed higher. "Faraz knows me. Knows how I think."

The admission chilled Joseph. "What aren't you telling me?"

Before Naveed could respond, his radio crackled with rapid Pashto. Listening intently, his expression darkened.

Joseph struggled to follow with his limited fluency. "What did they say?" he demanded.

"They've found this road." Naveed adjusted the radio volume. "Faraz is mobilizing more units."

The truck bounced through a shallow stream, cold water spraying through the open windows. Joseph wiped droplets from his face, studying Naveed's profile—the man whose daughter he had healed, whose son had accepted Christ.

"My wife still speaks of you," Naveed said suddenly. "She felt something change when you healed our daughter."

Joseph recalled the woman's grief and joy. "It wasn't me. I'm just—"

"I know what you are." An unfamiliar edge entered Naveed's tone. "That's why Rahman wants you dead."

"Rahman?" Joseph frowned. "The religious leader?"

"Maulana Hafiz Rahman." He maneuvered around another boulder. "He's been building power for decades, convincing officials to implement Shariah law. Your father's work threatened all that."

Joseph's phone buzzed again. This time it was Ian from the second vehicle.

"We've got company," Ian reported tersely. "Two vehicles on our tail, coming up fast."

Joseph craned his neck to look behind them, spotting two dust clouds gaining on Darius's vehicle.

"TLP militants," Naveed said grimly. "Old friends."

The truck swerved as Naveed took a hidden path off the main track. Scrub brushed against the doors, branches snapping against the windshield. Joseph gripped the overhead handle as they descended steeply.

Moments later, the second vehicle appeared behind them, following the treacherous descent. But Joseph noticed a third dust cloud, much larger, approaching from the east.

"Naveed, there's another group—"

"I see them."

The path narrowed, hugging a cliff face on one side with

a sheer drop on the other. Joseph's stomach lurched as stones dislodged by their tires disappeared over the edge.

"You said Rahman wants me dead. What about Faraz?"

"Faraz..." Naveed paused, navigating a particularly narrow section. "He has personal reasons."

"Such as?"

"Your father cost him everything. Rahman promised Faraz leadership of the TLP if he eliminated the Christian threat. But your father had something that changed everything."

Joseph sighed. "The petition Hassan kept hidden."

"Thirty-two signatures. Moderate Muslim leaders supporting your father's mission." Naveed let the weight of that sink in. "If those names had gone public after we destroyed the mission..."

"It would have undermined Rahman's entire platform."

"More than that. It would have ended Faraz's rise to power. Rahman would have abandoned him."

Joseph absorbed this revelation. His parents hadn't died due to general hatred—they had been targeted to prevent their allies from protecting them. "So my father never knew his petition was discovered?"

"No. But he died protecting those signatures," Naveed replied. "Rahman still doesn't know who signed it. If those names became public now..."

"Those people could hold power. Fifteen years is a long time."

"Or they could be dead," Naveed said. "Rahman's been eliminating moderate voices for years."

The path widened as they emerged onto a plateau revealing a breathtaking view—mountains stretching to the horizon, the valley below shrouded in mist. But the beauty was marred by multiple dust clouds converging on their position.

"They've surrounded us," he realized.

Naveed accelerated across the open ground, the truck's engine protesting. "Not yet. But soon."

The radio crackled again in urgent Pashto. This time, Naveed didn't translate immediately.

"What are they saying?" Joseph demanded.

"Rahman wants to make an example of you."

The plateau ended abruptly at a sheer cliff face. Naveed drove straight toward it, showing no signs of slowing.

"Naveed!"

At the last moment, a gap in the rock appeared—so narrow the truck scraped paint on both sides as it pushed into a ravine with steep walls rising on each side.

"My grandfather used this route during the wars," Naveed explained. "The British never found it."

Joseph exhaled shakily, watching as Darius's vehicle managed the same entry. "Will this get us to Peshawar?"

Naveed's expression was grim. "There's only one way through now."

He stopped the truck abruptly, raising his hand for silence.

In the distance, Joseph heard engines—many engines, growing closer. "How could they know about this route?"

Naveed's jaw tightened. "They don't. But they're checking everywhere."

Footsteps echoed off the ravine walls. Voices called out in Pashto. Naveed pointed ahead to where the ravine forked —and there, barely visible between two massive boulders, was a dark vertical cleft in the rock face.

"There's one way out," Naveed said. "The Widow's Pass.

My grandfather used it when he fought the British. Our family's secret for three generations."

Joseph stared at the narrow opening. "And Faraz?"

"Knows nothing about it." Naveed was already out of the truck, signaling the others. "Some secrets you keep, even when you're doing wrong."

Footsteps echoed closer. Shouts in Pashto grew louder. They were out of time.

"Abandon the vehicles," Naveed called to the others. "We go through on foot. Single file. Two hours to the other side."

Joseph's body went rigid as he stared at the dark cleft. Behind them, vehicle doors slammed. Men shouted orders. Ahead, a passage so narrow they would have to move sideways in places, trusting completely in Naveed's knowledge.

Naveed's phone began ringing.

He pulled it out, glanced at the screen. His face went white.

"It's Faraz," he whispered.

Joseph understood immediately. Faraz knew he'd lost the physical chase. That's why he was calling—desperation, not confidence.

Naveed answered on the fourth ring.

"Naveed." Faraz's voice was cold. "I know you're listening. I also know you have Freeman with you."

Naveed said nothing.

"I have men at every exit from that ravine. Every road to Peshawar is blocked. You think you can hide from me?" A pause. "You can't. But I'm a reasonable man. Turn around. Bring Freeman to me. And if you don't..."

Silence stretched.

"If you don't, your wife and children will join Freeman's parents in the ground."

The line went dead.

Naveed didn't react but moved to the gorge opening.

Joseph frowned at Naveed's calm. The man had just been threatened with his family's execution, yet his expression remained focused. "Hurry, hurry," he demanded in a low, intense tone. "Remember, single file."

Joseph placed a hand on his shoulder. "Your wife. Your children."

Naveed met his eyes. "They're safe. On the other side." He turned to face the gorge. "But Faraz doesn't know that. And when he discovers I've fooled him again..."

"Then we make sure you reach them first," Joseph said.

Naveed held Joseph's gaze, then glanced back at the team. When he turned toward the dark cleft, his shoulders squared. "Follow me," he said, stepping into the Widow's Pass. "Stay close and don't stop for anything."

Joseph and his team followed him into the darkness, leaving the vehicles and the approaching enemy behind. The gorge swallowed them, and the only sound was frantic breathing echoing off ancient stone.

# THIRTY-NINE

**Respite**

The walls were closing in.

Joseph knew it wasn't true—the passage was exactly as wide as it had been ten meters ago—but his lungs disagreed. The darkness swallowed them whole, and with each sideways shuffle through the Widow's Pass, his chest tightened further.

His shoulder scraped against cold stone. Ahead, Naveed's silhouette moved with practiced confidence, one hand trailing along the rock wall, the other holding a small flashlight that barely penetrated the gloom.

Behind Joseph, Maya's breathing echoed off the close walls, punctuated by an occasional grunt as someone stumbled on the uneven floor.

"How much further?" Darius called from somewhere back in the line.

"Halfway," Naveed's voice bounced between the stone faces. "The passage widens in another twenty meters."

Joseph's lungs pulled at the thin air. Dust hung thick

here, stirred by their passage after decades—perhaps centuries—of stillness. How many others had fled through this narrow cleft in the mountains? Refugees, smugglers, warriors? The worn stone beneath his boots suggested countless feet had passed this way before.

A hand touched Joseph's back. "You okay?" Maya whispered.

"Fine." He wasn't. The walls pressed close enough that he had to exhale to move forward in places. But complaining wouldn't widen the passage.

The gorge floor angled upward, forcing them to climb over tumbled boulders in near-total darkness. Someone's foot dislodged a stone that clattered down behind them, the sound magnifying in the confined space.

"Careful," Ian warned from the rear. "Stay close to the person in front of you."

Joseph's hand found a handhold, then another. His boots scraped for purchase on smooth rock. Ahead, Naveed's light bobbed and swayed, always moving forward, never hesitating.

"My grandfather brought me through here when I was ten," Naveed said, his voice carrying back. "To teach me our family's history. The British controlled the valleys, but they never controlled the mountains."

The passage began to widen. Joseph straightened, his spine grateful to be vertical again. Cool air touched his face —fresh air, not the stale breath of the gorge.

"Almost there," Naveed said.

The walls fell away on either side. Stars appeared overhead, brilliant against the black sky. Joseph stepped out of the gorge into a small valley cradled between two ridges, the moon casting silver light across scrub brush and scattered boulders.

One by one, the team emerged behind him, faces pale in the moonlight, clothes covered in rock dust. Rebecca bent over, hands on her knees, catching her breath. Thomas helped Leila over the last boulder. Darius stood blinking at the open sky as if he'd never seen it before.

"This way," Naveed pointed down the slope where distant lights flickered—cooking fires, perhaps, or oil lamps in windows. "The village."

They descended in silence, exhaustion making speech too costly. Joseph's legs trembled with each step. How long had they been walking? Two hours? Three? Time had lost meaning in the darkness of the Widow's Pass.

The village materialized from the shadows—a cluster of mud-brick homes built into the hillside, connected by narrow paths and stone walls. A dog barked at their approach, then went silent. A door opened, spilling lamp-light across packed earth.

A woman rushed out, her dupatta slipping from her head as she ran toward them. Naveed barely had time to brace himself before she threw her arms around him.

"Alhamdulillah," she breathed into his shoulder. "You're alive."

"I'm alive," he confirmed, holding her close. Then he pulled back, scanning the shadows behind her. "The children?"

"Safe. Inside." She turned to Joseph, and recognition flashed across her face. "You. The one who healed my daughter."

Joseph recognized her now—Naveed's wife, her face thinner than he remembered, etched with worry that even relief couldn't completely erase.

"Come," she said, gesturing toward the house. "All of you. We have food. Water. A place to rest."

Inside, the single room was lit by oil lamps that cast dancing shadows on whitewashed walls. Ayesha sat on a mat in the corner, a book open in her lap—alive, healthy, no trace of the fever that had nearly killed her. When she saw Joseph, she smiled.

"You came back," she said simply.

"I did."

Kamran emerged from the back room, taller somehow than Joseph remembered, his face carrying a new gravity. Their eyes met across the crowded space, and the boy's solemn expression broke into a grin.

"Joseph-sahib." He crossed the room, clasping Joseph's hand in both of his. "When we heard you were coming through the pass, I thought—" He stopped, composing himself. "I prayed you would make it."

"Your prayers were answered."

"Many prayers." Kamran glanced at his mother, who was already pressing cups of tea into the visitors' hands. "We've been praying for three days. Since Father sent word."

The team settled onto mats and low cushions. Naveed's wife brought out flatbread, lentils, yogurt—simple food that tasted like a feast after the long trek. Joseph ate mechanically, his body grateful even as his mind struggled to process their escape.

"The vehicles are ready," Naveed said between bites. "Kamran and my brother-in-law brought them two days ago. Hidden in a shed behind the mosque."

"Vehicles?" Darius asked.

"Old. Battered. But they run." Naveed smiled faintly. "They'll get us to Peshawar."

Maya leaned forward. "The tribunal is in two days. What time do we need to leave?"

"Dawn," Naveed replied. "It's a three-hour drive if we take the back roads. Four if we encounter trouble."

"We'll encounter trouble," Ian said flatly. "Faraz won't give up."

Silence settled over them. Outside, night insects chirped. Somewhere a goat bleated.

Joseph set down his cup and caught Kamran's eye. "Can we talk? Outside?"

The boy nodded and led Joseph through the back door into a small courtyard where a single acacia tree spread gnarled branches overhead. The moon hung low, painting everything in shades of silver and shadow.

"Your baptism," Joseph began. "How has it been?"

Kamran looked down at his hands. "Hard. My uncles know. My mother's brothers." He met Joseph's gaze. "They don't speak to me anymore. Some of them wanted—" He stopped.

"Wanted what?"

"To hurt me. To restore honor." Kamran's jaw tightened. "But my father stood between us. He told them I was still his son, and anyone who touched me would answer to him."

Joseph's chest tightened. "I'm sorry."

"Don't be." Kamran's voice strengthened. "I have something they don't have. Peace. Joy. Even when they curse me, even when they turn away—I have Jesus. And that's enough."

The simple declaration hit Joseph hard. This fifteen-year-old boy, who'd lost his extended family and risked his life, declaring Christ sufficient. What had Joseph been complaining about?

"You're braver than I am," Joseph said quietly.

"No." Kamran shook his head. "You came back. To

Pakistan. To rebuild what they destroyed. That's the bravest thing I've ever seen."

They stood in comfortable silence, the night air cool against their faces.

"I met a girl at the market," Kamran said suddenly, a smile tugging at his lips. "The day after my baptism. A Christian girl—her family moved here from Lahore after their church was burned."

"You met her?"

"She was selling bread with her mother. When I greeted them, she asked if I was the boy who'd been baptized at the Freeman mission." His smile widened. "Word travels fast here. We talked for maybe ten minutes. About faith. About what it means to follow Christ in Pakistan."

"And?"

"And I'd like to see her again. When this is over." He looked at Joseph. "Is that wrong? To think about the future when everything is so dangerous?"

Joseph thought of his own years of isolation, of burying himself in work to avoid the pain of loss. "No, Kamran. It's not wrong. It's hope. And hope is what keeps us alive."

A call came from inside—Naveed's wife announcing sleeping arrangements. The team would share the main room, the family taking the back. Simple hospitality offered without hesitation to people who'd brought danger to their door.

Joseph and Kamran returned inside to find mats being spread across the floor, blankets distributed. Darius was already lying down, eyes closed. Maya sat cross-legged, reviewing notes by lamplight. Ian stood by the window, watching the darkness beyond.

Naveed pulled Joseph aside. "The vehicles are old military trucks. Russian-made, from the Soviet era. They've been repainted, the markings removed. No one will know who we are until we're inside the city."

"And the route?"

"Shepherd paths. Dry wadis. Nothing Faraz will be watching." Naveed's expression hardened. "But once we get close to Peshawar, we'll have to join the main road. That's where he'll be waiting."

"Can we avoid it?"

"No. All the back roads dead-end in the foothills. The last ten kilometers, we're exposed."

Joseph absorbed this. "Then we'll have to be ready."

"We will be." Naveed gripped his shoulder. "Get some sleep, Joseph. Tomorrow, we finish what we started."

The lamps were extinguished one by one. Joseph lay on his mat, staring at the ceiling beams barely visible in the darkness. Around him, his team settled into sleep—Maya's quiet breathing, Darius's soft snore, the rustle of someone turning over.

He thought of his father's petition, tucked safely in Maya's bag. Thirty-two signatures. Thirty-two Muslims who'd risked everything to support the mission. In two days, in a courtroom in Peshawar, those names would either vindicate his father's faith or endanger everyone who'd signed.

*Father, guide us,* he prayed silently. *Give us wisdom. Give us courage. And whatever happens, let truth prevail.*

Sleep came eventually, fitful and shallow, troubled by dreams of fire and courtrooms and his father's face.

———

Joseph woke to Kamran's hand on his shoulder and the smell of tea brewing.

"It's time," the boy whispered.

Outside, the sky was beginning to lighten—not yet dawn, but the stars were fading. The team moved quietly, gathering their few belongings, accepting cups of steaming tea and warm flatbread from Naveed's wife.

"The trucks are this way," Kamran said, leading them down a narrow path behind the houses.

The shed leaned precariously against a stone wall, its wooden door hanging on leather hinges. Inside sat two vehicles that had clearly seen better days—Soviet-era trucks with cracked windshields, dented panels, and paint faded to indeterminate shades of brown and green. But when Naveed turned the key in the first one, the engine coughed to life with a reassuring rumble.

"They run," he said with satisfaction. "That's all that matters."

The team divided between the two trucks, the same configuration as when they'd left the compound. Joseph rode in the lead vehicle with Naveed, Maya, and Darius. Behind them, the second truck carried Ian and the rest of the team. As they pulled away from the village, Joseph looked back through the cracked rear window. Kamran stood in the road, hand raised in farewell, his mother and sister beside him, their figures growing smaller against the brightening sky.

The route Naveed chose wound through terrain that barely qualified as passable—rocky tracks that followed ridgelines, descended into dry streambeds, climbed through passes Joseph wouldn't have noticed existed. The trucks groaned and bounced, their suspension protesting every meter.

"Soviet engineering," Naveed said with grim humor as they lurched over another boulder. "Built for Afghan mountains. These trucks have carried weapons, refugees, smugglers—now missionaries."

The sun rose fully, painting the mountains in shades of copper and gold. Joseph watched the landscape roll past, trying to memorize it—the way the light caught the peaks, the shadows in the valleys, the distant villages clustered around water sources. His father had loved this country. Had died for it. And now Joseph was either about to vindicate that sacrifice or join him in martyrdom.

"How much further to the main road?" Maya asked. "The tribunal is in two days."

"Twenty minutes," Naveed replied. "Then another thirty to Peshawar if—"

The explosion came without warning.

The road ahead erupted in a geyser of dirt and rock. Naveed yanked the wheel hard right, the truck sliding sideways as debris rained down on the hood. Behind them, the second truck's horn blared a warning.

"Ambush!" Naveed shouted, throwing the truck into reverse.

Figures emerged from behind boulders on both sides of the road—men in traditional dress, but carrying modern weapons. Muzzle flashes lit up the morning shadows.

Bullets punched through the truck's door, the passenger window exploding inward. Joseph ducked as glass showered his lap. Darius grabbed Maya, pulling her down into the footwell.

Naveed accelerated in reverse, the engine screaming. The truck fishtailed as he fought for control on the loose gravel. More gunfire raked the hood, steam suddenly hissing from a ruptured radiator line.

"We can't go back!" Maya shouted over the chaos.

"We're not!" Naveed spun the wheel, executing a sliding

turn that pointed them toward a narrow gap between two boulders. "Hold on!"

The truck plunged through the gap, branches scraping both sides. Behind them, the second truck followed, its windshield now a spiderweb of cracks. Bullets continued to snap past, hitting rock, ricocheting with angry whines.

The terrain opened into a wadi—a dry riverbed that carved through the hills. Naveed followed it, the truck bouncing over smooth stones, the engine temperature gauge climbing into the red.

"They're following!" Darius called, looking back through the shattered rear window.

Two pickup trucks had joined the pursuit, men standing in the beds, firing as they came. The distance between them closed—fifty meters, forty, thirty.

Naveed pulled something from beneath his seat—a pistol, old but functional. He passed it to Joseph. "When I say, lean out and shoot at their tires."

"I'm not—"

"You healed my daughter. You baptized my son. You can shoot a tire." Naveed's eyes met his. "Now!"

Joseph leaned out the window, the wind tearing at his face. He aimed at the lead truck's front tire—or tried to. The bouncing made accuracy impossible. He squeezed the trigger. The gun kicked in his hand, the shot going wide.

"Again!" Naveed shouted.

Joseph fired twice more. The third shot hit something—the pursuing truck swerved violently, nearly rolling as the driver fought for control.

But the second truck was still coming.

The wadi narrowed ahead. The walls closed in. Naveed pushed the struggling truck faster, steam now pouring from under the hood. The temperature gauge was pinned.

"We won't make it much further," Naveed said through gritted teeth.

A checkpoint appeared ahead—government markings, but Joseph saw Naveed's face go pale.

"That's not official," Naveed said. "Faraz's men."

Three vehicles blocked the wadi, armed men taking positions behind them. Behind Joseph's truck, the pursuers closed in. They were trapped.

Naveed's hand moved to his phone, then to the gearshift. His jaw set with determination.

"Brace yourselves," he said.

He accelerated directly at the checkpoint. The men scrambled, not expecting a frontal assault. At the last second, Naveed yanked the wheel left, sending the truck up the wadi bank, tipping at a crazy angle.

Gunfire erupted from all sides.

The truck crashed back down onto four wheels, engine dying with a final shudder. Naveed's body jerked forward. Blood bloomed across his shirt, just above his hip.

"Naveed!" Joseph grabbed him as he slumped against the door.

"Drive," Naveed gasped, pressing his hand to the wound. Blood seeped between his fingers. "Take the wheel. Follow the wadi. Three kilometers to the main road."

Joseph's hands shook as he climbed over Naveed, taking the driver's seat. Behind them, the second truck rammed through the checkpoint, scattering men and vehicles. Darius was already in the back with Naveed, pressing bandages to the wound.

Joseph turned the key. The engine turned over once, twice—and caught. He stepped on the gas, the truck lurching forward, steam obscuring the windshield.

The wadi opened onto the main highway. Traffic flowed

normally here—cars, trucks, motorcycles. The chaos of the ambush might as well have been in another world. Joseph merged into the flow, the battered truck drawing stares but no intervention.

The second truck pulled alongside, the driver gesturing frantically. Joseph rolled down what remained of his window.

"Hospital?" the driver shouted.

Joseph looked at Naveed, pale and bleeding in the back seat. His hand found Joseph's shoulder, grip weak but insistent. "Peshawar," he whispered. "Get to... the compound. Protection."

"You need a hospital."

"I need..." Naveed's eyes fluttered. "I need you...to make it...to that courtroom. For my family."

Joseph pressed harder on the accelerator, the dying truck giving him everything it had left. The city of Peshawar rose ahead, minarets and government buildings piercing the haze.

"Hold on, Naveed," Joseph said, not knowing if the man could still hear him. "Just hold on."

# FORTY

**Overruled**

"They should be dead by now," Faraz said to no one.

He waited in the shadow of the compound's main building, focusing on the distant checkpoint where Freeman's convoy would arrive any moment. Bodies were supposed to be scattered across a mountain pass. Blood soaking into the earth. Justice finally served.

Instead, this. The phone call with the Interior Minister still burned in his ears. "The American's and British are involved now. Fix this without further embarrassment."

International pressure. Diplomatic interference. As if Pakistan's sovereignty meant nothing when Western powers decided otherwise.

His driver approached. "Director, the diplomatic vehicles are parked in the rear."

Of course they were. The West couldn't wait to interfere.

Movement at the checkpoint.

The first truck limped through the gate, engine steaming, diamond shards clinging to the frame. A second followed, metal punctured like a colander, oil bleeding onto asphalt.

Faraz's teeth clenched till his molars ached. They'd survived.

Joseph Freeman emerged from the lead vehicle, his dusty shirt smeared with blood. He braced himself against the car door, steadying his breathing before straightening. Despite the exhaustion evident in every movement, his eyes remained alert, scanning the compound with wary intelligence.

*They should be bodies on a mountain trail, feeding the buzzards.*

"Park behind the diplomatic vehicles," Faraz ordered his driver.

A flurry of activity drew his attention. Two men in Western suits approached Freeman's group. One tall and blond—clearly American—with the confident stride of someone who believed his nation could intervene anywhere on the globe. The other shorter, with watchful eyes that missed nothing.

Faraz exited his vehicle, catching fragments of their introduction.

"—Richard Harlow, Deputy Chief of Mission, U.S. Embassy," the American was saying, shaking Joseph's hand vigorously. "We've been expecting you since yesterday. When you didn't arrive, we feared the worst."

His companion, a compact man with graying temples, nodded. "Neville Thornton, British Consulate. Rather fortunate we received word of your predicament."

Faraz approached with measured steps, clipboard in hand. "Director Faraz Qureshi, Federal Investigation Agency. I'll be handling the processing of these individuals."

Harlow shifted subtly, positioning himself between Faraz and Joseph's group. "Director Qureshi, we appreciate Pakistan's cooperation in this sensitive matter." His voice carried the edge of a fierce negotiator beneath the veneer of courtesy.

The word "cooperation" landed like an insult. Faraz had not cooperated. He had been overruled.

"Of course," Faraz replied, keeping his voice flat. "The Islamic Republic of Pakistan takes its international obligations seriously." He allowed the faintest emphasis on "obligations"—a reminder that this was coercion, not choice.

His gaze moved past the diplomats to the rear vehicle where two men helped a third from the backseat. The traitor, Naveed. Blood-spotted bandages wrapped his midsection. The man who had once been Faraz's loyal subordinate now leaned heavily on Joseph Freeman's shoulder. Their eyes met briefly—Naveed's filled with defiance despite his pain, Faraz's with cold promise.

Faraz stepped forward. "That man requires immediate medical attention. Our facility at Peshawar Central has excellent trauma care. I'll arrange transport—"

"That won't be necessary," Joseph interrupted, his voice hoarse from dust and exhaustion. He winced as he shifted Naveed's weight, but his stance remained firm. "He stays with us."

Heat rose in Faraz's neck. "Mr. Freeman, this is not a request. The injured man is a Pakistani national requiring—"

"Director Qureshi," Thornton interjected, his accent crisp and authoritative. "I've already spoken with your Prime Minister about this matter. He has granted permission for our embassy physician to assess Mr. Naveed's condition here at the compound. The doctor is already inside."

The Prime Minister. Impossible.

"I have the authorization here, if you'd care to review it," Thornton continued, extending an official-looking document bearing the Prime Minister's seal.

Faraz scanned the paper, recognizing the authentic signature. His fingernails dug into his palm behind his clipboard.

"Until our physician say's its okay for this man to be moved," Thornton continued, "Mr. Naveed remains here."

The American diplomat nodded, a near-imperceptible smile touching the corner of his mouth.

Diplomacy—thinly veiled demands wrapped in polite courtesies. Any attempt to separate Naveed from the group would be reported, documented, and presented as Pakistan interfering with humanitarian aid.

"Very well," Faraz conceded, making a note on his clipboard. "Temporary medical assessment may proceed. But I must insist on having our own physician present as well."

"Of course," Thornton agreed. "Transparency benefits everyone." The subtle emphasis on "transparency" hung in the air—a warning that every action would be scrutinized.

Freeman's team moved to the guest quarters—a two-story colonial building with columned entrance. Maya Chaudhry, the attorney. Darius Karimi, the Iranian convert. Several others whose dossiers Faraz had memorized over the past months. None of them should have survived the mountain ambush. None of them should be walking into diplomatic housing in Peshawar.

"If you'll follow me," Harlow was saying to the group, "we've arranged appropriate accommodations. You'll find them most comfortable, I believe."

Faraz followed behind them, noting how the American consistently positioned himself between Faraz and

Joseph's team. The diplomatic quarters came into view—a remnant of British colonial architecture repurposed for government visitors. Faraz had intended them to be housed in the detention wing of the FIA regional headquarters.

Inside the building, staff had prepared several rooms along a wide hallway. Harlow gestured toward them. "You'll have the entire east wing. Kitchen facilities are at the end of the hall. My office has arranged for fresh clothing, food, and toiletries."

"What about the tribunal?" Joseph asked, leaning against the doorframe momentarily before straightening. His voice carried down the marble hallway despite its weariness.

"Scheduled for tomorrow at eleven," Faraz answered before either diplomat could respond. "The Bureau of Religious Affairs has expedited the hearing in light of international attention."

The injured Naveed had been settled onto a sofa in the common area, attended by embassy staff. Maya Chaudhry was already taking notes on a small pad. Darius stood nearby, arms folded. None of them behaved like people facing serious charges under Pakistani law.

"Director Qureshi," Harlow called. "Would you care to explain the security protocols to our guests?"

Faraz stepped forward, clipboard still in hand. "The compound is secure. Guards are posted at all entrances. For your safety, we ask that you remain within the designated areas. Any attempt to leave without escort will be considered a violation of your conditional release."

"Conditional release?" Maya Chaudhry questioned, her pen pausing above her notepad. "We haven't been charged with any crime requiring release conditions."

Faraz allowed himself a thin smile. "A matter of translation, perhaps. Consider it protective custody."

"House arrest," she translated flatly.

"As you wish." Faraz made another note on his clipboard. "The tribunal will clarify your status tomorrow."

The diplomats exchanged glances—silent communication of strategies and contingencies.

As the tour concluded in the main sitting area, Harlow addressed Joseph directly. "We have several matters to discuss with you and your team before we depart. Perhaps we could speak privately?"

The diplomat's eyes flicked meaningfully at Faraz.

Joseph glanced back at Naveed, where an embassy staff member was checking his bandages. "What about Naveed? Will he...?" He left the question hanging.

The staff member looked up, expression grim. "The bullet may have nicked his liver. His blood is dark. Our physician will need to assess him immediately, but he needs proper hospital care."

Maya Chaudhry stepped closer to Joseph and whispered. Faraz couldn't hear the words, but he could guess—her case would be significantly stronger if Naveed gave a firsthand account of his prior relationship with Faraz and the TLP.

Naveed tried to speak from the sofa but could only manage a pained whisper before his eyes fluttered closed. The staff member quickly checked his pulse and nodded that he was still stable, but unconscious.

Faraz's shoulders straightened. He made another note on his clipboard, keeping his expression neutral. Without Naveed's testimony, a crucial witness against him would be silenced.

He approached Joseph under the pretense of explaining

procedure. "Mr. Freeman," he said, lowering his voice. "Once the diplomatic presence withdraws, you will face Pakistani justice alone. I would advise you to consider what that means."

He expected a flinch or perhaps downcast eyes. Instead, Joseph met his gaze steadily.

"My father always believed truth would prevail in Pakistan," Joseph replied. A steady confidence in his eyes suggested knowledge—knowledge that should have died in the mountains. "I intend to honor his faith in your country's justice."

"Faith can be misplaced, Mr. Freeman," Faraz replied, leaning closer. "Your father died believing in things that weren't true. Justice takes many forms in Pakistan."

Joseph's jaw tightened, but his gaze didn't waver. "Truth is truth, Director Qureshi. It doesn't change based on who wields power."

The diplomats moved closer. Thornton cleared his throat. "I believe we have matters to discuss with Mr. Freeman before our meeting with the regional governor."

Faraz stepped back, studying the silent communication between Freeman and the diplomats. What were they planning? What evidence did Freeman possess?

Twenty minutes later, Faraz's government vehicle pulled away from the diplomatic compound. Through the tinted window, Christians gathered near the gates—drawn by news of Freeman's arrival. Women had brought flowers. Men stood in quiet conversation, occasionally glancing at the compound buildings.

Faraz punched a number into his phone.

"This is Director Qureshi," he said when his assistant answered. "Assemble the witnesses. I want everyone in my office in one hour."

The compound receded in the distance. The tribunal remained his last chance to eliminate Joseph Freeman and his mission permanently. The ambush had failed. The diplomatic intervention had complicated matters. But Naveed would not testify.

Tomorrow, in that courtroom, Faraz would destroy Freeman so thoroughly—the diplomats would be powerless to save him.

# FORTY-ONE

## The Muqadma

*Today changes everything.*

The thought had been pressing long before Joseph woke to Maya's knock at dawn. Through the window of his guest quarters, Peshawar's calls to prayer drifted across the diplomatic compound.

Everything he'd worked for. Everyone who'd sacrificed. It all came down to what happened in that courtroom.

"We need to leave in thirty minutes," she said when he opened the door. Dark circles shadowed her eyes—she'd been up most of the night preparing. "I'll meet you downstairs."

Joseph dressed in the only suit he'd brought from America. His hands fumbled the tie twice before getting it right.

In the courtyard, Maya briefed him while the security team loaded vehicles. "Naveed's stable, but he can't testify. Too weak. The embassy physician says attempting it could kill him."

Joseph's throat tightened. Naveed—who'd participated in the attack fifteen years ago, who'd risked everything to save them days ago—wouldn't be there to tell the judges what he knew about Faraz.

"So, we're on our own," Joseph said.

"We'll request Hassan as a witness. The judge will have to order him brought from detention." Maya met his gaze. "And we have the petition. But using those signatures puts thirty-two Muslims at risk. If we lose, Faraz will hunt every one of them. Are you certain?"

Joseph thought of his father's final letter: *Forgiveness does not mean silence.* "My father believed truth was worth dying for. I think it's worth the risk."

Maya offered a brief nod. "Then let's do this."

The team gathered—Joseph, Maya, Darius, Ian, and the others. Three vehicles waited with security escorts. Richard Harlow emerged from the main building, his expression professionally neutral but his eyes alert.

"The courthouse will be crowded," Harlow said. "Reporters, government officials, TLP sympathizers in the gallery. Stay close to your security detail."

The convoy moved through Peshawar's morning traffic, markets coming alive with vendors and shoppers. Mosques gathering men for prayer. Children heading to school. Ordinary life continuing while Joseph's fate hung in the balance.

"You ready for this?" Darius asked from beside him.

"No," Joseph admitted.

The courthouse rose ahead—a colonial-era building of stone and marble that had witnessed decades of Pakistan's legal struggles. Crowds gathered on the steps. Signs supporting religious freedom. Counter-protests demanding the foreigners be expelled.

Joseph's pulse quickened as the vehicle cleared the checkpoint.

This was it.

"Lord," he whispered as the vehicle stopped, "let truth win today."

Then the door opened and there was no more time for prayer.

————

Joseph's heart hammered as he stepped through the heavy wooden doors of Peshawar's Central Courthouse. Cold marble stretched beneath his feet. Hostile stares tracked him from every corner. Shafts of dusty sunlight cut through stained glass windows, casting jewel-toned patterns across the somber proceedings.

"Keep moving," Darius whispered behind him. "Don't let them see you hesitate."

Bailiffs directed Joseph and his team to a rectangular table positioned in the center of the room. The vulnerability wasn't accidental—they were meant to be scrutinized from every angle.

To his right, elevated on a platform three feet above the main floor, sat Faraz Qureshi. The man's face remained impassive, but his eyes followed Joseph with focused intensity. Beside him, Deputy Commissioner Asim Qadir shuffled papers with meticulous precision, never looking up.

The prosecution table sat higher than Joseph's, but still below the judges' bench.

"Theater," Maya whispered as she settled her briefcase on their table. "We're center stage in a pit, with the audience looking down."

Joseph nodded. Scanned the gallery. Local officials and curious onlookers filled the wooden benches. Along the left wall, behind polished wooden railing, sat Richard Harlow and Neville Thornton—relegated to observer status, physically separated from any ability to intervene.

At the far end of the chamber, on a raised dais dominating the room, three judges in black robes settled into high-backed chairs. The central judge—silver-streaked hair, wire-rimmed glasses—surveyed the room with cold indifference.

But the most unsettling presence was Maulana Hafiz Rahman. The religious leader sat in a special seat to the right of the judges' platform. Not quite at their level but distinctly separate from the regular gallery. His white beard and traditional dress commanded deference from everyone in the room.

"All rise," called the court officer.

Joseph stood. His legs unsteady.

The chief judge adjusted his microphone. "The Religious Affairs Court of Khyber Pakhtunkhwa Province is now in session. Case number 47-B-25, Federal Investigation Agency versus Joseph William Freeman and associates."

They sat.

The prosecutor—thin man, precisely trimmed mustache —approached the center of the court. "Honorable judges, today we present evidence of deliberate religious provocation, unauthorized religious teaching, and violations of the Blasphemy Provisions under the Pakistani Penal Code. These foreign nationals have systematically undermined the religious fabric of our nation under the guise of humanitarian work."

The chief judge nodded. "You may call your first witness."

A young man with nervous eyes was led to the witness stand. Couldn't have been more than twenty. Shoulders curved inward. Chin tucked low. He avoided looking at the defendants.

"Please state your name for the record," the prosecutor instructed.

"Abdul Waheed."

"And were you employed at the construction site known as the Freeman Mission Compound?"

"Yes, sir. I worked there for three weeks as a laborer."

The prosecutor paced methodically. "During your time there, did you hear the defendant Darius Karimi make statements regarding the Prophet Muhammad, peace be upon him?"

Abdul shifted. "Yes, sir. I heard him speaking to another worker. He said that the Prophet Muhammad was mistaken in his teachings and that Jesus was the true path to salvation."

Darius stiffened beside Joseph.

"And what was your reaction to hearing this?"

"I was deeply offended, sir. It is a grave insult to our faith."

The prosecutor nodded sympathetically. "No further questions."

The chief judge turned to Maya. "Does the defense wish to cross-examine?"

Maya rose. Calm confidence. "Yes, Your Honor."

She approached the witness stand. Manila folder in hand.

"Mr. Waheed, you testified that you worked at the mission compound for three weeks. Could you tell the court the exact dates of your employment?"

The young man hesitated. "I...I believe it was from July 12th to August 5th."

Maya consulted her notebook. "Interesting. Our records show no Abdul Waheed employed during that period. In fact, we have complete payroll documentation, counter-signed by your government's labor office."

She turned to the judges. "May I?"

The chief judge nodded.

She approached the bench. Presented the folder. "These are certified copies of all employment records."

The young man's color faded.

"Furthermore," Maya continued, "you claim to have heard Mr. Karimi make these statements, but Mr. Karimi was not at the compound during this period. He was in Islamabad, attending an interfaith conference." She presented more documents. "His credentials, letter of appointment, multiple receipts from Islamabad."

The chief judge examined the documents. Passed them to the other judges.

"Mr. Waheed," she gestured toward their table. "Could you please point out Mr. Karimi?"

The witness's eyes darted frantically over each man's face at the defendant's table. Long silence. Then he pointed at Ian.

Murmurs rippled through the courtroom.

Maya's expression remained neutral. "Let the record show that the witness has identified Ian Daniels, not Darius Karimi."

The prosecutor jumped up. "Objection! The witness is nervous. This is intimidation—"

"Overruled," the chief judge stated flatly. "The credibility of testimony is central to these proceedings."

Maya returned to her seat.

Joseph felt hope flicker.

The pattern repeated with the second witness. A middle-aged man claiming Joseph had distributed pamphlets ridiculing Islamic teachings. Maya systematically dismantled his testimony—produced sign-in sheets showing the man had never entered the compound grounds.

The third witness claimed Maya herself had argued that Sharia law was "backward and oppressive" to a group of local women.

Maya's response was surgical.

"Your Honor, I submit for the record my academic publications on comparative religious law, including my thesis on the progressive elements of classical Sharia jurisprudence as they relate to women's property rights." She presented the documents. "Additionally, letters from three Islamic law professors at Al-Azhar University commending my respectful approach to Islamic legal traditions."

The witness stammered as Maya questioned him about specific details of the alleged conversation. Tripped over inconsistencies. The prosecutor finally asked to dismiss him.

Joseph watched Maya work through Pakistani legal precedents with the familiarity of someone born to the system. Citing local case law that surprised even the judges.

The tension shifted perceptibly when Maulana Hafiz Rahman took the stand.

Unlike the previous witnesses, he exuded absolute confidence. His sonorous voice filled the chamber as he described the "dangerous foreign influence" the mission represented.

"These missionaries do not come merely to build structures," Rahman intoned gravely. "They come to dismantle the faith that has sustained our people for generations. They exploit poverty and suffering to lure vulnerable souls away from Allah's true path with promises of material aid."

The words swayed the room. Even the embassy officials shifted uncomfortably.

Joseph closed his eyes. Fighting the memory of smoke. His mother's final whispered instructions. When he opened them, he straightened his shoulders.

His parents had stood against such accusations. He would do no less.

When Maya rose to cross-examine Rahman, Joseph held his breath.

"Maulana Rahman," Maya began respectfully, "you speak eloquently about protecting Pakistan from foreign influence. Would you agree that all foreign influences are harmful to Pakistan?"

Rahman stroked his beard. "Those that undermine our Islamic character certainly are."

"Including foreign financial influence?" Maya asked.

"That depends on the source and intention," Rahman replied cautiously.

Maya nodded. "Investigative reports published last month by the International Corruption Watch document transfers from the Wahhabi Foundation in Saudi Arabia to accounts linked to several Pakistani religious leaders, including twelve million rupees to organizations you chair. Can you explain?"

Whispers swept through the gallery. Older men nodded with grim satisfaction. Younger Rahman supporters lurched forward in their seats. The court officer's staff struck the floor sharply, demanding order.

Rahman's face hardened. "Those contributions support my charitable works."

"Of course," Maya acknowledged. "Just as Mr. Freeman's foundation supports medical care and education." She paused. "I also have photographs published by Dawn and the Daily Pakistan taken at three different rallies organized by Tehreek-e-Labbaik Pakistan. Here you are..." she turned one photo to face Rahman, "addressing crowds alongside known TLP leaders. The same organization responsible for attacks on Christian communities throughout Pakistan."

"I speak at many gatherings," Rahman said dismissively. "I cannot control who else attends."

"Yet in this speech," Maya continued, holding up a newspaper article, "you are quoted as calling for 'decisive action against Christian infiltrators.' This was two days before three Christian homes were burned in Lahore."

Rahman's eyes narrowed dangerously. "You twist my words, woman."

"I'm simply quoting them verbatim, Maulana," Maya replied evenly. "No further questions."

Rahman stepped down, his face flushed with anger. Faraz Qureshi whispered in Asim Qadir ear. Qadir's face betrayed nothing.

The prosecutor rose. "The state rests its case, Your Honors."

The chief judge turned to Maya. "Does the defense wish to present evidence?"

Maya stood. "Yes, Your Honor. The defense is prepared to present evidence that will fundamentally alter the course of these proceedings."

The courtroom fell silent as Maya approached the bench with a manila envelope—the same one Joseph had retrieved from Hassan's safety deposit box.

"Your Honors, I present to the court a petition prepared

by William Freeman, the father of the accused, dated August 2010, just days before his murder. This petition, intended for presentation to the Pakistani National Assembly, contains thirty-two signatures from respected Muslim leaders in Khyber Pakhtunkhwa Province, all supporting the continued operation of the Freeman Mission and attesting to its positive impact on the community."

She handed the document to the court officer, who passed it to the judges. "These community leaders—imams, business owners, tribal elders—all testified to the mission's respect for local customs and Islamic beliefs. They specifically rejected claims that the mission engaged in forced conversions or disrespectful behavior."

The chief judge's eyes widened while examining the document. His finger moved down the list of signatures, then stopped abruptly. He looked up, his gaze darting to the prosecution table.

The silence stretched. The chief judge passed the document to the other judges. Urgent whispers. Heads bent together.

At the prosecution table, Qadir had gone perfectly still. Faraz's hands gripped the edge of the table.

The chief judge cleared his throat. "This court will take a thirty-minute recess to examine this evidence."

His gavel cracked.

Immediately, officials began conferring in urgent whispers. Faraz Qureshi's face contorted with barely contained rage. He snatched his phone and rushed to the exit, already dialing as he pushed through the doors.

The man who'd killed Joseph's parents. The man who'd hunted him for months. Now fleeing the courtroom like a cornered animal.

"What just happened?" he asked Maya.

"The chief judge just recognized Asim Qadir's signature on your father's petition."

At the prosecution table, Deputy Commissioner Qadir sat motionless, staring straight ahead as though the ground had opened beneath him.

# FORTY-TWO

**The Testimony**

Faraz pushed through the courtroom doors into the tiled hallway, pulling out his phone with shaking hands. Twenty minutes. He had twenty minutes to figure out how Freeman had obtained that petition—and how to contain the damage.

His heels clicked a restless rhythm—forward to the water fountain, back to the restroom entrance, forward again. The corridor lay empty, its occupants still gripped in the chaos he'd left behind.

The scar across his left cheek burned as if freshly cut. He tugged at his collar. That petition. Those signatures. How had they survived the fire?

Through the courtroom's small window, he could see Deputy Commissioner Qadir hunched at the prosecution table, shoulders curved inward, eyes darting between the judges and the exit.

*Come out, you coward.*

But Qadir remained inside, probably calculating his escape from this disaster.

Faraz's service pistol pressed against his ribs—a weight that usually steadied him. Today it only reminded him how far he'd fallen. From leading Rahman's righteous campaign to skulking in courthouse hallways, watching his carefully constructed case collapse.

A guard approached, nodding respectfully. "Director Qureshi, the judges are returning."

Faraz slipped back into the courtroom, taking a seat at the rear. Better to monitor the damage directly.

The judges filed in, their faces grim. The chief judge gaveled the room to order.

"After examining the petition submitted by the defense," the chief judge announced, "this court finds the document authentic and relevant to these proceedings." He looked directly at Qadir. "Deputy Commissioner, your signature appears on this document. The court will address this matter shortly."

Qadir's face went white.

"Furthermore," the chief judge continued, "the defense has requested Hassan Awan be brought from detention to testify regarding the history of this document and events surrounding the 2010 attack on the Freeman Mission."

Faraz's hands clenched. Hassan. The one witness he'd thought silenced.

"The prosecution objects," the prosecutor jumped up, desperation in his voice. "Hassan Awan has been transferred to a medical facility—"

"For what reason?" The female judge's eyebrow arched.

The prosecutor's collar looked too tight. "I...don't have those details."

"How convenient." Maya Chaudhry's voice cut through

the tension. "Your Honors, I have medical documentation from the detention center infirmary, taken when Hassan Awan was treated following his interrogation." She approached the bench. "These documents show severe trauma—injuries sustained while in FIA custody under Director Qureshi's direct supervision."

Conversations erupted in the gallery. The chief judge banged his gavel.

Faraz's breathing grew shallow. Those medical records—how had she obtained sealed files?

The middle judge, a stern woman with silver-streaked hair, examined the photographs attached to Maya's filing. Her expression turned to stone. "These injuries are extensive. Director Qureshi, you will explain this to the court when appropriate." She looked at the chief judge. "I recommend Hassan Awan be produced immediately."

"Agreed," the chief judge declared. His gavel cracked. "Court officers will retrieve Hassan Awan from detention. We'll recess for one hour."

Faraz stood, but his legs nearly buckled. Someone inside the detention center had betrayed him—someone with access to Hassan's medical files. When this was over, heads would roll.

He pushed through the corridor, needing air. Outside the courthouse, he dialed a number.

"It's worse than we thought," he said when Rahman answered. "They have Hassan. They have medical records. Qadir's signature is on the petition."

Rahman's silence was more terrifying than his anger. Finally: "Do what you must to contain this, Faraz. Our entire movement depends on it."

The line went dead.

Faraz leaned against the courthouse wall. Fifteen years

of careful work—eliminating witnesses, fabricating evidence, building his reputation on the Freeman raid—unraveling in a single morning.

Qadir emerged from a side entrance, heading for the men's room.

"A word, Commissioner," Faraz called.

Qadir's step faltered. He turned reluctantly, wiping his forehead with a white cloth.

Faraz grabbed his arm, steering him into an empty alcove. "Your signature is on that petition. Explain that to Rahman."

Qadir yanked his arm free, smoothing his expensive suit sleeve. "I was following orders to gather community input. Unlike you, I documented everything properly."

The implication struck Faraz like a gut punch. Qadir had covered his tracks while Faraz had left a trail of bodies.

"Freeman's son threatens everything we've built," Faraz hissed, stepping closer. "If Christians establish a foothold again—"

"Don't." Qadir backed away, his voice gaining strength. "I signed a petition as part of community outreach fifteen years ago. You led a mob that murdered his parents. We are not the same."

The scar on Faraz's cheek burned white-hot. "Careful with your accusations."

"They're not accusations—they're facts." Qadir straightened to his full height. "When Hassan Awan testifies about what he witnessed that night, I have documentation proving I followed proper procedures. What do you have?"

*Blood and screams. Flames and Freeman's final prayer.*

"I've been called to Islamabad," Qadir continued. "Whatever happens next is your problem."

He walked away, leaving Faraz alone in the alcove.

Faraz pressed his back against the cool stone, fighting nausea. This was about more than his career. Rahman had built his entire platform on opposition to Christian influence, using Faraz's raid as proof of community rejection. If Hassan testified about the petition—about Muslim leaders supporting Freeman's work—Rahman's narrative would collapse.

And Faraz would be the first sacrifice made to preserve the cleric's reputation.

———

When court reconvened, Joseph leaned forward, palms damp against his knees. The rear doors groaned open. Hassan entered between two officers, his steps small and uneven, as if each one hurt. A bloom of purple shadowed his left eye. A crusted cut split his lower lip. The man who had once carried him through smoke and fire now seemed shrunken, his shoulders caved, his hair streaked with gray. A decade older than his years.

The gallery fell silent.

Joseph's fingers found his mother's silver cross beneath his shirt collar. The edges worn smooth from years of touchning.

Hassan made his way to the witness stand. His eyes found Joseph's across the courtroom.

The chief judge gestured to the Bible on the stand—Joseph's father's Bible, still present from earlier testimony. "Please place your hand on the book and swear to speak the truth."

Hassan's hand settled on the worn leather cover.

"Do you swear in the name of God that the evidence you

give shall be the truth, the whole truth, and nothing but the truth?"

"I do." Hassan's voice was stronger than his appearance suggested.

Maya approached. "Mr. Awan, how long did you work for the Freeman Mission?"

"Eight years. I began as a groundskeeper when William Freeman first established the mission. Later, I became his assistant."

"And what services did the mission provide?"

"We had a medical clinic that treated anyone who came —Muslim, Christian, Hindu, it didn't matter. The school taught children to read and write. We distributed food during droughts." He touched his face gently. "The clinic removed a tumor from my cheek that would have killed me."

"How did the local community respond?"

Hassan straightened despite his injuries. "Many were grateful. Some opposed us. William Freeman knew tensions were rising. That's why he gathered signatures from local Muslim leaders who supported our work—thirty-two respected men who stated publicly that the mission bene-fited the community."

"The petition now in evidence before this court?"

"Yes. William gave it to me the night of the attack. He made me promise to protect it—to preserve the truth of what we'd built together."

Maya nodded. "What happened on the night of August 18, 2010?"

Hassan drew a breath. "Three trucks arrived just after dusk. White ones with TLP flags. They broke through our front gate." His voice faltered. "William knew what was happening. He told me to take Joseph through the escape tunnel while he and Lyla tried to buy us time."

Joseph closed his eyes. The acrid smell of smoke filled his nostrils as if he were there again—ten years old, confused and terrified as Hassan pulled him through the darkness.

"What did you do?" Maya asked gently.

"I took Joseph through an old tunnel beneath the mission. We could hear the attack above us—wood splintering, gunshots, screams..." Hassan's eyes glistened. "When we emerged from the tunnel, the mission was engulfed in flames."

"And you kept Joseph safe?"

"Yes. I got him to Islamabad. Then on a plane to his uncle in America. It's what William and Lyla wanted—for their son to survive, even if they couldn't."

Maya paused.

"Mr. Awan, after your recent arrest, who conducted your interrogation?"

"Director Qureshi." Hassan touched his bruised face. "He wanted to know what Joseph had retrieved from my safety deposit box. When I wouldn't tell him, he..." He trailed off.

"Take your time."

"He beat me for three days. Asking about the petition, about the signatures, about what I knew." Hassan stared down Faraz, his voice strengthening. "But I wouldn't tell him. Some truths are worth protecting."

At the prosecution table, Faraz sat rigid. His scar stood out white against flushed skin.

"No further questions, Your Honor," Maya said.

The prosecutor approached for cross-examination.

Asked about dates. About details. But his questions were weak, easily deflected.

Hassan's testimony stood unshaken.

As Hassan was helped from the witness stand, his face showed exhaustion but also something else—vindication. The truth had come out after fifteen years.

Joseph watched him settle into a seat in the gallery. Darius moved beside him, offering quiet words of support.

The courtroom hummed with whispered conversations. The judges conferred behind their bench, expressions unreadable. At the prosecution table, Qadir sat rigidly, staring at his folded hands. The prosecutor shuffled papers without purpose.

Maya remained standing at the defense table, her hand resting on her legal pad. She could rest their case now—the petition was authentic, Hassan's account unshakable, Qadir's signature undeniable.

A court officer approached their table. Handed Maya a folded note.

She opened it. Read quickly. Her expression went still—the kind of still that only appeared when something had gone very well or very badly.

"Your Honor," she said evenly. "May I have a brief moment to confer with my client?"

The chief judge nodded. "Five minutes."

Maya leaned close to Joseph. "This came from the American Embassy." She slid the note toward him.

*Ms. Chaudhry—Alexander Mercer is in the building and requests to testify.*

*He's willing to take the stand immediately if you'll call him.*
*—R. Harlow*

Joseph read it again. "Mercer? Why would he—"

"I don't know." Maya's voice was tight, almost a whisper.

"The note doesn't say. He might be here to explain why he pulled the funding—which could bury us. Or maybe to back us up. But Harlow wouldn't have sent this if it weren't critical."

"Can we even call him without knowing what he'll say?"

"Technically, yes. But it's reckless." Her eyes flicked toward the prosecution table. "If Mercer turns on us, even by accident, we're done. But if he's here to help..."

The rear doors opened. Christopher Rashid entered the room and took a seat in the back. Their eyes met. Christopher gave a single, deliberate nod, then raised his thumb.

"He's here to help," Joseph murmured.

"You can't know that from a thumbs-up," Maya hissed. "Joseph, this is the trial. We can't gamble everything on—"

"I trust Christopher," he said quietly. "And I trust that God didn't bring us this far to abandon us now." His gaze met hers, steady. "Call him."

Maya studied him for a long moment, searching for doubt and finding none. Then she exhaled slowly. "It goes against everything I learned in law school. But..."

"Ms. Chaudhry," the chief judge pressed.

Maya stood, facing the bench. Every line of her posture composed.

This was it—the moment she'd either vindicate Joseph or destroy everything they'd built. She glanced back at Joseph, who gave the slightest nod.

Trust.

"Your Honors," Maya's voice carried across the silent courtroom, "the defense calls Alexander Mercer to testify."

# FORTY-THREE

**The Verdict**

The doors swung wide.

Alexander Mercer entered. Expensive suit. Commanding presence. Behind him, Christopher Rashid remained seated, smiling.

The courtroom went silent. Then erupted. Then fell silent again as Mercer walked the center aisle, unhurried, owning every step.

At the prosecution table, Faraz Qureshi's hands went white against the wood. He half-rose. Froze. Touched the scar on his cheek.

Beside him, Qadir stared straight ahead, jaw working.

Joseph's heart hammered. Please, God, let this be right.

Mercer reached the witness stand. His eyes found Joseph's briefly—acknowledgment, almost a salute—then turned to the judges.

The chief judge leaned forward. "Mr. Mercer, you're prepared to testify?"

"I am, Your Honor."

The court officer approached with the Quran.

"The Bible, if one is available," Mercer said.

Maya offered Joseph's father's worn Bible. Mercer placed his hand on the leather cover.

"Do you swear in the name of God that the evidence you give shall be the truth, the whole truth, and nothing but the truth?"

"I do."

He settled into the chair. Adjusted his tie once. Went still.

Maya approached. "Mr. Mercer, please state your position and relationship to this case."

"I'm CEO of Stellarion Technologies. Until recently, primary funder of the Freeman Mission."

"Why did you withdraw support?"

Mercer's expression hardened. His gaze locked on Qadir. "Deputy Commissioner Qadir sent detailed reports to our legal department. Claims that Joseph Freeman was inciting religious insurrection. Illegal proselytizing. Creating dangerous tensions between Muslims and Christians."

Maya paused and turned pages on her legal pad before speaking. "Please, continue."

"These allegations could jeopardize our three-billion-dollar technology investment in Pakistan. Given the source —a senior government official—we withdrew funding immediately."

At the prosecution table, Qadir's head dropped. Faraz breathed shallow and quick.

"What changed?" Maya asked.

"The American Embassy investigated. Every allegation was fabricated."

The courtroom erupted.

The chief judge cracked his gavel. "Order!"

Mercer waited for silence. "The inspection failures were invented. The proselytizing claims were manufactured. Pure fiction." His gaze remained fixed on Qadir. "Deputy Commissioner Qadir lied to my company to eliminate an organization his office once supported."

Maya approached the bench. "Your Honors, the American Embassy's investigative report."

She handed over the folder. The judges examined it, expressions darkening.

Maya returned to the witness. "Mr. Mercer, why are you here today?"

"I'm in Pakistan for meetings with your Interior Minister about technology investments. When the Embassy briefed me on the fabrications, I flew here to clarify facts. Stellarion does not appreciate being manipulated."

"What is Stellarion's position now?"

"Full funding restored immediately. Mr. Freeman violated no Pakistani laws. He seeks to provide humanitarian services, medical care, education. The only crime was fabrication of evidence by government officials."

Mercer turned to address the judges directly. "Furthermore, Stellarion is conditioning our three-billion-dollar investment on measurable commitments to religious freedom. If officials can fabricate reports to eliminate Christian humanitarian work, they can fabricate reports to undermine any foreign investment. My board needs assurance that Pakistan is a reliable partner—where truth and rule of law matter."

The judges stared at Mercer. Then at Qadir. Then at each other.

Joseph barely breathed.

The chief judge turned to the prosecution table. "Does the state wish to cross-examine?"

The prosecutor stood. Hesitated. Looked at Qadir, who wouldn't meet his eyes. Looked at Faraz, whose face had become stone-rigid.

"No questions, Your Honor," the prosecutor replied.

Mercer was excused. He walked past the prosecution table without a glance. Faraz's hands curled tighter.

The chief judge cleared his throat. "This court will take a brief recess to deliberate and return with a verdict."

The gavel fell.

One hour felt like fifteen.

Joseph stood in the corridor. Couldn't sit. Couldn't speak. Maya reviewed her notes, but Joseph knew she wasn't reading them. Just moving her eyes across familiar words. Seeking control.

Darius prayed quietly. Ian stood watch. The others clustered nearby, waiting.

Through the courtroom windows, Joseph saw Faraz pacing. Alone. Qadir had disappeared somewhere. The FIA director moved like a caged animal—five steps one way, turn, five steps back. His hand kept going to his scar. Touching it. Pressing it.

"They're coming back," Ian said.

Joseph's stomach dropped.

They filed back into the courtroom. Every seat filled. Standing room only at the back. Reporters. Diplomats. Local officials. Believers from the village who'd risked being seen here.

The judges entered. Robes swishing. Faces unreadable.

Joseph sat. Maya on his left. Darius on his right.

At the prosecution table, Faraz and Qadir sat separated by an empty chair. Neither looking at the other.

The chief judge arranged papers. Adjusted his glasses. The silence stretched. Broke.

"In the matter of the Federal Investigation Agency versus Joseph Freeman and associates, this court has reached a verdict."

Joseph's heart stopped.

"After examining the evidence presented—the petition bearing thirty-two signatures from respected Muslim community leaders, the testimony of Hassan Awan regarding the mission's history, and the testimony of Alexander Mercer regarding fabricated reports—this court finds the accusations without merit."

A collective intake of breath. The chief judge continued.

"Furthermore, evidence suggests improper interference by government officials, including fabrication of evidence and witness intimidation. The court finds no basis for the charges of inciting religious hatred or illegal proselytization."

The female judge leaned forward. "Deputy Commissioner Qadir, your conduct in this matter is referred to the Interior Ministry for administrative review. Director Qureshi, your treatment of Hassan Awan while in FIA custody will be investigated by the appropriate authorities."

Qadir's eyes closed. Faraz sat perfectly still.

The chief judge's gavel rose. "The defendants are acquitted of all charges. This court is adjourned." He slammed his gavel.

The courtroom exploded.

Joseph couldn't move. Couldn't process. The word—acquitted—echoed in his skull but wouldn't connect to meaning.

Maya grabbed his arm. "We won. Joseph, we won."

Darius pulled him into an embrace. "Your father would be so proud."

Around them, believers wept. Embraced. Praised God in

whispers and shouts. The diplomatic observers stood, satisfied expressions on their faces. Reporters rushed for the exits—phones pressed to their ears.

Qadir remained seated. Head in his hands.

Faraz stood. Slowly. Every muscle coiled tight. His hands shook, his breathing came harsh and ragged. His eyes found Joseph's across the courtroom.

Hatred. Pure and absolute.

The man who'd killed his parents. Who'd haunted him for months. Who'd just been legally defeated. Turned—walked—then disappeared through the doors, humiliated.

Maya touched Joseph's shoulder. "You okay?"

He turned back to his team. His family. The people who'd risked everything. "It's done," he said. "The mission can continue."

"The mission will continue," Darius corrected. "We've won the right to finish rebuilding. Now we must do it."

Around them, believers gathered. Hands reached out. Voices offered congratulations and thanks and prayers. Joseph shook hands. Accepted embraces. Felt the weight of responsibility settle over him again.

They'd won the battle.

But what about the war?

But today—today they would celebrate.

The team were the last to file out of the courtroom. Into bright Pakistani sunlight. Into a future that moments ago had seemed impossible.

The chapel waited. Unfinished but standing.

Time to complete what they'd started.

# FORTY-FOUR

## Celebrating the Cross

*ONE MONTH LATER*

"Joseph? Samuel says we need to start now. Wind conditions are perfect."

Maya's voice pulled him from his letter. Joseph looked up from his makeshift desk, where morning sunlight filtered through the canvas walls of his tent. He'd been writing to Uncle David, trying to capture everything that had happened since the trial—the rebuilding, the completion, the miracle of simply surviving.

He set down his pen and touched the silver cross pendant hanging around his neck—his mother's necklace. She would have loved today.

"Is everyone here?" he asked, stretching.

"More than everyone," Maya said, her smile widening. " Half the village showed up."

The rhythmic ping of hammer against metal echoed across the compound. Someone laughed—a sound that would have been unthinkable a month ago.

He picked up his pen.

*Dear Uncle David,*

*I write as the sun rises behind the chapel—walls I once doubted we would ever see stand again. When we first returned to the ruins, our hearts were heavy with uncertainty. The land was scarred, our numbers scattered, and the memory of loss weighed on every step we took.*

*Yet, like our ancestors in exile, we set our hands to the work. This past month since the court's ruling has been a sprint to complete what we started. There were days when opposition from every side made me question whether we should continue. The sudden loss of Stellarion's funding, Miriam's forced betrayal, the ambush on the mountain road—each blow nearly broke us.*

*In those hours, I remembered the words of the prophet—"Rise up. This matter is in your hands. We will support you, so take courage and do it." I spoke them to our people, but I think I needed them most myself.*

*It was not only stones and timber that needed rebuilding, but faith and unity. One night, after a child asked me if God had left us, I prayed as I never have before. In that silence, I understood—our true task was to restore hope, not just buildings.*

*By God's grace, and with the help of friends near and far, we finished the chapel. But more than that, we found ourselves changed. We are no longer just survivors—we are a community bound by faith that endures beyond walls. The villagers who once watched us with suspicion now greet us with cautious respect. Our children sing again, though we remain watchful.*

*Faraz and his allies have gone quiet since the trial, but we know better than to mistake silence for surrender. Still, today belongs to celebration, not fear. I see God's grace and my father's legacy not only in the chapel, but in every act of kindness and courage among our people.*

Joseph paused, the pen hovering above the page. Through the tent opening, he could hear voices gathering— more than he'd expected. Much more.

"Joseph?" Maya appeared at the entrance, her expression caught between excitement and apprehension. " Samuel says we need to start now. The wind conditions are perfect, and he's worried about afternoon gusts."

Joseph looked up. "Is everyone here?"

"More than everyone." Maya's smile widened. "Half the village has shown up."

Joseph set down his pen carefully, his pulse quickening. Half the village. After everything they'd endured, half the village had come. "Any sign of trouble?"

"Nothing yet, but word is that the authorities know." She glanced over her shoulder. "Darius thinks we should proceed before any official response arrives. Hassan is already seated in the front row—he insisted on being here despite still recovering. And Naveed brought his entire family, including Kamran and Ayesha."

Joseph felt something tighten in his chest. Kamran, the boy who'd risked everything to help him escape Faraz's trap. Ayesha, the daughter he'd healed. Naveed, who'd taken a bullet meant for them all. They were here. They were safe.

"Give me two minutes."

Maya nodded and disappeared.

Joseph touched the silver cross one more time, then picked up the pen for a final paragraph.

*I am humbled, Uncle, by how suffering has deepened our faith and how hope has returned to us. I hope you find encouragement in our story, as we have found strength in your prayers.*

*With love and gratitude,*

*Joseph*

He folded the letter carefully and slipped it between the pages of the Bible. The rest could wait. The words he'd write tonight would be better—richer—for having lived through what came next.

Joseph stepped out of the tent into the brilliant morning. The smell of fresh bread drifted from the women's tables. Children darted between clusters of adults. And there, against the sky, stood the chapel—simple, humble, and whole.

Today belonged to the cross.

————

The completed chapel stood against the morning sky, its simple lines and local stone blending with the landscape as if it had grown from the earth itself. November's chill had begun creeping into the mornings, frost touching the edges of the marigolds in his mother's restored garden. One month of frantic work since the trial verdict—every daylight hour spent racing against the approaching winter and the possibility that permissions might be revoked. No grand cathedral—just a humble sanctuary risen from the ashes of his father's mission. Around the building, a crowd gathered —his international team mingling with local believers. Children darted between adults, their laughter carrying across the compound.

Near the chapel entrance, the silver cross leaned against the scaffold—twelve feet of polished metal, crafted in sections over weeks and assembled in darkness.

Darius approached, wiping dust from his hands, his eyes crinkling at the corners. "The children keep asking if it's made of real silver."

Joseph smiled. "Technically, it's stainless steel with a silver laminate. But I like your answer better."

Darius glanced toward the government vehicles that had appeared at the perimeter. "Ready for this?"

"I've been ready since we broke ground." Joseph followed his gaze. "You having second thoughts?"

"Not second thoughts. Just..." Darius gestured to the growing crowd. "This moment feels bigger than I expected. When we started, I thought we were just rebuilding walls."

"And now?"

"Now I see we're reclaiming something that can't be measured in square footage." Darius clapped him lightly on the shoulder. "Your father would be proud. Not of the building—of the people."

Across the clearing, Tariq directed two younger men as they secured guide ropes. The transformation in the once-bitter young man struck Joseph anew—movements now confident, without the angry edge that once defined him. When Tariq caught Joseph watching, he offered a brief nod before turning back to his task.

"He insisted on overseeing the rigging himself," Darius said. "Spent half the night calculating load vectors with Samuel."

Joseph chuckled. "Three months ago, he could barely sit in the same room with me."

"People change when they're given the chance to build something that matters." Darius squinted against the strengthening sunlight. "Especially when they thought they'd never get the opportunity."

People continued to arrive—more than Joseph had anticipated. Beyond their core group of believers, villagers gathered at the perimeter, some out of curiosity, others with expressions that suggested deeper interest. Joseph recognized the local carpenter who had refused their business initially, only to quietly provide tools when government pressure increased.

Near the back stood Naveed with his wife and children. Ayesha, her health fully restored, bounced on her toes trying to see over the adults. Beside her, Kamran stood close to a slender girl of perhaps fifteen wearing a pale green headscarf—the Christian girl from the market, Joseph realized, the one Kamran had mentioned meeting the day after his baptism.

The young couple maintained a careful distance, conscious of watching eyes, but their occasional glances spoke volumes. Naveed kept one protective arm around his wife, his expression guarded but present nonetheless, though Joseph noticed him watching his son with something between concern and resignation.

"They come for different reasons," Darius observed, following Joseph's gaze. "Some for the spectacle, some seeking hope."

"And some waiting to see what happens when we push back against the restrictions." Joseph touched the pendant beneath his shirt—his mother's silver cross, hidden but present. The familiar gesture steadied him, as it had during every pivotal moment since her death.

Miriam approached, her head covered with a blue scarf that brightened her care-worn face. In her hands, she carried a small tray of sweet bread. The dark circles under her eyes spoke of sleepless nights, but her movements held a steadiness Joseph hadn't seen before.

"For strength," she said, offering the tray to Joseph. "The women are preparing a celebration meal for afterward."

Joseph accepted a piece, noting the traditional patterns

baked into the crust—circles within circles, symbols of eternity. "Amir would be proud to see this day."

Her eyes glistened, and she pressed one hand briefly to her heart. "He believed it would come, even when I couldn't. Fifteen years in that cell, and he never stopped believing." Her voice caught. "At least...at least his suffering wasn't for nothing. At least I lived to hear the verdict, even if he couldn't—"

She couldn't finish. Joseph touched her shoulder gently.

"His faith preserved ours," he said quietly. "That's not nothing, Miriam."

She nodded, unable to speak, then moved away to offer bread to others, her back straighter than it had been in weeks despite the grief she carried.

Near the chapel entrance, Samuel Wong clapped his hands for attention.

"It's time," he called, his engineer's precision evident in every movement as he gestured for the workers to take their positions. "Wind conditions are optimal. We need to move before that changes."

Joseph touched the pendant once more, then stepped forward to address the gathering. The crowd quieted. Faces turned toward him expectantly. Heat rose from the ground, carrying the scent of dust and fresh mortar despite the morning chill.

"Fifteen years ago, a mission stood on this ground," he began, his voice carrying across the morning air. "My father and mother gave their lives here, believing that what they built would outlast them. They were right—but not in the way they imagined."

He gestured to the people assembled before him.

"You are what survived. Not walls or roofs, but faith and community. This chapel is not a monument to the past, but a commitment to the future. And this—" he turned toward the twelve-foot beam of polished metal "—this is our declaration that what was meant for destruction has instead brought new life."

A murmur rippled through the crowd. Several officials watched from their vehicles, writing in notebooks, but none approached.

"Samuel," Joseph nodded. "Let's raise it."

Four teams took positions at the guide ropes while Samuel oversaw the main pulley. The massive symbol lifted slowly, winter sunlight blazing cold and brilliant across its surface as it rose. Joseph found himself holding his breath, watching it ascend the chapel wall. Each inch upward felt like reclaiming ground that had been lost—not just physical space, but the right to worship openly, to stand firm in faith without fear.

Halfway up, it caught on something, tilting precariously to one side. A collective gasp rose from the crowd. The rope groaned under the shifting weight. Metal scraped against stone.

Tariq darted forward, adjusting one of the guide ropes with swift precision.

"Hold steady!" he called to his team. "Don't force it!"

For a breathless moment, the beam hung suspended, neither rising nor falling. Joseph found himself whispering his father's favorite psalm—"I lift my eyes to the hills. Where does my help come from?"

The symbol straightened, continuing its ascent until it reached the peak of the chapel roof. Workers moved quickly to secure it in place, locking it into the mounting bracket Samuel had designed. Metal rang against metal. When the final bolt was tightened, Tariq gave the signal for the ropes to be released.

The silver cross stood radiant against the blue sky, gleaming in the thin sunlight. From this angle, it looked impossibly large, a beacon visible for miles across the valley.

Someone began to sing—a Pakistani hymn Joseph recognized from his childhood. Others joined in, the melody swelling as it passed from person to person. Even some of the Muslim observers nodded in rhythm, respecting the moment if not sharing the faith it represented.

Joseph felt a presence beside him and turned to find Hassan there, recently released from the hospital, his face still bearing faint bruises from his detention. The older man leaned slightly on a walking stick, but his eyes were clear and fixed on the gleaming symbol overhead, tears streaming unashamedly down his cheeks.

"Your father once told me," Hassan said softly, "the mission would someday belong to the people, not to him. I didn't understand."

"And now?"

Hassan gestured to the gathered community—international workers standing shoulder to shoulder with local believers, villagers who had once been hostile now watching with respectful curiosity, children playing freely in a space that had been defined by fear for so long.

"Now I see he was a prophet." Hassan's expression softened. "The petition signatories have been calling," he added quietly. "At first, they were afraid—worried about retaliation now that their names are public record."

Joseph's stomach tightened. The decision to use those signatures had haunted him through the trial. "And now?"

"Now?" Hassan's smile widened. "Three have asked permission to attend Friday prayers here. Two sent donations for the clinic fund. Mercer's investment announcement changed everything—international pressure won't let

Pakistan risk that money over domestic religious disputes. The spotlight protects them as much as it protects us."

"For now," Joseph said carefully.

"For now," Hassan agreed. "But 'for now' is more than we've had in fifteen years."

A government official approached—not Faraz, but a younger man Joseph recognized from the tribunal. The crowd tensed. Conversation faltered.

"This is not covered in your permit." The official's words carried no heat. His eyes moved to the symbol overhead, then back to Joseph. "Official notification will follow."

Joseph waited for the threat, the demand for removal, but the man simply gave a slight nod before turning away. Not approval, but not immediate opposition either. A space to breathe, at least for today.

As the official departed, Maya joined Joseph and Hassan. "Different tone than Qadir used to take."

"What happened to him?" Joseph asked. "After the trial?"

"Demoted. Transferred to a records office in Islamabad —stamping forms in a basement somewhere." Maya's expression held no satisfaction, only weary acknowledgment. "The Interior Ministry review found... irregularities. Apparently fabricating reports to international investors doesn't sit well when billions are at stake."

"And Rahman?"

Maya's jaw tightened. "Silent. No Friday sermons, no public statements. Ian says that's when we should worry most—like a cobra before it strikes." She glanced around at the celebrating crowd. "But not today. Today we've earned this."

The community began to move toward the tables

Miriam and the women had prepared. The atmosphere shifted from solemn ceremony to celebration.

Naveed approached with Ayesha clinging to his hand. The girl beamed up at Joseph, then pointed overhead at the gleaming cross.

"It's beautiful," she said in Urdu. "Like the stars, but in daytime."

"Your daughter has a poet's heart," Joseph said to Naveed.

Naveed's expression softened slightly. "She gets that from her mother." He hesitated, then added quietly, "My son asks permission to bring his friend to future gatherings. The girl from the Christian family."

Joseph glanced toward Kamran, who stood with the green-scarfed girl, both suddenly fascinated by something on the ground.

"What did you tell him?"

"That it's not my permission he needs." Naveed met Joseph's eyes. "That faith makes its own choices, and fathers can only love their children through them."

"Wise words."

"Difficult words," Naveed corrected, then managed a slight smile before leading Ayesha to the food tables.

Tariq approached, wiping sweat from his brow, his gaze repeatedly drawn to what now stood overhead. "My father would have wept to see this," he said, his voice rough with emotion. "He died believing it would never happen again."

"He died so it could happen again," Joseph corrected gently. "There's a difference."

Tariq considered this, then extended his hand. When Joseph clasped it, Tariq pulled him into a brief, fierce embrace.

"Thank you for coming back," he whispered, then released Joseph and walked away before he could respond.

The celebration spread across the compound, people sharing food and conversation in clusters. Joseph noticed Leila, their Muslim linguist, deep in discussion with Darius, her questions earnest and unguarded. Nearby, Kamran explained something to his sister, pointing occasionally overhead.

Samuel joined Joseph, his clipboard finally set aside. "Structurally sound," he reported with professional satisfaction. "It will withstand the wind and weather."

"And the opposition?"

Samuel's expression softened. "That's not an engineering question. But if you're asking my opinion..." He looked around at the gathered community. "I'd say we've built something stronger than metal and stone."

As the morning wore on, Joseph found a moment to stand alone before the chapel, looking up at what marked its completion. The silver gleamed against the sky, reminiscent of the small pendant that had been his mother's, now hanging around his neck. Two crosses—one personal and hidden, one public and defiant—both declaring the same truth.

He pressed his palm against the chapel wall, feeling the sun-warmed stone beneath his fingers. "It's done," he whispered, uncertain whether he was speaking to his parents, to God, or to himself. "Not finished—but begun again."

In the distance, a truck's engine growled to life, drawing his attention to the hills overlooking the compound. Someone was watching—had been watching, perhaps, throughout the ceremony. Joseph thought of Faraz, of the man's implacable hatred and the threat that still lingered. Winter was coming—the season when his father used to say faith was tested most—and today's victory didn't end their struggle. In some ways, it only marked the beginning of a new chapter.

But for now, the symbol stood. The community gathered. And in the space between what had been destroyed and what was being rebuilt, hope had found root again—as stubborn and resilient as the wildflowers that had reclaimed his mother's garden.

Joseph turned back to join his people, the letter to Uncle David waiting to be completed. There would be time enough tonight to put into words what today had demonstrated through action—

They had returned. They had rebuilt. And whatever came next, they would face it together.

# EPILOGUE

Faraz Qureshi's knuckles whitened around his binoculars. The setting sun painted the valley in shades of amber and crimson, casting long shadows across what was no longer a blackened ruin. Where scorched timbers and collapsed walls had once marked his victory, a gleaming white chapel now stood, its silver cross catching the dying light.

*Fifteen years ago, I burned it all to the ground.*

Below, at least fifty people gathered in the courtyard of the rebuilt Freeman Mission. Tables laden with food stretched across the space where he had once directed his men to pour gasoline. Children—Pakistani children—darted between adults, their laughter carried upward on the evening breeze. At the center of it all stood Joseph Freeman, moving through the crowd, clasping hands, embracing locals. The son possessed the same dangerous charisma as the father—perhaps even more potent.

The scar on Faraz's cheek burned with phantom pain. A month since his dismissal from the Federal Investigation Agency, his government authority stripped, forcing him back to the shadows of his militant past. His spectacular failure in the tribunal had been too public, too embarrassing for his superiors to ignore. Deputy Commissioner Qadir had distanced himself immediately. Maulana Rahman had called only once, his disappointment colder than any rage.

"You promised to eliminate the threat," Rahman had said. "Instead, you made him a martyr while he still lives."

Through the binoculars, Faraz spotted Hassan Awan—the missionary's assistant who had survived the original attack and helped the boy escape. The old man moved with difficulty, his injuries from Faraz's interrogation still evident. Yet his face shone with unmistakable joy as he surveyed the rebuilt compound.

Faraz shifted position, feeling the same stones dig into his knee that had fifteen years before. He was still watching, still plotting, still determined to eradicate the Christian presence from this land. Only now he operated from the shadows again, stripped of his authority but not his resolve.

As dusk deepened, spotlights illuminated the cross atop the chapel—a deliberate choice, ensuring the symbol remained visible day and night. Faraz's jaw clenched until pain shot through his temples.

*They were supposed to stay hidden. They were supposed to disappear.*

Joseph Freeman mounted the chapel steps and raised his hands for attention. The crowd quieted, faces turning toward him with expressions of admiration and respect.

"This chapel," Joseph's voice carried clearly in the evening air, "stands not just as a place of worship, but as a testament to endurance. What was destroyed has been rebuilt. What was meant to silence us has only made our voices stronger."

A murmur of agreement rippled through the crowd. Faraz recognized faces among them—Muslims from the neighboring villages, some who had once been sympathetic to the TLP's cause. Now they stood alongside Christians, sharing bread and conversation as if the boundaries between them had dissolved.

Movement near the western edge of the compound caught his attention. A young man slipped away from the celebration, moving with purpose toward the perimeter fence. Kamran—Naveed's son. The boy who had been baptized despite the consequences.

Kamran opened a gate, admitting five more Muslim youths who greeted him with embraces before being led toward the chapel. New converts. The mission wasn't just rebuilding—it was expanding.

"This isn't over," Faraz whispered. "This will never be over."

Below, Joseph concluded his speech. The gathering broke into spontaneous song—an Urdu Christian hymn Faraz recognized from his intelligence work. The melody floated upward, carrying words of triumph over suffering, light overwhelming darkness.

Faraz stood abruptly, no longer concerned about being spotted. Night had fallen fully, cloaking him in protective darkness. He slipped the binoculars into their case, his movements betraying none of the rage that coursed through him.

The scar on his cheek throbbed in time with his heartbeat as he turned toward his waiting motorcycle. The official channels were closed to him now, but other paths remained. The TLP had welcomed him back, eager to utilize his insider knowledge. Already, they were planning their response to this Christian provocation.

As he descended the rocky path, Faraz cast one last look over his shoulder at the illuminated cross. William Freeman he had silenced with bullets and fire. Joseph Freeman would require a more sophisticated approach.

The night enveloped him, his resolve hardening with each step. The Christians celebrated their victory, believing the battle won. They did not understand that for men like Faraz Qureshi, there was no surrender, only strategic retreat before the next advance.

The cross might shine tonight, but darkness always returned.

And Faraz would be waiting when it did.

# PLEASE LEAVE A REVIEW

If you have enjoyed this book, it would be a tremendous help if your could leave a review.

Reviews help me gain visibility and bring my books to the attention of other readers who may enjoy them. You can leave a review on the Determined Souls Amazon book page.

# GET EXCLUSIVE WILL MARLER MATERIAL

THANK YOU FOR READING! Building a relationship with my readers is the best thing about writing.

Join my LEGACY READERS CLUB and get:

🕮 FREE Book 1 of the Eli Colt Series (The Worst Kind of Evil)

🕮 Exclusive deleted scenes and character backgrounds

◎ Early access to new releases and special deals

✍ Behind-the-scenes updates from my writing journey

Sign up now: www.willmarler.com

Connect with me: Facebook | Instagram | Amazon

# ABOUT THE AUTHOR

Will Marler is a seasoned author of Christian suspense thrillers, best known for his gripping Eli Colt series and The Joseph Chronicles. His stories weave high-stakes drama with profound themes of faith, resilience, and redemption. In addition to his writing, Will is the founder of Legacy Acres, a Christian organization dedicated to supporting abused, abandoned, and neglected children.

A native of New Orleans, Will brings the vibrant culture and rich history of the Gulf South into his work, infusing his novels with a vivid sense of place. He now resides on the Mississippi Gulf Coast with his wife, Wendie.

For more information:
www.willmarler.com
will@willmarler.com

# ALSO BY WILL MARLER